ALSO BY LYNN RODOLICO

Two Seas

Intimates

Heart and Soul

SMALL CHANGE

Lynn Rodolico

Eccolo Editions

Grateful acknowledgement is made for permission to reprint previously published material: excerpts from Josh Groban's *The Prayer;* Thornton Wilder's *Our Town*; Andrew Marvell's *To His Coy Mistress;* W.H. Auden's *Musée des Beaux Arts*; Thomas Mc Carty *Poetry and Politic; Pennies from Heaven* lyrics by Johnny Burke and Arthur Johnston; *My One and Only Love* lyrics by Robert Mellin.

Cover photo: Amber Shereen Photography
www.ambershereen.com

Published by Eccolo Editions
www.eccoloeditions.com
ISBN   978-88-906986-6-8
Epub ISBN 978-88-906986-5-1

per Antonino

I pray you'll be our eyes
And watch us where we go
And help us to be wise
In times when we don't know.

Let this be our prayer
When we lose our way
Lead us to a place
Guide us with your grace
To a place where we'll be safe...

The Prayer, Josh Groban

Prologue

The pain was her punishment.

She screamed her agony into the hand held over her mouth. She pushed. She tore. Out with the blood came an angry, unforgiving child. But the pain didn't stop. The blood continued, and out came another baby. And still the pain wouldn't stop. She pushed again and out came a third baby, deformed.

Finally, the pain relented, and her sister removed her hand from her mouth, now that she was sure she wouldn't scream anymore, and cut the long rubbery cords that tied her to her sins. Her sister wrapped the whole mess into the blanket on which she had bled. Whimpering, the girl curled into a ball, a fetus herself, wanting only to die, of shame and exhaustion.

Her sister slapped her face hard, twice. With the same scissors she had used to separate the babies from the cord, she cut through the long, white-blonde braids Jo had worn her whole life, and tossed them into the bloody mess in the center of the blanket; folded it together and dumped it into an apple box.

"Be dressed by the time I get back and ready to leave."

"Where are you going?"

"Does it matter?"

"Jackie?"

"To take care of this mess."

"You won't tell mum?"

"Nor will you, Jo. Never."

CHAPTER ONE

In her hurry to get to work on time, Elizabeth hadn't dropped the trash in the bin at the side of her house which was covered in snow. Instead, she had thrown it into the back of her car, along with her purse, and would have left it all there while she spent the day at work, if the trash bag hadn't been full of chicken bones from last night's roast. The smell emanating from the trunk of her car reminded her, just as she was driving into the hospital parking lot. She pulled over, popped open the boot of her car, and retrieved the small, pungent bag of trash.

If it hadn't been for the snow she might have missed them altogether, but there had been a storm last night, a hefty ten inches, and she pauses to brush off enough from the top of the dumpster so she can open the lid without a cascade of snow tipping back on her clothes. From inside she hears a kitten's meow. What on earth? She stands on tiptoe and peers inside, but can't see anything in the dark interior except bulky black bags of trash, full of disposable diapers, she concludes, from the smell. Still, she hears it again, a muffled meow.

Her eyes adjust to the dark, dim interior and she sees a grocery box propped on top of the black mountain of trash bags. It looks to be full of crumpled newspaper. Her eyes adjust again and she sees there is a blanket, stiff to her touch. Under the crusty folds her fingers touch something fleshy. Blindly, her fingers identify a baby, sticky with after-birth.

Her hands are shaking so hard she has trouble lifting the box out of the bin. It slips from her numbing fingers and falls back onto the black, knotted bags of rubbish. She grips the edges of the apple box more firmly and lifts it over the edge of the dumpster. She hurries the surprisingly heavy box to her car.

She can't imagine that this baby is still alive, out here in the cold for how long, who knows, but she heard it mew. There is hope. She must hurry. With the box filling the front seat of her little car, she overrides the impulse to take it home, call it her own. Instead, full of intent and responsibility, with the heater blasting, she speeds the last fifty meters to the closest entrance, the children's admission unit. She leaves her car parked in the middle of the emergency entrance and hurries the box in through the automatic doors.

Its eyes are squeezed shut. Its lips are blue.

As she stumbles into the hall, snow falling off the tops of her boots, she throws her keys to the security guard. "Can you move my car, please?" Even in her hurry, there is always time for civility. It is the key to effectiveness in a large public institute like a hospital. She calls to Jess, the first nurse she sees. She knows them all here, all the doctors and nurses. Last month she was stationed here herself. "I found a baby in the snow."

Jess hurries her into the treatment room, and an instant later they are joined by a junior doctor, Ricky. Elizabeth sets the heavy, sodden box on the table. With extreme care—a care mixed with urgency and fear—she lifts the neonate out of its cardboard box.

"Beep the Registrar, Jenny," the nurse tells the health care assistant, as she helps Elizabeth untangle the baby from the blanket in which it is wrapped. "It's a girl," the nurse identifies, as she initiates the obs machine. "Can't be more than an hour or two old."

The temptation to reach for this baby, to cradle it in her arms, despite its need of immediate medical care, is palpable for Elizabeth. Always maternal, in the last few months her desire for a baby has risen like a high fever. She forces her attention away from the baby, back to the box on the table, and then blinks in amazement at the sight of a tiny, splayed, starfish hand peeking out of the cover. Tucked into the blanket is a second baby, also a girl, as blue as the first, a hand-knitted cap pulled down over its eyes and ears. Its mouth is open in feeble protest—a meow. The frenzy of activity in the room stops mid-step as Elizabeth lifts the second baby from the box.

"My God."

The health care assistant returns to the small room with both a forced-air warming blanket and a warming crib. "Actually, we're going to need two of those warming cribs," Elizabeth says, quickly handing the second baby to the junior doctor. By the time Ricky has inserted an IV line into back of the baby's hand, Dr. Singer, the Registrar has arrived.

"Temperature is 34.3 degrees," the nurse reports.

"Blood pressure?"

"First girl or second?"

"I'll start an obs chart on Rosy here. Jess, if you'll start one on Pinkie."

"Heart rate?"

"90 for Pinkie"

"110 for Rosy."

"Weight?"

"Rosy here weighs 2146 grams—4 pounds, 7 ounces." Jenny is gently rubbing the tiny feet and hands to increase circulation. "And Pinkie weighs—" Dr. Singer adjusts the scale, "2240 grams—4 pounds, 15 ounces."

"How premature are they?"

"My guess is they are thirty-four weeks—maybe thirty-five."

3

"Fortunate. There could be real complications for preemies with this cold."

The babies have been wrapped in the forced-air warming blankets to prevent worsening hypothermia. Oxygen masks cover their tiny faces. Already, pink is replacing the immobile blue facial tones.

"What do you want me to do with this?" Elizabeth holds up a third object in the box, an angry mass of meat red placenta.

"Recycle bin?"

"Compost?"

"I wonder what it would do to my undernourished camellia bush?"

"The police are going to want everything in the box," the consultant offers. "They will want to speak with you, Elizabeth, when you are ready."

"Of course." Elizabeth lifts out the blanket and shakes it gently. Out fall two long, blonde braids.

"Someone's idea of a good luck charm?"

Christine puts the phone back on its base.

"What's wrong?" her husband asks, distractedly. He is putting the last of his papers into his computer case. He is speaking at a conference this afternoon in Geneva. His plane leaves in two hours, if the snow doesn't cause a delay. Fortunately, the subway to City Airport is reliable—and quick.

"I'm not sure that anything is wrong."

"What is it?" He is wondering if he should bring his computer or his iPad. His colleagues deliver their speeches from their iPads or their Kindles but he is a man of habit and wonders how his delivery would change without a handful of ruffling papers. He appreciates technological advancements. He can't last a day anymore without an internet connection. But technology has gotten ahead of him. He has more toys than he can play with at one time. He wonders if this is a sign he is getting old.

"I think we are going to be parents," Christine says quietly.

They have been on the waiting list for over two years. They could have adopted sooner if they had been willing to take an older child, but Thomas's only criteria for adoption has been that the child be newborn. Race, sex, physical defects, nothing else had mattered to him when Christine proposed adoption as a means to resolve their inability to have children. However, he has refused to budge on age. It must be a newborn.

"That was the social services officer calling from the Norwich & Norfolk Hospital. This morning one of their doctors found a newborn. In the trash bin."

"Good God. In this day and age? Is it all right?"

"It seems to be fine. They want us to come up straight away. If we don't want it, they will notify the next family on the list."

"Let's get going."

"What about your conference?"

"What about it? Come on. I'll get the car keys."

"The car?" They have an old Saab, but they never use it. It sits in a garage two blocks from their house, and every few weeks Thomas drops by to make sure the battery hasn't died. A car in London is a bad idea. However modern the city has become, the streets are better suited for the occasional carriage, not single use automobiles. Now that they have broken themselves of their car dependency, they use public transportation when they leave the city, too, when they travel on weekends to their little cottage in the Epping Forest in Essex. "Not the train?"

Thomas smiles brightly and the reality of their situation dawns on her. They might need their car to bring home a baby.

Christine has gathered her woolly hat and winter gloves. She has one arm into her coat but hesitates. "There's another thing."

"Yes?" Thomas is holding her coat. He positions it so that her left hand can locate the arm hole.

"It wasn't alone. It is a twin. What are we going to do?"

"We will decide when we get there."

"What's wrong with me?" Christine asks, looking back into the apartment, wondering what she has forgotten. "I didn't ask if they are boys or girls or one of each."

"What does it matter? Let's go!"

By the time Christine and Thomas see the newborns through the glass of the hospital nursery, the twins have been cleaned and fed, and are nestled side by side in a double bassinet. The cardboard cradle and birth stained blanket, the bagged placenta, the hand-knitted cap and the two braids are in the custody of the Norwich police.

They sit in awe at the sight in front of them. Every miniature movement, every jerky reflex elicits a sigh of disbelief. They look more like Beluga baby whale pups than humans, Thomas thinks, so pale, so otherworldly. The more they watch the tiny twins, the more they know they must adopt them both.

"They are going to need each other."

"They are," Thomas says, lowering his voice to a whisper, leaning close to his wife. The faint, familiar residue of shampoo gives him comfort, reminds him he isn't alone in making these complex decisions. "All adoption cases have sad stories. All adopted children have trauma they must overcome, regardless of how lovingly they are brought into their new homes. But a child thrown into the trash—"

"That's attempted murder—" Christine has lowered her voice, as well, as if softening her voice can lessen the gravity of the transgression against these two innocents. "Neonaticide."

"These children will need everything we can give them and more."

"Together, maybe they won't feel so decidedly abandoned."

On principle, there is no question but to take them both.

But practically, twins! Two newborns all at once. How will they manage?

6

Natural parents have nine months in which to prepare for the arrival of their child. Christine and Thomas have been preparing themselves, too, in a way, but they never considered they would need more than two arms at any time to hold their eventual child. Thomas has a demanding job. He is often out of the country. Even when he is in London, he works long hours. Neither of them has relatives in England. "We will have to hire help," Christine says. "I don't see how I could manage two on my own."

"Of course we'll find help." He frowns at the idea of sharing his home with a stranger. Their apartment is large by London standards. There is a room for the babies, if he moves his study down the hall into a corner of Christine's office. They had always planned to use his office as a nursery.

"It shouldn't be hard to find help in a city the size of London," she says doubtfully.

"Someone from the neighborhood, perhaps, so we don't have to think about live-in help."

"I wish your mother lived in London. She would be a trustworthy presence. She is so good with children."

"Hmmm." He has had the same thought.

"Do you think she could come up to stay with us, at least at the start, until we get used to being parents?"

"We don't really have room."

"For your mother I would give up my studio."

"I was planning to move in with you, to give the babies my study."

"You and I could set up at one end of the dining room. I have a feeling I won't have time to work for a while anyway." She laughs, a mixture of irony and fatigue lifting and tingling like dual-tone chimes in an overhead breeze. "We probably won't be having dinner parties for a while, either."

There are moments when they speak, as the logistics of their adventure present themselves, but equally they are silent, trying to come to terms with the reality of their situation. The social service worker interrupts their meditation and invites them down into her office to initiate the bureaucratic process. They are visited by the police who

7

are as clueless about the situation as they are, and just as indignant. The video surveillance cameras showed an average height female dressed in a black parka, the hood pulled up against the snow, its fur border blowing to obscure the facial features. A close up shows pale skin and an expression of distaste, an upturned, ski slope nose. It could be anyone.

Each of the doctors and nurses who participated in the reception and recovery of the babies has stopped by to check on the newborns and to chat with the new parents. Reporters have tried to speak with them, but the hospital is keeping them at a distance. It is all quite overwhelming. When they are alone together, they sit quietly, watching their daughters, watching the other new parents, hoping for clues, their thoughts navigating the tributaries of their new responsibilities.

To be honest, joy isn't the primary emotion coursing between them, but it will gain ground, will pick up speed, and elation will surface like salt in fresh water to dominate the other emotions that are pouring over them at present.

"How will we tell the children that they are adopted?"

"We will wait until they ask. Then we will answer the specific question they ask. *They* will know how much information they want and when they are ready to handle it."

"What will we say?"

"The truth."

"We must never say they were found in the trash."

"No, that information won't help them. But that they were left at a hospital, yes, that much of the truth they can hear."

"You know, Tommy, in one way—and one way only—I am glad that the mother put them in the trash instead of bringing them to a safe place. She will assume they died and will never come looking for them. And even if she doesn't assume they are dead, she is guilty of attempted murder and can't risk showing herself to the authorities to start a search."

"You are giving their mother a rational line of thought, but the only thing we know about her for certain is that she was desperate—desperate enough to want to destroy two babies. Desperate people do desperate things. They don't think rationally, as we are giving her credit for now." He shifts his chair so that he is looking at his wife instead of into the nursery. "We will tell them they were found at the hospital. When they are old enough, we can bring them here; show them this lovely, clean room. Don't frown, Christy. This is going to be great, for them and for us."

"But what do we tell them about their parents?"

"We don't know anything about their mother or their father." With his thumb, he soothes the double crease from between her eyes. "What is there to tell?" With the tips of his fingers he moves her fair, silky hair back from her face. "We will let them create whatever stories they need to make them feel secure as our children."

"They are going to *need* each other," Christine says again, taking his hand and holding it tightly.

"They are going to *have* each other," he confirms, interlocking his fingers with hers. "And us."

Christine sits in a chair beside the cot, one hand resting on the back of each of her daughters. They breathe differently, she notices. One with a hurried hiccup, and one—how can she describe this subtle breath—as if without conviction. Perhaps she is wrong. Perhaps babies just breathe differently depending on their stages of digestion, or the positions in which they sleep. Christine realizes once again how little she knows about babies. She has read a dozen books in the last several years, preparing for this day that she can't believe has finally arrived. The day after tomorrow when Thomas returns from Geneva, they will bring the babies back to London. She is sorry the babies have had to stay in hospital these last three days, but a part of her is relieved that she isn't at home with them alone. Not yet. She needs time to acquaint herself with the reality of what has happened to them. It is such a different scenario than that for which she has rehearsed.

"Those are the cutest babies I have ever seen," Dr. Aragona says, bringing a current of fresh air into the overheated, incubated room. She smiles at Christine, then at the baby who has hoisted its bottom up into the air.

Christine looks at the two sleeping babies. They have almost no hair. The little bit of fuzz on top of their heads is almost translucent, like newborn chicks. Their cheeks are blotchy red; their eyes are tightly shut, as if afraid to view the world into which they have found themselves unwelcome. Identically, their lashes are long and matted, as pale as the insignificant wisps of hair. Christine wouldn't call them cute. Vulnerable, yes. In need of care, definitely. But cute? Not yet. "I was wondering why they never cry?"

Elizabeth has noticed that, too. Each night, at the end of her shift, before she drives herself home, she stops in to see them. *Her twins* is how she refers to them. She has stood at the foot of their cot, watching their mouths work up into a wrinkle, hungry to suck. She has studied how their tiny bodies twist with discomfort—passing a bubble of gas or pooing their nappies, an acidic diarrhea irritating the thin tissue of skin before they can be changed. But neither of them has cried. The one on the left, the one with less hair, she has heard mew, like a tired, lost kitten, but the other one hasn't made any sound. The babies have been examined extensively. Considering that they are five weeks early and weigh about two kilo each—and have spent the first hours of their life in the cold in a trash bin—they are miraculously healthy. Their not crying is not physiological.

Elizabeth jokes, "Once they start crying, it may be one of those questions you wished you hadn't asked?" Immediately, she is sorry for her joke. New mothers, especially new mothers in exceptional conditions, are not prone to humor. Elizabeth speaks more seriously. "They are healthy babies. They need time to finish developing, that's all. I can see a considerable improvement already."

"You are the one who found them?" Christine studies the confident, pretty young doctor. She removes her coat and purse from the chair where Thomas sits when he is with her, inviting her to sit.

"I am!" Elizabeth sits for the first time in eight hours, and immediately recognizes her mistake: weariness takes advantage of a moment to relax, and exhaustion surges through her body like a bad blood transfusion. She slumps back against the chair.

"If it weren't for you—"

"Let's not go there." Elizabeth makes herself sit up straight. She is not off duty, not at home, not with friends. Even if she is tired, she must remain professional. "Let's give your daughters every positive thought you can muster. They are going to need a strong mother. I think they have been lucky they have been given to you."

Her pager interrupts their conversation. "Sorry, I've gotta run—"

"An emergency?"

"Always." She checks the screen of her pager to see which department has called. "An emergency thrombolysis. The window is closing."

Christine hasn't understood the doctor's explanation, only that she needs to leave.

"I'll come back at the end of my shift."

"What should I do in the meantime?"

"Exactly what you are doing now."

"Which is—?"

"Let them become acquainted with your scent, with your voice. Talk to them. Sing. Don't be afraid to hold them. Ciao."

This woman has offered a salve to her maternal doubts.

She is afraid. Tomorrow Thomas will return from the conference she insisted he attend. Tomorrow they will take their babies home. She sits beside these two sleeping infants and wonders how on earth she will know what to do with them. By giving her twins, she feels the universe is laughing at her. There should be classes, not only how to give birth painlessly but how to raise children. Birth control or Lamaze on one side of their arrival, psychiatry on the other. But a basic maternal instruction course? Even with Thomas, the person she loves more dearly than anyone, sometimes, when she is tired or taken by surprise or stressed, she says things she doesn't mean. What will she do if that irrational voice invades her body to scream at her children, these two innocent babies who merit unconditional love? Is she up to the task? She is going to need help.

"Christine? Everything all right here?"

"Oh, Dr. Aragona."

"Please, call me Elizabeth." She brings another chair to sit beside Christine and positions it so she can be close to the babies.

"You are here late tonight, Elizabeth."

"I've had the ten to ten shift this week."

"Grueling."

"It's not so bad, really. I hardly have time to notice I'm tired until I have a day off, which is tomorrow." She covers a yawn with the back of hand. "I am on my way home but I wanted to see the twins. They look wonderful."

"They do, don't they?" They have both gained weight. Together, they weigh more than five kilograms. "We are taking them home tomorrow, late afternoon."

"I will miss them." She has found an excuse every day to come to see them. She has often found Christine asleep in this chair. "May I ask you a question?"

"Of course." She brushes the hair out of her face. She must look a mess. "Please do."

"When was the last time you slept? In a bed?"

Christine laughs but even her laughter is tired. "The night before you found the babies."

"Why don't you get some sleep now, while you have the nurses to care for them? You are going to need to be rested when you return home."

"I hate to leave them."

"I understand. But no one is going to harm them. And no one is going to take them from you. They are as much yours now as if they came from your womb."

Christine lowers her head into her hands. Her voice is quiet, barely audible. "I am worried I won't know how to take care of them."

"Every new mother's fear."

"I'm afraid I won't know how to love them properly."

"You will learn. This isn't an exam you pass or fail, Christine. It is a work in progress. Every day you will learn from your children what they need. And when you make mistakes, you can correct your errors by not repeating them."

"I am so tired, and I haven't even started."

"Christine." Elizabeth stands up and hooks her bag on her shoulder. "Come home with me tonight. I live five minutes from here, literally, and I have a lovely guest room. You can get a good night's sleep. My fiancé, Stephen, can bring you back tomorrow morning, if you are up early. Otherwise, I can bring you in whenever you want."

"Are you sure?"

"All your doubts will disappear with a good night's sleep, you'll see. Your babies will be grateful to have a well rested mother."

Stephen is surprised that Elizabeth has returned home at this late hour with the adopted mother of the twins she found. He has waited up for her, even though he has to be in hospital on an early shift in the morning. Their schedules match infrequently. They are lucky if they have a weekend off together, but they knew these first few years of practice would be hard. A few quiet minutes at the end of the day renew their devotion, and usually they are reluctant to share it with others. They have stopped meeting friends for drinks after work on Fridays, as they did in medical school. They have stopped inviting in guests for dinner on the weekends, even when they have a weekend free. Until they are both established in their specializations, they focus all their energies on their work and each other. Everything else has been put on hold.

Stephen covers his disappointment graciously. After all, he is a doctor. His life is dedicated to helping people, a service that doesn't cease when he leaves the hospital. He crosses his arms over his broad chest and smiles. "I have put water to boil. Would you ladies like a cup of tea?"

"Tea would be lovely. I have persuaded Christine that she needs a proper night's sleep."

"Good idea. You mustn't let yourself get under the weather."

Elizabeth says, "I am going to make toast. Christine, would you like a couple of slices?"

"I would, thank you. I'm afraid I forgot about dinner again tonight."

"I can make the tea, *Amore*, if you want to get to bed. I know you have to be up early."

"All right then. It is lovely to see you again, Christine. Good luck with your daughters." He shakes Christine's hand, then kisses Elizabeth. "I will see you upstairs."

Christine follows her hostess into the kitchen. Elizabeth pours the nearly boiling water into the Brown Betty tea pot with chamomile and prepares two cups. "What do you like with your tea?"

"Lemon, if you have it."

Elizabeth pops four slices of bread into the toaster, and then opens the refrigerator door to look for jam. "Orange marmalade? Apricot? Or fig?"

"Whichever you are having. They all sound delicious."

"My mother made them. You should try them all."

"I heard you call your fiancé *Amore*. I assumed you had Italian roots—"

"There can be no doubt with a name like Aragona—"

"But your accent is confusing. It sounds American or British."

"My father is Italian. My mother is American. I was born in Italy, but moved to England eight years ago to attend medical school. I have been working here since I graduated. Stephen is British. I guess the accent rubs off."

"Where are you from in Italy?"

"Florence."

"How nice. My husband's mother lives in Florence. In San Domenico. Do you know it? Just below Fiesole?"

"We are on the other side of the valley, also in the hills."

14

"It must have been hard to leave such a beautiful place."

"It was, and I am very close to my family. But I love living in England. The medical system is superb. The people are so nice. And Stephen and I fly home every time we can coordinate a long weekend off."

Elizabeth is very tired and would like nothing more than to climb into bed beside Stephen before he is too asleep to enjoy her company. She looks at Christine seated at the other end of the sofa. She looks more worried than tired. "Do you think you can sleep?"

"I will try."

"You look worried."

"I feel overwhelmed. And I haven't even started."

"You can arrange with London Social Services to have a health visitor drop by your apartment each morning for the first weeks. They are generally wonderful people and very helpful."

"That would be useful." But she doesn't look convinced. "My problem is that I don't know where to start. I know I need to find full-time help but I don't know where to start looking."

"There are agencies. Local church bulletin boards. Ask mothers with strollers in the park."

"I don't even have car seats—or whatever we need to bring them home."

Elizabeth brightens. "These are the fun bits to resolve. If you would like, I'll take you shopping tomorrow morning. There is a sweet little shop in Norwich that has everything you will need to furnish your nest."

"My nest." Christine thinks of their home in London, their cottage in Epping Forest. "I think I might feel less anxious if I were better organized. This has all happened so fast, I feel unprepared."

"I would love to shop with you for baby things. As you are falling asleep tonight, think of what you might need. I will do the same. We will make a list over breakfast tomorrow morning and by noon you will be back in the hospital with your babies."

"But tomorrow is your day off."

"Exactly. I can't think of anything more fun to do than shop for babies. And while we are shopping, we can talk about how to solve all your other questions."

CHAPTER
TWO

Thomas has delivered his speech in Geneva, and by all measures it has been a success. It didn't make any difference that he arrived at the conference a day late, or that he has had to step out of meetings to receive Christine's periodical updates on the twins. He has had calls from his lawyers, too, who are working with the adoption agency to guarantee that nothing will interfere with their bringing the babies home this afternoon. He has only been away from England for four days but it feels like a lifetime. He packs his suit into his garment bag and his papers and computer into his briefcase. He hopes his flight isn't cancelled because of the snow. He wants to see these babies who are going to change their lives. He wants to be close to Christine, to share this transformation. He hears something in her voice that makes him need to hold her.

He collects the abstracts from the conference, thinking to review them on the flight home, to see if there is anything that might be worth remembering, but he has his doubts. As a young man, he had thought he could make a difference, could bring about significant changes. But despite whatever successes he has had, the truth is the world needs an overhaul, not a checkup. If he believed in the traditional God, he would think it well time to build an ark and flood the perversity of mankind. It is time to be done with religious differences. It is well past time to be done with racial intolerance and corrupt politicians. They are long overdue to rid the world of poverty, infant mortality, starvation, child abuse. The list of things gone wrong is longer than the list of what's right with the world. All the charities, all the caring, all the church choirs chanting praise and love, are a minor fraction of the overall sum. He doesn't love the world they live in.

Despite his reservations, Thomas persists in his labors. He has been a champion of children's rights since he was a child, when his father was stationed in Italy. Trailing a stick along the shallow water of the Arno, poking at the ducks feeding at the banks, he stumbled, literally, upon a battered child lying in the mud. Panicked, he sprinted home and insisted his mother return to the river with him. And to her merit, despite the blood and the mud and the terrible odor of decay, she picked up the filthy child, hugged him close to her chest and carried him home.

How many thousands of children has she helped?

But for every child that she—and later he—have helped save, how many are left to be cold, hungry and unloved? He can't understand how, in this day and age, in a civilized, first world country like the UK, with birth control available to anyone who wants it, and abortion available to those who lacked foresight, with the adoption agencies holding long lists of parents waiting for babies, who on earth would throw babies into a dumpster?

He shakes his head, discouraged. He can understand a religious or moral objection to birth control. Adoption agencies have been formed to help people who can't keep their children, for whatever reason. But to dump babies into the trash bin fifty meters away from a hospital entrance? To condemn babies to die in the snow? Thomas needs to return to his wife and children in order to renew his belief that the world is a place worth inhabiting.

Thomas finds Christine transformed. When he left, she was white with worry. Now she is radiant with joy. The babies, too, have lost any traces of their unhappy start. They look like the other babies in the nursery except they are as pale as snow.

He sits beside her, relieved. Emotion floods over him and he holds himself very still until he can contain it.

"I think I've found names for them." Christine offers, shyly.

"You have?" His voice hails unfamiliarly from high registers.

"Anna—"

"My mother will be pleased—"

"And Elle—" She pronounces the two syllables separately, distinctly.

"For your mother, Eleanor, how perfect."

"Light and Grace. They start where they finish, finish where they start. There is no chance of our daughters ever getting lost again."

"You look wonderful, darling." The frown marks have disappeared; her eyes are clear, her face is smooth and relaxed. Her hair isn't clean but it has been brushed and pulled back with an unfamiliar red enamel barrette.

"I feel wonderful. I have found my purpose."

Thomas parks his old Saab next to Elizabeth's little FIAT 500 and helps Christine and Elizabeth transfer their purchases from her car to his. There is an hour before they can pick up their babies so they invite the young doctor to join them in the cafeteria for a snack before they drive back to London. If they eat now, they won't have to think about food the minute they return home. Thomas orders a full meal, steak and potatoes and mushy peas, which he eats with relish, as if enjoying his last meal. Christine nibbles on a triangle of spinach quiche. She accepts the bite size pieces of beef that Thomas cuts and deposits on her plate. She is obviously relieved to be with him again, and is gaining nourishment from his presence, at least as much as from the calories she's encouraged to consume.

"Do you mind if I ask how you met?" Elizabeth is touched by their intimacy, as if silently but steadfastly gaining strength from each other.

"At a Children's Rights symposium in London," Christine says, laying the tips of her fork and knife on opposite edges of her plate. "He was the last speaker at a conference for which I was translating. All the other participants were so political, so abstract, and in disgust, Thomas threw out his speech and spoke off the cuff—which is so much more difficult to translate because of its unpredictability, unfamiliarity. But he was so passionately outraged by the committee's refusal to look the situation directly in the eye, to focus on the children themselves that I almost froze in my tracks. I was so moved that I almost forgot to translate what he was saying, which would have been terribly embarrassing as we were being televised, live."

"My quarter-hour of fame indecipherable."

"I would have been fired in an instant if I had failed to do my job, which was to translate his address into Swedish."

"Even though every Swede speaks English better than I do," Thomas says.

He recalls his disappointment in the symposium. Blame passers, he called them. How on earth did they expect to make progress when all they could do was throw the ball of blame back and forth into each other's court? Like those walruses who fight against each other to maintain their dominance, at the expense of crushing the next generation underfoot in the battle. Power at its most absurd. "There are children dying in every corner of the world, children who might be spared their suffering if we would stop our internal bickering."

"Darling—"

"Forgive me. The soap box is my greatest weakness."

"So how did you get together?" Elizabeth asks. She has finished her quiche and is enjoying her dessert: a moist, sticky square of dark chocolate cake.

"Well, I did something I had never done before," Christine admits. "I went up to him after the conference, after everyone else had finished congratulating him, and told him how very moved I had been with his speech. He listened patiently, wearing this little smile he has—that one, there. I thought he was being terrifically polite and patient to listen to my ramblings, and when I finally finished, he said he was terribly thirsty and in need of a drink. He asked if I would care to join him."

"You should have seen her," Thomas interrupts. "She was obviously trying to contain her nervousness but she was shaking, she was so passionate. Her face, that lovely, creamy white skin, flushed red with determination."

"All red and blotchy. What a fright I must have been."

"You must understand," Thomas continues, "this conference was the height of sophistication, a place where words were strung together for the sound of the cadence rather than content. And here was this woman telling me about the months she had lived in Botswana, telling me the names of the children who had died while she was there. She had tears in her eyes—"

"Probably a leaky nose as well."

"And we have been together ever since."

How bold she had been! "You were the star of the conference," she had told him, carried away by the enthusiasm he had conveyed in his off-the-cuff speech. "The north star, by which we will all find our course, if we keep you in sight."

"Do you like stars?" he had asked.

Christine stepped back, risked collision with the pin-striped back of another man from the conference. "I'm sorry. I am not a groupie. I didn't mean to give you the wrong impression."

"I'm afraid I've given you the wrong impression. You mentioned stars. I lost my train of thought." He studied her, as shy and reticent as an unspoken wish. "I would very much like to continue this conversation with you, but I am seriously parched. Would you care to join me for a drink?"

She hesitated only briefly before accepting his invitation, a shallow breath's attempt to extinguish the flame, but when they arrived at the conference center's lounge, it was crowded and boisterous. People were laughing raucously, the same people who had been so serious, so outraged upstairs a few minutes before. He sensed her hesitation. "It is a bit noisy, isn't it?"

"It is. I don't know if I'll be able to hear myself think in there."

"I know another place where we can talk. If you don't mind a bit of a drive?"

"Not at all."

"It might be a little cold."

"Are there stars?"

"More than you can count."

At that time of night, Epping Forest was only a thirty minute drive from the Royal Victoria Dock Conference Center in east London. Thomas left his car at the old beech pollard at the end of his driveway, and took Christine's hand to guide her along the bank of the river to the front of the cottage. The stars were as he had promised, despite the presence of a bright, three-quarter moon, but it was too cold to stand still to start the count.

They rounded the corner in time to see a gray heron lift from his perch at the edge of the river. Its great wing span was almost as wide as the river itself. With a sound like muffled wind, it flew low, close to the water, an unhurried glide, until it rounded the bend and disappeared out of sight.

"I can't believe what we've just seen," Thomas said breathlessly, rubbing her hand vigorously between his. "I have lived here for four years and I've never seen a heron at this spot of the river."

"We are fortunate there was enough moonlight to see it," she said, shivering, either from the cold or the thrill. "I think this may be one of the most magical moments of my life."

All that was about to change. Like a frozen waterfall about to thaw, the magical moments in her life would begin to flow with extraordinary, unstoppable force.

"Your house is lovely," she said, as he opened the front door and switched on the lights.

"It was the Old Mill House. I bought it several years ago from my friend, Julian, who lives in The Surdans, the Manor House." He looked at his rooms, as if for the first time. He had furnished the house simply, mostly from the pieces he had collected from his father's house in London: a sturdy library table, an old kid glove leather sofa and two large, overstuffed chairs; a long, narrow dining room table where he deposited the groceries he bought on his way out of London. Sometimes he cooked, sometimes he nibbled. Mostly he read and wrote, looked out his window and tried to make sense of the world.

He wondered how much of him she would understand by entering his house, but she wasn't looking around. She was wholly absorbed by the multi-faceted face of the grandfather clock in the entry hall.

"1820?" she asked.

"1825. How do you know?"

"It's quite easy to date a painted dial long case."

Thomas looked at her, waiting for her to continue.

"My father collected clocks, mostly English. In the 1800s, dials started to lose the five minute markings and were replaced with fifteen minute numbering—" she pointed to the fifteen, the thirty, the forty-five minute marks. "The hour numerals were often in Arabic rather than Roman style."

"Fascinating."

"I could bore you for hours!" she laughed self-consciously. "Your house is lovely. And quite grand."

"It's miniscule compared to The Surdans, but if one resists the comparison, it is spacious."

"Was it like this when you moved in?"

"More or less." He had taken her coat and briefcase, had hung it in the hall closet. "There was a wall here, between the front parlor and the kitchen. I knocked it down to create one large living space. Easier to heat. I installed this half-bath beneath the stairs," he opened the door to show the efficient use of a small space, "so I wouldn't have to run upstairs to the cottage's only bathroom." He had refrained from telling her more, how he had sanded the timber beams and painted them with a resin that restored their patina. How he had knocked down the wall between the two smallest bedrooms upstairs to create one large bedroom, with a fine, open view of the river Lea. He had accessed the flue from the fireplace on the first floor and added a fireplace in the new, enlarged bedroom, and installed glass-fronted wood-burning stoves in both rooms to solve the problem of heating. The other two bedrooms upstairs he kept closed, opening them only in summer to access the cross-breeze.

He saw that she was shivering.

"The only drawback is that before we can have our drink, we need to light the stove." He could see their breath mingling in the space between them. He returned to the entry hall closet, and handed her a heavy Irish fishing sweater in exchange for her light suit jacket. He grabbed a second sweater off the shelf in the closet and pulled it over his head.

Christine noticed the bin of seasoned wood stored beside the fireplace. "I don't mind starting the fire if you want to fix the drinks."

Surprised, he raised his eyebrows. "If you are sure?" She nodded. "What would you like to drink?"

"What do you have?"

"Good question." He opened a cupboard in a storage room off the entry hall and rummaged through a collection of bottles. "Nothing very interesting, I'm afraid." He moved bottles so he could see better. "Gin but no tonic. Scotch. Brandy. I have a fairly decent bottle of red wine, a Chianti," he added with enthusiasm.

"Do you have tea?"

"I do. A good, strong Irish breakfast tea or an herbal mix, some kind of berries, I think?"

"Berries. Once I warm up, I will switch to red wine, if that's what you are drinking."

"If you are cold we can go back into town."

"I wouldn't think of it," she said, already on her knees in front of the stove, her sleeves pushed up so she wouldn't soil her white silk blouse or the white wool cuffs of his sweater. "I am happy here. It feels like home."

A simple, understated contentment, perhaps the first uncomplicated happiness she had known in years.

And that is when he first kissed her.

That night she dreamt she found a cache of baby tortoises. Everywhere she looked she discovered another one until the little basket she carried was full of tiny tortoises, their shells curved in an obtuse oval shape. Inexplicably, when she woke from this dream, she felt an abundance of happiness. When she opened her eyes and found herself in bed with Thomas, the man who yesterday was a stranger but today was her intimate, her sense of well being increased.

She hadn't intended to stay the night. She wasn't in the habit of sleeping with a man whose words she had translated. But nothing that had transpired last night was what she was accustomed to.

She waited until he opened his eyes to see if his first reaction reflected his promises of last night. She watched closely, knowing that the first look would give her all the information she needed, before he had time to guard his thoughts, polish his act, and cover his bets. That first look would tell her if she should hurry out of his soft cotton shirt and into her own clothes—once she could remember where she had put them. She lay beside him, willing him to wake, willing him to wake happily, happy to see her.

Then he was awake and his response to finding her beside him in bed was relief, as if he had dreamed a wonderful dream but had feared it had only been a dream.

"Stay right there," he said, slipping out from under the covers and hurrying across the room. Quickly, he filled the stove with wood. She recalled he had done the same thing last night. She had assumed he had gotten up from the sofa to visit the loo, but when he returned a few minutes later, she noticed a faint whiff of smoke, and later, when he brought her upstairs to his bedroom, it was warm and welcoming as he had already lit the stove. Undressing was luxuriously slow, unhurried in the warm, fire-lit glow. The bed was warm, too. He had turned on a heating blanket and the flannel sheets were toasty. By comparison, their hands were a degree colder, and they both shivered with pleasure.

Last night, when they had exhausted their need for each other, she heard him humming softly, half under his breath, a tune she had heard before but which she couldn't quite place. Before they had fallen asleep, he had whispered, "Now we can count the stars."

She lay next to him and looked up at the ceiling. A skylight the size of the double bed was animated with bright pin pricks of light. "Do you ever see shooting stars?"

"In August, all the time." He couldn't wait to shower her with August stars. "More rarely in the winter."

She wondered if she would have the occasion to see the stars in August. "I am going to try to stay awake until I see one," she said, settling on her back, forcing herself to keep open her eyes. Don't let yourself fall in love, Christine warned herself. Not until you are sure it's reciprocal. But as she admonished herself, she knew that she had as much of a chance of avoiding love as she did of staying awake to see an eventual falling star. She wished she could identify the song he was humming.

In the morning, after several false attempts to get out of bed, Christine asked if she might make breakfast. "I have one of those high metabolisms," she confessed. "I require food every few hours. Not a lot," she hastened to add, not wanting him to think she was a glutton, "just regular."

"Let's see what we have. We might need to drive into town for breakfast. I don't keep a lot of food here."

They found a bushel of apples on the doorstep. "That will be my neighbor, Julian," Thomas explained, as they lugged the heavy basket indoors. "He kind of looks after me. He brings me quantities for a family of ten. I never quite know what to do with all the food he brings me."

"Stored in a cool, dark place, most of these apples will last throughout the winter. Most winter fruit stores well."

"I wish I had known. I've been giving almost everything away to the woman who cleans my house in town, Cynthia. She has ten kids."

"Does she really?"

"Well, maybe not ten." Their laughter collided overhead, his baritone bumping against her alto. "Last time I was here, Jules sent over a ten pound bag of flour. The week before, honey to satisfy a bear. Quite good, actually."

"Did you keep any of the flour and honey?"

"I did."

"I could make apple pancakes. It's my national obligation."

"Norwegian or Swedish?"

"Swedish."

"That would explain your height." And the gorgeous eyes, he thought, the creamy skin, the silky hair. "You *do* have a national obligation to make pancakes."

Her raised eyebrow asked for his details. "I am American," he said, "but I haven't lived in the US since I was a baby. My father was born in Germany. He moved to Washington, D.C. during the Second World War."

"Where did you live if not in the USA?"

"All over. My father was in the diplomatic corps."

"Your mother?"

"She was studying literature in Boston when she met my father. They met in that park where the ducks live."

"Sorry?"

"You know that children's story about the ducks that pass through a park in Boston?"

"I'm afraid I've missed that one."

"It was my favorite childhood tale. I naturally assumed my parents had known the ducks. Instead, they both had appointments with other people in that park, but mistook

27

each other for the people they were supposed to meet. It wasn't until they were settled in a restaurant and had ordered their meal that they discovered the travesty."

"Are the other two people, the ones they were supposed to meet, also happily married?"

"I never thought to ask. You can ask my mother when you meet her."

His words surprised her. She could feel herself blushing. "What other ingredients do you have in there?"

"My family?"

"The pantry." Their laughter was less awkward as it collided this time.

Thomas rummaged through the larder, putting words to the tune he had been humming last night:

> *When I fall in love, it will be forever*
> *Or I'll never fall in love*

and then caught himself, as if he'd revealed a secret, and switched back to the safe anonymity of humming. "I have eggs. How many do you need?"

"How hungry are you?"

"Starved, suddenly, now that you've mentioned apple pancakes." He set six eggs on the counter.

"I'll make a full batch. We can snack on them later, or send a batch over to your friend, Julian."

"Or Cynthia's ten kids, if you make tons."

"Are those walnuts?"

"They are." He pulled out a heavy burlap bag.

"If you don't mind cracking open some?"

It took her a minute to locate a whisk and a large enough bowl, a pan and some butter, but once she started assembling ingredients, from where Thomas sat at the table shelling nuts, she looked at home in his kitchen, as if they had been waking up hungry together for years. He could hardly keep himself from singing.

CHAPTER THREE

"How long did you say you have lived here?"

"I know. It's shameful." They were putting on their coats, preparing to go out for a walk along the river. He saw her looking at the stacked boxes in the storage room. "I bought this house four years ago. I'll admit I've been slow getting my books out of their boxes."

"Funny. That's always the first thing I do when I move house. I can better cope with a transition if I have walls lined with old, familiar books. It tends to buffer the drafts, as well."

"I don't know why I've been reluctant. It isn't a very demanding task. And it would buffer the drafts, as you say. The disadvantage of being so close to the river is the humidity."

"Too bad you don't have bookshelves." She picked up a heavy Atlas, obviously old and probably valuable.

"Actually, I have bookcases." He pulled a heavy blanket away from the wall where the shelving was stored. "They only need to be assembled."

"These are lovely." She touched the smooth veneer of old wood, tripped her fingers against an inlaid design, an interwoven **I** and **R** in fancy script.

"They were my father's." He touched the intarsia initials lovingly. "He set up a studio in London when he retired. It was beautiful. Just those two chairs, this table, and all these grand old bookcases. He said he wanted to reread every book in his library, cover to cover, now that he had time." There was reverence in his voice. "Unfortunately, he didn't have as much time as he thought. I doubt he read past Blake."

"This house will do them honor. Have you thought where to position them?"

"I hadn't thought." He had. He had mentally assembled them in the living room part of the big front room. But before he spoke, he wanted to hear where she would put them.

"I think they would look nice in there, at the end of your big room, if you aren't afraid that the cooking odors and oils will damage the books." She stepped back and squinted the storage room out of focus, into possibility. "If you wanted to use this room as a library instead of for storage, the books would help insulate the house." She touched her hand to the north wall and shivered at the chill that passed through the thick, stone wall. "This room is wide enough that you could leave a space between the backs of the bookcases and the wall, where you could insert insulation panels, eventually. You could move the library table and your father's arm chairs from the living room."

"How do you know about things like insulation?"

"I've lived in cold places and wanted a warm house, and haven't wanted to give my hard earned money to the oil magnates. Insulation isn't astrophysics. Old, crumpled newspaper works pretty well, too."

"Seal skins?"

"The best solution, if your conscience allows. It's a little like veal or lamb: It's a great flavor treat, as long as you don't think about what it was before it became your meal. If you have a screwdriver, we could assemble one of the bookcases and position it, to see where you like it best."

He liked the idea of a library, a place to work and leave his clutter at the end of a day, without it staring him in the face when he was trying to relax. He liked the idea of erecting his father's bookcases and unboxing his books. "Let's move the larder into the cupboard in the kitchen and set up the first bookcase here."

The first bookcase took over an hour to assemble and they were tired when they finished. Leftover apple pancakes satisfied their appetites and restored their enthusiasm for the project. The second bookcase was standing in under an hour. In the third hour the last two were standing beside their brothers, transforming the room from a cluttered, unused shed into a dignified library.

"There is still enough daylight for our walk," he said.

"We could walk, if you would like to. For myself, I think I would prefer to put these lovely books into their proper homes. They seem so forlorn stuffed into these boxes."

"Then let's do it," he had said, suddenly enthusiastic. "Should I put on water for tea?"

"Tea would be lovely. Shall we finish the last apple pancakes?"

Thomas retrieved an old cane chair that had been stored in the corner of the room, and positioned it for Christine at the end of the pile of books. She removed the first book from the box. *"For Every Child: UN Convention on the Rights of the Child,* by Caroline Castle. How would you like to organize them? By subject? Fiction, philosophy, poetry, biography, economics, etc."

"I am afraid eighty percent of these books concern human rights, and all its branches." His tone was apologetic: "Children's Rights, Social and Economic rights, Children and the law, International humanitarian law. All non-fiction, all written—or at least translated—into English."

She held up a volume of essays, *The European Union and Human Rights.* "In that case, maybe you would prefer to shelf alphabetically?"

"How convenient to start with the A's."

She picked up a slim volume of poetry, brushed it with a cloth to free it of dust. Curiously, she opened the marbled cover. On the front page, in sepia colored ink, there was a delicate scrawl. She checked the front cover again, the inside pages. "This is a signed first edition."

"Father loved poetry."

"Did he know Auden personally? Or was he a collector of first editions?"

"I don't know if he knew Auden personally but I remember poets at our house, in whatever country we were stationed."

"Is that a polite way of saying your father was an ambassador?"

"Well, at the end of his career he was. But the diplomatic corps starts you at the bottom of the barrel and if you are successful, you end up a consul general or an ambassador. If you aren't successful—and it doesn't always depend on you— you are out of a job. No second chances. My father had many close friends who were very good diplomats, but found themselves stationed in the wrong country at the wrong time. With the diplomatic corps, it is either up or out."

She envisioned a large barrel being pushed down a steep hill with a cartoon head and legs sticking out. "What does an ex-diplomat do?"

"They join the private sector. Universities like to hire them. They can work for the government, just not in the diplomatic corps."

She picked up the next book and dusted it. "Do you want to alphabetize by author or book title?"

"Either way."

"Are you good at remembering author's names? Otherwise we should alphabetize by title."

"I have met many of these writers. We tend to be invited to speak at the same conferences. Even when I don't agree with them, I remember their names."

"What if you were to keep your poetry separate from your other books?"

"Like two separate libraries?"

"Exactly. You probably won't reach for Rilke when reading Castle."

"Actually, I do, but I like your idea of creating separate shelves for Father's collection."

"Or we could place it on the top shelves on each of the four bookcases." She dusted a book as she lifted it from its box. "After all, poetry is considered to be the most elevated of all literature."

"Why is that, do you think?" He placed two volumes of Auden on the top left shelf of the first bookcase.

"I think it is because poetry isn't dated. The urgency Andrew Marvell expressed in *To His Coy Mistress* is no less urgent today than it was in the mid 1600's—"

"While the youthful hue," Thomas recited, *"sits on thy skin like morning dew. . . ."*

Christine was impressed that he had committed lines of the poem to memory, but she didn't let it interrupt the point she wanted to make. "Our speech has changed, we don't say Thou or Thee—"

". . . and while thy willing soul transpires, at every pore with instant fires. . ."

"And women aren't coy in the way they once were," she said, "making their suitors wait endlessly." Their eyes met and twinkled, remembering their mutual urgency. "But the sentiment is the same. We are still concerned with immortality, with our race against time."

". . . though we cannot make our sun stand still, yet we will make him run!"

"That's what I love about poetry. A quote for every occasion. Instead, a novel—even a really good novel—"

"Like *Robinson Crusoe*—" Thomas held up a leather bound copy that was clearly part of his father's collection.

"Or *The Age of Innocence*—" Christine added, handing him a volume of Edith Wharton.

"—becomes outdated, because it is situated in a time period."

"Exactly. It depicts its characters' current attitudes and dress, the events of the day."

"In other words, it might be a pleasure to read Dickens, but *Oliver Twist* is a period piece. Even though it concerns the fate of an orphan, it isn't relevant to anything in our own lives."

"We might be at this task an entire lifetime, if we stop to discuss every book," Christine remarked.

"I could think of worse ways to pass a lifetime, actually." His comment lingered in the air between them, but she passed him the next several books silently, without opening their covers. Simply, she read out the authors' names, and he positioned them on their appropriate shelves.

"What do you have on your bookshelves?" He had asked to get the conversation moving again.

She laughed and he was happy to hear the merriment in her voice. "I have an embarrassingly large collection of children's books."

"But no Boston Ducks."

"No Boston Ducks. I can't resist the illustrations, especially the water colors. I also have a lot of biographies, a fair amount of fiction; sometimes the same novel in five or six languages."

"How many languages do you speak?"

She handed him two dusted volumes of Goethe. "Fluently, five."

"Which five?"

"Swedish, English, Dutch, Norwegian, and French."

"And not fluently?"

"I can translate from German, Danish and Russian into English, as well as from Chinese, Japanese, and Suomi—"

"Which is?"

"Finnish. But I am totally useless with the Arabic languages. I can't make heads or tails of them."

"I'm glad to hear it. I was beginning to feel inadequate."

"How many languages do you speak?"

"One."

"I assume that would be English."

They laughed, and their laughter rattled around each other like dice in a cup. "I can stumble around in Italian," he added "—my mother lives in Florence—and sometimes I can make myself understood in Spanish, but I'm an embarrassment, really. I've lived in a dozen countries and have never been able to learn more than a few, rudimentary phrases. How do you do it?"

His look of admiration embarrassed her. "It isn't anything I do, really. I just understand different languages in the way that a person who plays the piano can pick up other instruments to play them without studying. Some people paint and sculpt and draw, some people are good at making money in whatever field they try. I just hear the words and they make sense. It used to drive my sister crazy. She is like you. She can't hear the different sounds."

"Is your sister older or younger than you?"

"She is older by five years."

"Are you close?"

"Very, even if we rarely see each other. She and her husband have about ten kids—"

"You are sure her name isn't Cynthia?"

"Janelle. I wish she lived in London so I could see her more. She lives in Karlstad—"

"Which is where exactly?"

"It is in Sweden, where we grew up. On Lake Vänern. I try to visit her every Christmas."

"It must be beautiful."

"It is, and even better in the summer months when the sun never sets. I sometimes visit for the summer solstice. Lake Vänern is the largest fresh water lake in Europe." She shivered.

He waited for an invitation but none was forthcoming. She hadn't yet accepted what he knew to be a truth: that they were going to spend the rest of their lives together. True, it had all happened very quickly, but why should he pretend otherwise when he knew for certain that she was the person he had been waiting for all these years? Still, he didn't want to scare her. If she hadn't figured it out for herself, if she hadn't picked up his clues by the time they must part, he would speak plainly. But she was a smart girl and he doubted it would take her long to understand that his intentions were in their mutual best interests.

"Did I understand you said you never studied?"

"An inaccurate figure of speech. Of course I studied, once I was convinced I should become a simultaneous translator."

"Convinced?"

She tucked a blonde strand of hair behind her ear. "I had thought I would teach elementary school, like my mother. I've always liked children and teaching would have suited me. But my mother told me I had a gift and therefore a responsibility to use it."

"My mother gave me the same speech. We should introduce them to one another. It sounds like they would agree on many points."

Christine grimaced but continued. "My mother was the one who researched all the translation institutes, and decided I should go to Geneva to study instead of Brussels. It wasn't the obvious choice but she knew I was shy and thought the smaller school would be better for me."

"Where did you study?"

"At the *Ecole de traduction et d'interprétation*. Their preparation is very thorough. Unfortunately, their base language is French, not English."

"What do you mean?"

"We learned to translate from French to German, French to Italian, French to English—"

"You forgot to put Italian on your list."

"My Italian isn't bad." She used two hands to pass him a heavy tome of collected poems. "After ETI, I went to the UN in New York, where I got a lot of practice translating into English, and where I had the belated study of how to overcome my shyness."

"And now you live in London?"

"I do!" she said brightly. "I will invite you over, if you'd like. I, too, have a skylight."

"So it wasn't just a line. You do love stars."

"I do. I live in a tiny but amazing mansard in Kensington."

"Kensington? I live in Kensington."

"But don't you live here?"

"On weekends and such. But for all practical purposes, I live in Kensington. On Lansdowne Road."

"Lansdowne, you're kidding."

They were neighbors. Their streets backed up onto one another so that Thomas, if he had known to look, might have gazed out the window of his study across the green to see light shining from under her book-lined rooftop apartment.

"This whim of mine," Thomas stuttered, "to bring you here last night. I don't mean to presume. If you need to get back to town, I will understand. If you tell me in simple English, that is."

36

"I have to be at a conference in Brussels on the 16th."

"Today is the 10th?"

"It is. What is your schedule?"

"I need to be in New York on the 17th. Can you stay here for another few days?"

"If you aren't worried about lending me another of your shirts and sweatpants." She tried to keep her voice even. It tended to squeak when she was uncertain. "I have some reading I need to do, in preparation for the conference."

"We can work in the new library, once we have these last books up off the floor." He picked up a copy of *Vulnerable Children and the Law* and placed it on a shelf with the S's. He positioned *The Challenge of Child Labour* with the H's. "What kind of prep work do you do?"

"I read the papers that will be presented, of course. But I also research the speakers. I read their essays, other speeches from past conferences. I try to understand their breathing patterns, their syntax. It all helps to facilitate translation."

"Did you research me?" He spoke with his back to her, as if his full attention was needed to straighten the spines of the books on the shelf.

"I did. But not too much."

"Why is that?"

"Because I already knew your speech patterns."

"You did?"

"I have translated your work before."

"When? Where?"

"Last year. At the Hague."

"The Rights of the Child."

"I could recite it for you, if you'd like."

"You are kidding."

"I am, actually. But you did make an impression on me. And I told myself if I ever had the opportunity to meet you, I wouldn't let myself be shy."

"I'm glad you came to speak with me." He left the book lying flat on the shelf to take a step toward her.

"And I am glad you invited me here." Her hands met his hands first, a touch of recognition, before his arms enclosed her. They spoke from within their embrace.

"When are you back from New York?"

"On the twentieth."

"You?"

"On the twenty-first."

"I could pick you up from the airport, if you'd like. Show you my apartment."

They had been together for less than twenty-four hours and were making plans like they had been married for decades. In the light of the day they were more reserved with each other than they had been last night. Trust, the hardest component to build between two strangers, was already present, a base on which they could build their daily habits. Respect was present, too, but as it had been established before they knew each other, it needed to be brought down from the podium and into the living room without letting the limitations of an individual destroy the illusion of greatness. Christine had seen Thomas lose his temper. She had seen his impatience with colleagues who were more interested in making points in a debate than with the issues themselves. Equally, she didn't know what to make of the overly tidy closet, work shirts ironed and hung neatly beside his suits, all the wooden hangers matching, turned in the same direction. His shoes were lined up and polished, even old work boots. Black and white photos of a previous generation shown in recently polished silver frames. She hadn't thought of herself as particularly messy, but her late mother's tarnished tea service was proof positive. She would be embarrassed to let him see her closet!

It was dark and they were tired by the time the titles were alphabetized. Arbour stood erect beside Arnet, Carney next to Dagne, Wollstonecraft near Yeats beside Yoham. Nonetheless, before they quit they carried the two heavy arm chairs from the living room to the library, and positioned the table into the center of the room. While Thomas stacked his work papers onto the table, Christine broke down the cardboard boxes, and stacked them sideways behind the bookcases, creating the first layer of insulation. The room was already noticeably warmer. Transformed.

"Enough work for one day!" Thomas said. "I'm taking you into town for dinner."

She changed out of his sweat pants and work shirt and put on her own clothes again, her skin feeling different under the clothes she had worn to the congress the day before. Thomas left his suit in the closet and put on dark corduroys, a shirt and the Irish wool sweater Christine had been wearing all day. At the front door, they paused to appraise their work, pleased with the overall effect.

"The living room looks better now, too, don't you think?" he had said, his hand on the door handle.

"It's a handsome room. Very welcoming."

"If we did all this in one day, imagine what we could accomplish in a life together."

Christine tried not to take him too seriously, but she felt herself flush at his declaration. "Once the pantry is put in order, I can't think of anything else to change. Everything is perfect. I really hate to leave, even for the promise of dinner."

He took her declaration seriously.

At her suggestion, they bought groceries at the little shop in town and hurried home to cook. They uncorked a bottle of Chardonnay and worked together in the small, compact space between the sink, counter and stove without bumping into each other. She prepared *Blomkalsuppe*, a creamy cauliflower soup, breaking tradition by sautéing a half pound of shrimp at the last minute, and while it was cooking, she riced boiled potatoes and mixed them with butter, milk and salt to make *Lefse*, another national favorite. When everything was nearly ready, Thomas braved the cold in the back garden to grill the salmon steaks he had marinated in oil, lemon and dill.

After dinner, they finished the last of the wine in front of the fire, and when they ran out of things they wanted to tell each other, they went upstairs, to be closer to the stars.

> *. . . while the youthful hue*
> *Sits on thy skin like morning dew,*

And while thy willing soul transpires
At every pore with instant fires...
...though we cannot make our sun
Stand still, yet we will make him run.

They fell asleep to a sky full of enigmatic, mobile stars and woke to bright blue beckoning skies and high flying white cotton clouds. The sunshine helped bring them to their feet, and over breakfast Thomas said, "Let's take that walk we've been promising ourselves."

"If you don't mind lending me your sweatpants and work shirt again, and that handsome fisherman's sweater." Her conference clothes were entirely wrong for this excursion into country living. It was funny really, since most of the time she dressed in the kind of clothes that would be right here, tweed and wool, and warm, tall, weatherproof boots. She only wore a suit for conferences.

"It's a good thing we are more or less the same size." Thomas commented. What a pleasure to look a woman straight in the eye. Even their coloring was similar. The shirts he wore to complement his pale blue eyes made her eyes brighten to turquoise, like the sea in Sardinia. When she pulled on his plum colored sweater, her eyes darkened to a royal, cobalt blue. He forced himself to stop staring. "Shoes might be a bit of a problem. What size do you wear?"

"Definitely smaller than yours," she said, looking down at the pairs of boots by the rear door of the mudroom. "Perhaps if I add another pair of thick socks?"

She stumbled as she tried to walk in the ungainly boots, and he took her arm. A few more incoherent steps and they realized the boots weren't going to work: they lifted and flopped from her foot with each smacking step. "Let me see if I can borrow a pair from Jules. Do you want to wait here or limp along?"

"I think I'll wait here, if you don't mind." She leaned against the huge base of a veteran coppiced beech at the rear of his house, reaching down into her boot to pull up the thick sock that had slid under her heel. She looked across the closely cropped expanse of green pasture to see longhorn cattle grazing in the distance. She could hear the water rumbling over the rocks in the river, but couldn't see it from this side of the cottage. Apart from the gurgling river and a distant progression of wings overhead from a chevron of migrating geese, there was only silence. She savored this rare interlude, an interval to the incessant cacophony of modern civilization. She closed her eyes and gave in to the concert of pure nature.

"Has someone been keeping you from sleeping at night?" Thomas was beside her before she heard him approach.

"I'm to blame." She hadn't noticed till now exactly how good looking he was. "I see you found boots."

"Yes. And Jules has invited us to dinner tonight, if you would like."

He looked so happy, so pleased with himself. "Whatever you would like to do is fine with me." She would have gone anywhere with him. It would have suited her to stay in his cottage, warm in front of the glass-fronted stove, reading and talking, interrupting themselves with a kiss or a caress, another hour of abandoned pleasure. Equally, she was curious to see him in company. And she had to admit she was intrigued to see the insides of The Surdans, that magnificent, post-Edwardian palace built on the edge of a lake so that its reflection filled the water and the sky, not unlike the Taj Mahal in its reflected splendor.

"Good. Let's see if the slipper fits."

"Like a glove."

He set the too large pair of boots at the back door of the cottage, and they walked toward the river. As they rounded the corner, they saw the heron lift, leaving its post on the river bank in a slow, gracious *glissade.*

Thomas stopped abruptly. The heron maneuvered his large wing span down the narrow river, and disappeared around the bend.

Eventually, without speaking, which might have broken the spell they found themselves in, they began to walk across the great pasture into the distant woods.

"Do these cattle belong to your friend Julian?" she finally asked, as they left the pasture and entered the woodlands.

"No. They belong to a local farmer."

"Are they here year round?"

"No. In the summer months they graze in the High Beach area of the Forest." He slowed his step, shifted his position so that she was on his right side. "Tell me about your family."

"Not much to tell, really. I have one sister—"

"Cynthia with the ten kids."

"You've been listening. My father taught nuclear engineering at the University in Karlstad and my mother was an elementary school teacher."

"Are they retired?"

"My mother died in my last year of university. My father died a few weeks later." Christine was silent for a long time.

"May I ask how they died?"

"My mother had leukemia. She was forty-eight when she died. My father was forty-nine. He died of a broken heart."

"Both so young."

"Yes. Terribly young. You should have seen them. My mother was so fit, so healthy. At the summer solstice she was swimming in Lake Vänern with my nephew on her back. In early August she couldn't bend over to lace her shoes. I wouldn't have wanted her to suffer, I wouldn't have wanted a long, drawn out death, but I wish I could have had time to come to grips with what was happening to her."

She had felt so bereft when her mother died, so thankful she had her father for comfort, so sad and confused when he was suddenly gone, and she was orphaned. Her sadness was complicated by irrational anger and relentless guilt— directed as much at her parents as herself. She was too old and independent to be experiencing infantile emotions like abandonment. Her sister did what she could to comfort Christine, but she had her own family to think about. Christine was all too aware of the background noise of babies and running water, dishes clinking as her sister attempted to set the table one-handed. Besides, comfort transmitted long distance via satellites doesn't warm the cockles of an aching, human heart.

"To be honest," Christine continued, "I think that's why I accepted your invitation for a drink, why I came up to speak with you in the first place. There are too many things left unsaid in my life."

"I am listening."

"It isn't easy for me to find words. Perhaps that is why I translate, so I don't need to rely on my own words but can use others."

"For myself, as capable as I know you to be as a translator, I would prefer to hear what you are thinking."

"I will keep that in mind." She was thinking of her father, but as much as she would have liked to speak, to tell Thomas the story, she couldn't bring herself to introduce sadness into this idyllic setting. "Tell me about your parents."

"Father was an extremely positive and influential figure in my life. I admired him as much as I loved him. I love my mother, as well, but it is a more material love, built on affection and joint adventures, shared secrets. Father, instead, inspired principles and values."

"He must have been very proud of you."

"Perhaps. But never as proud as I was of him."

"How long ago did he die?"

"Father died five years ago. A month after he retired. He was on his bicycle in the Cotswold's with my mother, and he forgot he was in England. He looked left instead of right."

"He was killed?"

"No. He broke his shoulder. I flew back early from a conference at the Hague and was relieved to see him looking so well. I remember that my mother and he were planning a trip to Bruges when he died. Pulmonary embolism. Gone before we understood he wasn't paused in thought."

"Your mother must have been devastated."

"She was. I think she blamed England. In any event, she left straight away. She moved into the house they kept in Florence. I lost both my parents in one fell swoop and never saw the talons flexed to kill."

"Where is your mother now?"

"Still in Florence. She had an interesting group of friends—la Signora Gronau, who started Sotheby's in

Florence, and Niccolai Rubens, the eminent Renaissance scholar—both of whom are dead now, which leaves her with few friends, most of whom she dismisses as more clever than intelligent. She has her routines, and doesn't complain about being lonely, but she isn't one to complain, really, not about anything. I try to see her as often as I can, but at best I see her three or four times a year, and even that is hard, with my schedule. There aren't a lot of conferences scheduled in Florence. I love my mother and I miss her, even though I probably shouldn't admit that at my age." He grimaced and looked to Christine for her reaction.

"You are fortunate to have parents who merit your love and respect. That isn't always the case."

"In that sense, too, I have been privileged. As an only child, with my father so engaged with his work, Mother and I would explore whatever new country we were in. She was never too busy for me, although looking back I see that she must have had a busy schedule as a diplomat's wife. She's the one who got me interested in children's rights, if truth be told."

"How did it happen?"

"We were living in Italy. I don't know how well you know Florence, but the American Consulate is really beautiful. Right on the river. Italy was the first European country in which my father had been stationed, after a long stretch of assignments in some terribly underdeveloped third-world countries. I had seen poverty, I had been aware of it everywhere we had lived. I guess that's what threw me off guard in Florence. It was so beautiful, I wasn't expecting it.

"From the terrace of the Consulate I had this magnificent view up and down the Arno. I felt I could see forever. If I used Father's binoculars I could see even farther down the river, past that long park, *Le Cascine*, past a suspension bridge named after some famous Indian Raj who had died in Florence. It was like living in a fairy tale."

"It sounds lovely."

"It was." He shivered from repulsion. "Until one day I convinced Mother that I was old enough to go out exploring on my own, and down at the river I found a kid who had been

44

beaten and left on the river bank. I should have called the police, I was old enough to know that was the right thing to do, but instead I ran home and got my mother. And she, bless her ever generous soul, brought him home to nurse.

"Things were different then in Italy. Sure, there were laws, a law for everything in fact. My father complained about the endless bureaucracy, but there were so many laws, it was hard to keep track of them. In the general chaos, people pretty much did what they pleased, and no one paid them any attention. Every now and then there would be a roundup and tickets would be issued, but for the most part, there was a kind of benevolent anarchy.

"So my mother brought home this little kid and nursed him until he was well. He spoke some but trust me when I say he wasn't talking! I would have told everything after a beating like he had suffered, but he kept his mouth shut. The police left us alone. Things would have been very different if he had been Italian, but he was assumed to be a gypsy and no one had come looking for him. My father agreed to let him stay if my mother took full responsibility for him. And that was the beginning of my long march for children's rights.

"It was also the end of my own childhood, so to speak. It would have ended soon enough anyway, I suspect. I was enrolled in middle school at the International School of Florence, a pretty sophisticated place, if you consider that I had been attending schools in Sri Lanka, Guatemala and the Philippines. I was an only child and whatever difficulties I found outside the home, in whatever country we found ourselves, at home I was my mother and father's pride and joy, their little prince.

"But when Rikki moved in with us, I became the gatekeeper. 'Tommy, take Rikki with you, Tommy, read to Rikki, Tommy, let Rikki play with you and your friends.' I don't know exactly how old he was but around eight, I'd guess, although in some ways he seemed much older than I was, and in other ways, absolutely infantile. He refused to sleep alone in the room my mother had prepared for him, so she had an additional bed moved into my room. I could have lived with it all, I did feel sorry for him, but he lied about everything. He refused to admit that he cried in his sleep. He stole things, too, and lied about that, as well. The cook was always catching him red-handed, and I found Mother's compact hidden under his bed. Mother—my own mother—took his side against me when I tried to explain how things really were. She said she was disappointed in me! So I stopped telling on him and I stopped caring if he cried in his sleep."

"How long did he stay with you?"

"Four miserable years."

"And why did he leave."

"Ha! He burnt down the consulate!"

"No!"

"He had stayed home from school, pretending to be ill. He hated school, couldn't get along with the other kids, and my mother let him stay home more than I thought healthy. But this time I was home, too, with a stomach flu. I woke up because I smelled sulphur and lacquer. I looked up in time to see him sitting cross-legged on his bed, playing with matches and hairspray. It shouldn't have taken a genius to understand that the feather comforter would burst into flames. I pulled him off the bed and out of the room before the curtains caught fire.

"The guards called the fire department, and they arrived pretty fast, but the second story of the Consulate was badly damaged. My mother cried. My father was stunned, and then furious when Rikki denied it was his fault. He laid down the law to Rikki, saying. 'If you can admit responsibility for what you have done, we will let you continue to live with us. But if you can't accept responsibility, you must live with a family that can supervise you more closely.' In the end, the best Rikki could manage was to say he was sorry, but he could never admit that the fire was his fault."

"Pathological."

"I was glad when he left, although my relief was compromised with a heavy sense of guilt. I was the lucky one, born into privilege. No one would ever beat or abuse me. I had no reason to lie, no need to not trust the truth. I guess a lot of my work is thanks to Rikki, who gave me a close-up view of what poverty and abuse does to kids. And that the problems need to be solved before kids are old enough to play with matches, so to speak, because by that point, well, it is too late."

"What happened to Rikki?"

"I am ashamed to say I don't know. My mother kept in touch for several years with the family that adopted him but eventually she lost contact. But Rikki stays present in my life in peculiar ways."

"How is that?"

"I can't tolerate lies, not even white ones, and the smell of hairspray inevitably makes me nauseated."

CHAPTER FOUR

They arrived punctually at seven, a short walk through a snowy patch of woods along a crushed stone pathway. They passed the stables and heard horses whinny in alert; passed the winter kitchen garden where they caught sight of a rabbit burrowing beneath the snow in search of food. The doors to the gabled garages were ajar and deep in the shadows they saw tractors and farm equipment stored neatly. In another barn there were bales of hay stacked one atop of another, disappearing into the height of the upper loft. Christine was wearing the dark suit she had worn to the conference. Thomas took her hand and assured her she looked lovely. Their time together had brought high color to her face and she couldn't stop herself from smiling.

At the front door, they removed their boots and thick socks to slip on their proper shoes. "Shall we leave them here?" Christine tucked the two pairs side by side near a snow powdered camellia bush.

Thomas rang the bell and heard a dozen chimes resonate from indoors. "I think we can give them to Gregory. He will store them someplace warm."

Gregory gave their coats and boots to another, younger member of staff and led them down an expansive hallway into the library to meet Julian.

"Just like ours," Thomas whispered to Christine.

"A wee bit bigger," she said, surprised but pleased to hear him referring collectively to his new library as theirs.

"All right?" Julian rose to greet them, setting down the large orange cat he had been holding. He was a dignified figure several years younger than Thomas and almost as tall—perhaps taller, Christine noted, if his shoulders hadn't been slightly rounded.

"All right," Thomas answered. "Christine, this is my dear friend, Julian." He brought Christine forward proudly. "We've been erecting a library in the cottage, but I'm afraid it is rather humble compared to yours."

Julian bowed over Christine's hand, then shook hands with Thomas while Gregory opened a bottle of Champagne and poured them a drink. Julian would have liked to postpone dinner to share the wonders of this book-lined room. He and Thomas often spent entire evenings lost in the company of these great books. Henry James had once said that The Surdans library was one of the best private libraries in England. It was a subject of great interest to Julian, and he had to be careful or he could bore his guests by assuming a shared passion. Besides, Gregory had already warned him that dinner was almost ready; there was time only for a quick drink. He had reminded him that Marion wouldn't suffer silently a collapsed soufflé. "He's put you to work already, has he?" Julian gestured for them to sit.

"He has." Christine seated herself on the sofa beside the cat, hoping its orange fur wouldn't attach itself to her black suit.

"I am happy to meet you," Julian said, sitting beside her. "I was beginning to wonder if our Thomas had gone off girls."

"Behave, Jules," Thomas warned, lowering himself into an overstuffed armchair by the fire.

Christine looked up, startled. The cat leapt from the couch and scurried across the room, disappearing behind a heavy stand of drapery.

50

"It's undoubtedly my fault." Color flushed into Julian's face and fanned into his short-cropped, reddish-brown hair.

Thomas was equally embarrassed. He picked up a framed photo to study it but instead of looking more closely, he set it back down in the same spot, unseen. "Don't be ridiculous, Jules. You aren't to blame."

Christine didn't know what to make of their suddenly chilled behavior. "I don't understand."

"What a way to start an evening." Thomas rose as Gregory invited them into the dining room, but Christine stared at him with confused interest. Julian was wearing a puckish, apologetic grin. "I brought a woman here when I first moved in," Thomas explained to her, as Julian led them out of the library, toward the dining room. "It was a mistake I realized as soon as we got here. Cheryl didn't like nature, and she was bored to tears with me. However, she quickly became interested in The Surdans. Jules here made the mistake of inviting us to dinner."

"Mistake?"

"Well. Yes, I guess you would have to call it a mistake."

"Did she steal the silver tea service?" Christine asked, as Julian pulled out the chair to his right.

"No." Color crept up his neck again. "She convinced me to marry her."

"She did?"

"She did," Julian said, taking his seat at the head of the table. "Not the first night but shortly thereafter. We were married for almost a year. It took her that long to figure out I wasn't the kind of Earl she had in mind. I guess she expected fancy parties every night, but I'm almost as solitary as Thomas."

"That's why folks like us live out in the middle of a forest," Thomas said, finishing his Champagne and setting his empty flute beside a large bowled wine glass which Gregory had half-filled with red wine. They were laughing. Whatever Cheryl's powers of persuasion, she had not left a mark on these two old friends. "She was a stupid girl, really. She was in such a frenzied search for riches she was blind to everything around her."

They were laughing again, already at ease. "Fortunately," Julian added, "she was stupid enough to sign a pre-nup."

"Otherwise, you would have had to divide the house right down the middle."

"And that end of the table—" Julian gestured toward the other end of the long, formal dining table, "—would be frequented by well-dressed socialites."

Christine raised her chin in question. Thomas, embarrassed, shrugged. "That is why I don't invite people here. One must be careful who one invites into his inner sanctuary."

"Better off alone than in the wrong company."

"I'll drink to that."

"Me, too."

"I can understand *her* attraction, if, as you say, she was interested in your riches," Christine said after a moment, "but what persuaded you to marry *her*, if I may ask?"

"Funnily enough, it's a question I have asked myself a million times, and have never found a satisfactory answer."

"I have a theory," Thomas said.

Julian ducked his head between raised shoulders and said, "It wasn't just the sex."

"I wasn't going to further debase your weak character by suggesting it was, Jules. Besides, Cheryl was pretty in a cold, calculated kind of way, but I wouldn't have ever thought to call her sexy."

"So what is your opinion as to why I rushed to marry her?"

Thomas set down his fork and knife. "I think you were lonely, Jules. Your father had just died and this old house was echoing with loneliness. The promise of company was attractive. And because you are an honorable man, you proposed, and because she was less honorable than you, she accepted."

"I've spent most of my life alone," Julian confessed, "even when living at boarding school I found ways to be alone. Solitude becomes me. You, too, I might add, are guilty of enjoying it a bit too much."

"I do. But I've also come to realize that too much solitude can create instability. If I am alone too much, I lose my perspective. At the same time, if I push myself to be too social, I find it can cause ineptitude." He turned to Christine. "Would you agree?"

Christine had been silent, listening with interest as the men aired their personal beliefs. "I would agree, actually. I have spent much of my life in search of the balance between solitude and company. I have often asked myself why I can't be content with crowds, in the way that so many other people are. Do you think it is a kind of snobbism?"

Thomas scoffed. How many times he had asked himself the same question. "Not snobbism, but perhaps romanticism. I believe those of us who prefer solitude to random company are in search of a country that doesn't exist."

"How do you mean?"

"I think we are looking for a kind of Utopia. And in this Utopia we hope to find our Antigone—our ideal partner. As long as we are alone with our thoughts, our ideals, we can imagine it exists, but once we move into a crowd and can't find even a trace of the world we imagined, much less the goddess we dreamed of, we are disappointed, are shown to be fools."

"So we return to our solitary search," Julian contributed, "where we can think ourselves clever rather than be proven fools."

"Like Milton's Lucifer who would rather reign in hell than serve in Heaven?" Christine offers.

"That's a whole other can of worms," Thomas said, "which I suggest we save for another occasion." He smiled at her across the table, and then directed his next comment to Julian. "By nature, the perfect woman can't exist," he says, "no more than Utopia exists. As soon as we embrace the romantic ideal, we find it has left its slippers in the middle of the bedroom to be tripped over. She becomes human, therefore flawed, and we are therefore disappointed. Either we give up, or we continue our search in earnest."

"So you are suggesting that the search for love, for a life of value, is a mistake?" Christine dared to ask, despite her fear of being confirmed. "That we are destined to be disillusioned?

"My response to that question is different tonight than it would have been a week ago." He spoke directly to Christine, as if they were alone in the room, as matter-of-factly as if they were preparing a grocery list. "Tonight I would risk to suggest that reality can excel an imagined Utopia."

"And if you were to find your Antigone," Julian asked, "would you be able to avoid tripping over her misplaced slippers?"

"I believe she doesn't wear slippers after all, and if she does, I suspect she would tuck them neatly under the edge of our bed."

Relaxed at one end of the long, undivided dining room table, at the end of a delicious and elegantly presented meal, Christine asked. "May I ask how you two know each other?" Christine glanced at both men. "Or is that another indelicate question?"

"Our fathers were friends. Colleagues."

"Your father was in the diplomatic corps, as well?" Christine wondered if he was one of the successful ones or not, but from the size of his estate, by all accounts he would have been successful.

"Lord Berryrose was in Parliament," Thomas explained.

"Actually," Julian giggled, "our fathers were spies together."

"You are telling tales out of school tonight, aren't you, Jules?"

They had all had quite a lot to drink. Even Christine, who usually limited herself to a glass of red, had joined in the spirit of the long evening, had kept up with them through a second bottle of Pinot Noir. Uncharacteristically, she accepted a snifter of cognac after dessert had been cleared from the table.

"You can't pretend it isn't true."

Thomas exhaled a deep breath. "My father worked against the Reich at the start of the Second World War, but as you can deduce from the history books, he wasn't successful. When he failed, he fled to Washington, D.C., where he was given sanction. That was the beginning of his career in the diplomatic corps."

"True to his nature, he looked after his friends in Europe," Julian continued, "and after the war, my father was very happy to see him again." He rose from his seat at the table. "Now darling, would you like a tour of the house?"

"Not so familiar, Jules. Remember, my women have a weakness for you."

"Actually, I was speaking to you, dear."

"A tour would be lovely," Christine replied. "Do you mind if I bring my drink?"

"Let me refill it for you," he said, adding another inch to her half empty glass. "Thomas?"

"Why not?"

"Many of the rooms on the ground floor have been closed off," Julian explained, as they started the tour, opening doors to reveal splendid furnishings draped with cloth and cloaked in perpetual shadow. The frescoed walls were beautiful but in need of restoration. "The entire east wing is closed. I have no need for all these parlors and reception halls. Upstairs," he said, holding the railing to steady himself, "all of the rooms on the second floor are closed, except for my suite of rooms. The third floor is inhabited by ghosts. I never go up. Even Gregory and the rest of the staff have transformed rooms at the rear of the ground floor into living quarters. Much more comfortable, many fewer stairs."

"I don't recall ever having seen the third floor," Thomas said.

"I believe we spied on a maid or two when we were boys. I was only a child but Thomas is older than me by—what, ten years?" he said to Christine. "And should have known better." He continued up the stairs.

"I'm sure you were just as interested as I was."

Julian giggled. "We could have a look at the top floor, if you don't mind a bit of dust."

In comparison to the rest of the house, the third floor rooms were bare and uninviting. The ceilings were low and slanted; the single windows were comparatively small, as if the working class didn't need an enlarged view. There was space in each room for a bed and a bureau, a chest of drawers and a sink. The bathrooms were at either end of the long corridor, and while they were large, they, too, left much to be desired. "Mother and Father would have been appalled to see the conditions in which their house staff lived, but it never occurred to them to come up to inspect. They just assumed the smiles worn by the staff were sincere."

"In a way, they probably were," Thomas added. "The conditions back at home were far worse for most of the staff. No one had their own room, and they would have found indoor plumbing a luxury, even at the end of a long, cold corridor. I am sure they were glad for the wages and the honor of working in an important and honorable household."

"You are undoubtedly right," Christine contributed. "It is a mistake to judge the past by present standards."

"I know that the staff didn't change. People who worked for my grandfather worked for my father, and were given a room and assured a place at the servants' table, even when they were old and couldn't do more than polish the silver. Gregory came to work for my father when he was a young man and he seems content to work for me. I give him an annual increase in pay above the inflation rate. He is free to use the car on his days off. He eats what I do. I think Marion serves larger proportions to the staff than I am served at table. They insist on keeping me trim." He smoothed his shirt front, made sure it was neatly tucked into his trousers. "In all, I think everyone is fairly pleased with the life he has here."

They descended a flight of stairs where the guest rooms, by all standards, were grand; opulent. Those to the front of the house had large double windows with a view of the lake. The furnishings were substantial and intricately carved. Many of the beds had elaborate canopies, all of which were draped in dust coverings. Ornate mirrors, crystal sconces, dark paintings and tapestries adorned the walls.

Julian's house had an intimate feel to it, contrary to what its size and status might have predicted. Christine would have expected to feel intimidated by such an imposing structure, that awe-like feeling in the shadow of Michelangelo's David, but instead she felt at home, at ease, as if its Goliath-like stature could protect her from all concerns, all potential threats of danger. She slipped her hand into Thomas's.

"I seem to remember there used to be animals on the walls," Thomas said, squeezing Christine's hand affectionately. "Horns, that kind of thing."

"Yes, creepy, weren't they? When Father passed, I had all the taxidermy sold at auction, for quite a tidy sum, all of which came in handy to pay taxes and such." They continued along the vast corridor. The rooms to the rear of the house were equally spacious and had their large windows overlooking the rear gardens and the river Lea, which reflected silently, almost motionlessly, in the bright light of the moon.

"How many rooms are there, do you know?" Christine asked.

"Too many," Julian said, "for little me." He started down the upstairs hall, pausing occasionally to point out the more famous portraits of ancestors along the gallery. Christine was impressed by the quality and size of the collection of paintings and statues: no one painting would feel out of place in the National Gallery, and all would be considered Mona Lisas in the museum of her home town of Karlstad.

"I find myself in a difficult situation," Julian said. "I would like to do something useful with The Surdans. I don't relish being an anachronism. At the same time, I am caught between my regard for tradition—respect for those who built and developed this house—and the desire to do something useful. The question is how do I balance the two disparate needs? I loathe the idea of transforming Father's house into a boarding school for prepubescent, foul-mouthed boys."

"But there is something you could do, Jules, that would embrace both needs," Thomas said. They had paused at a large set of windows to admire the frozen lake bathed in moonlight. "I remember Father's stories of when this house was a gathering place for your father's friends, before the war. He said that the conversations here helped determine

Britain's position in the Second World War." He turned excitedly to Christine to explain. "It was like an informal UN, where people of importance could meet to discuss their feelings, form their ideas, before they were forced to present them publicly."

"Are you anticipating another war?" Julian teased, to lower the tension that was flashing like holiday sparklers between them. "Is there something I haven't heard about?"

"There are issues that need resolving, Jules. The problem with the conferences that Christine and I attend is that decisions have already been made and are merely presented *fait accompli*. People need a place to gather, to speak informally, to make up their minds as they walk through the woods, relax after dinner. I can't think of any place more conducive to profound thought than The Surdans. Think of the tradition you'd be maintaining. And so close to London."

"And who would sponsor this retreat?"

"You would. That would be your contribution. It needn't be expensive. You already have the staff to cook and change the linens."

"I'm not worried about the linens, darling. But who would organize it all? Who would tell Marion what to cook and for how many? Whatever talent I have for organizing is being taxed to the limit trying to follow the grain production, the sheep, the horses—the bees, for Heaven's sake."

"You do all of that yourself?" Christine asked, looking out the large windows at the end of the gallery. The moon was high but not yet full, as if an artist's hand had tried but failed to create a perfect circle. The white was imperfect, too, full of shadows, as if the ridges and valleys of the moon were visible and ready for a cartographer's pen.

"I employ people who follow my instructions, but they need to be organized. I am often at the books or on the phone late into the evening."

"You would need a coordinator, that's true. But it needn't be an enormous expense."

"I can't find someone I want to invite to dinner twice," Julian complained. "How would it be possible to find someone to work with me day after day?"

"Don't create obstacles to keep yourself from getting involved, Julian."

"Find me someone trustworthy to manage the programming at a reasonable salary, and I will open my house to the thinkers of our time."

"I have a witness, Jules."

"And I will hold you to your word," Christine said, touching her hand to his heart, as if in a mutual pledge.

Julian took her hand from his heart and held it in his. "If Thomas will release you from rebuilding his house, we could all go skating on the lake tomorrow morning."

Christine shivered, and withdrew her hand. "I would rather not, thank you."

"Not a skater, are you?" He led them back down the grand, circular staircase to the front entry. "I thought all Swedes were born on skates."

"We are, under normal conditions." She took a final sip of her cognac and placed it on a tray by the front door. She hoped it wasn't intended for the mail but feared it was. She feared her refusal to skate had been rude. Too cold. Too abrupt. She explained, "My father died on a lake, sailing."

Julian set his glass on the tray beside hers. "I am terribly sorry to hear that. You have my condolences."

"It was many years ago, but it keeps me fairly landlocked." To fill an embarrassed silence, she suggested, "Perhaps you would like to come to lunch tomorrow?" She looked at Thomas for his reaction but she couldn't catch his eye. "I've promised Thomas I'd make meatballs."

"Swedish meatballs?"

"Is there any other kind?" Christine removed her shoes and replaced them with thick socks. She leaned down to pull on Julian's borrowed boots. They had been stored near a radiator and were warm and dry.

Thomas pulled on his boots and accepted his coat from Julian. Gregory and the rest of the staff had long ago retired for the night. "Thanks, Jules. Thank Marion for us, as well. Dinner was excellent, especially the soufflé."

"I will. And I'll bring the wine tomorrow." He said to Christine, "Thomas thinks a Chianti is the answer to everything. For meatballs, we will need a vintage Cabernet Sauvignon. Until tomorrow, then."

"Goodnight."

The moon had whitened the snow as if with a celestial searchlight. Each individual crystal was accented so that one sparkled, one reflected, one detracted, one absorbed. The overall effect was a smooth, sparkling expanse of unadulterated whiteness. It seemed a shame to trespass.

"You've grown rather quiet," Christine remarked, as they made their way back to his cottage. "Have I overstepped my welcome by inviting Julian to lunch?"

"No, not at all." He walked on. The only sound was from the weight of his boots as it broke the thin crust that had formed over the snow. Isolated in the silent night, the crunching of their boots reverberated loudly. It needed another sound by which to reestablish its dimension. "I just realized how little we know each other, that's all."

"We know each other quite well, considering we met four days ago," she answered, struggling to keep up with his hastened pace. "What in particular is troubling you?"

"Tonight you said your father died in a sailing accident."

She stopped walking, and waited for him to stop, too, to turn to face her. It was cold but this was a subject to address face to face, not a comment that could be casually thrown over a shoulder as they strolled into the whiteness. "Yes?"

"I thought you told me your father died of a heart attack." He stood at a slight distance, his feet planted firmly in the snow.

"No." She resisted the temptation to reach out to touch him. "I said he died of a broken heart."

"Why do I feel you aren't telling me the truth?" He folded his arms tightly over his chest.

"I am sorry if I have made you mistrust me." She plunged her hands deeply into the pockets of her coat. She wished she had worn a scarf or gloves or both. Thomas trudged on ahead of her. She spoke to his back. "I should never have said anything while we were at Julian's tonight."

"Do you want to tell me now?" he said, bending to remove the front door key from under a pot of snow-dusted pansies.

"It isn't an easy story to tell," she said reluctantly, entering the soft halo of light at the cottage's front door. "Let me put a log on the fire and warm up," she said, patiently. "Then I will tell you everything."

They ate meatballs and freshly baked bread for lunch, and had a long, leisurely, indulgent nap after Julian left in the afternoon. In the evening they were content with leftovers, but didn't open the second bottle of wine that Julian brought as they both needed to work for a few hours before bed. Christine settled herself at one end of the sofa, Thomas at the other, their feet close enough to touch, but they restrained themselves from distracting one another. Their need to speak had been satisfied last night. If Thomas looked up, as he often did, he saw her engrossed in her work, her lips moving imperceptibly as she silently read the speeches she would translate at the end of the week. She kept a cup of herbal tea beside her and occasionally got up to refill it. When Christine looked up, she saw a slide show of emotions flashing across Thomas's face as he read the papers of his colleagues who would be presenting in New York. He made notes on a yellow legal pad, and crossed out and added phrases in the margins of his printed speech. By the time he had finished, it was indecipherable.

"I hope you will reprint that or your translator is going to kill you before you have a chance to speak."

"I'll print up a readable, final copy," he said, flipping through the legal pages back to the start, changing a line, then setting the pad on the floor. "How much easier it would be if I could always work with the same person. Sometimes I spend hours trying to straighten out an impression gained from an incorrect interpretation."

"You can ask for the same translator, you know."

"I could, I suppose, if I worked in the same country or even on the same continent. But I move around too much to have access to the same person, and I am not important enough to hire a translator of my own. You people are quite expensive."

"We are rather costly, I'll admit."

"Do you love your work?"

"I do." She looked to see if that was enough of an answer, but he was waiting for more. Their resolved misunderstanding had brought them closer. She set her computer on the table next to the sofa and tried to explain. "Something happens to me when I translate. I disappear into a line of verbal energy between myself and my subject," she described, like the taut line between the two tin cans of primitive communication of her childhood. In this capacity, she had no need to feel self-conscious about her fly away hair, her too pale eyelashes. She didn't need to worry if she was standing up straight or chewing a nail. All her attention was focused on hearing the words her clients were speaking, letting the words transform themselves as they travelled from her ear to her mouth, speaking them as quickly on her client's heels as was possible.

"When I am focused, when I am having a good day, it feels more like gliding the thermals across a perfectly clear sky than work. A bad day, on the other hand, when I am out of sync or a client isn't cooperating, isn't leaving those tiny spaces between sentences, well, that can feel more like rock climbing, with the mountain beneath my feet crumbling as I hold tight to a rope."

"Do you have a favorite city to work in?"

"Brussels, without a doubt. The more international the group, the easier the translating. People used to speaking and listening to a variety of languages inherently understand that a translator needs that split second lapse in which to interpret and repeat before the next phrase needs attention. The work is always demanding but is usually exciting."

"Anything you don't like about it?"

"I hate the crowded booths. They are tiny and two translators occupy a single booth."

"Why is that?" He had lifted her foot into his hand and was admiring its long, high arch, the even row of toes. His second toe was longer than the rest, which had always embarrassed him as unsightly, but Christine's feet, like everything else about her, were perfectly aligned and graceful.

"We always have a backup, in case the translator has a coughing fit or forgets a term. For those of us who suffer claustrophobia, the booths can be rather tight."

"I can imagine."

"But once I start translating, I forget where I am, and the size of the booth becomes irrelevant."

"Have you ever considered working one-on-one, whispered interpreting?"

"*Chuchoteuse*? That is my dream. One day I hope to sit behind just one person, a single individual whose rhythms and words I know well, to translate for one voice only."

"I think you have identified a dream for me, too. Perhaps we could work together to make this dream come true for both of us."

"You aren't afraid of being together too much of the time? It is very close work."

"To be honest, I am trying to figure out how I am going to manage to be away from you any of the time."

They had time to figure things out after all, together and separately. Christine had a contract with the British Bureau of Simultaneous Translators that required she continue to translate for them for another five months, until June. Thomas was already scheduled to work with translators until mid-May. They moved forward through their separate obligations, keeping an eye open to how they would organize things differently, once they worked together. Christine also watched for clues that might reveal the imprudence of their decision to work together, and Thomas checked his certainty against his conviction to make sure it didn't diminish in the harsh light of reality.

More often than they expected, at least several days a month, they found themselves in London at the same time, and their reunions were charged with professional details and personal revelations. In those few, precious days, they were inseparable. Twice they were lucky enough to be present at the same conference, once at The Hague, once in Helsinki, but frustrated that she had been assigned to interpret for another speaker. In mid-April, the lease expired on Christine's mansard, and Thomas convinced her of the futility of paying two rents. His apartment was large enough for them both. The first thing they did was to line the second bedroom with her books, to set up her study. He moved some of his clothes into the closet in his office down the hall to give her half the closet in their bedroom. She hung a favorite illustration in the breakfast nook and another two in their bedroom; the rest of her art she hung on the walls of her study. The shelf above the kitchen sink which had until now only hosted salt and pepper grew crowded with unpronounceable spices: *persilja, salvia, rosmarin and timjarm.*

In June, at the end of her contract, they moved to the Old Mill House and neither of them worked for a week. They celebrated her retirement, as she called it, with Champagne and caviar, and long, uninterrupted forays into intimacy. When they rose from their bed of familiarity, as they walked through the flowering woods, admiring the carpets of bluebells and the scent of woodbine, they were planning their future together.

At the end of June, at the Royal Victoria Dock Conference Centre in London where they had first met, Christine worked as a *chuchotage*—a personal, individual interpreter—for Thomas for the first time as he conversed with a Finnish diplomat. It was a magnificent experience. Later, as she translated his speech for the Swedish national news, his high energy helped keep her own wire taut, and he built in pauses for his audience to consider the information he was providing, which left Christine more than enough time to translate his words. Once Christine fell into rhythm, translating for him was like speaking her own thoughts out loud, regardless if she was deciphering his words to one other person or translating his speeches to large, international crowds. Their word choices were similar, his pauses matched hers. It was like riding on the back of a dolphin; and feeling as strong as that dolphin, she forgot that it wasn't she who was powering them through the waves. Their compatibility confirmed, they decided she would work with him exclusively—or not at all.

Externally, while they were both pale-skinned and bright-eyed, that was the end of their similarities. Christine prided herself on blending into a crowd, on her invisibility, whereas Thomas drew a room's attention simply by entering it. That attention turned to enthusiasm as soon as he started to speak, and more often than not it rose to a standing ovation. Christine watched people stumble over themselves to be near him, men and women alike. Important people were excited by his words, his ideas, his commitment. Children of every nation clamored to be near him, too, to touch the hem of his jacket, the leg of a trouser, to rub the dust off his shoes, as he stood in their dry, dusty village talking to their chief. Mistrustful children, hungry children, angry children, sad, they all responded to him quickly, as if his optimism was contagious. In his presence, they seemed to believe he could make a difference in their lives, until after he was gone and the dust covered his footprint of hope and settled over their hopelessness again.

When they travelled in Europe or North America, they stayed in modest accommodations rather than at the conference hotels. "How can I justify spending so much a night for a room in a luxury hotel, even, especially, when my organization pays the bill, when I am asking people to reconsider their priorities, to forgo that expensive bottle of wine or that extra weekend of skiing so that children might be given the few basic essentials for their survival?"

"I quite agree with you," Christine said. "I've just never seen the ideas put into practice, that's all. And I attend a lot of these conferences."

The money they saved personally, they donated to their favorite children's fund, sometimes as much as six or seven hundred dollars a conference, which they stored in a jar hidden under the sink in Thomas's bathroom. But when they travelled to third world countries, they were rarely given the option of an expensive hotel. They were lucky if there was a trickle of water in the bathroom. They stopped expecting minibars and counted themselves lucky if the mosquito netting was intact. Sometimes the ride from the airport to the village they were visiting was longer than the transcontinental flight itself. It was always bumpier. In Africa, Christine learnt to eat what Thomas ate when the villagers offered hospitality. After her first willful attempt at independence, when she dipped her fingers into the communal bowl of thick stew called wat, which looked irresistibly appetizing after their steady diet of oromo potatoes and injera bread, she also learnt to refuse what he refused, mimicking his artful, diplomatic phrases.

The compassion with which he tended her when she was sick was almost worth being unwell. She had known his ability to be tender, she had experienced it since their first night together, but when she was ill, her hair matted against her forehead, her breath stale and her body ripe with perspiration, he washed her face and her hands and her neck with the corner of his only clean tee-shirt. He held her in such a way that made her feel loved—and as lovely—as an Ethiopian desert rose. Thereafter, she stayed with the *teff* and she was never ill again.

Surrounded by the ominous buzz of mosquitoes circling outside their net, they lay together in the dark, as close as the heat allowed. They were in East Africa again, at the end of a frustrating, inconclusive visit. They would be returning to England in the morning, and in all truth they were looking forward to leaving this horrid place. Last night, the authorities of this miserable village made it clear that the care of children was not their concern: it was woman's business, and women, Thomas understood, had no voice in this unhappy, unhealthy, over-populated village. To add insult to injury, late last night, after a lengthy, pointless harangue with the inner echelon of the village elders, the old chief had pulled Thomas to one side and whispered, "half-half." He jabbed Thomas hard on the chest bone.

"What do you mean *half-half?*" Thomas's eyes brightened with the possibility of renewed negotiation. Perhaps with the other villagers at a safe distance, the chief would turn a benevolent eye toward the next generation.

"You bring money, we share." He made a gesture like he was pulling apart two sides of a wishing bone. "Half half."

"I don't think so, Chief," Thomas kept a smile fixed on his face. He didn't have to agree to the old man's plan but he couldn't show outright disrespect, not in front of his tribe, all of whom were as rotten, as crooked, as the old chief's teeth.

The chief chose to see the smile rather than hearing the words. He was not deterred. "Tomorrow you leave." Thomas nodded. "I give you two girl. You take home. You sell. You make good money. We share. Half half."

Thomas shook his head no, adamantly, the smile fixed but fragile; in danger of splintering like glass in a mirror.

"No girl? No problem." He winked a rheumy eye. "I give you boy. Small change."

Under the netting in their sweltering hut, Christine and Thomas had been trying to figure out what had gone wrong, why the people in charge were refusing their help. Self interest and control were the obvious reasons, but Thomas and Christine were trying hard to understand the dynamics that had defeated them here, not so they would be able to convince the chief to change his mind—they understand that was fruitless—but to avoid this same error with the next chief they encountered. They had appraised the situation from every angle but hadn't drawn any useful conclusions. As for the *half half* offer, Christine would have liked to report the bastard to the UN, but Thomas knew that nothing would ever come of it. They had no proof, no evidence. It could all be explained as a miscommunication, *their* wicked inter- pretation of an old chief's generous offer of a *she* or *he* goat. The sadness of the situation infiltrated their protective netting, like the sting of a malignant mosquito, and left them both drenched in lethargy. Ineffectiveness was the malaise of their profession, and despite their many successes, hundreds of thousands of children remained beyond their reach. If they didn't focus on the children they had managed to help, they could be defeated by the job left undone.

"Did you see the old chiefs new bride?" Thomas said, hoping to change the course of the conversation into a less stagnant direction. Humor had lifted their spirits before—even black humor. They would sleep better if they stopped rehashing the *wal* of the evening's meeting.

"That poor girl," Christine said, wiping the perspiration from her forehead before it dripped into her eyes. "She couldn't have been more than fourteen."

"Some would say she was fortunate. Her future isn't bright, no matter whom she marries. Being the chiefs wife will give her a certain status, perhaps more food for her children."

Christine shook her head. "Marriage should be outlawed."

"Here or in general?" This wasn't the light conversation he had hoped for.

"Marriage is outdated," Christine argued, wishing for a breeze. She tried to imagine herself standing under a cool jet-stream of water, rinsing away the coating of dirt and despair that had accumulated during this trip, but sweat dripped into her eyes despite her best efforts, and she couldn't focus on the image. Somehow a mosquito had found its way into their inner sanctuary. She swatted at it but missed.

"You don't want to marry me?"

"Why would we want to participate in an institution that doesn't work?" She poured water from her thermos into its cap and offered it to him. "Would you put your money into a bank that was going under?"

"A bank doesn't depend on us." He accepted a sip, and then sipped again, even though he knew that the more he drank, the more he would perspire. "But what happens in a marriage does depend on us." He handed back the cup and watched her take a tiny sip. "Were your parents happily married?"

"Yes," she confided, sitting up. It was too hot to lean against the folded towels they used as pillows. "I think so." She was thirsty but restrained herself from finishing the contents of the thermos: she didn't want to climb out of the netting to fetch their last sterilized bottle of water. She wished they had a fan, and then remembered they did. She rose onto her knees beside Thomas and waved the small palm frond he had cut yesterday, stirring the air inside their netting. "I wouldn't want to duplicate their dependencies, but I think it worked well enough for them."

"My parents were blissfully happy," he said, taking the palm frond to share the work of circulating the air.

"It shows." She took another tiny sip of water. "You assume you are entitled to happiness."

"Is that a fault? A false presumption? I've always wanted that kind of relationship for myself."

"And here you are nearing forty and still single." The mosquito buzzed near her ear and instinctively she slapped the side of her face.

"It has been worth the wait."

"Has it?"

"Most definitely."

"You really want to marry me?" Her nose had started to run. She was hot and miserable. She was sure she was at her least attractive.

"I do! Say you will marry me. Make me an honest man."

"You are an honest man." She looked at him and realized what she had said was true. "All right."

"All right, what?"

"I will marry you if you promise I won't have to walk down the aisle to Wagner's *Ulich Geführt*."

"No Lohengrin's Bridal Chorus?" She was agreeing to marry him! "I can live with that." He was silent for a minute, the weight of her agreement beginning to sink in, making him oddly inarticulate. "Would Handel's Water Music suit you?" He hummed the refrain, then slapped at his leg to squish the trespassing mosquito before it could draw more than a drop of blood.

"Lovely," she said, but he could see she was sad. He didn't fill the silence with questions or chatter. He waited for her to speak. "It is times like this that I wish my father were still alive," she offered eventually. "He would have enjoyed walking me down the aisle, delivering me to you."

"If we marry in the chapel at Mother's house, the aisle is about six feet long. I could meet you halfway."

"You are sure?" she repeated.

"I'd marry you tonight if you'd let me."

She laughed. She wouldn't ask the mean-spirited, inhospitable chief of this village to pronounce their sacred vows if he were the last cow in India. "Would you be willing to wait?"

"Until we are home?" Thomas was not even sure a marriage by the tribe's chief would be considered legal in the UK. "Of course."

"I would like to wait to make sure we aren't going to wake abruptly from this lovely dream."

"For you, I would wait forever," Thomas said patiently.

"Then we have no need to marry."

"If you feel strongly against marriage, we can wait. But once we have children—you do want to have children, don't you?"

"Yes, absolutely. At least three but more if you are in agreement. And you?"

"As many as we can manage. However, I want them to start their lives in a secure home."

"When we have children, I will marry you."

"Then let's start that first baby."

The question of when they were to marry was settled in May when Christine discovered she was pregnant. They called her sister, who flew from Stockholm to Florence, where they were married in the little 17th century chapel on his mother's estate. Standing beside Thomas, with Thomas's mother, Anne, and her sister, Janelle, as her witnesses, in front of a priest who was half as tall as she was and stone deaf, in the company of Thomas's witnesses, Julian and Giuseppe, Anne's aged gardener, Christine enunciated her vows of love, trust and loyalty, as if the whole world was present to bear witness to their commitment.

They had their first argument in July when Thomas was invited to speak in Nepal, and didn't want Christine to accompany him because she was pregnant. The first months of mild morning sickness had passed and she was feeling fine and energetic. Pregnant, she had translated for him in Belgium, Holland, and America, without problem. She didn't understand his reservation, and didn't agree with his logic that Nepal should be different. He thought it was time she gave up translating. How did she expect to continue after their child was born? It was time to step sideways into written translations. Backwards, not sideways, she insisted. Written translating, despite its obvious difficulties, was slow and tedious work, especially when compared to the high wire act of simultaneous translating. Written translation gave her time to bite her nails and reprimand herself for it. Besides, she would miss him. He insisted that it would be a sacrifice for him, too. He had become dependent on their seamless work together. He would not benefit from working with another translator. Stubbornly, they maintained their different points of view for twenty interminable hours, through a long night in which they lay side by side without touching, until Thomas yielded the next morning over breakfast and agreed to let her come to Nepal.

She travelled with him on all his assignments, believing that the good they were doing for the undernourished children would somehow be absorbed by their developing child so that it, too, would care enough to make a change in its lifetime. When she miscarried in Kathmandu, she blamed herself for her impudence. In addition to her sorrow over losing the baby, she was convinced that Thomas would regret his decision to have married her.

"But I wanted to marry you all along," he insisted. "It was only you who resisted. Are you regretting your decision to marry me?" he asked.

"No," she said. He had become her whole world. "I only regret that I have lost our child."

"We will start another one, as soon as you are strong again. We have plenty of time."

A year later, when she became pregnant again, she stayed in England while Thomas travelled abroad, her head bowed in submission over tedious written documents. He was in Indonesia when she miscarried the second time. And she was alone in London. It was a bloody shame.

She had been pregnant three times in the last seven years. Getting pregnant wasn't their difficulty, but staying pregnant had been impossible. At four months, like clockwork, down the drain flushed all their plans for a family. After the second miscarriage, she froze every time Thomas wanted to make love, but his touch was convincing, full of hope and love, and she was convinced to try again. After the third miscarriage, her hope disappeared altogether, no matter how loving and patient Thomas proved himself to be; no matter how she wanted to lie with him. It was the sadness in his eyes at her refusal to hope that led her eventually to propose adoption. He was willing to do anything to erase the terror as they made love. His only condition was that the baby they adopted would be a newborn.

CHAPTER
FIVE

Elizabeth escorts them from the cafeteria to the nursery and stays with them until she is sure there won't be any last minute tangle of red tape to trip their departure. She carries Christine's heavy bag while the new parents carry their children to the car, and stays with them while they load the babies into the backseat. She hugs Christine with genuine affection, and then repeats herself with Thomas, even though she barely knows him.

Christine takes her seat beside Thomas in the front seat, then reconsiders and settles herself in the back seat, nestled between the babies, in case they wake. In the front seat beside Thomas they put the large canvas bag that holds the bottles of warm formula, towels, swipes, and nappies, everything they need for the ride down to London. The trunk is packed with boxes of tiny clothes, diapers, dried formula; a grasshopper mobile; muted nightlights; and the roller bases that fit under the beds in which they are sleeping, which can also be used for wheeling them around the neighborhood in London. There will be other things they need to buy to complete this transition, but wisely Elizabeth has suggested Christine shop again in London, to avoid shipping costs and to double-check measurements in their house before they invest in cribs, changing tables, etc. For the first couple of weeks, the babies can sleep in these snug, portable cradles.

Thomas speeds along the dual carriageway, shifting from one lane to the next, overtaking a lorry or letting another car pass, as automatically as if this were a trip the four of them take daily rather than a journey that is about to transform their lives. As they pass Cambridge, Thomas says, "Do you remember those pancakes you made me the first morning we knew each other?"

"Funny, I was just thinking about them."

"Why did you stop making them?"

"You told me they were making you fat."

"And you believed me?"

"It's still apple season. I can make them as soon as we return home."

Anna grimaces herself awake, as if she has understood the reference to food. Christine feeds her a bottle of formula before she can cry and wake her sister, then burps her against her shoulder. She lays Anna back into her padded bed just as Elle puckers her lips in a hungry cry.

"How civilized of them to take turns," Thomas offers, taking the third exit at the roundabout that brings them onto the M1.

"They obviously understand my limitations."

The sound of tires on asphalt creates a constant white noise which facilitates the babies' sleep. Christine dozes, too, her head against the headrest behind Elle's cradle. She wakes to find Thomas watching her in the rearview mirror. "Have I been drooling?" she asks.

"Not that I noticed, but there are towels in your bag, if you need one." His look is tender, loving. He returns his attention to the road in front of them.

Christine tries to imagine the details of their soon-to-be altered lives, but like Thomas's reflection in the rearview mirror, focused on the road in front of them, it is unreadable. Everything is an uncertainty. Apple pancakes are the least of their concerns.

But like the face in the mirror, even if it is focused elsewhere, the thought of apple pancakes keeps her on track.

They are on a journey to amplify their happiness, not decrease it, so no matter what logistical problems they are forced to face, apple pancakes will be part of the eventual outcome.

At the city limits, Christine says, "We must remember to call your mother when we get home."

"She is going to be thrilled!" There is real affection in his voice as he anticipates his mother's response.

"Thomas, I've always wondered why your mother calls you *Bunny*."

He laughs. "I never thought to ask. It's just a childhood name." Traffic has increased but it isn't heavy. "Didn't your parents have a nickname for you?"

"Yes." She looks over her shoulder. "You're clear on the left, if you want to merge." She waits until Thomas has completed his maneuver, and then says, "My father had a pet name for me."

"What was it?"

"Promise you'll never use it."

"Promise."

"He called me Cricket."

"Cricket!"

"You promised, remember."

"Not quite as bad as *Bunny*, I should think."

"No, *Bunny* is adorable. It suits you." He cringes. "I must remember to ask your mother why she calls you *Bunny*," she says, then adds a thought that has just occurred to her, "Maybe we could ask your mother to come stay with us?" They are off the highway and into the start-and-stop of city traffic. She peers into the folds of the babies' beds and admires their peacefully sleeping faces. Thomas speeds up to pass through a yellow light, then reconsiders his cargo and comes to a full stop, a little too abruptly. The bag on the passenger seat tumbles onto the floor.

"With her diminishing eyesight, I'm not sure she would relish a move," he says, uprighting the bag on the seat beside him before the light turns green.

"It shouldn't be hard to acquaint herself with our house," Christine perseveres. They have reached Kensington. In another few minutes they will be home. "Think how useful an extra set of arms would be to hold our daughters."

"It would give her something to think about other than her declining health." He rubs his hands against the steering wheel. "I will ask her."

"Would you enjoy having your mother live with us?" she asks, as Thomas turns off Holland Park onto Claredon. Miraculously, there is a parking spot available in front of their house.

"I think I would." He pulls on the hand brake and pops open the trunk. "I think it could be good for us all."

Even before they unload the boxes and bags of baby accessories into the entry hall, their home feels different to them. Their needs have changed and their perspectives have been altered. They have always felt grandiose to have a proper entry hall in their London apartment, but it is quickly filled with boxes and bags of baby paraphernalia. Their large apartment shrinks before their eyes.

"You were thinking to invite my mother to stay with us?"

They don't keep a cluttered, fussy house, but there are no empty surfaces on which they can station the snug cradles in which the babies sleep. Thomas carries them down the hall to the bedroom, careful not to bump their beds against the narrow walls. Until his study has been transformed into a nursery, the babies will sleep in Thomas and Christine's bedroom, side by side on top of their bureau. He looks at their bed, still unmade from the morning they drove to Norwich, the duvet corners symmetrically thrown back into the center of the bed, like the first wing folds of a paper airplane. Uncharacteristically, he resists the temptation to make the bed. He isn't in a hurry to erase the traces of their last childless morning.

"Let's take advantage of this quiet minute while it lasts," Christine says, depositing two heavy bags onto the kitchen counter. "If you want to shower before they wake, go ahead." She unloads the boxes of formula and places them on the lower shelf beside the sink. "I will start to organize these things."

"Excellent." He picks up his briefcase and garment bag and starts down the hall. "I'll be quick. I know you will want to shower, too."

"I am dying for a wash and clean clothes."

Quickly, Christine empties the shelf above the washer and dryer, putting aside the bottles of detergents and replacing them with diapers, liners, mild soaps, etc., all the supplies Elizabeth helped her shop for in Norwich. Next, she takes the protective felt pad from under the dining room table cloth, folds it neatly so that it covers both appliances, and then covers it all with two fluffy bathroom towels. In a few minutes, she has improvised a diaper changing station.

She will need more time than she has at the moment to transform her study into a nursery, but they can do that later, when the more immediate problems have been solved. For the next few days, the babies will sleep in their bedroom anyway. What she needs is a drawer in which to put all their little clothes. Double-checking to make sure they are both asleep, she transfers the fruit from its three-tiered wire mesh trolley in the kitchen into a big basket and puts the basket in the center of their little breakfast table. Wiping away the dried orange leaves and shriveled tomato stems, she unpacks the clothes into the trolley. Undergarments are placed in the top basket and warm, fluffy tops in the middle section. Tiny trousers with snaps and overalls are stored in the bottom bin. There will be no division between Anna's clothes or Elle's. They will not tell them apart by the clothes they are wearing. They will have to look closely at their features. Distinguishing them is not going to be easy. Their differences are subtle and characteristic rather than physical. Christine is tempted to paint one of Anna's miniscule fingernails red, if she could be sure which one is Anna. Then she remembers, Anna has a faint red spot at the back of her neck, and Elle has a pale miniature map of Australia at the side of her left hip, the pale blue black of a bruise.

"Your turn, Sweets." Thomas's hair is wet but combed. He has on clean clothes but is barefoot. "Show me what needs doing."

"If you can set up the bottle sterilizer in the kitchen and organize what we need to make formula. Maybe invent something for dinner, so that we don't have to think about that later."

"Any ideas?"

"Something we can eat one-handed, if necessary."

"Is there any of your yellow pea soup in the freezer?"

"*Ärtsoppa* or vegetable soup. Maybe both. I think I froze a loaf of the bread I made on Tuesday." She pauses. Tuesday seems a lifetime ago.

"I'll take a look."

"Perfect. I'll be back in five minutes."

The spray of hot water is cathartic; perhaps the best shower of her life. She indulges herself longer than necessary, just because the jet stream feels so good. Her frugalities are different than her husband's. She will use a tea bag until it loses its power to color boiling water, and put on an extra sweater after dinner instead of turning up the heat in their apartment. However, she will luxuriate under the torrent of hot water until it starts to turn cold, and refuses to change her ways. Everyone should have something they can waste and hers is water. Thomas uses quantities of soap and shaving cream, but doesn't let the water run unnecessarily long. They both splurge on marmalade, and the big jars of honey that Julian supplies empty as quickly as if bears had invaded their pantry.

She wraps a towel around her wet hair, dresses quickly in jeans and a cardigan, kicks on a warm pair of slippers and hurries into the living room where she finds Thomas sitting on the sofa with both babies in his arms.

"Were they crying?"

"No. But I needed to hold them. We have waited so long for this moment, Christy, and here I was rushing around thinking about soup. I haven't disturbed them. They are both sleeping. Come, take Anna."

"I think that is Elle." She cradles her tiny daughter in her arms. She is so small, so light, so insubstantial, little more than a half-grown cat or a *nano* rabbit. She lets its perfect orb rest in the fold of her elbow. "You are right," she whispers. "We can rush around later."

They sit close together on the sofa, touching only incidentally where their shoulders brush. Christine stares at the baby in her arms, and then studies the baby in Thomas's arms. She lifts her eyes to view the expression in her husband's face as he watches their babies and her. Their communion is complete. They will never be anything less than a family. "Dear Lord," she prays silently, "let us be worthy of this task."

Later, they paid for their indulgence. Both babies woke hungry and angry that their hunger wasn't answered immediately. Elle finished her bottle quickly, gulping it down before her tears had subsided. Anna sipped more slowly and steadily and produced a long satisfying belch. But Elle wouldn't burp, no matter how Thomas thumped her little back, and then she spewed undigested, curdled milk down the back of his shirt and onto the arm of the sofa.

Side by side, Thomas and Christine changed their daughters' diapers, initiating a competition as to who could fit the nappy better, who could pack up the soiled diaper tighter and toss it into the bin first. Thomas's large hands fumbled to close the tiny buttons on the shoulders of Elle's shirt, and again down the snaps at the back of the jumpsuit. Just as they were congratulating themselves on their expertise, Anna soiled her diaper again, which leaked out of her nappy onto the leg of her tiny trousers. Christine felt sorry for Thomas but was glad she didn't need to change Elle again, when Elle made a rude noise and dirtied her diaper.

Smelly Elle, Christine thought but didn't speak. What a mistake it would be to ruin a perfect name with a cruel rhyme.

"Good thing these appliances are front loading," Thomas joked. "I think we are going to be doing a lot of wash."

In the early evening, when they have recovered their equilibrium, Thomas calls to give his mother their news. However, before they can make their announcement, Anne surprises her son with an unprecedented complaint.

"Every day I can see less," Anne tells him. She doesn't know that Thomas has put the call on the speakerphone and Christine can hear her confession. If she did, she would undoubtedly stop herself. She is a proud woman, and stoic. "I am fine in the house. Ha! I could find my way around it with my eyes closed, which is how it will be soon enough, if this keeps progressing."

"Have you seen a doctor, Mother?"

"An ignorant, arrogant bastard."

"Mother, certainly there are doctors who can help you."

"I have seen them all already, known them all, the eyes that fix you in a formulated phrase, and when I am formulated, sprawling on a—"

"Mother, are you quoting Prufrock?"

She doesn't bother to acknowledge the obvious. "They are all self-centered prima donnas, Thomas. You know what the last one said to me?" She shimmies her voice up to the top of a haughty pole. 'What can you expect at your age?' Oh, the sheer audacity!"

Christine and Thomas exchange puzzled looks. This is not the woman they know and love.

"Oh, Bunny, I can't seem to remember anything anymore."

"Nor can I, Mother."

"Yes, well, you've always had some of that, but I've always been able to remember everything. The other day I asked Rosa something and she looked at me as if I were insane. When I challenged her stare, she said I told her the exact opposite two minutes prior. It's embarrassing."

"Can you give me an example?"

"For instance, 'I'd like lamb chops and spinach for lunch' when she says I've asked a moment earlier that she prepare minestrone and garlic toast."

"Sounds like you are hungry."

Or lonely, Christine thinks.

"Maybe you should be getting out more," Thomas suggests.

"Perhaps when the weather improves. I don't really like going out alone when it's cold."

"You could ask Rosa to accompany you."

"That would make me feel old."

But you *are* old, Christine thinks, and then wonders if she will do any better when she is eighty-four. Will she be reluctant to walk down the street using a cane? On the arm of some small, dark-skinned caregiver? Thomas would laugh, would urge her to hire a tall, handsome young man to lean on, to laugh in the face of respectability and enjoy the fresh air. However, if Thomas's mother can't do it, a woman who has led her life running against convention, has acted on her convictions even when they weren't immediately applauded, if she is having a hard time confronting old age, then how will pale, cold-blooded Christine fare?

"Mother, I have some very exciting news to share." He picks up Elle from her bed, as if holding her in his arms will make the news more real. "We have twin daughters."

"I don't remember you telling me Christine was pregnant again."

"We've adopted, Mother." He shifts his daughter higher onto his shoulder, closer to the phone. He hopes she will make that little gurgling sound so his mother can hear. "Two baby girls."

"Wouldn't one have been easier?"

"Yes. Of course. But we didn't want to separate them."

"Yes, of course," she echoes. "How old are your daughters?"

"Five days. We brought them home today."

"Are they white?"

"Like the snow," Thomas answers quickly, even though the question, coming from his mother who has always been culturally color-blind, has shocked him.

"I haven't turned racist, *Bunny*, you needn't be alarmed. It's just easier on everyone if children resemble their parents. Have you named your snow babies yet?"

81

"We have." Thomas is beaming. "Anna—after you, Mother. And Elle, after Christine's mother, Eleanor."

"Pronounced El-le, rhyming with jelly, I understand, but how is it spelled?"

"E-l-l-e."

"How clever! You have found two pronounceable pachyderms. Well done."

"Elephants, Mother?"

"Not elephants. What is the word for a name that is the same—oh, palindromes?"

Thomas doesn't know if she is teasing him or not. She has always had a peculiar sense of humor but this time it is hard to tell. He tries to steer back on track. "Mother, we were wondering if you would come to stay with us for a while."

"Oh, *Bunny*. Think what you are asking."

"An extra set of arms would be very welcome, Mother." Elle starts to fuss, and he hands her back to Christine. "And we would like you to know your granddaughters."

"But England, no."

"England isn't responsible for Father's death."

"I know that, but I can't come back to England. Don't ask, Thomas."

"All right, Mother. It was just an idea. Don't upset yourself. We will bring the babies to see you, as soon as they are old enough to fly."

"Are the twins identical?"

"They are. At the moment we can't tell them apart. We hope their personalities will be distinct enough to distinguish them." He accepts Anna from Christine, and he leans her against his chest to keep her head from wobbling. "Are you sure you won't reconsider coming up for a visit, Mother?"

"Why don't you move south to live with me? The house is large enough for the four of you, plus a babysitter, if you want a live-in."

He laughs. "You don't think Rosa would quit if a family of four arrived, expecting to be fed?"

"Rosa complained the other day that I am no fun to cook for anymore. I rarely have guests. I suspect she would relish having a family to cook for again."

"We can't uproot ourselves on a whim, Mother. We are settled here."

"You and Christine don't really need to be in London, Thomas. You just need to be near an airport so you can travel to your meetings."

"It's not as simple as that, Mother."

"It would be easier for you to move to Italy than for me to move to London. Consider your options."

At six a.m., the babies wake with urgent, ravenous cries. Thomas blinks awake first. Christine opens her eyes an instant later. It takes them a second to focus on each other, another second to mobilize themselves out of bed and into their current state of parenthood. Christine pulls a bathrobe over her thin nightgown. Thomas hands her one of the twins and takes the other with him into the kitchen to collect their bottles. "How often did you say these kids eat?"

"The books say newborns eat every couple of hours."

"These two eat every twenty minutes."

"The sooner they put on weight, the sooner they will sleep through the night." She wonders where she left their burping towel. She thought she had folded it on the edge of the sofa.

"Can we give them extra quantity during the day?"

"I don't think it works that way." She searches the room and finally locates the cloth behind a sofa cushion.

"I think I am going to have to cancel my next conference."

"I have already cancelled mine. We need to find a babysitter, too, or that shower we had yesterday may be our last."

"You aren't having regrets, are you?"

"None at all." She wishes she had remembered to put on her slippers, her feet are cold. "I'm just wondering how we will manage."

They lean their heads against each other and doze as the babies greedily nurse from their bottles.

"We should be fine if we don't try to do anything else."

"That will be our strategy, then, at least until they start sleeping through the night. I have to be in Geneva in two weeks' time. It's a meeting I can't miss as I helped organize it. But everything before then can be cancelled, and afterwards, too, if necessary."

"We should be old pros in two weeks' time." She burps Elle and then puts her back into her bed, then collects the empty bottles to sterilize them for the next feeding while Thomas places Anna beside her sister. "If the weather is good, let's take the girls out this morning. I want to stop at St. Barnabas Church."

"Turning religious?"

"Elizabeth—Dr. Aragona—suggested we might find a babysitter notice on the bulletin board in the local church."

Thomas returned home late last night. Christine heard him across the hall, kissing his daughters who have been moved into his study, and a minute later, she felt him leaning over her with another kiss. "Sleeping?"

"Hmmm."

"Miss me?"

"Silly question." She has missed him more than she could ever have imagined possible. She has been alone with the twins for three very long days. And nights. The babysitter, Lori, that indispensable additional pair of arms on which they had quickly come to rely, hasn't shown up; nor has she called to explain her absence. She hasn't answered any of Christine's repeated calls.

Christine hasn't been a very good mother in these days. She has lagged behind every chore, never getting their diapers changed before their bottoms turned red, never heating their food fast enough to keep them from wailing. She has felt like a mother bird with a nest full of fledglings, their mouths constantly open and impatient for nourishment. She hasn't enjoyed motherhood very much these past few days. "Good conference?" she asks, wearily.

"Good enough," he says, pulling off his tie.

"Who was there?" She can hear him undressing; can hear from the sluggishness of his movements that he, too, is tired.

"The usual crowd." He folds his trousers over the back of the chair, slides his shoes beneath it, and sits to pull off his socks.

"Tired?"

"Very."

"Come to bed." They used to sit up for hours whenever one of them returned from a conference, no matter how late it was or how tired they were. Together they replayed the minute details: who was present, what had been said; what, if anything had been accomplished. Since the twins have arrived, all they seem to talk about is the babies. "Leave the unpacking till the morning, Tommy."

"I think I will."

She moves over to give him more room, but once he is under the covers, his pillow adjusted beneath his head, he pulls her closer. "I've missed you." His arms are around her, his hands regaining familiarity. Suddenly, she isn't tired anymore. The closeness of his breath in her ear restores her energy more effectively than a long, undisturbed sleep, something neither of them has known since they have had children. The conviction of his hands creates a need for closeness. The avalanche of her thoughts is overruled by pure sensation. Their heightened, synchronized breathing is the only soundtrack to their private, unarticulated exchange of trust.

A call of pleasure escapes and she is immediately sorry for her lack of restraint. A startled duet of indignation emanates from across the hall. "I must have frightened them." She hurries herself out of bed, throws her tangled nightgown over her head, and struggles as her head lodges in a sleeve.

Thomas is laughing as he tugs softly at the fabric, disengages her from her twisted nightgown.

"This is not funny," she insists. She feels like crying herself.

He adjusts the neck so it slides easily over her head. "It is hilarious," he says. "You should have seen yourself." He ruffles her hair, in a way he knows she doesn't like. "Heat their bottles. I'll bring our babies into bed with us. We can feed them here."

"What if we fall asleep and crush them?"

"We won't. We'll put them back into their crib when they've finished eating."

He is so sure, so confident, she thinks, shuffling along the corridor to the kitchen. She locates the bottles in the dim light of the fridge and heats them in a pot of boiling water on the stove. Expertly, she tests the temperature on the inside of her wrist, and then shuffles back down the hall.

Thomas has a baby in each arm. He is two-stepping them around the bedroom, singing to quiet their tears.

Heaven, I'm in Heaven,
And my heart beats so that I can hardly speak;
And I seem to find the happiness I seek
When we're out together dancing, cheek to cheek.

It is early for their two o'clock feeding but since they are up, they will feed them, and perhaps they will sleep until six. Now that Thomas is home, she feels more courageous, more certain that she is up to the job. The memory of yesterday's nightmare fades into a momentary shortcoming rather than a forewarning of a permanent state of affairs. It is unrealistic to think she can manage two babies alone. Anyone would lose their patience. She just has to make sure she has a reliable babysitter.

Back in their warm bed, propped up against a mountain of pillows, Thomas feeds Elle while Christine feeds Anna. They are close enough so that the babies' feet touch. Thomas is left-handed and cradles Elle in the fold of his right elbow while Christine feeds Anna with her right hand, cradling her in her left. When the babies have finished with their bottles, Christine hands Anna to Thomas in exchange for Elle. They are deliberately trying not to bond more closely with one than the other. Anna produces her little burp as soon as she is put into position against Thomas's shoulder, but Elle fusses against Christine's neck, is slower to release the little bubble that will let her sleep quietly through the night.

When she finally does release, curdled milk spills over the shoulder of Christine's nightgown. "You would think I would learn."

"You will." He takes Elle, hoists her up onto the towel on his shoulder and taps her back lightly as he carries both babies back into their room. Christine can hear him singing again, subdued.

Heaven, I'm in Heaven,
And the cares that hang around me through the week
Seem to vanish like a gambler's lucky streak
When we're out together dancing, cheek to cheek.

Christine has changed into a freshly laundered nightgown by the time he returns, has stripped off the soiled pillow case and deposited the soiled items in the laundry room where they will soak overnight. "It is so good to have you home. I don't think I could have gone another day without you."

Thomas notes that her nails have been chewed ragged, an old habit he had thought had disappeared. His invincible Christy is showing signs of wear and tear. "But you are the woman who can bake bread while assembling bookshelves while keeping the fire going, all the while chatting up a storm and falling in love, knocking my socks off. I know it is hard taking care of the twins, but I would have thought you could manage with the babysitter to help."

"Lori didn't show up."

"What? You're kidding. You have been alone with the twins?"

"I have."

"What excuse did she offer?"

"She didn't call to say she wasn't coming. She never even sent a message."

"You called her?"

"Of course, but she didn't answer her phone. I even tried Cynthia but her kids are home with the flu. Tommy, I have never felt so incompetent in all my life."

"No wonder you are exhausted, Christy." He holds her tightly. He can hear her attempts to steady her breathing. "What would you say if I were to stop travelling?"

"Don't tempt me with a question for which you won't like the answer, especially after three days alone with our twins."

"Yes or no."

"Yes. Yes. But how?"

"I've been offered a chair at the European University Institute."

"In Florence?"

"We could stay with my mother. I would have reasonable hours. I would be able to watch my daughters grow, perhaps save my wife's sanity."

"You are qualifying for sainthood."

"I would be aiming for a simpler life with my family."

"It's a complicated proposition. What would we do with this apartment?"

"We could let it go. It doesn't really suit us anymore, does it?"

"It has become a bit cramped." Their needs have changed: what was once an ideal setting is now less than adequate. "The cottage? We couldn't let that go."

"No. But we can let it sit empty for awhile. I can ask Julian's gatekeeper to keep an eye on it, to make sure the pipes don't burst if there is a freeze. Once the girls are older and settled in a routine, once we have good, reliable help, we can leave them for an occasional weekend."

"When they are old enough to travel, we will bring them with us."

"It will be a perfect place for school holidays," he says. "Florence can be unbearably hot in the summer."

"Do you think you would be happy living in Florence?" she asks him.

"I will be happy anywhere with you. So why not Florence? It's a beautiful little city."

"It would require an adjustment on your mother's part. She is used to quiet now. We as a family can be quite noisy. At all hours."

"She has told us more than once that we are welcome. Her house has room for quiet, even with us there. I think it's worth a try. If it doesn't work, we can find another house for ourselves."

"When would the assignment begin?"

"That's the challenge." He fiddles with his cell phone on the bedside table, retrieves a saved message. "It's all last minute. I would be taking over for Martin Oliver, who has fallen in Cortina and broken his hip."

"Poor old Martin. He shouldn't be skiing at his age."

"Snowboarding, actually. I would be taking over his course *Fundamental Rights in the European Union*, as a member of the law department."

"It sounds important."

"If I accept, I need to be there for the start of term, on the 21st of February."

"You are kidding." Her ragged thumbnail finds itself into her mouth. "That's ten days from now."

"I could go ahead, start my lectures. You could follow with the girls."

She is chewing furiously. "I don't think I can manage on my own, Tommy."

"Then let's pack what we need, as if we are going on holiday to Florence." He takes her hands and studies her nails. "We will settle in, acquaint Mother with the twins—"

"Hire a reliable babysitter?"

"Straight away. We can relax a bit—"

"Let Rosa fatten us up, fuss over the babies."

"Once we are calm again—"

"Once my nails have grown back—"

"Exactly. Then we can fly back to London to box up our things and arrange for the shipping. It's not that Mother's house lacks for furniture."

"Listen." She takes her hand and settles it in her lap. "If you are available for the next week, if you can help me with the babies, I can box up what we need. It isn't much. All we need are our clothes, our books and the babie's things."

"That's my girl. We can ship things down so they are there when we arrive."

"We can pack them in the car and drive down. How long would it take?"

"If we take turns driving, we can be there in eighteen hours. Two long days."

"We can stop when we are tired and need to rest."

"Oddly enough, it's probably easier to travel with the girls now than it will be when they are mobile."

Face to face, they slip down beneath the covers, their eyes wide and glistening in the shadows of the room. It won't be hard to leave London, Christine thinks. The idea of a big city is better than the reality, where the traffic offsets the metropolis's other incalculable charms. A small city will offer them more because what it does have is easily accessible. And a city like Florence, in which half of Italy's riches are housed, with a historical center that can be traversed in fifteen Medieval to Renaissance minutes, mostly without cars, that is a city they can happily and easily explore. Anne's house is wonderfully large, set in the country on extensive grounds, with the Duomo in the near distance, almost close enough to touch on a clear day.

Thomas sings in her ear, softly, a little off key:

Dance with me
I want my arms about you;
The charms about you
Will carry me through to . . . Heaven

CHAPTER SIX

Christine finds Thomas's mother looking old. She tries to remember how much time has passed since she last saw Anne. Nine months? Thomas has seen her several times recently. He has attended two conferences at the *Palazzo dei Congressi*, and last fall he delivered a guest lecture at the European University Institute. He has told Christine about his mother's deteriorating eyesight, but he hasn't mentioned the sudden aging. Perhaps it is the comparison to the smooth-skinned newborn in her arms that accentuates the wrinkles in her mother-in-law's face. Perhaps it is the badly applied make-up, an uneven coat of unnatural pancake color that stops abruptly at the jaw bone, leaving the untouched neck a pallid, vulnerable white.

Anne's hair has been recently done, which helps restore an illusion of youth. The hairdresser drives down from Fiesole every Friday afternoon, as she has every week since Anne started living here. The color has altered slightly over the years, has become less platinum, a softer blonde, even if no gray tones have been allowed to infiltrate the mesh. Anne, for all her accomplishments, is relentlessly vain, and her hair is always as perfect as her sense of style. Today, dressed to stay home, to play with her grandchildren, she is wearing

Chanel. It isn't a new outfit, but Anne has stored it carefully in her closet, and the tight-fitting jacket has come back into fashion. Christine notices that the pink and green Emilio Pucci scarf knotted neatly at her neck clashes with the cranberry red of her outfit. Otherwise, from the game she is playing, one wouldn't know that Anne has trouble seeing.

At lunch, alone in the company of her husband and his mother, without the distraction of the twins who are upstairs in the nursery with their new babysitter, Allegra, Christine notices another difference: Anne isn't wearing her jewelry.

No matter what Anne wears during the day, she always accents it with jewelry. Christine's best necklace and ring shine palely in comparison to her mother-in-law's rock-sized jewels. And while Christine wears her best jewelry only when Thomas takes her out for a special occasion, Anne wears hers all the time. Today, however, she is wearing a strand of costume jewelry. Her watch, a heavy, gold Rolex she wears loose on her wrist like a bracelet, has been replaced by a plastic Swatch. "Anne. You aren't wearing your watch," Christine can't help but comment.

"It's too heavy," she confesses and then catches herself. "It hasn't been keeping time accurately," she says, then adds, anticipating her son's criticism. "Yes, I have kept it wound."

"Mother, it is mechanical. You needn't wind it. It reacts to your movement. It will slow if you stop wearing it."

"I think it needs to be cleaned. I will take it into town."

"I can take it, if you'd like," Christine offers. "I have an interview at the *Palazzo dei Congressi* next Tuesday."

"No, thank you," Anne says, holding herself erectly. "I can manage. I need to go into town myself next week."

After lunch, Christine excuses herself to check on the babies. Their babysitter, Allegra, is exactly as her name suggests. Christine always finds Allegra in good spirits and the babies fed and changed and happy. After her bad experience in London, she is watching closely to make sure that Allegra is trustworthy, and if she is, Christine hopes that she will be able to accept translating work at some of the conferences in Florence. Allegra hasn't shown reluctance to working long hours, but Christine doesn't want to take advantage of her goodwill. "Go have your lunch," she says, picking up Anna and then accepting Elle from Allegra. She is aware that they are holding up their heads better, are less wobbly. They seem to have grown sturdier in the two hours she has been away from them. And they have gotten heavier, Christine thinks, carrying her daughters downstairs to visit their grandmother. She wonders for how much longer she will be able to carry them both at the same time?

She finds Thomas and his mother in the sitting room. Someone has put an old Guy Wood recording on the stereo. Thomas takes the twins from Christine and dances them around the room, as smoothly as if he were Fred Astaire's understudy. Christine can hear their daughters' gurgles of pleasure as a counterpoint to Thomas's song. She hopes he won't swirl them. Elle's digestion isn't always steady and spilt milk on Anne's Persian carpets would not make anyone happy. Christine holds out her arms to take Elle, but rather than relinquishing one of the twins, Thomas includes her in his dance. He sings along as they dance.

The touch of your hand is like heaven.
A heaven I've never known
The blush on your cheek, whenever I speak
Tells me that you are my own.

Thomas lets his wife take Elle and continues to dance alone with Anna, pressing her doughy little face against his cheek. He exchanges Anna for Elle and counter-clocks his steps to keep from getting dizzy, and then brings them all back together again, as if the choreography wasn't complete until it included the entire family.

Christine catches her mother-in-law's admiring eye, reads her look to say, that's just how he is. She is right. Even when Thomas isn't dancing, even when Christine's hands are soapy with bathwater, even when they are separated across a busy conference room or faced with a bin of dirty diapers, tired from too many interrupted nights' sleep, he focuses on her as if she were his one and only love.

The very thought of you makes my heart sing
Like an April breeze on the wings of spring
And you appear in all your splendour
My one and only love.

Christine would never have chosen a song like this. She would have been afraid that one of the twins might feel excluded, even if she knows, realistically, that babies don't understand the lyrics. Still, she would have worried that someone, anyone, would have felt excluded, offended. Instead, Thomas proceeds under the assumption that the twins are an extension of his love for her, not a replacement. For him, they are all *his one and only love.*

As they settle the twins into their shared bassinet, Christine wonders how people can become jealous of their babies when they are so obviously the culmination of a couple's love. She follows Thomas's example, in this as in so many other ways. When she kisses her daughters, one hand is placed on Thomas's arm. When she passes a child to him, her hand lingers to caress his before moving on to the next chore. And when they are alone together, no matter how tired they are, they focus their attention directly on one another, however briefly.

In the hush of night while you are in my arms
I feel your lips, so warm and tender, yes
My one and only love

Thomas helps his mother out of her chair and begins to turn her around the room, singing along with the words. They dance together, acting it up to cover any embarrassment. Anne is out of breath when the song finishes and Thomas guides her back to her chair. "Oh, Ian. You are a sentimental fool."

Thomas freezes. Ian is his father's name. "I'm Thomas, Mother."

"Of course you are." She doesn't miss a beat. "And you dance as badly as your father did."

CHAPTER SEVEN

"I've received a text message saying that Elizabeth Aragona and her fiancé will be in Florence at the end of the month," Christine says to Thomas, as she brings the babies into the kitchen. She closes the door and lowers the twins on the floor, then straightens up to ease the pain in her lower back. Thomas pours oatmeal from the pan on the stove into brightly-colored, durable plastic bowls for the twins, and Christine retrieves the slices of bread as they pop up from the toaster. "She asked if she might see the twins."

"Nice of her to continue her interest," Thomas says, mashing banana into the oatmeal. With flourish, he improvises a smiley face of raisins in both bowls.

"None for Elle, remember?"

"Right." Elle picks them out and throws them onto the floor. He scoops them out of Elle's bowl and shakes them into Anna's, a suggestion of dot curls above raisin eyes.

"Elizabeth will be amazed to see how much they have grown." Christine catches Anna before she can crawl under the table and secures her into her high chair. She ties a Sylvester the Cat bib around her neck as Anna bangs her flattened palms against the tray of her chair, impatient for breakfast. Beside her, Elle picks up the rhythm, only louder, then misses on the uptake and presses her Tweety Bird bib against her face. Before she can cry, Christine tucks the bib back into place and puts a spoon into her fist. At fifteen months Elle is determined that she will feed herself. She refuses all help, and is content with the amount of oatmeal she gets into her mouth. Christine seats herself beside Elle and eats a piece of toast. When her daughter gets distracted, she guides the spoon toward her mouth. "Do you think your mother would mind if I invited them to lunch?"

"It might not be a bad idea to have a couple of doctors at the table with Mother," he says, spooning oatmeal into Anna's eager, open mouth. Anna, too, likes to feed herself, but left alone she would finish breakfast at lunchtime, so they feed her in between what she can feed herself. "We might discreetly solicit an opinion about Mother," Thomas adds. This is a subject they have not openly discussed, but it is an issue that concerns them both.

Christine wipes Elle's face with a damp cloth. It seems to Christine that more food goes into her ears and nose than into her mouth. At least Elle doesn't try to spoon it into her eyes.

She wonders what kind of child she had been, passive and wanting to please, like Anna, or willful and independent like Elle. She experiences a flush of regret that she will never know. What a luxury it would be to pick up the phone to ask her mother a simple question, to receive a simple answer. In this way—if only in this way—she and her adopted daughters share the frustration of not knowing their early details. Christine will be able to answer most of her daughters' questions—she has known them since birth except for a couple of hours. Christine lived with her mother for eighteen years but never bothered to ask, and now the questions that form themselves will never be answered.

As if reading her mind, Thomas asks, "Have you called Janelle recently?"

"No, actually, I haven't called since the summer solstice." And that had been to say that they wouldn't be coming up again this year. They had spent their summer holiday at the Old Mill House. "But I should," she says, brightly. Her sister would know what kind of baby she had been. "I will." She finishes cleaning Elle's sticky hands and puts her back down on the floor. "Are you here for lunch today?"

"No. I have lectures until five," he says, scraping the last bit of cereal from the bowl and spooning it neatly into Anna's willing mouth. His cleanup is minimal; a napkin patted perfunctorily against Anna's cupid bow lips. He lifts her out of her chair, raises her high into the air before lowering her onto the floor, where she crawls behind Elle to disappear under the table. Downstairs, the doorbell sounds. "That will be Allegra, right on time." He leans over to kiss his wife, and then kisses her again. "Ask Mother when you see her, but I am sure she won't mind if Elizabeth and her fiancé join us for lunch when they are here."

Christine has invited Elizabeth and Stephen to lunch on the last Saturday in April. She has suggested they come up an hour early so they can see the children before they join Anne for lunch. Allegra, who usually has Saturdays free, has agreed to sit with the children until the adults finish eating.

In this way as many others, Christine has been brought up differently from Thomas. She and her sister were always at the table with her parents, for every meal, even when there was company. They were expected to behave, they were expected to sit up straight, to say please and thank you as food was received and passed. A quick glance from their mother brought them to their feet to clear away the dinner dishes, and once they were old enough to be trusted, they had the job of bringing the dessert to the table. They were encouraged to speak up when answering a guest's question but never to speak uninvited, unless they had something significant or entertaining to contribute to the conversation. Christine's mother had been a good cook, and her father had been a fine storyteller, so they were happy to participate passively at the dinner table.

Thomas, on the other hand, had been fed his meals in the company of a nanny until he was ten, when he was invited to sit at the table with his parents at their evening meal, if they were home without guests. At fourteen, he was invited to join them in company, and was encouraged to speak to the guests, if and when he had something of value to say. Enthusiasm eventually overcame reservation, and after the first stilted company dinners, Thomas asked questions of the women who sat to his left or right, occasionally throwing a query across the table to be fielded by a visiting diplomat.

Thomas and Christine have talked about the advantages and disadvantages of the family meal. He agrees that eating together is an important element of the day. Religiously, they start each morning together over breakfast, and even when they are rushed, they sit down together to have their meal. If Christine and Thomas aren't invited to dinner with Anne, as happens sometimes when she has a guest, they eat their evening meal with their children, in the kitchen, where the floor is easy to clean. Where they disagree is that Thomas doesn't see any reason to bring babies into the dining room. He believes it would only distract from their conversation as the children can't yet participate in any meaningful way, so they are bounced on Anne's knees until they are called to the table, and Allegra feeds them upstairs and keeps them happy until Christine or Thomas retrieve them for an after-meal visit. Christine wants to know when Thomas thinks they will be old enough to join them at the table, and Thomas reassures her that as soon as they can eat without smearing food onto their faces, the tablecloth and their clothes, they will be welcome. Cleaning up the smear of oatmeal from the trays on their high chairs, Christine understands that they have a long way to go before their children can join them in the dining room.

At noon on Saturday, Elizabeth and Stephen ring the bell at the gate. Christine opens the door to greet them. "Don't you two look radiant!" she says, ushering them into the courtyard.

"As do you!" Elizabeth says brightly, kissing Christine on both cheeks.

"Parenthood obviously becomes you," Stephen says, grasping her hand.

"You should have seen the circles under our eyes the whole first year! Come in. Thomas is with the girls in the loggia. If it isn't too chilly for you, we thought we could have a drink outdoors. Oh, I can't wait for you to see the twins."

Stephen and Elizabeth follow Christine into the inner courtyard. Under the three tall arches, Thomas stands, holding the hand of each of his daughters.

"Look how much they have grown," Elizabeth says. It is a truism but too exact a statement not to be voiced.

"Are they walking yet?" Stephen asks.

"Anna pulled herself up a couple of months ago," Christine explains, offering them chairs under the loggia. "She keeps hold of the seat of a chair, whatever is near at hand. She has yet to take her first steps but we suspect she will, any day now. Is fifteen months terribly late for a child to start walking?"

"All children have their own sense of timing. Anna will walk when she is ready."

"Elle pulled herself to standing months ago and has been running ever since, like one of those Duracell wind-up toys." Thomas lets go of Elle's hand and she propels forward, as if on command, moving across the room like a little robot.

"A slightly inebriated robot," Stephen comments, watching the little girl stagger toward him. "Hello, darling," he says, kneeling down so that he is closer to her height. "It's a challenging time for children, when their world changes from horizontal to vertical."

"I hadn't thought of that. It must be dizzying."

"Like a hall of mirrors."

"How long does it last?"

"Once they stop toddling, once they can walk and run without hesitation, their world will be righted and the adjustment period will have finished."

Elizabeth bends down, too, and holds out her hand. "Hi there! What's your name?"

"Baby." Elle stumbles forward, and stops in front of Elizabeth.

"And what is your name?" she asks Anna, who is standing still at her father's side, smiling uncertainly.

"Baby." Anna answers shyly.

"And who am I?" Christine steps forward.

"Mommy!" they chorus together.

"And who is that?" Christine points to Thomas.

"Daddy!"

"And what does a cow say?"

"Moo!"

Thomas interrupts, "Before they get started on their barnyard sounds, what can I offer you to drink?"

"Do you think I might hold one of them?" Elizabeth asks. Her maternal instincts, always smoking close to the surface, bubble up like lava in the presence of the twins. Almost a year and a half has passed since she saw them last but the instinct returns, as if it has always been present but dormant.

"Take your pick. Elle likes to be picked up but won't stay still for long. Anna is a bit more reticent but once she decides you are trustworthy, you can't put her down without a fuss."

"In that case, I'll start with Elle and end with Anna."

"Stephen? Something to drink?"

"We have brought a bottle of Champagne," Stephen says, holding up a bright orange box of *Veuve Clicquot*. "Already chilled. I was hoping I could convince you to open it."

"Coerce us, please."

"Is there a special occasion?"

"Indeed, there is." Stephen takes Elizabeth's hand. "Elizabeth and I have been married this morning."

"This is fantastic news!"

"Congratulations!"

"I thought you were planning to marry next year."

"You remember correctly. Next June we will marry in the church," Elizabeth explains, "but in order to marry in St. James Church, which is Episcopalian, not Catholic, we need to be married in the *Comune*—in the courthouse. That is what we have done today."

"Well, congratulations. If we had known, we would have planned a proper celebratory meal."

"We prefer it like this, actually. There will be endless celebration when we marry next year. It is nice that today is quiet, between us, with friends," Stephen says.

"This is going to be a huge surprise to my parents, who think we've been out shopping this morning," adds Elizabeth, bringing a little, loosely wrapped package out of her pocket and handing it to Elle who is fidgeting on her lap. She hands another identical present to Stephen, who gives it to Anna, who is now seated on a cushion at her father's feet.

Thomas pops the cork out of the Champagne and fills four glasses. "We are honored to be the first to share your excellent news." He lifts his glass. "To your never-ending happiness. May today be the first of many joyful days in your long and purposeful life together. *Salute!*"

"*Salute!*"

"Will you have a large wedding?" Christine asks, sitting beside Stephen.

"Extremely," Stephen says, wincing. "Lizzy has ordered thousands of invitations."

"It only seems that way because each envelope takes time and concentration to address. I am happy if I can complete five in an evening. Stephen has a beautiful script, so he has been addressing envelopes, too."

"I repeat, thousands."

"We are expecting about two hundred guests," Elizabeth clarifies.

"How nice."

"I've always dreamed of a large wedding," Elizabeth says, unobtrusively helping Elle open the present. "Stephen would have been happier with a smaller crowd, but he's been wonderfully indulgent, letting me have as many bridesmaids as I want, assisting with the seating arrangements for the reception, helping to select the menu for the dinner."

"It sounds like a lot of work," Thomas says, looking at Stephen.

"It sounds lovely," says Christine.

101

"Did you have a large wedding?" Elizabeth asks Christine, while helping Elle remove a little stuffed owl from its paper wrapping.

She laughs. "It couldn't have been smaller. The law requires two witnesses each. If you count the priest, we were a total of seven."

"Sounds good to me," Stephen says.

"A little like what you've done today."

"*Salute!*" They raise their glasses and drink.

Christine looks down at the stream of bubbles rising in her glass. She can feel their presence as they break the surface, splattering slightly as they meet the warmer air. Suddenly, she sees her own wedding in a new light. True, they achieved the intimacy they wanted, as well as the simplicity. She doubts she would be any happier now if she had married in front of a room full of people, but what dawns on her, with the Champagne warming in her glass, is that they didn't consider that option. Thomas had Anne's gardener as his second witness. Aside from Julian, who are their friends? The realization stuns her, like little slaps across her face. It has taken her all these years to understand that her very popular, sought-after husband doesn't have a second friend to stand witness to his marriage. And she is even worse. She was fortunate that her sister flew down to stand witness for her, but who are her friends? She looks down into the columns of rising bubbles and realizes she has none.

Of course they have numerous colleagues and professional acquaintances, long lists of names to scroll through in their phonebooks, but is there anyone listed they would care to invite to dinner? If Elizabeth hadn't called to see the twins, they wouldn't be sitting here together now, enjoying the spring sun as it slants low across their laps. When their babies were newborn, it was necessary—even right—to focus their full attention on the family, but what was a practical strategy at the start doesn't necessarily apply to the rest of their lives. The danger, Christine realizes, of perfect familial happiness is that it can isolate them from the rest of the world. She must expand their tiny circle before it shrinks to the size of a Champagne bubble.

Thomas puts Elle, who is fussing, into her bouncy chair, but that's not what she wants, and she continues to fuss. She reaches up to grab his glass with small, sticky hands. Thomas lets her touch her lips to the rim but doesn't tip it forward. "We made the mistake of letting her have a sip of Champagne once, and it gave her diaper rash."

"They are a little young to be indulging."

"We just don't like to exclude them from anything that they so obviously want to join in."

"Wait until they are asking to skydive and bungee jump," Stephen says.

"Actually, Thomas skydives," Christine admits.

"I did, until I became a father. Now I don't take gratuitous risks."

"Well, I would suggest that you get them out of diapers before you take them skydiving. And if you don't mind my saying so, you might want to keep an eye on things like alcoholic tolerance when they are a bit older, since you don't know their parents' origins. Some populations don't tolerate alcohol well, are missing an enzyme that allows for proper alcohol absorption. It can become a problem if one is unaware."

"A very wise idea." Thomas hasn't wanted to ask but since they are on the subject, he voices a question that has been nagging him since they left East Anglia. "We haven't heard anything from the police in Norwich, but I was wondering, since you live there, if anything has ever been discovered."

"The story was in the news at the start. It was a big deal when it happened," Stephen says, then takes a sip of the *Veuve Clicquot*, which engages his taste buds like no previous Champagne. He looks at his hours-old wife to confirm. "I don't think anything has been reported since."

"I had the police visit me twice in the hospital," Elizabeth states. She has been talking to the twins, has heard every animal sound at least twice. She holds the stem of her glass but doesn't drink. "They wanted me to look at the video surveillance tapes."

"You never told me this." Stephen stops dangling the ribbon in front of Elle's hands. He has been moving it from left to right, up and down, testing her reflexes. Even off duty, he is a doctor.

"Sorry, I thought I had." She sets her drink on the table beside her, back from the edge so a toddler can't overturn it. "Anyway, there wasn't much to see. A blur of a woman in a dark parka, a fur-lined hood pulled up. The police brought an enlarged, still photograph from the video."

"What did you see?" Christine and Thomas have both leaned forward in their chairs.

"Pale skin. A wisp of blonde hair. Lots of snow. Except for the height, which seemed average, it could have been your twin, Christine, or any other fair-skinned, blonde Anglican."

"You said the police visited you twice?"

"Yes. The second time they showed me the photograph again and asked me to call them if I saw anyone similar. I told them I see girls like that every day. It could be any of a million former English milkmaids or anyone from Eastern Europe. They agreed they were searching for a needle in a haystack. They didn't say so specifically, but I was led to believe that they had closed the case."

Christine says, "For me, the case has been closed since we brought the babies home." She lowers her voice. "A mother who abandons her babies in that way isn't likely to come looking for them later."

"You are assuming rational behavior from an unknown commodity," Elizabeth says, then hastens to add, "I think you are right to proceed with your lives as you are, to stay in the present. The past, especially in a case like this, isn't going to serve you or your daughters." She strokes the pale fluff on Anna's head and asks, "Where are your ears?"

Anna claps her hands on the side of her head.

"And where is your nose?" she continues, managing to give the twins her undivided attention while continuing her discussion with their parents. "In my own case, as a doctor, I can't be looking at every blonde in a fur-hooded parka, wondering if she is guilty of attempted neonaticide. Hands?

Where are your hands, Anna? It would sidetrack me from my duty to serve those who have come to me in need."

"I agree with you wholeheartedly," Thomas says, satisfied with the answers he has received and ready to bring this conversation to a close. "Before we are called to lunch I wanted to ask if you could take notice of my mother while we are at the table. If it isn't an imposition."

"What are you looking for?"

"I don't mean to have you sing for your supper, especially on your wedding day, but we've noticed a decline in her memory. Perhaps we could confer after she leaves us for her afternoon nap?"

They are interrupted by Rosa, who calls them to the table, followed by Allegra, who lifts both twins into her arms to take them upstairs for their lunch.

Elizabeth runs her hand lovingly over the soft down covering Anna's head. Anna rewards her with "happy baby." Instantly, Elle joins in: "hug baby!"

"Their first sentences," Thomas says proudly.

"Oh, I hate to say goodbye to them," Elizabeth says. "There are so many more body parts to name!"

"I will bring them back as soon as you've had your lunch," Allegra says, adjusting one on each hip. "Starting to get heavy, these two," she adds, burying her nose in the folds of soft skin on Elle's neck.

Thomas guides Elizabeth and Stephen into the dining room and says, "Mother, we have very special guests today. May I present Dr. Aragona—"

"Elizabeth, please."

"And her husband, Dr. Fleming. They were married this morning."

"You don't say. Heartfelt congratulations." Anne allows her hand to be taken and pressed. "Dr. Fleming, if you would care to sit on my right? Elizabeth, dear, I've put you next to Ian."

"Thomas, Mother."

"Yes, how silly of me. Ian won't be here for lunch. Christine, you are next to Stephen."

"What a beautiful table you have set," Elizabeth says, running her hand familiarly over the gold rim of the china. Her mother has the same *Vecchio Ginori* service, and for a moment Elizabeth regrets being on the other side of the valley from her family. She has so few holidays, when she comes to Florence she likes to spend as much time as she can with them. Torn, she has also wanted to see the twins. She wishes her sister could see them. Electra would have them charmed in an instant. They would toddle after her, as if she were the Pied Piper of Hamelin.

From the platter Rosa presents on her left, Elizabeth helps herself to a portion of melon and *prosciutto*. "My favorite antipasto," she says, admiring the glistening ripe fruit, its little beads of sweet perspiration mingling with the paper-thin smoked ham. She imagines her parents, across the valley, eating the same appetizer. Even though she is only ten kilometers across the valley as the crow flies, she is suddenly homesick. She can't wait to share her news with her parents. The rest of their friends won't know they have married today. They don't want anything to detract from the importance of the ceremony next year, but she can't wait to share the news with her parents and her sister. They are going to be so pleased. She forces her attention back to the table. "Signora, where have you found freesia at this time of year?"

"I have a greenhouse, and that lets me anticipate and prolong the season of each flower."

"You have a gardener who has a greenhouse."

"Are you contradicting me, Bunny?"

"Are you calling me *Bunny* in front of our guests?"

Elizabeth redirects her attention to her hostess at the head of the table. She is a small woman, neatly kept, with a determination several sizes larger than the body she inhabits. In some ways, she reminds her of her grandmother. They are not the same age but are of the same class and generation, which would explain the stately, familiar surroundings. She looks beyond her hostess to survey the dining room. Between the traditional, almost transparent *Capo di Monte* porcelain positioned on the two sideboards of the large room and the brightly handpainted antique ceramic plates from Orvieto and Montelupo, lit and displayed, one to a shelf, in tall showcases along the other side of the room, there is a wall covered in masks, an incongruity her grandmother would never allow in her classical decor. The masks are diverse, and if Elizabeth looks at them carefully, she has to admit that some of them are quite frightening.

"Have you collected these masks in your travels?" Elizabeth asks her hostess.

"I have." Anne glances over her shoulder at them. "One from every country we have visited, sometimes two, if they were particularly unusual."

"Some of them are quite—"

"Intimidating?" Anne finishes. "That is their purpose, I suppose. Masks allow the wearer to become larger than life. *Different* from life. They let the shy man become bold, the religious woman sin, the poor to pose as a baron and the rich to unburden himself momentarily of his reputation.

"Every culture has its need for masks. In Italy, in Brazil, to name just two countries, they have their *carnevale*—the last day before Lent where all prohibitions are possible, before restrictions must be observed. A tightening of the belt in every sense—"

"—certainly no more *Feijoada*," Thomas adds. He considers the abundant meals they have had all through Lent, no different than the meal they are having in early spring.

"An economy to get through the last barren months of winter. Think of the foods: fried dough with a sprinkling of the last sugar scraped from the bottom of the barrel; *cenci*, more fried dough, twisted like a bow to make it festive, using the last of the powered sugar."

"We call those *Fattigman*, in Sweden. Poor Man Cookies."

"Lent requires sacrifice."

"Even if Brazil, below the Equator, starts Lent in autumn, in a moment of abundance," Thomas challenges.

"Yes, but the tradition was born in the original Catholic countries, Italy, Portugal and Spain. South American carnivals are an afterthought, even if their festivities have become renowned."

"In Sweden, Lent was strictly observed, even if Carnival and masks were absent—more of a Catholic celebration, I believe. Nowadays, with the advent of supermarkets, any kind of food is available at any time of the year. But when I was a child, the only fruit and vegetables we had during Lent were those my mother had canned during the summer months. Lent was an agricultural necessity as much as a religious one."

"Pagan rites adopted by the Christians."

"The need for restraint until the first spring crops could be harvested is the same, no matter what god is being worshiped."

"That was true until we started worshiping the god of World Globalization," Thomas says.

"Where anything can be found at any time," Stephen says.

"As long as one doesn't live in a Third World country," adds Christine.

"Certainly traditions have suffered," Anne says. "What point is there to eating *Frittelle di San Giuseppe* in June?"

"Doughnut holes," Elizabeth says enthusiastically. "You can buy them any day of the week at a supermarket in England."

"England?" Anne's eyes darken. "You are not Italian?" She studies Elizabeth's light coloring, then looks across the table to Stephen's olive complexion, dark hair and handsome, impenetrable eyes. "He is Italian," she decides, "but you aren't."

"The other way around, Mother. Elizabeth was born in Florence. She has lived here all her life."

"My father is Italian, my mother is American," Elizabeth explains. "I studied medicine in England, where I met Stephen. We live and work in Norwich."

"Elizabeth is the one who found the twins, Mother."

"Found the twins?"

"Remember, Mother? At the hospital in East Anglia?"

"Of course. Of course." She is obviously flustered. "I am so accustomed to my granddaughters. I forget they aren't blood related."

"That is how it should be," Elizabeth says, gently.

Stephen adds, "They certainly look like Thomas and Christine."

"And their eyes," Elizabeth adds, "are exactly the color of their grandmother's."

"So you live in England?" Anne asks, her pretty blue eyes glistening with tears. "Are you married?"

"Yes, Mother. They were married this morning."

As Rosa removes her plate and silverware, Anne recovers. "Yes, of course. But so few people feel the necessity of marriage these days."

"Yes, we have noticed that, too," Stephen answers, laying his fork and knife side by side on his plate, so that Rosa can remove his plate more easily. "Many of our friends have been together for years but have declined to marry."

"It's a pity," Anne lifts her wine glass, swirls the dark red liquid but sets down the glass without taking a sip. "In my day, everyone married."

"How many of them divorced, Mother?"

"Too many, unfortunately," she brings her elbows close to her body so Rosa can lay the plate for the next course. "But still people married. People who didn't marry were calling attention to themselves; were considered odd." She adjusts her fork and knife so they are perfectly aligned, moves her wine glass so that it is directly above the knife's point. "Shall we move onto the terrace for coffee?"

"After dessert, Mother. Rosa has baked a sweet."

While Thomas is upstairs collecting the babies from Allegra and Christine is pouring an inch of *espresso* into *demitasse* cups, Elizabeth and Stephen confer between themselves for a moment. They are seated again in the loggia, happily anticipating the digestive drop of Italian coffee after an elaborate three course meal. Thomas returns, humming, and gives Christine and Elizabeth each a child to hold on their laps.

"Your mother is a lovely woman," Elizabeth says, adjusting the baby's weight on her knees. She isn't sure if she is holding Elle or Anna, and she doesn't want to offend Thomas or Christine by asking. She runs her hand over the top of the baby's head. The hair is as soft as goose down and almost as short. If it weren't for the feminine frocks the girls are wearing, it would be easy to mistake them for boys. By all accounts, Elizabeth was practically bald until she was two, and now her hair is thick and abundant. She'll have to tell Christine that babies with little or no hair at the start are the ones most likely to have a thick head of hair later in life.

"Thank you," Thomas answers. "But what do you think of her condition?"

"Your mother is obviously an extremely intelligent, cultured woman," Stephen begins. "Some memory loss is normal as we move on in years, in the same way that our strength diminishes as our muscles weaken. I sometimes wonder if the more intelligent a person, the more striking and therefore disconcerting is their decline. Much of what you are seeing is behavior typical of the old."

"How do you mean?" Thomas pulls his chair closer to Stephen, leans forward.

"Like teenagers and two-year-olds, all age groups have some things in common. So do the old. Some of your mother's characteristics are unique to her, but many are a factor of her advancing years."

"But the memory loss?" Thomas asks. He doesn't want his need for reassurance to dull his inquisitive eye.

"How old did you say your mother is?" Stephen says.

"Eighty-five."

"How long have you been seeing signs of memory loss?"

"She has always had a formidable memory. I remember teasing her about something she had forgotten—what, about three months ago. It was so unlike her to forget anything. She was terribly embarrassed."

"Looking back, can you see other forgetfulness?"

"In retrospect, there have been signs for at least a year."

"The December before last, she sent us a Christmas card, twice," Christine remembers.

"What you have been noticing," Stephen says, "are very slight signs of dementia."

Thomas folds his arms tightly over his chest and crosses his legs. "I was afraid of this."

"It's not to become alarmed," Stephen adds. "To some extent it happens to us all. In your mother's case, it doesn't appear as if it is progressing rapidly," he continues, "and although she's extremely fit and doesn't show her years, she isn't young. She isn't in danger to herself or to others but you might not want to leave your children alone with her." Stephen sees alarm register in Thomas's face. "Not that she would ever hurt them, I'm not suggesting that, but she might take herself off on an errand—to the bathroom, to the library—and leave them unattended."

"That's easily resolved," Christine says. "If we aren't with the children, their babysitter is. Anne has been perfectly clear from the start that she couldn't manage even one of the twins alone."

"What will be harder to reconcile is the damage to her self-esteem," Elizabeth says, a child's foot in each hand.

"Yes, she's always terribly embarrassed when she realizes her error."

"It is especially hard on those who have had an infallible memory in the past," Stephen says. He looks at Elizabeth—his wife!—with a baby in her arms, as radiant as a Renaissance Madonna holding her beloved child. The idea of a child frightens him, but the idea of marriage made him uncomfortable until a few years ago, and now he couldn't be happier. Fatherhood looms on his horizon, but it is still a small spot in the far distance.

"When we first moved in with her, she had started a project—" Christine starts.

"She has always set herself a winter project," Thomas interjects. "Something to occupy the long indoor hours at the start of the year, before she can start her gardening projects."

111

Christine continues, "This year, she was determined to organize the photographs she had taken over the years of all the orphans she has helped situate. It is a large box, perhaps two feet long, eight or ten inches wide, crammed full of photographs."

"Oh dear," Elizabeth says, "my mother has one of those boxes of photos of my sister and me. She'll never get them sorted."

"On the contrary, Mother had those photographs organized and into albums before the first tulip greens appeared: one for Sri Lankan orphans, one for the kids in the Philippines, seven albums in all, with over a thousand photographs neatly cornered."

"That's amazing."

"What is amazing is that in each book, under each photograph, she had penned in the names of the children, as if she had met them yesterday instead of thirty or forty years ago."

"What you are describing," Stephen leans forward, his elbows on his knees, his hands under his chin, "is fairly typical. Not the extraordinary memory—I don't want to detract from that—but when people lose their memory, it is the present memory that goes, while the past memory remains intact."

Elizabeth says, "I have noticed in hospital that people who have dementia, even advanced dementia, can hold on to one thread of thought for a relatively long time, actually, if their thought isn't interrupted. For example, if I maintain eye contact with Mrs. Doe, she will remember me and our conversation until the end. But if I turn away to check her chart or to read the blood pressure gauge, when I look at her again, she will ask me my name and what I am doing there, as if the eye contact helps keep the thread from snapping."

"I have noticed that with Mother. While we are at the table together, she is less likely to forget things, but if I go out of the room and return, I can see a startled expression in her eyes, as if she's trying to remember who I am, or at least what I am doing in her house."

"I have noticed that, too," Christine says, "after lunch, when I go upstairs to collect the twins. When I reenter the room I can see a question in her eyes, as if she is wondering who is this woman with two squirming children in her arms? If I sit with her to watch a television program, if I am not in her sight line, she forgets I'm in the room."

"Does she have someone she trusts implicitly?" Stephen asks. "Aside from the two of you?"

"Rosa," Thomas and Christine say simultaneously.

"The woman who served lunch?"

"Yes. Rosa worked for Mother and Father when he was stationed in Italy many years ago. At Mother's urging, Rosa came out of retirement when Mother returned to live in Florence."

"A link between the present and the past. That's good."

"Would your mother accept her company during the day, in addition to Rosa's kitchen responsibilities?"

"That might present a problem. Mother guards her independence jealously, and she doesn't welcome anyone as witness to her idleness."

The slipping of the mask, Elizabeth thinks, and then asks. "Does your Rosa sew, by chance?"

"She does," Christine chimes. "Anne is always having Rosa alter her clothes. She won't admit it but she's getting smaller. Everything needs a button moved or a hem raised."

"That might be a place to start. Speak with Rosa. Let her in on the plan, if she's discreet."

"She is. And she adores Mother. She will want to help."

Elizabeth apologizes as they stand to leave. "We really should be going. I don't want to keep my parents waiting any longer for our news." Reluctantly, she shifts the sleeping child into its carriage. Again, she wishes she could take at least one of them home with her. Her maternal instincts are, at times like this, at odds with her passion for her work, and she has to remind herself that soon it will be her turn, too, to take time off from doctoring to start a family. Both she and Stephen are planning their careers so that they will be able to raise their children themselves rather than leave them all day in childcare. It means they won't rise to the top of their professions or be the richest of their doctor friends, but as long as they can do the medical work for which they were trained, why can't there be time for a family? Three or four years from now, when they are both well established in their specializations, that will be the perfect time to start a family. One step at a time, she reminds herself, looking up from the perfection of the sleeping child. "Thank you for inviting us up today. It has been so nice to see you as a family."

"I hope we haven't made you sing for your supper," Thomas says.

"Not at all," Stephen says. "Try not to worry about your mother. She is in remarkably good shape for a woman her age."

Christine places sleeping Anna beside her sister, and says to their guests, "I hope you will call us the next time you are in Florence. We would love to see you again."

"We will, although it probably won't be until next year, as we are saving our holiday leave for the wedding celebration. You will come to the wedding, of course."

"We would be thrilled to attend, if you have time to address one more invitation."

CHAPTER EIGHT

"Anne?"

"Yes, dear?"

"Would you mind if I invite friends to lunch on Saturday?" Christine asks, depositing a stack of mail in the silver tray on the table in front of where Anne sits, even though her mother-in-law never reads the mail anymore. Thomas sorts through it, makes sure the bills have been paid.

"Do I know them?"

"You do." Christine sits beside her mother-in-law in the late morning sun. The cushions are warm and she is tempted to stay, to relax, with the excuse of keeping her mother-in-law company. "Elizabeth Aragona and her husband, Stephen Fleming."

"The doctors," Anne nods. "Weren't they just here last week?"

"It was almost a year ago."

"Yes, we had melon and *prosciutto* as *antipasti*, even though it was only April, and freesia on the table."

"We did. I am sure everyone would be pleased with the same menu."

"Speak with Rosa. Tell her you have already spoken with me."

"I will. Thank you."

"Will Thomas be here?"

"I am sure he will be."

Stephen has brought Champagne again, another chilled bottle of *Veuve Clicquot*.

"This could become a habit," Thomas greets him.

"There are worse habits to have than great taste in Champagne," Christine says, leaning in to kiss Elizabeth, then Stephen. "What is the occasion this time?"

"It's our first year anniversary."

Christine guides them toward the loggia. "And how are you faring after a year of clandestine marriage?"

"Wonderfully committed, ready to get married next month." There is decidedly more enthusiasm in his voice this year.

"Did you manage to address all the invitations?" Thomas asks Elizabeth.

"We did," she says, smoothing her hair away from her face. "I received your R.S.V.P. If only everyone would respond so punctually."

"It is easier for us to confirm, I imagine, being in the same town. I gather many of your guests are coming from abroad."

"They are. But you would think they would know their plans by now, no? I'm just glad we don't have to give notice to a venue as to how many guests will be attending. The caterer only needs ten days' notice. By then we should know how many people will be at the reception, I hope!"

"It must be stressful planning such a big party."

"We are working hard so that all the details are in order now, so we won't be stressed for the wedding itself. We want to enjoy our party!" Elizabeth says, seating herself beside Christine. "But where are your girls?"

"They are having their lunch. They tried to wait but they were up early this morning and were cranky, so we decided to give them an early lunch, and if that improves their humor, Allegra will bring them down before their nap."

"I can't wait to see them. They must be what— two and a half?"

"Nearly. Twenty-seven months."

"That's the terrible twos times two," Thomas says.

"Are they terrible?" Elizabeth asks.

"Not at all. Just lively."

"As they should be."

"Exactly. Independent and determined and willful at every turn."

"How long does it last?" Thomas asks, hope and trepidation occupying equal space in his question.

Elizabeth laughs. "If you ask my grandmother, she'll say my father never outgrew the terrible twos."

"Oh, dear!"

"Then again, my grandmother said there was nothing terrible about my twos. So there you have it, no easy answer. Speaking of mothers, how is your mother, Thomas?"

"She will be joining us for lunch. I will be interested to hear what you think."

Rosa appears to announce lunch before the twins make their appearance, but Christine promises Elizabeth she will see them afterwards. "They will be rested, we will be fed, the reunion will be much more pleasurable," she says, escorting her guests from the loggia into the dining room. "Elizabeth, you remember Thomas's mother, Anne."

"Of course I do," Elizabeth says affectionately, taking the woman's proffered hand. "I have often thought about our discussion of masks last year, and have shared your ideas repeatedly with friends and colleagues."

"Masks?"

Elizabeth sees by the puzzled expression on the old woman's face that she doesn't recall the conversation at all; probably couldn't make an educated guess as to whether or not she and Elizabeth have ever met. "It's nice to see you again," Elizabeth says, providing a clue. "And I see you have freesia on the table again. How do you do it?"

"I have a greenhouse, and that lets me anticipate and prolong the season of each flower."

"You have a gardener who has a greenhouse," Thomas says.

"Are you contradicting me, Bunny?"

"Are you calling me *Bunny* again in front of our guests?"

Elizabeth shudders, as if to dislodge an odd sense of *déjà vu*. She looks around the room to see if there are any details that can tell her if she has slipped into the past. The room is exactly as it was a year ago: the plates are the same Richard Ginori; the centerpiece is composed of freesia, and for a moment Elizabeth is caught between what she knows to be reality and a slip through the cracks into the past. She looks at her husband, dressed today in chino trousers and a blue blazer, and remembers that the last time they were here, on the occasion of their marriage, he was wearing dark trousers and a white shirt, a navy blazer. Her vision cleared, she notices that Christine is wearing a dark red dress and Thomas is in shirt sleeves, his cuffs rolled back to show the light hairs on his forearms, all details she doesn't remember from their previous visit. Thomas's mother, who was clearly the bright and shining star of their luncheon last year, is pale and eclipsed in comparison, dressed neatly but anonymously in black, as if in mourning for a former, more colorful self. The confusion has passed and Elizabeth is firmly rooted in the present again, amused at her momentary lapse in perspective. But it still remains that the words she has heard are the same words she heard last year, as if a recording of last year's lunch is being overlaid on this year's reunion.

The meal that Rosa brings to the table is different from last year's. Rosa keeps a book of each meal she serves to Anne's guests so she won't risk *la brutta figura* of repeating herself, of letting people think she has a limited repertoire. Last year's melon and *prosciutto* has been replaced with chicken liver *patè* on fried bread, a heavy starter, Rosa knows, but a reliable Chianti Sangiovese will cut through the richness; will help everyone digest. Besides, the first course is light, Rosa figures: little dumplings of spinach and ricotta she spent the morning forming with her thumb and forefinger in the palm of her hand, cooking the *strozzaprete* only until they floated to the surface, then rescuing them one by one with a slotted spoon. A drizzle of olive oil, a sprinkling of parmesan, they won't weigh heavy on anyone's stomach, won't keep anyone from welcoming the main course of *inzimino*. Rosa loses points for allowing spinach to show itself twice in the same meal, but from the way everyone is taking second helpings no one seems to mind; besides, the spinach in the *strozzaprete* is more of an element to which the ricotta can adhere rather than an ingredient in and of itself. No, no one is complaining. She probably should have set aside a portion of the moscardini for herself. It looks like they will finish everything on the platter, and from the way Signor Thomas is looking at her, she suspects he will ask if there is more set aside in the kitchen. Best to take their appetites as a compliment, that's the trick. She can cook *moscardini* for herself anytime.

It is easy for Elizabeth and Stephen to notice the change in Anne. Last year, the conversation was more important than the food. This year, Anne starts eating before the rest have been served, is almost finished with the food on her plate before her company have started eating. Her vision has worsened, Elizabeth can tell, when she urges Rosa to offer a second serving before Stephen and Christine have finished their first serving. Last year's perfect manners have fallen away; have stained the front of Anne's impeccably preserved presence. She is not looking forward to sharing her opinion with Thomas after lunch.

As if by osmosis, by the time they move into the library for coffee, Thomas understands clearly how much his mother's condition has worsened. Observing his mother in the company of these two young doctors, Thomas has gained objectivity that he hasn't had in his day-by-day encounters with his mother. Until today, his vision has been clouded by his desire for his mother's infallibility. This is unrealistic, he knows. He is a grown man, his mother is an old woman, and he should be prepared for her demise. But the less rational part of Thomas, the child who adores his mother and needs her to stay strong and present, resents her regression, and blames her as if she had a choice.

"So what's the verdict?" Thomas asks, his legs crossed, his arms folded tightly over his chest. It is better to know the truth than to worry over the possibilities. Once the twins arrive, there will be no uninterrupted conversation.

Stephen and Elizabeth exchange looks, and Elizabeth reluctantly takes the lead. "I don't need to tell you that your mother has aged since the last time we met. You live in the same house, you see her every day."

"Yes, but simply for that reason I am able to delude myself, focus on her better moments. She still has good days."

"I am sure she does. And even today, if I were to meet your mother for the first time, I would be impressed with her overall condition. She's remarkably young-looking for her years."

"Yes—and terribly vain about her appearance still."

"But having seen her a year ago," Elizabeth continues, "it is hard to forget how impressive she was."

"You should have seen her when I was a boy. She was a dynamo."

"I am sure she was. But she has a right to age and you mustn't hold it against her. What you are seeing, unfortunately, is a natural decline."

"It can't be treated?"

"It might be slowed a bit, and I would certainly recommend she see a doctor. There are tests to determine her condition, medications to slow the process."

Thomas shakes his head. "If only she would agree to see a doctor."

"She should be encouraged. In some cases, memory loss can be halted altogether. However, to be honest, I am seeing something different with your mother."

"What is that?"

Elizabeth glances at Stephen, then proceeds. "She seems tired. Like she has lost her enthusiasm for life." Thomas nods. "Does she brighten up when your daughters are with her?"

"Sometimes. A little. But increasingly, I think, their company tires her more than anything. I see her glancing at her watch, even though I know she can't read the time, as if she wishes she had an appointment to escape to."

"The twins can be overwhelming," Christine adds, apologetically.

"It's not just the twins. If I call to say I will be home for lunch, even if I call mid-morning, which is enough time for Rosa to adjust to another presence at the table, I can hear annoyance in Mother's voice. If I ask her if she'd rather I not come home for lunch, she's further annoyed. She wants the company, I think, but has lost the flexibility to alter her plans for the day. Last week I tried another tactic. I told her I would be home every day for lunch, but once I couldn't get away in time, and she was furious with me, as if I had stood her up for a date."

"This isn't unusual behavior for the elderly. They have less to think about, so the few things that occupy their day become more important."

"It isn't easy."

"I'm sure it isn't."

"What can I do?"

"Let her get old. Expect nothing, and be happy for whatever bits of her personality surface. Sit with her. Be as patient with her as she was with you when you were a two-year-old."

"So now I have triplets," Thomas says, resignedly.

"Something like that."

"Speaking of the devil, here come the twins."

The serious, dignified march of lunch is overturned by the joyful melody of childhood: the quickened pace, the noisy laughter, the high notes of innocence intertwine with the deeper voices of responsibility in the moments before the two groups merge. Elizabeth listens closely to the assured sound of their voices, appraises their elongated sentences, applauds the more complex syntax structure, but none of their sounds prepare her for how much the little girls have grown. They round the corner to the loggia at a dizzying pace, undisputed masters of their vertical world.

Elizabeth knows what to expect at twenty-seven months. She knows the standards, she knows the measures, but in the hospital she is often in contact with children who have problems, children out of the norm, and she is quite unprepared for the appearance of these two healthy, nurtured, adorable girls.

There is no doubt they are girls, their halo of wispy blonde hair almost touches their shoulders and is held back from their animated faces with pink sequin headbands. They are not dressed alike but are wearing similar fairy princess costumes. The starchy tutus are short enough that Elizabeth notes their diapers have been replaced by thick cotton training pants. They each hold a star-shaped wand, and from the way they are swinging them, Elizabeth is either being sprinkled with fairy dust or being knighted.

"Hello, darlings!"

"Elle," Christine brings the taller twin forward, "Do you remember Dr. Elizabeth?" She brings forward the other twin, "Anna?"

"I be a doctor when I big," Elle announces, nodding her head in agreement with her assertion.

"Me, too." Anna says.

"A little premature to be deciding a profession, don't you think?" Thomas teases.

"Actually, I knew at their age that I wanted to be a doctor."

"You did?"

"I did."

"And you never changed your mind?"

"Well, except when preparing for year-end exams, no. I've always been convinced I wanted to be a doctor."

"You could do worse than to have two charming doctors in the family," Stephen says.

There is no sitting still this time, no bouncing babies on their knees. The children have moved on to sprinkle their joy across the garden, blessing the flowers, a terrified cat, a wrought-iron bench situated beneath a weeping willow tree at the far edge of the courtyard. The girls are carefree and articulate, distilling a trail of babbling nonsense as light-hearted as a Puccini duet.

Elizabeth feels a tightening in her throat. She remembers finding them half-buried in the depths of the trash bin. What if she hadn't stopped? She had almost forgotten the trash, would have let it sit in the trunk of her car all day if it hadn't been for those smelly chicken bones. What if she hadn't found them? What if she hadn't heard one of them mew?

She watches the girls leave the courtyard, traipse through the garden, two little fairies determined to sprinkle their magic on everything they touch. There is nothing damaged about them, she realizes, and swallows her concerns. They are whole and healthy, untouched by *what ifs*, as if they have been protected all along by the magic in their wands.

"Lizzy?" Stephen says. "We should probably be leaving soon. Your parents are going to want to discuss wedding details with us."

"How are you holding up?" Thomas wants to know.

"Remarkably well, actually," Stephen says. "Much better since we've been married. Being married, I understand the ceremony we are preparing for." He laughs.

"You are saying that everyone should get married before they get married, so they will understand what they are letting themselves in for?"

Stephen laughs again. "In a sense, yes. It does take the strain off, if you know what I mean."

"Thank you for a lovely lunch. It was wonderful to see you all again." Elizabeth's gaze returns to the garden, lingers on the simple beauty of the two perfect twins. "Please thank your mother again, Thomas. And try not to worry about her. This is all part of the process."

"I'll try. I appreciate your point of view."

"We are planning to be in London the last weekend in April," Christine says. "Why don't you come to see us?"

Thomas is surprised by his wife's unprecedented invitation, but he isn't annoyed. Surprisingly, he likes this young couple and would enjoy seeing them again. "Yes, come to lunch on Sunday, if you are free. There is a train from London Liverpool Street Station to Chingford. Epping Forest. We are between Woodcote and Epson Downs."

Elizabeth checks her schedule on her phone agenda. "As hard as it is to believe, I am free both the 27th and 28th. Are you, Stephen?"

"I believe I am." He checks his schedule. "Sunday lunch would be lovely."

"Are you walkers?" Christine asks.

"When we aren't running the corridors, answering our pagers, we are, yes."

"Why not come down Saturday night for dinner—we have a nice guest room," Christine says, echoing Elizabeth's long ago invitation. "We can walk on Sunday to High Beach. I will pack a picnic."

"What a lovely idea, thank you."

"Perfect." Thomas is smiling. "We can have Swedish pancakes for breakfast."

CHAPTER NINE

Rosa has fitted a jacket for Anne, and has marked how much the sleeves need to be shortened. "Signora, do you mind if I stitch the sleeve hem here in the room with you, so that I can have you try it on again once it has been basted."

"Wouldn't you prefer to work in your own room, Rosa?"

"To be honest, Signora, the stairs are hard on my knees. And the light is better in here, not as hard on my eyes when I am stitching with black thread on black fabric."

"You are getting old, Rosa." Anne fumbles for her glasses until she finds them. It isn't that they help her see better but they serve as a prop; give her the pretense of sight. She must remember to replace them in exactly the same place each time she takes them off; this fumbling is a dead giveaway that her vision is failing.

"I am. It is true. I will be eighty-three next month."

"But you are younger than I am, Rosa. You mustn't give in to your years."

"You are the exception, Signora. You never age. You have the gift of eternal youth."

"Don't paint an exaggerated picture, Rosa. I am no Dorian Gray."

"Look at my ankles, Signora, and my knees." She lifts her skirt several inches. "So fat and swollen. Painful."

"My ankles never swell. Nor do I have protruding veins."

"You have lovely legs, Signora. As shapely and pretty as when his Excellency was alive."

Anne looks down at her legs. She can see the outline and is pleased with the shape. She would never allow herself to have swollen ankles. Refusing to acknowledge the ache in her joints, she runs a hand down over her knees and down her shin. She flinches. "Another bruise," she says, startling herself that she has spoken out loud.

Rosa clutches her sewing in one hand, presses it against her ample stomach, and leans down to examine the bruise. "That's a new one," she observes.

"I don't know where they come from," Anne says sadly. "But every day I feel another bruise."

"I'll fetch some makeup. We can cover it up, make it disappear altogether. In another few weeks, it will be warm enough to sit out in the sun. A little color on your legs will mask the bruises."

"I have missed the summer sun." Anne turns her face to the window into which streams a half-hearted spring sun, but the glare burns her eyes. She gropes for her sunglasses, and puts them on, annoyed at another in an endless stream of interruptions to her well-being. She listens—her hearing is as sharp as ever—but apart from the noise on the television, there is nothing to hear. The house is far too quiet with Ian away.

"We'll enjoy the sun soon enough, Signora, and the day after tomorrow we will be seeking the shade. May I sit with you?"

"Yes, you can do your work in here, in that chair near the window." She clicks up the volume on the television.

"Do you mind if I watch as I sew, Signora? This was my favorite program when I was retired, before I returned to work for you."

"If you don't chatter. I can't stand people who talk while they watch television."

126

If she closes her eyes, she can see them all, every child she has ever known. The details of their rescue have been lost over the years; she can't recall if it was Luai who went to live with the Austrian couple or Michele. One of them went on to Queen's College, but she can't remember which. Nor can she remember how many orphans she prepped for exams or for how many she found funding to continue their schooling. The details, like her sight, have blurred into an indistinct haze. When she closes her eyes and allows herself to drift, what remains is the look in their eyes, the whites yellowed by fear, the big black orbs gleaming with hope. She is relieved they are all collected into albums where they won't be lost. She regrets that she can't see the photographs well enough to distinguish Linaio from Lesotho from Tenagne in Ethiopia. Thank God she put them in order before her eyesight failed. Now, when Christine brings her an album of her granddaughters, she opens the book and flips the pages, murmuring gratuitous endearments. She isn't blind, she just can't see. Thank God she has her memory.

She would have liked to have had many children but Ian wasn't keen on a brood. Although he never said so directly, she was sure he believed that children would have hindered his career, would have inhibited their mobility. He wasn't concerned when she didn't conceive in the first years of their marriage. On the contrary, he might well have been relieved, although it wasn't a subject of conversation between them. Nowadays, judging from the television programs, everyone discusses every detail of every bowel movement. Fortunately, they weren't like that. She kept her counsel, he kept his. Personal privacy didn't mean that they cared less for each other. It just didn't occur to Anne that she might mention her growing concern or a subsequent visit to a doctor when they had stopped in Australia enroute to his post in Bali. How vividly she remembers the doctor in Sydney: the walrus moustache, with its ends turned up and twisted with wax in an outdated Edwardian manner and his wild, corkscrew eyebrows that rose and fell with each exclamation. He assured her that she was fine. He told her that if she relaxed and stopped worrying, she would conceive. He promised her a healthy *Heir*. That is how he had phrased it, emphasizing the H, like they were on a hunting expedition, hunting for Hare.

They stayed in Bali for two years and she never conceived, although she did her best to relax and enjoy Ian's weekly sojourns into amorous territory.

She remembers the dinner they had with Ian's colleagues the night before they were transferred to Colombo, when the vice-consulate's wife mentioned an outbreak of measles in the school where she volunteered. Ian said, "If you haven't already had them, keep your distance, John. I caught measles when I was seventeen and it was more uncomfortable than anything I've experienced before or since, even worse than dengue fever."

"Nothing can be worse than dengue," John had responded, and the conversation disappeared into the jungle of tropical ailments.

In the car on their way back to their house, Anne said, "You never told me you had the measles as a young man."

"I didn't know it was worth recounting. Have you had the measles?"

"I believe I have, as a child."

"I suppose I've had most of the childhood illnesses, as well, if I stop to think about it."

He obviously didn't know that measles could cause sterility in young men. She didn't think it her place to inform him. What good would it have done? The last thing she wanted was to humiliate him. But as they drove along the avenue, she formed a plan. She would have her child; he would have his *Heir*. No one would ever need to know. If she couldn't have a brood of ducklings, at least she could have one chick.

She didn't consider it a betrayal. She didn't plan to enjoy herself in another man's company or to run off to start a family with someone else. She clocked her monthlies carefully so she wouldn't have to repeat the act, so her plan could be realized in one fell swoop. She kept her eyes open until she found a man who resembled Ian, someone he didn't know, would never encounter, not even in passing. And when she was fairly certain it was a fortuitous moment to conceive, she went to the piano bar where she had heard the man play, and bought him a drink at the end of each set. She watched closely to make sure he wasn't clumsy or stupid. His face lit up as he played, and as the evening progressed, he sang as if directly to her. If she was honest with herself, she would have to admit that she found him to be genuinely attractive, but she didn't lower her critical eye to indulge sentiment. By the time she had achieved her goal, after she was dressed and on her way home, she was convinced she had planted the seed for an intelligent, kind and giving child.

She promised she would never share her secret with anyone, and she has kept her word. She knows she was a good wife to her husband, and over the years she has come to think of her episode with the piano player as her sacrifice, so that Ian would have the pleasure of being a father. It was all for a good cause. Ian loved his son. He never regretted his presence. He would have considered his life incomplete without Thomas's devotion. And Thomas, bless him, has always honored his father, as becomes an only son.

How young she was. How old she has become. If she closes her eyes, they will think she is sleeping. Only the old nap in their chairs after lunch. She has never taken a nap midday in all her life, even when they lived in those hot, humid countries where everyone, even the servants, ceased work at midday to lie in a darkened room. Even then, she had insisted that the shutters be left open a crack so that she could read a novel or write letters. There was too much to do in one day to lose an hour to sleep. Nowadays, if she could lose an hour a day to sleep, it would be a blessing. Who would have ever thought she would find herself with too much time on her hands?

CHAPTER TEN

Thomas has unlocked the Old Mill House before Christine appears with the twins. He stands at the front door to glimpse their expressions before going indoors to open the windows and light the fire. He and Christine haven't been here in months, and it is the first time the girls are old enough to realize where they are.

Christine rounds the corner, holding each daughter by the hand, walking slowly so they won't trip over the uneven cobblestones on the pathway. She closes her eyes while Anna stalls to tug on a sock. She hears the new leaves overhead in the trees, a gentle rustling that differs in spring and autumn.

Thomas knows it is unrealistic but he wants to see by his daughters' expression if they appreciate the magic of this place. Anna disappoints him: she is wholly absorbed by a sock that has slid down under the heel of her foot. But Elle stops walking and stands up straight, seeing the world through her ears: "*Gurgle gurgle gurgle*," she sings, caressing her father's heart by producing the sound of the water in the river. Anna looks up and repeats her sister's words: "*Gorgle gorgle gorgle*."

"If we can teach Anna an *A* sound, she could audition for a mouthwash advertisement," Thomas says to his wife.

"Shall I set them on the lawn or do you think it is too damp?"

Thomas lays his palm flat on the ground. "It's dry enough at the moment to let them play on the lawn. If you will stay with them, I'll air the house."

"If you put on water, we can have tea outdoors. What do you think?"

He looks at the sky. There are clouds gathering but the wind is high, the air is warm. "Probably better to have tea indoors but let's keep them outside until it's ready. Would you prefer the role of Royal Guard or Custodian of the Mill?"

"If you put it that way, I will loll on the lawn with our daughters until the tea water boils, then we can change roles."

"I can make the tea."

"I know you can. But I want to start bread rising, and I want to air the guest room. We mustn't forget to call Julian. I would like to invite him tonight for dinner with Elizabeth and Stephen."

"I'll call him now. What time shall I tell him?"

"Around eight. We can phone him as soon as the children are asleep. Or he can come at 7:30, if he would like to see the girls."

Anna is playing with her bear, pulling its blanket up around its neck in a fastidious fashion, which Christine hopes isn't a reflection of her parental skills. In contrast, Elle is sitting stock still, as if absorbing the elements with all her senses. Christine can practically see the breeze tickling her skin and caressing her fine blonde hair. Her seashell ears seem to capture every sound: the water cascading in the river, a rock pulled loose, tumbling with the water before becoming lodged again; the first bird song before the migration sounds become insistent. She sits so intently, it is almost as if Christine can see the rays of the sun as they warm the pile of her daughter's playsuit. She looks like a lamb, dressed from head-to-toe in woolly fleece, with rounded ears on top of the cap, which at the moment lies down on her back. Christine feels a little guilty for buying Elle the darker version of this cute, lamblike outfit, but if she had bought her the white one, as she did for Anna, it would have been dingy in minutes. She hopes she hasn't cast her daughter into the role of black sheep in order to save a few cycles in the washing machine, but Charles Schulz might have had Elle in mind when he created his dust-cloud character, Pig Pen.

"Elle?"

Elle breaks from a trance, lifts her ten fingers to the air and sings "wa-*ter*-wa-*ter*—"

"Do you hear water, darling?"

"Da!"

Christine understands abruptly, inexplicably, that it will be Elle who carries on her gift of languages.

"Would you like Mommy to show you the water?"

"Da!"

"Anna? Would you like to see the water?"

Anna nods, her head bobbing up and down deliberately. Christine takes hold of Anna and Elle's hands as they walk toward the river. "You must never come to see the water without Mommy or Daddy. Understand?"

Anna nods. Elle either hasn't heard or is ignoring her, it isn't possible to tell. Christine knows that their understanding of what she says is limited. She will have to repeat her warnings many times before she is sure they understand, but it can't hurt to start young, while they are still willing to listen. She wants them to be obedient children but not without ideas of their own. How can she convey potential danger without making them fearful? Thomas isn't afraid of anything—except perhaps fire—and she wasn't afraid as a child, until life gave her reason to fear.

"Water's boiling," Thomas calls, crossing the lawn. "And I've called Julian, who asked if he could bring a friend to dinner."

Christine raises an eyebrow. As far as she knows, Julian hasn't brought a woman to The Surdans since she has known him. "Anything serious?"

"No idea." He lifts Elle onto his shoulders, and she lifts her hands over her head, as if to touch the sky. "Hold on, Elle," he instructs, and Elle puts her hands on his head. "But don't pull. Daddy wants to keep all the hair he has left."

"I'll bring Anna inside with me while I make the tea and start the bread rising. Would you like biscuits?"

"Yours?" he asks. She nods. "You're kidding?"

"I packed a tin of *pepparkarkor* into my suitcase."

"I knew I loved you. Now I know why."

"**D**inner tonight will not be as planned," Christine announces, when Thomas brings Elle in from outdoors for tea.

"What have you burnt?" He pulls off Elle's lamb suit which is wet at the feet and sleeves, rubs her dry with a towel and dresses her quickly in another fluffy playsuit. He piles books and then a cushion into two chairs before helping his daughters to sit, before pushing them close to the table.

Christine hands each child a ginger cookie and passes Thomas the plate. "Elizabeth's sister is in London unexpectedly. Understandably, she will want to see her." She pours apple juice into the girls' cups and screws on the tops.

"Have you suggested she bring her along?" Thomas pours tea for himself and his wife, adding to hers a wedge of lemon and to his a spoonful of honey. "It wouldn't be any trouble to have an extra person to dinner, would it?"

"Not at all. I told Elizabeth to bring her along." She frowns for a moment. "I hope we have enough place settings."

"There is another leaf to the table, if you want to extend it, but it should be all right, as is. Do you want me to run into town for anything?"

"You might ask Julian to bring an extra bottle of wine. We need to restock, by the way. We have emptied our cellar." They laugh. Their cellar is a shoe rack at the bottom of the entry hall closet. "And perhaps he could bring us a pint of his cider. I seem to remember Elizabeth doesn't drink wine."

"What are you preparing tonight?" Thomas brings two extra straight back chairs from the library into the dining room. The house has become richly furnished, having inherited many of the contents of their apartment in London.

"Janssons Frestelse."

"Translation?" He pauses, tying a thick blue cushion onto the hardwood seat.

"Potatoes, onions and anchovies—"

"Right, I remember. Delicious. Anything else?"

"You can't expect people to travel a distance for a single course." She is dusting the wine glasses, setting them on a tray which she will bring to the table when the children have finished their snack. "I'm making *Vitkals-och Lingonsallas.*"

"Cranberry and cabbage salad?"

"Who says you aren't good with languages?"

"Dessert?" He crosses his fingers behind his back and hopes she is baking apples with almond paste, his favorite.

"*Mandelfyllda Steak Applen.*"

"Bless you."

"*Gesundheit!*" She touches her finger to the tip of his nose. "To finish, if I have time, and if we have any sherry and brandy left, I will make *Glögg.*"

"I will drive into town if necessary to buy sherry and brandy. Your *Glögg* is an excellent finish to any meal."

"Thank you. I should probably start cooking. Would you mind giving the girls their baths?"

The house is fragrant with rich northern scents when the doorbell rings. Christine listens to the single chime resonating through the room where she has been cooking, where they will enjoy their evening meal. For the last moment this evening the house is silent. The clock pendulum is the loudest sound in the room. Quickly, she lights the two tall white candles in their simple silver holders, brushes back her hair, even though she knows it is useless, and opens the door to greet Julian and his guest.

"Are we the first ones here?" Julian says, handing Christine a canvas bag holding several bottles of wine and cider.

"You are. Welcome. Come in." She kisses Julian. She is happy to see him again after all this time. "You must be Julian's friend."

"Denise." She hands Christine her coat, a heavy, full length sable. "I hope we will all fit into your little house," she says, looking around, ignoring Christine. "Julian, why didn't you insist they come to The Surdans for dinner?"

Christine pauses, her arm extended, her hand buried in animal fur, waiting to receive Julian's coat. She tries to decipher the tone of her guest's remark. "I think we will all fit in," Christine answers cheerfully, "if we park the animal in the hall closet."

Julian brings the fresh outdoor air into the warm, cozy room. "Where are my girls?"

"Thomas is putting them into their pajamas. They should be down in a moment. Come in where it's warm. I have a couple of things to finish up in the kitchen."

"You didn't tell me there would be children tonight," Denise hisses. "And are we to eat in the kitchen?"

"Tommy!" Christine calls up the stairs, her voice two tones too bright. "Julian is here. And his guest."

By the time Thomas has arrived with their daughters, Christine has decided that her tactic will be to ignore Julian's guest. She is not going to let her ruin this evening, no matter what.

Thomas proudly presents his pride-and-joys, Elle, whom he calls Anna, and Anna whom he calls Elle, just to set them giggling. It is impossible to confuse them anymore. It is hard to understand how they could ever have confused them. They are as different as red from orange.

Julian holds out his arms and Elle clamors out of Thomas's grasp and tries to climb up onto Julian's shoulders. "She's a little monkey, isn't she?"

"She is," Thomas agrees. "Watch out for your hair. She can hasten hair loss by the handful." He picks up Anna, who is clinging to his leg. "Would you like to hold her?" he offers Julian's guest. Denise is model-thin and smartly dressed; her hair and too-perfect features seem to have been improved cosmetically. "Anna's a bit calmer."

"No. I don't do children," Denise says. "Is that cabbage I smell or does someone's nappy need changing?"

Thomas swings Anna up onto his hip and hugs her closely. "Sounds like you could use a drink," he says to Denise. Bending down to reach into the cupboard, he pulls out a dusty bottle of vodka. Thomas looks at Julian and makes a wry face. "I think we should all have a drink. With or without orange juice, mate?"

The bell rings again and Christine hears it differently, sounding into a room full of people, bouncing off bodies and competing with voices instead of resonating clearly through an empty space. She excuses herself from the group and opens the front door to find Elizabeth and Stephen, holding between them a large and bountiful camellia bush. Behind them, holding another camellia bush, equally profuse but flowering white instead of pink, is Elizabeth's sister, Electra. "Thank you for including me like this last minute. I hope I haven't been an imposition."

"On the contrary, welcome. Come in, Elizabeth. Stephen, come in. We are very happy to have you all here. What gorgeous camellias."

Quickly, Thomas makes the introductions. "Elizabeth was the one who found the twins," he says proudly, handing everyone a drink.

Elizabeth removes her gloves and shakes hands with Julian and Denise, laughing. "It is my one claim to fame."

"That one isn't too bad," Denise says. "But this one is a little dopey looking, don't you agree?"

Before Christine can cover little Elle's ears, Anna says, "She Snow White, you Dopey!"

Before anyone can jump to the poison apple conclusion, Christine intervenes, barely bothering to hide her smile. "Elizabeth, if you would like to put your bag upstairs, your room is the first door on the right. You'll find towels in the bathroom at the end of the hall, if you would like to freshen up."

"We'll just be a second," Stephen says, carrying their overnight bag up the steep steps.

"Would you mind if I hold your adorable daughter?" Electra interrupts. "Would you come to me, sweetheart?" she says, holding out her arms and wiggling her fingers.

"You might want to be careful," Elizabeth calls down the stairs. "My little sister loves children even more than I do. Check her pockets to make sure they are empty of twins before she leaves."

Christine invites everyone to sit. Denise sits in the center of the sofa and Julian and Thomas squeeze in on either side. Electra stands, jiggling Anna on her hip. "If you need any help, Christine, please let me know."

"Everything is ready, but thanks." Christine brings a loaf of warm bread to the table together with a tub of freshly churned butter, and sets them beside the *Janssons Frestelse*. "Tommy, will you open the wine Julian brought? Electra, if you could help Anna into her booster chair. Elizabeth, Elle sits here. Good. We are ready to eat."

Thomas steers Denise to his left and places Elizabeth on his right. He puts Electra next to Julian, and Stephen next to Christine. His daughters together make an eighth at the other end of the table. They have already eaten. Usually they are asleep at this hour, but they had a late nap, they are in good spirits, most of their guests seem to enjoy their company, so they can stay, until they are tired and ready to sleep. Christine has cut them a thick piece of bread crust which they can chew on, without making an unsightly mess.

Julian fills the wine glasses while Christine serves the first course. "This is *Janssons Frestelse*, a favorite of ours. I hope you will like it."

"What's in it?" Denise asks, suspiciously.

"I won't try to describe it," Christine says, taking her place and laying her napkin across her lap. She has made an effort tonight, and she is pleased with how the table looks. "As with so many Swedish foods, it's the mingling of flavors that makes a dish agreeable rather than the individual ingredients."

"It is delicious," Stephen is the first to say. "I wish you would teach Elizabeth to make this—what did you call it?"

"*Janssons Frestelse*," she says, then laughs. "It is easier to make than it is to pronounce."

"I'll call it *Christine's Supreme*," Elizabeth says. "And I would love to know how you make it. It is excellent."

Christine blushes. She takes a bite of the hearty potato dish her mother taught her to make, and agrees it is tasty. But what makes it a special meal is that they are seated at the table with friends—and their daughters. And no one has smeared anything into their hair.

Thomas addresses Electra across the table as he passes Denise the basket of bread. "What brings you to London?"

"An extended stopover. I am flying to Argentina tomorrow morning from Heathrow." She accepts the warm bread willingly from Julian, sets it to the left of her plate, and passes the butter on to Stephen.

"What are you doing in Argentina, if I may ask?" Julian inquires.

"I will be working as a volunteer with an organization that provides after-school tutoring; a program to keep kids in school, off the streets, that kind of thing." She breaks off a small piece of bread and pops it into her mouth. "Delicious."

"She's one of us!" Thomas says, lifting his glass.

"In what way?" Electra asks.

"Thomas is a human rights' activist," Julian says. "Specifically, children's rights."

"You make me sound as if I march in protests and throw rocks at police."

"What *do* you do, exactly?" Electra asks.

"Quite simply, I speak on behalf of underprivileged children."

"He shines light into otherwise dark and hopeless corners of the world," Christine says.

"She's my greatest fan." He lifts his glass again to Christine. "She is the one who makes it possible for me to continue this terribly frustrating work. As she says, I shine the light, but if no one is looking, all the light in the world won't filter down to make a difference to a hungry or misused child."

"Do you know this organization in Argentina?" She tells him its name.

"I have heard of it. It is relatively new but it has been proven effective. Education is the key, I believe, to breaking out of the chains of poverty. It isn't supported well because it doesn't feed the hungry child today, but it will feed him tomorrow—and his children, too. We need to teach our children and keep them in school, help them learn important issues, not the decadent subjects that have flooded European and American schools, like trigonometry and—"

"Latin!" Elizabeth says.

"And Greek!" Electra adds. "A total waste of time."

"I loved Latin," Denise says, moving her food from one side of her plate to the other. "Veni, Vidi, Vici." She hasn't eaten anything but has stirred it into an unappetizing mash. "And Greek. Essential for a classical education."

"Especially in the Third World countries," continues Thomas, "we need basic economics, agricultural courses, mechanical courses, nutrition, and fundamental health care. Basic education is the simple secret to solving poverty."

"Well, if you are talking about Third World countries, I can see how Greek and Latin wouldn't be useful."

Thomas ignores Denise's remark. He asks Electra, "How long will you be in Argentina?"

"Only a month. I had planned to stay longer but Elizabeth and Stephen are getting married in June and—"

"And I would never forgive Electra if she were absent for our wedding. She's my Maid of Honor."

"One of six bridesmaids," Electra teases. "My sister doesn't do anything on a small scale." She addresses Thomas. "If I like the work in Argentina, if I'm not wasting my time or theirs, I will return in July and stay indefinitely."

"Lucky you, you don't need to work," Denise says.

"Actually, I hope I will be working very hard."

"I meant the pay check, ducky. The career."

"There is time to worry about both those things, once I figure out how I can be useful, in what area I am capable."

"Electra finished graduate school in October and went straight to work for Armani."

"It was a six month internship."

"And—?"

"The purpose of an internship is to let the employee and the employer see if the fit is right, if it is a relationship to be developed, continued. Six months was enough to show me I don't want to work for a corporation, no matter how prestigious the name. Armani was great, I'm not saying otherwise, and I liked my boss and colleagues, but I wasn't accomplishing anything I could be proud of. It was all just—"

"Fashion?"

"Exactly. There has to be more to life than the quality of leather."

"What did you major in?"

"Business and Economics. Management."

"She's a great organizer," Elizabeth says, laughing, taking a sip of apple cider. "Lizzy do this, Lizzy do that."

"I know how to get things done, that's all. I can't write perfectly in English, nor can I write a flawless letter in Italian. But I can evaluate problems and see how to resolve them where others are blinded by obstacles. Everyone has their talents. I like to organize."

"And tomorrow you will be in Argentina."

"I will! Any suggestions of things I should be aware of?"

"Is this to be your first practical encounter with children at the poverty level?"

"Yes." Electra fingers the pretty little heart hanging from a chain around her neck.

Thomas sets down his fork and knife before he speaks. "You are going to Argentina to tutor. Stay focused on education." He sees his answer has puzzled her. "If you don't, if you get distracted from your goal, if you get pulled in by all the brutal aspects of poverty, you will accomplish less."

"Could you be more specific?" she asks.

"My whole campaign is focused on hunger," Thomas says. "Let's feed the hungry children of the world." He fiddles with the dessert spoon lying above his plate, aligns it perfectly with the small, three-tong fork. "Even if hunger isn't the worst of the problems."

Thomas is usually more articulate. Christine doesn't understand his vagueness. "We concentrate on hunger," she explains, "not because it is the only problem children are faced with, but if we can resolve the hunger issue, other problems, worse problems, like slavery and prostitution, will resolve themselves."

"Parents who can feed their children are less inclined to sell one or two of them to feed the others," Thomas resumes. "They won't let themselves be hoodwinked by the agents' false promises of good jobs in rich countries.

"By focusing on hunger, it gives us a very real need to address, one that isn't as evil as prostitution or the bands that buy kids for a couple of dollars to teach them to steal, to beg.

"The situation can be so grim that if I look it directly in the eye, I won't be able to get out of bed in the morning," Thomas continues. "Instead, if I focus on hunger—an essential human need—it's a problem I feel capable of addressing. In the face of an issue like hunger, I am motivated to work tirelessly until I've made a significant difference.

"A lot of the committee work we do is simply to inform children of their fundamental human rights. They need to know they are entitled to the basic human rights."

"Basic human rights," repeats Denise. Everyone looks at her expectantly, waits to hear what she has to add. She finishes, "there's a lot of committee work."

"It is complicated, of course," Thomas continues. "When a culture permits an eight-year-old girl to be wed to a fifty-year-old-man, how is that different from a man selling his daughter into prostitution? But if he can afford to feed his family, if he is solvent enough to allow his daughter to attend school, or to stay in school beyond the first elementary years, he might perceive her as an asset to his family instead of expensive chattel to feed, worth something more than a few coins to feed the rest of his family."

"You paint a grim picture," Electra says. "Are you speaking specifically about Argentina or the world in general?"

"The world in general, although you will find all these evils wherever you deal with impoverished children. This is why I suggest you focus on education. In the long run, it really is the solution to the world's problems."

"Dare I ask for any other advice?"

"Are you travelling alone?"

"I am."

"Don't take taxis at night, and if you must, make sure you aren't alone."

"I'll heed your advice, but if you could see how I'll look tomorrow when I step off the plane, you wouldn't worry about me being kidnapped." She pulls a face as she ties her hair up into a disorderly knot.

"No good, I would kidnap you in an instant," Julian says, and then blushes. "I should lend you a stocking hat. Not that it will help much but at least it will hide your gorgeous hair."

Electra shushes him. "Christine, may I help you take your sleepyheads upstairs to bed?"

Everyone turns to look at the end of the table. Both twins are fast asleep in their chairs, Anna erect, her heavy head bobbing, and Elle with her forehead on the tray, lying in soggy bread crusts.

"I somehow knew we couldn't get through a meal without one of them getting food in her hair."

"Hair?" Denise challenges. "Their hair is as wispy as a bald old man." Hastily, she looks at Thomas, then Julian. "No offense intended."

Thomas runs a hand through his thinning hair. "You couldn't offend us if you tried." He decides he isn't going to waste time being polite to someone as inherently rude as this woman. "But I am sure that won't keep you from trying."

Elizabeth and Electra both help Thomas bring the children upstairs to bed, and are back as Christine brings the *Vitkals-och Lingonsallas* to the table.

"I thought I smelled cabbage," Denise says to no one in particular. Julian refills her wine glass. He has developed a strategy to make her company less onerous: a refill for every off-colored remark. At least he will have something on which to blame her bad behavior.

"Yes, cabbage and cranberries," Christine explains. "It is another favorite of ours."

"What an unusual combination. I only know cranberries as a side dish to turkey," Elizabeth says, taking a bite.

"Exactly. Cranberries are like spice, they brighten up any number of bland foods, like turkey, cabbage...."

"Scrumptious. Where did you learn how to cook?"

"My mother was a wonderful cook. I learned simply by being in the kitchen with her. She always prepared the same dishes—plus a few that were reserved for the holidays. There was never any doubt that our dinner would be delicious, and we always came to the table willingly."

"Our mother is a good cook, too," Elizabeth says, "but she never cooks the same thing twice. She's always taking chances. She'll play with a recipe that we all know and love and transform it. Most of the time we are pleasantly surprised."

"We call the successes *Keepers,*" Electra adds, "although that isn't an accurate term in her case, as she never writes down the improvements."

"And even if she can remember them," Elizabeth says, "she's always tempted to improve on them. Her cooking is an evolution."

"Evolution is right. Sometimes you would swear that the fish we are eating has crawled onto land and is breathing air for the first time," Electra says.

"I still say it smells like cabbage," Denise says, her speech distinctly slurred. Julian and Stephen both reach for the wine bottle to refill her glass.

"I am impressed by people who can cook," Thomas says. "Mother never set foot into the kitchen, except to give instructions to the cook."

"My mother was the same way," Julian adds, "although I think she would have enjoyed cooking, if she'd been allowed in the kitchen."

"The workings of a kitchen are a mystery to me."

"Me, too."

"The impressive thing about Rosa—my mother's cook," Thomas says, "is that her kitchen is totally void of the usual equipment. The refrigerator is always empty, except for the two or three things she needs for the day. She has a set of knives but she only uses one of them. She squeezes lemons by hand, whips up egg whites with a fork, peels and chops an onion in the palm of her hand. She has two pans, one for the pasta and one for whatever else she's cooking."

"How dependent I have become on my kitchen toys, even the little things," Christine says. "I ran out of paper towels the other day and almost couldn't function." Everyone laughs. "I am exaggerating of course, but I found myself at a disadvantage."

"I feel the same way about my grapefruit knife," Julian says, earnestly. "Silly, really, but my day is off to a bad start if it isn't at its place on the table, and I have to defend myself with a regular knife against the sections."

"And I thought my dependencies were silly!" Christine says. There is something different about Julian, she senses, then realizes he is sitting up straight; he's taller.

"Marion spoils you rotten," Thomas says, helping himself to a second portion of the cabbage dish.

"If Marion spoilt me, he would section the grapefruit before presenting it to me at breakfast. Honestly, you don't know the things I'm expected to do for myself."

"Julian, you are beyond redemption."

"I know I am an easy target, but this life of privilege isn't as easy as it looks." He pats his lips with his napkin, and then pouts. "I am completely out of my element in the 21st century. An Earl without an era."

At the mention of Julian's title, Denise speaks, as if awakening from a coma. "What would I be called if I were your wife?" Her voice is too loud, her words imprecise.

"Oh dear!" Christine says, covering her mouth with her hand.

"I expect I'd call you *precious*."

When the dishes have been cleared and the dessert is brought to the table, Denise rises unsteadily and wobbles across the room. She throws herself down on the sofa, unceremoniously.

"That's the third female to leave this table in a stupor," Stephen reflects.

"It must be my cooking," Christine says, getting up from the table to collect Denise's coat, which she drapes over her haphazardly.

"Or my company," Julian laments.

"Where on earth did you find her, Jules?" Thomas looks at the mound of animal fur on his sofa. "She's horrid."

"Cousin Sissy introduced us." Julian covers his laughter with the back of his hand. "She sounded nice enough on the phone. We chatted online, we met for drinks, and I invited her out to dinner. But she's been like this since she arrived this afternoon. It must be something about The Surdans that brings out the bitchiness in a woman."

"What is The Surdans?" Electra asks.

"Do you remember that illuminated palace we passed driving in?" Stephen clarifies.

"I do." She turns to Julian. "You live there?"

"If I admit it, promise you won't turn bitchy?"

"I'll do my best."

"Then I'll give you the tour." Color flushes up his neck and into his face.

"I'd love to see it."

"Any time you like." He adjusts his collar; takes a sip of cool water, but nothing helps disguise the blush.

"Perhaps the next time I pass through London."

"When you return for the wedding?"

"Yes. I arrive a few days ahead of time. I've promised Elizabeth I'll help keep our mother from suffering last minute stress."

"Why don't you fly down for our wedding?" Elizabeth says to Julian, glancing at Stephen. She has lowered her voice instinctively. She doesn't want to offend Julian's date, but she doesn't want her at the wedding, either.

"You might as well come," Electra says. "She's invited the rest of the world."

"Just the people I want near us to celebrate," Elizabeth clarifies.

"Two hundred of our closest friends," Stephen says.

"Where will the wedding be held?"

"The church service is in Florence, at St. James Church."

"I assume that's a Catholic church?"

"No, it is Episcopalian—one of the few Protestant churches in Florence. I am Catholic but we thought it would make things simpler to marry in a Protestant church—in English."

"I take it you are Protestant," Thomas says to Stephen.

"I'm not much of a church-goer, I'm afraid. But yes, I was baptized Church of England."

"I don't attend church regularly either," Elizabeth says, "but I have lovely childhood memories of the American Church, as St. James is called. It has such a good, generous feel to it, like open arms offering a blessing."

"What is the difference between Catholic and Protestant?" Christine asks. "In a nutshell."

"Well, in the beginning—" Elizabeth starts to explain.

"God said, *let there be light*," Electra teases.

"In the beginning," Elizabeth ignores her sister. "The Protestants broke away from the Catholic church because it was considered too politic, too indulgent. Too many taxes, too much control, too little religion. Martin Luther protested against the Pope and formed the Lutheran church, which branched out into Calvinism and eventually all the other Protestant religions. But more fundamentally, the churches have two significant differences. First, the Catholics believe that the taking of communion is literally partaking of Christ's body."

"That requires a leap of faith."

"All religion is based on faith. In Christianity in particular, we are taking the Apostles' word. But I am getting sidetracked from your original question."

"And you don't even have the excuse of having consumed too much wine," Julian says.

"True." Elizabeth lifts her glass of apple juice.

"Elizabeth doesn't drink," Stephen explains.

"Unfortunately, even an excellent wine has a metallic taste to me, and it just puts me to sleep."

"I suspect Elizabeth has a slight intolerance," Stephen says, "but we've never bothered to investigate it, as she doesn't miss drinking."

"Lucky you," Julian says to Stephen.

"Yes, she is always the designated driver." He smiles shyly. "What was the second difference between the two religions?"

"Protestants pray directly to God. Catholics have the Pope intervene on their behalf."

"There is another difference," Electra adds. "In the Catholic religion, the Madonna plays a more significant role—almost as important as Christ—whereas the Protestants revere Mary but focus on Christ."

Christine says, "I was reading an interesting book the other day about the Nordic Gods—how they swept down upon occasion and mated with mortals, which resulted in offspring that were half human, half god-like. And then it occurred to me that the Virgin Mary was visited by God, by whom she begot Jesus. He was the son of God as well as Mary's son—half God, half human." She looks at her guests. "I hope I haven't committed a blasphemy."

"All religions have their roots in the pagan myths, even Christianity."

"If you look at paintings and statues of the Madonna, she is often depicted as having a star by her forehead, which comes straight from the Babylonian goddess Ishtar. Ishtar—as well as the Sumerian goddess Inanna—were goddesses of love, piety, fertility and maternity, but also, somewhat surprisingly I might add, of war.

"I don't know the truth of any of it but it makes for interesting study," Christine says, hoping she hasn't offended anyone. "Anyway, sorry to have interrupted you, Elizabeth. You were telling us about your wedding. Where did you say it was to be?"

"The reception, the dinner, will be at my grandmother's summer house, Villa L'Antica, in the hills just outside Florence. It's where my parents live, where I grew up."

"Near Anne's villa?" Julian asks. He looks from Christine to Thomas.

"Across the valley from us," Thomas explains. "Why don't you come, Jules? It will be fun. You can stay with us. Mother would be delighted to see you again."

Julian turns to Electra and says, "If you know your travel dates, if you know when you will be passing through London, we could fly down to Florence together."

Electra is surprised, but tries not to show it. She checks the calendar on her cell phone. "I land at Heathrow on the morning of the 29th at 9:00. I fly from Stansted at 18:40. We'd arrive in Pisa at 21:00. Florence an hour later."

"Perfect." He brings out his phone and makes a note on his calendar; then places his phone beside hers on the table. "I will pick you up at Heathrow on the 29th at 9:00. We can have lunch here, you can sleep off some of your jet lag, and I'll drive us to Stansted in time for the evening flight."

"Is he trustworthy?" Electra says, glancing around the table for general approval. She finds a smile on everyone's face, and a thumbs up from Thomas. "*Va bene.* I'll meet you outside of Terminal Four. If you tell me your number, I will call you when I am through customs." She presses the numbers on her phone as he dictates them and hangs up after his phone rings once. "Now you have my number, in case we can't find each other on the 29th."

"Don't expect to hear from her before the 29th," Elizabeth says. "Our parents will be lucky to hear if she's arrived safely." She shakes her head at her sister, indulgently. "By the way," she shifts her attention to her hosts. "I wanted to tell you that we have a babysitter hired to watch the children during the church service and again in the evening of the wedding, so please bring Elle and Anna. I would love to show them off."

"Would it help if I bring our babysitter, too? The twins can be a handful and Allegra could help your babysitter with the other children, as well."

"That would be great. There is a room upstairs for the children to play in, and a room for those who want to sleep."

"Will the party run late, do you think?"

"We have breakfast scheduled for the sunrise hour."

"5:23 a.m." Electra says, checking her phone.

"Not everyone will stay until the end. Many of my parents' friends will leave earlier, I suspect. But I hope most people will stay for the Champagne breakfast."

"Shall we move into the library, since the sitting area is occupied?" Christine rises from the table. The tall tapers have been reduced to stubs. The flames flicker around char-blackened wicks, sputter in the wax that has fed them throughout the meal. Christine extinguishes them between a dampened fingertip and thumb. A thin line of smoke rises and disappears in the air. "We can have our coffee in here," she says, leading the group into the library. "Thomas, do you mind putting another log into the stove?"

"This is a handsome room," Stephen says, pulling out a chair for Christine.

"It is one of those rooms you don't dare walk into for a moment only." She lights a tall, fat candle in the middle of the library table. Its flame doesn't increase the light from the lamps but gives the room a purposeful glow, a focal point.

Thomas offers chairs to his guests. "My wife has been known to come down from bed to find a book, and I have to resuscitate her several hours later."

"We made this room together, the first weekend we met," Christine says, sitting beside Stephen. "The rest of the house was pretty much as it is now but this room was buried in storage. All these lovely books shut closed in their boxes."

"I had the bookcases from my father's estate but they were disassembled." Thomas looks at Christine fondly. "How many hours did it take us to complete the first one?"

"Quite a few, I seem to remember. But we improved as we progressed, as we learned to work together. It was quite illuminating, really, to find we were compatible in a practical sense, not just in theory or physically," she finishes, blushing.

"Our parents did the same thing," Elizabeth offers. She runs her hand over the smooth grain of the library table. She can feel the inlaid design rising slightly under her palm, like baby teeth beneath the gum. One day she would like to have a room like this in which to adjourn after dinner with friends or to sit with a book on a rare day off. "My father was in the midst of transforming a cantina into a ground floor living room when he met my mother."

"He still shows everyone who enters our house the parallel line she drew freehand that divides the lower quarter of the room from the sloping ceiling." Electra wishes she could curl up in the comfort of the oversized arm chair, tuck her feet up under her and ask for a blanket. She hasn't had much sleep in the past couple of days, suspended as she is between departure and arrival, an old chapter and a new one.

"Our father is good with the broad stroke, our mother is better at the details," Elizabeth says. She looks at her sister and wishes they were in the same room more often. The winds of fate that have carried Elizabeth to England are whisking Electra to South America. Who knows where she will settle? They can stay in touch quite easily thanks to the internet, but it isn't the same as sitting together in a cozy room at the end of a pleasant evening.

"Your parents sound lovely."

"They are particular. Not everyone's cup of tea. But they are very happy with each other."

"That is already saying a lot in this complicated world," Thomas says.

"Do your parents continue to work together?" Julian asks.

"They do. They have olive orchards in Tuscany. They produce olive oil."

"That is what keeps them fit, but our father is an investor," Electra explains. "He champions new companies, helps them find seed money. Our mother is a photographer."

"Will your mother be photographing the wedding?"

"No. We want to see her with tears in her eyes; not have her squinting behind a lens."

"She doesn't usually photograph people. She specializes in nature—clouds, wind blowing through grain, that kind of thing. You might have seen her work in calendars of Tuscany."

"Actually, their mother was quite famous before she came to Italy," Stephen says. "She did a series of books called Divas and Daughters."

Christine sits up straight in her chair. She looks at Elizabeth and Electra. "Your mother is Kate Griffitts?"

"You've heard of her?"

"My mother had all of her books. When I was little, I fashioned my idea of motherhood based on the photos in your mother's books. I'm impressed."

"You can tell her at the wedding. She will be happy to be recognized. Nowadays, her claim to fame, according to her, is that she assisted Electra and me to adulthood."

"I don't want to interrupt this lovely evening, but I should probably catch the train back into London," Electra says, "I saw that the trains aren't regular after midnight, and I would hate to miss the last one."

"What time is your flight tomorrow?"

"Bright and early, six a.m. And I have to check in two hours earlier."

"Do you have a hotel?"

"No, I'll lean against my suitcase and doze."

"She can sleep anywhere," Elizabeth says. "One of our shared attributes."

"Enviable. But wouldn't you rather stay here, and I will drive you to the airport very early tomorrow morning," Julian offers.

"I wouldn't think to ask anyone to drive me anywhere at such an ungodly hour."

"I have to drive into town anyway. I am not letting her—" he gestures toward the other room where the snoring mound of fur occupies the sofa, "—stay in my house overnight."

"Let's let Ducky sleep it off, and when she wakes, if you aren't too tired, you can drive us both in. To be honest, I would much rather be here in good company than in a chair at Heathrow airport, especially if I could ask for another slice of your apple almond dessert?"

"Of course. I can make you an espresso as well, if you like, since you will be awake all night."

"Perfect. I will sleep on the plane. I want to be rested when I arrive. I have less than a month to help Argentina resolve all its problems," she says laughing "—at least those concerning its children."

Thomas raises his glass to offer a final toast. "To Evita!"

Julian raises his glass and silently toasts: To Pippa! The loveliest sister of the bride.

CHAPTER ELEVEN

The next day Christine wakes early, with a terrible sense of dread. She listens carefully, trying to understand if the fear is inside or outside herself. Something flips inside her stomach, causing a terrible, queasy feeling, as if she has eaten something spoilt. Her stomach flips again. Is it fear or nausea?

She opens her eyes and looks at Thomas who is peacefully at sleep beside her, his face as smooth and unstressed as Anna's. She listens closely, tries to hear if there is any noise from the guest room down the hall, the bathroom in use, any sounds of discomfort, but as far as her ears can reach, it sounds as if their overnight guests are still asleep. The only noise is the insistent ticking of the downstairs clock. She looks again at Thomas. If she has cooked something venomous, he isn't feeling it yet. If she dares to speculate, it looks as if he is dreaming of pancakes.

The very thought brings bile to her throat. She shifts onto her back but the unpleasantness in her stomach repeats itself. She turns on her left side and snuggles back into the curve of her husband's sleeping warmth, hoping his nearness will quiet this disturbance. She lies very still and listens. She can practically hear the cells dividing.

Either she has cancer or she's pregnant again. In both cases, the news is bad. She swallows hard and presses closer to Thomas. Instinctively, he wraps an arm around her, without lifting out of his deep sleep cycle. She is alone with her fears. She is sure she has inherited her mother's fate.

How would Thomas ever manage the twins without her? He would need help, more than a babysitter. Would she want him to remarry? She can envision him with a woman like Elizabeth who would know how to raise their daughters. But the Elizabeths of the world are few and far between. It is much easier to find a Denise. As much as she would want her daughters to have a good mother, as much as she would like to be altruistic, the thought of Thomas lying beside another woman in their bed makes her stomach flip again.

She feels the cells divide somewhere deep inside her, one splitting into two as clearly as if she is watching the process on a large screen in a darkened room.

She struggles to her feet. Vertically, she is in less danger of being sick. She peeks into the babies' room and is comforted by their sleeping forms. She can't imagine her day without them present. At the same time, she is relieved to have a minute to herself before they wake. Quickly, she undresses and steps into the shower. The spray of hot water helps dilute whatever is bothering her, and by the time she is dressed, she feels quite a lot better.

As long as she keeps her eye on the horizon, she can keep her stomach quiet enough to accommodate her guests with a pancake breakfast. She keeps the window in the kitchen open and the fresh, circulating air helps her cope with the odors of breakfast. She conserves her movements, using as little energy as possible. She feels like she is moving through water, not gracefully like a mermaid but slow and ungainly, as if she were swimming with heavy bags of sand.

It is mid-morning before everyone is ready for their walk. The children have crawled under the table, are hiding themselves behind the edges of the table cloth. Stephen is finishing his second cup of coffee as Julian arrives.

"Did Electra get to the airport on time?"

"She did." Julian has chosen to sleep late after his trip into London rather than breakfast. "I wanted to accompany her inside the terminal, but she said it was an unnecessary expense to pay for parking. She sent me a message to say her flight departed on time."

"This is unprecedented," Elizabeth says. She has brought her suitcase down from their bedroom and leaves it by the front door. Their train back to Norwich leaves from London Liverpool at 6 p.m.

Julian is grinning like a cat that has discovered spilt milk. "I convinced her to leave me her heart," he says, opening the neck of his shirt to show the necklace Electra was wearing the previous evening. "I told her it was too valuable to risk having ripped off her pretty neck, and promised to take care of it until she returned."

"You have bewitched my little sister," Elizabeth says, tucking a lightweight windbreaker into the bag she will bring on their walk. She takes a seat beside Stephen at the table, and then lifts the edge of the tablecloth to peek at the twins.

"I even convinced her to take the stocking cap. Her hair is irresistible, you know." He reaches across the table and lifts a sand-dollar-sized pancake from the pile remaining on the plate. Powdered sugar dusts his brown corduroy shirt and khaki trousers. "And guess who called me this morning to ask when she'd see me again? Denise!"

"Lucky stars!" Christine hands him a napkin. "There is time for a drop of tea, if you'd like."

"No, I propose we go." He folds another pancake into the napkin. "There is the Grand Prix race this afternoon at two. I'd rather not miss it."

Stephen perks up. "Do you think—?"

"—that we might join you?" Thomas finishes. He doesn't have a television in the Old Mill House and doesn't miss it, except when there is a car race or a soccer match. Julian has a large screen, high definition television—and beer.

Christine has been putting their lunch into a hamper. Her hands stop mid-air, awaiting a decision. No one says anything but their wishes are as tangible as if they were waving brightly painted placards. "Shall we walk until noon and return here for lunch?"

"Does that upset your plans?" Thomas asks, looking at the assortment of plastic containers filled with food.

"It makes things easier, actually." She removes a container of gravadlax—cured salmon— and a loaf of rye bread from the hamper. "I'll just bring biscuits and tea. We won't get as far as High Beach if we are to be back by noon, but we can see how far we get, before we need to turn back."

"**R**ight then!" Thomas says, grabbing a last pancake. "Who is riding first?"

Anna scrambles out from under the table and holds up her arms. "Me, ride, me!"

"I'll take Elle," Julian says, bending down to lift her under her arms. He straightens up and holds her at eye level. "If she promises not to pull my hair."

"She can hold on to your ears," Thomas teases. "They are good sized handles."

Julian reddens. "My moniker at college was *Saucer Ears*— later shortened to *Sauce*. I might never forgive you for bringing it up."

"Accept my apologies," Thomas says, handing Julian another pancake. "This will set everything right." He ducks low so that his appendage won't hit her head on the door jam.

Stephen holds out his hand to take the food hamper, as Christine grabs her bag. Following Thomas's example, she grabs a pancake for herself, hoping to set everything right.

"We couldn't have chosen a better day for a walk," Elizabeth says. She has stayed with Christine as she closes the house. The three men have hurried ahead, as if late for an appointment.

"Isn't it glorious?" Christine turns down the collar and unbuttons her blazer. "It is supposed to rain tomorrow but today is gorgeous."

"Somehow it makes today even more special, knowing tomorrow will be wet and cold. Look at the roses, aren't they beautiful?" Elizabeth says, as they distance themselves from the house. They have taken the path away from the river in order to walk in the sun. "Someone has a green thumb."

"Julian's gardener can poke a stick in the ground and it will flourish like Eden," Christine says, "but I've always had an aversion to roses," she confesses, studying the roses in their walled garden. She sets down her bag on the old flint wall and looks inside to make sure she has remembered everything. "I know it's irrational. I appreciate the color— that palest pink at the start of spring—but roses, well, even the scent annoys me."

"Is it the thorn versus beauty issue?" Elizabeth tests the flint to make sure it is dry and then sits while Christine rummages through her bag.

"No, it is simpler than that." She hoists her bag up more securely onto her shoulder. She hasn't taken a walk without it since she has had children. It contains everything they might need or want in the next few hours, but because it is so full, she is always afraid she has forgotten something. "When I was a child, my mother cultivated roses. Nothing as fancy as Julian's gardens but a nice border of roses along the front of the garden. You have to understand that in Sweden flowers are absent nine months of the year, and when they arrive, they are received like visiting royalty. My mother had been watching this one particular rose for days. As she described it: first a tight bud wrapped in green, then a glimpse of dark red color, then the unfolding, the delicate petals opening just a little. That is the point at which I picked it and proudly presented it to her, with almost no stem. Poor Mother burst into tears—a final frustration, I now realize—and said, 'Alright you! You picked it, you eat it.'"

"You're kidding?" Elizabeth stands and dusts the seat of her trousers.

"I sat at the table nibbling on those bitter petals until I thought I would choke, as much from the unpleasant flavor as from the unhappy reaction my gift had brought my mother."

"Did you eat it all?" Elizabeth picks a rose and removes the thorns along the stem with a flick of her thumb nail.

"No. After a few petals I threw it under the table and hoped she wouldn't see it. Of course she did, but by then she had gotten a grip on herself and didn't say anything more. Since then, the sight of roses fills me with shame instead of pleasure."

"How old were you?"

"I was probably four."

"I'm sure your mother regretted her harsh words." Elizabeth pulls her hair back into a ponytail to keep it from blowing in her face.

"I imagine she did. I don't blame her. I see how easy it is to lose one's patience. I have to watch myself all the time with the twins, to make sure I don't holler at them just because I am tired. I try very hard to only correct them when they have done something wrong. Picking a rose wasn't wrong, and I shouldn't have been punished, even if I had spoilt my mother's pleasure."

"Yes. An explanation would have worked just as well."

"I try hard to resist that initial angry response which creeps to the surface sometimes, especially if I am tired or hungry."

"It's natural enough," Elizabeth agrees. "I have to guard against it myself in hospital, especially at the end of a twelve hour shift."

"Thomas doesn't have it." She points ahead to see him lifting Anna from up high on his shoulders, easing her down as if she were prancing from cloud to cloud until her feet touch the ground. He wraps her small fingers in his large hand and slows his pace to match her smaller steps. "I've never seen him lose his temper with anyone."

"He must have some shortcomings."

Christine thinks, quite a long time Elizabeth notes, considering that they have been married for many years.

"Thomas can only do one thing at a time; he's extremely methodical, and he doesn't like to be interrupted while he's writing." Christine thinks again. "And he's much too tidy."

"Those are hardly faults."

"And he can't tolerate a lie."

"All virtues. You will have to do better than that."

Christine shakes her head, apologetically.

"He's the exception, then," Elizabeth says. "But it sounds like you have it fairly well under control. The good thing about parenting is that it isn't written in stone. If you make a mistake, you can correct it." Elizabeth breaks the stem of the rose and inserts it into Christine's lapel. "Apologies and explanations go a long way toward setting things straight."

"How true," Christine says, leaning down to inhale the soft fragrance. "A short-stemmed rose can still look good as a corsage."

"Exactly." Elizabeth inserts the other rose into her own buttonhole. "My mother and I disagree at times but we always manage to clear the air, to say what we intended rather than what rushed out of our mouths in a fury. You will have a dialogue with your daughters that lets you step back to retrieve words you regret, not erase them exactly but cushion them with caring."

"I can watch Thomas. I can learn from him."

"You can be sure he is watching you, too, that he is learning from you. You are lucky to have each other."

"We are. We are."

"But?"

"No, there is no but. I just worry that I am too dependent on him, that we are too dependent on each other."

"You strike me as a very capable, independent woman, Christine. I don't see that you have anything serious to worry about."

"I *am* strong, usually. I don't know what is wrong with me today. Even my perfect marriage seems like an invitation to error."

"Marriage invites a certain co-dependency, don't you think? Part of the attraction is doing things together, as well as letting the other one take charge of some of the details, dividing the burden. Why does that frighten you?"

They have left the open fields, have entered the woods. The light changes from bright and clear to a premature twilight. It shifts down through the tall trees like solid shafts of pale color. Christine extends her hand, expecting to touch something material, but the light passes through her fingers like ghosts. "My mother died when I was twenty-two. Cancer: very ugly, very quick. The only comfort I had at the end was the presence of my father."

"You were fortunate to have someone to count on."

"So I thought. But he couldn't live without her—literally. Three weeks after we buried my mother, a week after I had flown back to New York, he took himself sailing. And drowned."

"It was an accident?"

"He had lived at the edge of that lake for twenty-six years. He had spoken with my sister that morning, had told her a storm was brewing. He chose death by drowning over a life without my mother." The image of her father alone on the lake grieves her, a figure alone in a too large, too dark seascape. She shudders. "That is why dependency frightens me."

"Suicide is a tough one."

"It's our national anthem."

"I can imagine how upsetting your father's death has been for you," she says, taking Christine's hand and holding it in hers, "especially on the heels of your mother's death." She adjusts the rose in Christine's lapel, tucks it more securely into the buttonhole so it won't slip out. "But you needn't replay your parents' mistakes. You should be able to enjoy your marriage and its dependencies, without the fear of capsizing."

"More than anything, my father's death robbed me of an illusion." Christine bends down to pick up a tightly closed pinecone from the forest floor. It would take an insistent squirrel to crack this cone, she thinks, free the kernels locked inside. "I had always thought of Mother and Father, first and foremost as my parents, but when my father couldn't tolerate

160

life without my mother, I understood that my sister and I were merely by-products of his love for her. I lost the sense of being foremost in my parent's eyes."

"But you and your sister were gone. It might have been loneliness that killed him. Futility. I doubt it was an absence of love for you or your sister."

"I know he loved me." Absently, she tucks the pinecone into the pocket of her jacket as they emerge from the filtered forest light to reenter the fields of bright sunshine. "I just wasn't as important to him as I had always thought. I lost the leisure of assuming first place in anyone's life."

Elizabeth doesn't know what to say. She lets silence settle between them, a comfort in its own right. Across the meadow she sees a flock of sheep grazing.

Christine follows her gaze. It would be a pastoral image, a Swedish painter's scene, except Christine knows that Julian doesn't allow sheep to graze on this corner of his property.

"Look," Elizabeth says. "A single dog to corral that huge flock of sheep."

They watch the dog move the sheep forward between two timber posts until they are settled in a meadow beyond Julian's garden. "The dogs know better than their owners in which fields the sheep are permitted to graze."

"Christine, you are looking a little pale. Should we sit for a minute?"

"No. I'm fine. Really." She catches her breath, swallows bile. "I woke feeling nauseated this morning. I hope I didn't cook something poisonous last night."

"Everyone seems to be fine." Ahead of them, beneath a stand of towering oak trees, the men have stopped with the children. Stephen has blown up balloons and has tied them onto a half-yard of string to the twins' shoelaces. Each time they move, the balloons move. They are trying to catch something they are propelling out of reach. Julian is knotting balloons onto his shoelaces, as well. He takes big, clown steps. The girls run behind him. Thomas squints behind a small video camera. "But you, on the other hand, are a little green."

161

"To be honest, I feel like I'm in the center of a kaleidoscope."

"Christine, might you be pregnant?"

"I shouldn't think so. I've had my last monthlies two, two-and-a-half weeks ago. I'm always regular."

"Some people feel the difference quite quickly after they conceive."

"Oh dear. I would hate to be pregnant."

"It happens quite often after adoption. People who couldn't conceive finally get pregnant."

"But I have been pregnant," she says sadly, "three times."

"You have?" Elizabeth looks at Christine, trying to incorporate this new information with the history she has drawn of her. "What went wrong?"

"I miscarry at four months. It's a terrible experience: hope cheated by disappointment. I thought I had resolved the problem definitively when we adopted the twins."

"At sixteen weeks, how unusual. Have you had your condition diagnosed?"

"I've heard a different theory from every doctor I've consulted, but nothing convinces me, and doctors won't investigate until after a third miscarriage."

"Would you mind if I spoke about this with Stephen?"

"I wouldn't want to ruin his weekend off."

"Are you kidding? Doctors love to talk medicine. It's hard to get us talking about anything else. It solves shyness issues for us."

"Even if I knew the cause, it would be a mistake to hope again."

"Cautious hope is always useful."

"Is it?"

"Even if you are pregnant, even if you were to lose this baby—and it isn't at all certain you are or will—enjoy the process, as if you are awaiting the birth of your twins. Acquaint yourself with every phase: how long the nausea lasts each morning? In what month does it pass? Do you feel the baby move? Pay attention to the details. If nothing else, your daughters will have questions you will want to answer when they are waiting for children of their own."

"I hope I will be around." Elizabeth looks at her so strangely Christine feels ashamed of this bout into pessimism. She feels the need to explain. "My mother was forty-eight when she died. It leaves scars."

"Of course it does." Elizabeth's expression softens with compassion. "I don't mean to criticize. Fear is a natural reaction in a situation like yours." She reaches down to gather a perfect oak leaf, its bright orange surface not disturbed by the long winter, insects or frost. "Knowing her problem, you will need to have regular checkups, but her fate isn't necessarily yours. I want to stress that point."

"The temptation is to stick my head into the sand when a symptom appears."

"That's everyone's first response, but resist it. Pay attention. If you discover you have something, get it treated straight away. Even cancer doesn't need to be fatal," she says, as they near the group.

Elle has fallen and scraped her knee. Thomas brings her to Christine who kisses it better. Elizabeth dabs it with the disinfectant gel she keeps in her purse, and brings out a bright red Band-Aid with white stars. When Anna sees her sister's Band-Aid, she wants one, too, and then Elle wants another, to put on her balloon. Christine shakes out an old blue and white bedspread and they settle themselves onto the ground in a patch of sun. She brings out a thermos of tea and a tin of *Kringlor* cookies.

Elle grabs a ring cookie in each hand and runs off across the pasture. Anna stuffs her cookie into her mouth and runs behind her sister.

"Do you want me to run after them?" Stephen asks.

"No, they can't do more than fall again, and the grass will pad a fall."

"We'll give them the illusion of independence," Thomas says, lying on his side, shading his hand over his eyes to keep his daughters in sight. "Let them build esteem."

"My father was always talking about building esteem," Julian says. "He sent me to some god-awful boarding schools with the intention of giving me self-esteem."

"You can't *give* self-esteem," Stephen says. "By nature it has to be earned. By giving them simple tasks, like maneuvering through a field alone, which tomorrow will assure they can manage an airport alone or a drive across country, you are giving your daughters the opportunity to feel good about themselves."

"And if they are incapable?"

"Eventually they will figure it out. We all did. And think how proud they will be of themselves. That's how we build self-esteem."

"At this distance, it is hard to tell them apart," Elizabeth says.

Not for me, Christine thinks. She can't see how she ever confused them. "Anna's movements are different from Elle's, watch how she moves."

"Their personalities are certainly different," Thomas adds. "Anna is docile in everything she does; Elle is rebellious. I never have to tell Anna anything twice, and it's pointless to tell Elle something even once, she never listens."

Christine asks, "Do you think all parents of twins make this mistake of expecting similar behavior?"

"I think all *parents* make this assumption. 'It worked with the first child, why doesn't it work with the second or third?' Instead, each child needs to be considered individually," Elizabeth says, "even when they physically resemble each other."

"It sounds like you are speaking from experience," Julian says.

"Yes." She shakes loose her hair from its ponytail and leaves it hanging over her shoulders. "If one looks closely, my sister and I look nothing alike, but people see *tall* and *ash blond hair* and it's as though the brain atrophies and ignores further distinctions. Then people are astonished to find we have different personalities. Some hold it against me that I am less outgoing than Electra, and Electra complains that people are disappointed to learn she isn't me."

"How are you different?" Julian shifts on the picnic spread to move closer to Elizabeth. "How are you the same?"

"I was a better student at school. I brought home good grades while Electra struggled. No one doubted that Electra was intelligent but *I* was the good student. When my parents transferred me into the International School of Florence—"

Thomas stops throwing acorns across the expanse of lawn. "I went to that same school when Father was stationed in Florence. They called it The American School then, ages before you were born. Was Miss Brooks still there?"

"She was, although I've heard she's since retired." She reaches for another *Kringlor*. She would like to ask Christine for the recipe for these ring cookies, too, but realistically she knows that her schedule will not allow time to bake. She and Stephen are fortunate if they have a proper evening meal each night. "When my parents transferred me into the International Baccalaureate program, it was a difficult adjustment for me, and not only because the classes were in English rather than Italian. Instead, for Electra, it was like opening a window in her learning process. It took her a minute to acquaint herself with success but then there was no stopping her. She graduated high school with almost the same marks as I had, and bypassed me in university by graduating at the top of her class. To be honest, it has taken me a minute to adjust to the reversal of roles. I quite liked being considered the capable one."

"Her success doesn't deter from yours any more than her beauty makes you less attractive," Thomas says.

"A born diplomat," Elizabeth says. "I understand why you like this man, Christine."

"You said you were different?" Julian says. He, too, is tossing acorns across the lawn, as if he and Thomas are in competition to hit some unseen object. "In what way?"

Elizabeth looks at Julian a moment before continuing. "The one real difference between Electra and me is that I have a vocation. I have always known I wanted to be a doctor. An alternative profession has never suggested itself to me. Instead, Electra is good at so many things, in so many different areas, her sense of direction hasn't developed. I keep waiting for her to take flight."

"The larger the wing span, the harder the takeoff."

"Like an albatross, once she is airborne she may not touch ground for years."

"Look at that!" Stephen says. They see a solitary sheep that has returned to graze on the nearside of the railing, away from the flock. A pack of shaggy white dogs approach it from all sides and expertly move it along so that it joins the other sheep on the far side of the fencing. "A single dog to corral a flock of sheep. A single sheep to occupy an entire pack of dogs."

"**E**lizabeth?" Thomas asks, when they have finished their tea and are lounging on the blanket. Elle and Anna are tearing up grass and throwing it in each other's hair. As long as it doesn't go into their eyes, there shouldn't be a problem, Thomas thinks, although they are going to need a bath after lunch. "Would you have any way of knowing which twin is older?"

"I wouldn't be able to offer any more than a guess," Elizabeth says, looking from Anna to Elle. "Anna is a little more advanced in her hand-to-eye coordination and is more vocal, but Elle has more teeth and is taller, none of which definitively answers your question."

"It's probably one of those questions you won't be able to answer for them," Stephen adds.

"Does it matter?" Julian asks, looking between Christine and Thomas for consensus. "Which one seems older to you?" He directs his question to Thomas.

"To me, Anna seems older."

"OK, so Anna is older," Julian says matter-of-factly. "What's the big deal?" He responds to their shocked looks. "We are talking about what—a couple of minutes?" He looks to Elizabeth and Stephen for confirmation. "An invented truth doesn't need to be a lie."

"Personalities develop according to birth order, although it may be different with twins," Stephen says. "You know the stereotypes: the bossy big sister, the younger sibling impatient to catch up. I don't know that I would want to tamper with that particular bit of information. Maybe you can let them decide, between the two of them, when they are older."

"Which one is older is the least of the unanswerable questions," Thomas says. "We don't know what family illnesses there have been."

"Christine and I were just talking about that," Elizabeth says. "Not knowing might be liberating. Too often we assume our parents' fates are our own."

"It's more the idea that you can't know rather than anything else," Christine says. "I can think of a million questions I should have asked my mother while I still had the chance but didn't. Now I will never know."

"How many things are unknowable?"

"The stars. That is part of their attraction."

They are silent a moment as they ponder their private constellations. "If we study them," Thomas says, "if we understand them beyond being able to identify Orion and the Big Dipper, some of the magic disappears, don't you think?"

"Yes, that's true with music, too," Julian says. "If I understand a composer's intent, if I know the structure and technique, I listen with my head rather than giving in to my senses, and part of the magic is lost."

"Actually, I prefer to know how things work," Stephen says, looking at his phone. "Information enhances the process for me." He brings up a quote. "Listen to what Feynman says:

Poets say science takes away from the beauty of the stars....What is the pattern or the meaning or the why? It does not do harm to the mystery to know a little more about it. For far more marvelous is the truth than any artists of the past imagined it.

Christine would like to agree, but wonders if knowing makes things better. I know why my father took his life but

167

that doesn't make me miss him less. I still feel like I should have been able to prevent his suicide.

Thomas answers, as if she had spoken out loud. "Even when you understand it, you still wish you could have done something to prevent it." She looks at him, stunned, and then realizes he hasn't spoken at all. She has just read his words as if they were her own.

Anna scrambles after Elle across the middle of the blanket, overturning the tin of cookies.

"Are you tempted to have another child?" Stephen asks. "Try for a boy?"

"No," Thomas says, laughing, anxious to protect his wife from this sensitive subject. "It would undoubtedly be another *girl* and even if it wasn't," he finishes replacing the cookies into their container, "it would still be another *kid*."

Christine pushes herself off the blanket in time to be sick at a distance.

CHAPTER TWELVE

The race is over and two out of three of the men are pleased. On a big screen, car racing is as graceful, as powerful as thundering stallions. Instead, on those miniscule, back-of-airplane-seat screens, where Thomas usually sees the races, the drama is reduced to a frenzy, like noisy toy cars, hard to take seriously.

Stephen and Julian have been cheering for Hamilton, their national hero, and just to keep the tension keen, Thomas has been cheering Ferrari's driver, Alonzo. There are many empty beer bottles on the tray behind the sofa. Thomas and Julian are slouched on the sofa and Stephen has made himself comfortable in an adjacent chair. The race is over but they are waiting for the awards ceremony. Gregory brings in a pot of coffee and three cups, and while the door is open, a cat comes in, crosses the room confidently, and jumps up onto the sofa beside Julian.

Julian struggles to his feet. Having not slept much last night, plus the walk and fresh air of this morning, the beer and television this afternoon, he definitely needs a coffee.

His head is beginning to clear when his phone vibrates. "Maybe it is Electra," he says, pulling his phone out of his pocket. He touches the screen, retrieves the message. "Oh, dear." His mouth turns down at the corners, an expression of disapproval and dismay.

"Electra wrote to you?" Stephen says, astonished. He, too, could use a coffee. He sits up straight, runs his hands back through his short, dark hair. "This is positively a first." He glances at his watch. It seems too early for Electra to have landed in Buenos Aires, and he doesn't understand Julian's dismay. "What has she said?"

"She wants to see me again. Tonight."

"Sorry?"

"I hope I won't have to change my number. She's texted me three times already this morning. Such a nuisance."

"Didn't you drop her at the airport this morning?"

"No—not Electra." He looks dismayed. "Denise."

"Denise!" Thomas laughs. "The phoenix has risen from its stupor." His face shows concern. "How will you answer?"

"I was thinking to ignore her. Do you think she will eventually get the idea I'm not interested in continuing our non-dialogue?"

"I doubt it."

"I was hoping it was Electra," he says, putting his phone on the table in front of him. The large cat steps onto his lap. Julian runs his hand along its back and its arched tail, and uncrosses his legs to give it room to curl itself up for a nap. "Electra said she will call when she lands. Do you think she will?"

"If she said she will, she will," Stephen says.

Thomas accepts a cup of hot, steaming coffee. "I think you have found your organizer, Jules. No more postponing the conferences."

"Organizer?" Stephen asks. "Are we talking about Denise or Electra now?"

Thomas explains to Stephen. "Julian has agreed to open The Surdans for informal conferences, where ideas can be discussed before they are presented *fait accompli* at the international conferences. A place where people can express their doubts, be convinced, change their minds, all in relative privacy, without damage to their reputations, their egos or their self-esteem." He sips his coffee, grateful that it is both hot and strong. "You've seen what happens if a public figure voices a thought in public that hasn't been proofed and re-proofed against all possible conflicts of interests. The press are so alert to what they consider indecision or inconsistency, they pick up on a double meaning or an ambiguity, anything that can provide them with a good headline, a quirky story, even when the result destroys a potentially good cause."

"No wonder politicians rely on platitudes," Stephen says.

"Exactly." Thomas reaches over to refill his cup of coffee. "But if we invite a small group of individuals who are willing to discuss their ideas as they evolve, we stand a better chance of finding new solutions to old, irresolvable problems."

"And you want to involve Electra? As far as I have seen, she's not at all political."

Thomas starts to talk at the same time as Julian, then retreats. "You explain," he tells his friend. He starts to pour himself another cup of coffee, and then reconsiders. He won't sleep tonight if he has any more. He picks up a biscuit and smiles. It appears that Marion has appropriated Christine's Tepparkakar recipe. He takes a bite, and knows instantly by the texture and the sharp blend of spices that his wife has baked these cookies herself. He passes the plate around to Stephen and Julian, as proudly as if he had baked them himself.

Julian explains. "I agreed to make my house available, but I am incapable of organizing an event like this. I need someone who can make a schedule so we know who arrives when, so we can have them picked up; someone who will know in what room they will stay. If they have particular needs or food allergies. Marion can cook but I wouldn't trust him to plan menus on this scale. We will need to bring in extra staff for serving and cleaning, which is fine with me, but I need help interviewing them and then supervising them. Breakfast will be at eight but how will I know if someone rises earlier and needs tea in his room? I can't just throw open the doors and expect people to take care of themselves."

"Of course you can't," Stephen agrees. "And you think Electra could help you organize?"

"That is the proposition I will make when she returns," he says, stroking the cat.

"Good," Thomas pronounces. "It is time we moved forward on this plan. Christine and I have been drafting the invitation list."

"How's it coming?"

"Excellent. We have about sixty names."

"Ouch."

"We will narrow it down, don't worry. It is wise to start small," he says. "Just hard to know who to eliminate."

"The names you bump, you can put them on a list for the second conference, or the third, assuming the first goes well."

Julian turns his attention to the television screen in time to see three young men in jumpsuits approach the platform where they will receive their trophies. Their hair is still wet with perspiration, and they tilt back bottles of water as casually as if they were offstage instead of in front of a vast audience. Julian hasn't restored the volume, he doesn't want to startle his old cat, but he can tell from the sudden shift to solemnity that the national anthem is being played. First-place Hamilton closes his eyes, his lips moving imperceptibly to the song played in his honor. In this pose, he does not seem like a daredevil driver but a serious, respectful young man. However, as soon as the unheard music finishes, he throws up his arms in a victory salute, and Thomas glimpses the taut nerves that bring him to victory on this platform. Magnums of Champagne are shaken and sprayed—boys being boys. It seems that these three men are drinking pals instead of strict competitors.

"By the way," Julian asks, "how is Christine feeling?"

"Better. She was fine when I left. Must have had too much Glögg last night."

"I hardly noticed her drinking," Stephen says. "But then I was enjoying the *Glögg* last night, and therefore can't be responsible for any accurate observations." He refills his coffee cup. There will be no more alcohol today. He works tomorrow and must be perfectly clear. "So you need someone to set up the conference, and you are thinking of Electra."

"Yes. And once the conference is in session," Julian continues, "I need someone present but not imposing, someone elegant but not standoffish, someone eminently presentable—"

"That's Electra—"

"Who will make sure things are running according to plan, who can direct Marion and Gregory without seeming to direct—without trespassing on their territory, without usurping their power."

"Without stepping on toes," Thomas adds.

"Electra can do that," Stephen says. "I've watched her organize our wedding party. She's been extremely tactful with her Italian grandmother, who can be difficult at times. It's basically the same thing, organizing a wedding, organizing a conference, although I hope you will have fewer bridesmaid's dresses to distract you."

"She's well organized?" Thomas asks.

"Extremely. She had everything taken care of in advance so that she could travel to Argentina without having to worry about details left undone."

"You said she is diplomatic?"

"Yes. Especially if you aren't marrying her sister."

"What do you mean?" Julian looks up, attentive.

"When I first met her, she viewed me as the interloper, as if I were stealing away Elizabeth's affections. She and Lizzy are very close, and Electra was afraid I would end all that."

"Resolved?" Thomas asks.

"Absolutely. We are really good friends now. Have been for years."

"You know her quite well then?" Julian shifts himself under the weight of his cat to lean closer to Stephen.

"Between stories from Elizabeth and holidays with her family, I would say I know Electra very well—like a sister."

"Do you know if she is seeing anyone?" Julian shuts off the television and without the shifting light from the large screen, the room darkens to natural daylight.

Stephen looks at his host in a new way. "Are you gathering information about a future co-worker or are you asking out of other interests?"

Julian can feel the blush rise but as there is nothing he can do to stop it, he tries to ignore it, and hopes the others will do the same.

"I find her fascinating," he confesses. "Really attractive." He pauses to think, as if analyzing her appeal for the first time. "She is beautiful, yes, but it isn't just that. There are lots of beautiful woman who don't catch my attention. But Electra is, well, attractive inside, don't you think?"

Thomas nods his assent. "Absolutely."

Stephen agrees. "Without a doubt."

Encouraged, Julian continues. "It's like she's transparent, that her beauty shines from some inner source. She's so enthusiastic about everything, as if she's in love with life. It's hard not to share her fervor." He tries to contain himself. He's afraid he's said too much. He doesn't want to embarrass himself, but he needs to ask the question again. "So, is she seeing anyone?"

"No," Stephen says quickly. "Unless she's less transparent than you say, and she has a secret life she's not sharing. I've met many of her friends in the six years I've known Electra, but I have never seen her interested in any one male."

"I think you have found your mate, mate," Thomas says, standing. He would like to go home to see how Christine is feeling.

"I hope you are right."

"A word of warning, if I may?" Stephen says.

Thomas resumes his seat. Julian sits up straighter. The cat uncoils himself and leaps onto the floor. Without a backward glance he carries himself out of the room. "Tell me everything I need to know."

"I doubt I can do that, but here's what I do know." Stephen shares his knowledge of Electra. "She is loyal, trustworthy, and dedicated—as long as you don't assume familiarity. Electra needs her time. She won't consider you a friend until she has known you for months and has held up various hoops for you to jump through." He closes his eyes and remembers the hoops she made him jump through. "But if you can jump through those hoops, and if you are patient enough to let her come close, you will have a friend for life."

"I had rather hoped for more," Julian says, frowning. At present, the possibility of a relationship with Electra feels as inaccessible as the Sloan Great Wall.

"If that is your intention, lock it deep into your heart and don't let it leak out, no matter how you are tempted, until you see clear welcoming signs from her. If you approach her romantically before she is ready, your moves will be received with suspicion. You definitely need to travel the route of colleagues and friendship. And whatever you do, don't expect a subordinate: she's everybody's equal."

"Will she have me taking out the trash and doing the dishes?"

"She won't expect you to do anything she won't do herself. She won't be your superior, just your equal. It takes a minute to get used to, but it's quite refreshing, in the long run."

"It's odd that she doesn't have a long line of suitors. Is there a problem?"

"Not that I know of. But sentimentally, she's at odds with the 21st century. In business, logic, she's quick as a wink but romantically, well, she still expects courtship. Anything fast seems like a violation."

"She sounds like my kind of girl."

"Tread carefully, Jules," Thomas counsels. "Any business you have in mind, focus it on transforming The Surdans into a conference center. See what kind of line she paints across your horizon."

"Actually," Stephen says, "better to expect broad strokes and plan to supply the precision yourself. Electra's genius is that she always thinks out of the box and her logic, while brilliant, is sometimes messy."

CHAPTER THIRTEEN

"**H**ow was Argentina?" Julian asks, once Electra's bags have been stowed into the boot of the car. He wants to embrace her, but he remembers Stephen's warning and extends his hand.

Electra accepts his hand, then leans forward and kisses him twice, once on each cheek.

"It was pretty grim. I can't believe how naive I was—am." She shakes her head to clear an unwanted image. "But the nature was amazing—unstoppable—and the kids were also great—and unstoppable." She savors a memory momentarily, and then continues. "Buenos Aires was both chaotic and striking, but I have to admit I am not a city person. And definitely not political." She glances around her, and despite the airport concrete, she admires the trees in their full spring finery, the same bare-limbed boughs she remembers from the day of her departure. "It feels good to be back in Europe."

"Did you learn any Spanish?"

"*Hola, Julio, como estas?*"

"That's it?"

"Just about. Spanish and Italian are close enough so that I could understand most of what was being said, and most people could understand me, if they were listening. But the closeness of the two languages is actually a disadvantage for learning it. Or maybe that's just me. I am not particularly good with languages."

"Did you solve the country's problems?"

"Don't even joke. I had no idea what real poverty looked like. I was expecting an extended Naples, but Argentina has serious problems to resolve. Intimidating, really, even though I tried to follow Thomas's advice to stay focused on education."

"You don't look too jet-lagged." He thinks she looks wonderful.

"I slept a lot on the plane," she says, running her fingers through her hair. She wishes she hadn't given her brush to a child at the school, she could use it now, but Magda and her friends had never had a hairbrush and Electra has another one at home. "I wouldn't mind a cup of coffee, though, if there's a place to stop."

"I brought you a thermos," Julian offers shyly, "and a croissant. I thought you might be hungry for real food after the airplane fare."

"I am starving, actually."

"Good. Marion is preparing us a lovely English roast. And then you can nap, if you like."

"I think I will try to stay awake until night, to get back on schedule as quickly as possible."

"Perhaps a walk then?"

"After fourteen hours on the plane, a walk would be very welcome."

"After a lunch like this and half a bottle of wine, I am in need of another walk," Electra says, laying her napkin to the right of her plate.

"I still need to pack," Julian says. "I've waited to ask your opinion on what I should bring."

"Let's take advantage of this glorious sun to walk for half an hour, then I'll be happy to help you pack."

"Fair enough," Julian stands. "Would you like me to take you out rowing on the lake?"

"Another time. Today I'd rather walk."

"Come then, I'll show you the farm."

The light on the lake is so perfect, the water so still, such a dark, articulate blue, Electra regrets declining Julian's offer for a boat ride. However, she has eaten so much savory roast and Yorkshire pudding that if she doesn't start to move before her digestion sets in, she will fall asleep wherever she is and not wake until morning. Still, her eyes linger on the lake. As they walk through the front gardens, she is physically drawn to the little boat bobbing at its edge, its nose nestled into a bank of tall grasses like a feeding doe, and hopes there will be another occasion. Her eyes move beyond the lake to the vast stretch of green pastures that lie between the woods and the lake, where they walked for an hour before lunch, and wishes she hadn't been so tired, so jet-lagged; she would have loved to walk farther.

At the southeastern corner of The Surdans, Julian steers her away from the lake, the pastures and the woods, and leads her back along a wide, well-cared-for path between two walled rose gardens.

"I see the colors of the roses haven't been left to chance," Electra comments, admiring the artful bloom of white, then red, then orange then pink roses, as if they had been planted so that no two colors would clash.

"Well, a good Englishman would never plant red and white roses in the same bed."

"People don't still give heed to the War of the Roses, do they?"

"Do Americans from the south still begrudge the loss of their plantations? Do Germans regret losing the Second World War? It isn't politically correct, I know, but if you scratch the surface, national pride still bleeds from its carefully dressed wounds. No Brit in his right mind would regret the end of slavery, but the end of our empire remains a thorn in our side."

"Can't have a rose without thorns," Electra says, impressed with the variety of the blooms, the seemingly endless variation in a single species. "Who would have ever thought such diversity could be possible in a single rose garden. Miraculous."

"Not unlike humanity, thorns and all." Julian unfolds a pen knife from his pocket and cuts three perfect specimens.

"Are you sure you want to pick roses right before you travel? Won't they just die?"

"Marion loves roses, and I do what I can to keep Marion happy. Besides, Weatherstaff, the gardener, says that the more we pick the roses, the more they produce."

"You have a gardener named Weatherstaff?"

"Yes, Ben. He's been here longer than I have, and his father before him. Weatherstaff says he doesn't create miracles; he just cultivates God's glory. You should see his orchids in the conservatory."

"I'd like to."

"If we have time," he says, glancing at his watch as he leads her off the main lane, down a smaller path toward a large barn. "Remember, I still have to pack, and I want to show you this barn."

Julian pulls back a heavy wooden door. It creaks with age and humidity and lodges stubbornly in its track. Electra leans in and together they slide the door open.

In the time it takes for her eyes to adjust to the dimness, her nose tells her that the barn she has entered isn't used for storing tractors. The combination of odors isn't motor oil and diesel fuel but herbs: thyme and tarragon, sage and marjoram, plus many other scents she can't name. As the details of the barn's interior come into focus, she sees bouquets of dried herbs hanging from the rafters, lemon grass and rosemary, coriander and chervil, and others, many she doesn't know. Her eyes adjust to the shadows and she finds herself in a large, well-equipped barn, her eyes confirming what her nose has already told her.

"What a beautiful room. I feel like a bee in an herbal bouquet."

"How intuitive you are. This is the room where we prepare our herbs and honey."

She looks at the clean surfaces and floors, her eyes catching up with her nose. She doubts a tractor has ever entered this barn. "How much of this work do you do yourself?"

"Can you keep a secret?"

"Cross my heart," she says, making the childhood movement against her chest, a sloppy, unorthodox Catholic cross.

"I actually spend a lot of time out here. Undoubtedly, I drive my staff to distraction, but I love to witness the working side to this estate. I love being present when the honeycombs are removed from the hives, when the walnuts are harvested. I hung these herbs myself. I wish you could have seen them when they were still fresh. That was a sight to convert an atheist."

She looks at the herbal bouquets, the tarragon tied with a pale pink ribbon, the thyme with dark green; the lemon grass has been bound with dried winter grasses, and the coriander distinct in dark red. In addition to the herbs, there are handsome river reeds drying, their elongated dark brown heads inviting a caress. "And why exactly is this a secret?"

"The only whipping I received as a child from my father was when he found me mucking out my horse's stall. He would have fired the groom for letting me get my hands dirty, but if he had, he would have had to find someone else to clean the stalls, and already that was too close to manure for his taste."

"I don't understand."

"He explained it to me very clearly, as he was strapping my behind. People of our position must never dirty their hands."

Electra is shocked. "Do you agree with that?" She has moved further into the barn and has stopped along an aisle of large vats.

"No, actually, not then, not now," he says, lifting a lid. "But I have come to appreciate his point of view and therefore I keep it a secret when I dirty my hands with work." He leans forward and breathes deeply, steps back, clearly satisfied.

"May I?" She follows his example and is surprised to find herself inhaling the dark, mysterious fragrance of honey. "Do you mind if I have a taste? My hands are clean." She runs her finger against the thick, dark honey. She looks down the row and sees a dozen more vats. "How much do you produce?"

"Several hundred pounds."

"Have you thought of packaging your products for retail?"

"I haven't thought it worth the effort. What can a jar of honey bring? Two pounds?"

"Are you kidding?" she dips her finger again, as if another taste is essential to an appraisal. "Honey like this, unprocessed, if you can find it, costs four times that." She moves to the next vat and dips again. "This is amazing. A completely different taste."

"Would you like to see the hives? The bees are busy bringing in the first pollen."

"If you didn't have to pack, I'd say yes. Another time?" She moves to the other side of the room, to where huge vats of nuts are stored. "You have a small gold mine in here, you know. Walnuts cost like gold, practically. Shelled, they are like diamonds. You really should sell your products."

"I would have to invest in machinery."

"Step by baby-step. Even if you sell only a hundred jars of honey in the first year—something that Marion and you, in secret, naturally, could do in the kitchen—that's a lot of money for kids who have nothing. Think small. If you can help two kids in one year, that's two fewer who will go to bed hungry—all because of industrious little bees in Epping Forest."

"Actually, Thomas and Christine and I have been looking at another way to help sponsor children. It is less direct than your plan of selling honey and walnuts but perhaps more far-reaching, if we can get it to work."

"Let's walk and you can tell me," she says. She is reluctant to leave the barn, with its many intriguing, shadowed corners to explore, but if she doesn't walk, she will fall asleep. She needs to move out of this dark, cozy barn and into the daylight. She places her hand on the heavy door to assist closing it, but it slides easily, effortlessly.

"We'll walk back to the house along the river," he says, taking her elbow and guiding her onto another, smaller path. As they walk, he tells her the plan, sketching it quickly, with more optimism and enthusiasm than concrete details. "We were thinking to host the first conference in October."

"It would have to be quite small to be set up in four months, but it could be done."

"Would you be willing to give us a hand?"

She answers his question with a question that implies her consent. "Would you be willing to make an investment straight off?"

Julian stuffs his hands into his pocket before she can empty them. He hopes she won't suggest he refurnish the house. He is attached to the family furnishings, even if they are a bit tattered and worn. He hopes she won't suggest a new state-of-the-art kitchen and a celebrated staff of chefs. How could he break such news to Marion?

"You will need to buy a fleet of bicycles."

"Bicycles?"

"For your visitors. Their inclination will be to go out walking, and that should be encouraged in the first days, but once they have been here a day or two, they should be given bicycles. It will speed up their thought process, gear up their motivation, help them reach concrete decisions."

"Following your logic, wouldn't motorbikes motivate them more?"

"No, engine-operated vehicles encourage passivity." She answers his puzzled expression with an example. "Like the difference between television and theatre." He still frowns. "Radio and a live concert."

"So you'd be willing to help organize this affair?"

"Let me get my sister married next week and then we can talk details. Now, we should probably get you packed."

He wants to hug her to him like a bear embracing a honey pot, but he restrains himself. He contents himself with a prolonged touch to her arm as he guides her around the front of the house.

"Considering the discrepancy between yesterday and today's time zones," Julian says, as they ascend the stairs to his living quarters, "you are holding up remarkably well."

"The walk helped. You live in a beautiful place. I hope you appreciate how fortunate you are."

"I do. I walk every day and never grow tired of this quiet beauty."

"England's beauty is restful rather than dramatic, don't you think? Such a soft, gentle green." Electra seats herself on the sofa in Julian's bedroom while Julian decides between two suitcases positioned near the door to his room. "The smaller one will be enough," she says. "You can wear the same suit to the rehearsal dinner as to the wedding."

"I hadn't thought to be invited to the rehearsal dinner," he says, looking at the clothes Gregory has laid out on his bed for consideration. He lays a bright red tie against the starched white shirt. "Are you sure?"

"It's up to you. We are inviting all the guests who have come from out-of-town. There will be an activity every day for the out-of-town guests, a tour of the vineyards in Chianti, lunch at a cheese farm in the Saline di Volterra, a tour of the Vasari Corridor—"

"Vasari—?"

"It's the corridor that Cosimo dei Medici had constructed so that he and his family could pass from one side of town to the other without having to rub shoulders with the town's people. Its attraction—apart from being one of the best kept secrets in Florence—is that it is lined with self-portraits of the painters who have their works in the Uffizi. You'd be impressed by who is there: Rubens and van Dyck, Rembrandt and Sargent and Marc Chagall. None of the guests will be obliged to join in but since most of the people coming to the wedding don't live in Italy and will want to see

184

Tuscany, we thought it would be easier to organize excursions for them."

"I would love to join in. But Christine and Thomas aren't really out-of-town guests, are they?"

"But they will be invited to join in, if they are free."

"You think one suit is enough then?"

"Yes. One suit, two shirts, two ties. Something comfortable and lightweight for the days."

How easy it is to be with her, he thinks, setting aside the second suit in favor of chino trousers and polo shirts. As he closes his suitcase, he watches her relaxing on the sofa, leaning back under the open windows, a gossamer veil lifting and falling behind her, as if measuring and replicating the rhythm of her breath. Light falls and shifts across her stationary form as if it were she who is moving, not the shadows, as if this were an intimate moment in a shared life rather than an interlude to their separate lives. He feels as comfortable, as relaxed, as if he has known her for years.

What has happened to women these days? The last woman who came into this room was so impressed with his four-poster bed that she suggested she tie him up with silk handkerchiefs! He doesn't believe women should hide their ankles or pretend virtues they don't have—he isn't wishing for duplicity—but what's wrong with a little human modesty? If it is all on display, what is left to discover? He walks down the streets of London and feels he's in the red light district of Amsterdam. Last week, sitting in a pub waiting for his accountant to return from lunch, in the time it took to finish a half pint, he was accosted twice by women in tight, aggressive jeans. The proposals they made were startling.

Electra interrupts his thoughts. "Who is the woman?"

It takes him an instant to realize she hasn't read his thoughts. He follows her gaze to the portrait on the west wall of the room. "That would be my great-great-great grandmother, Juliet—"

"Your namesake?"

"Yes, actually."

"It looks like a Sargent."

"It is."

"You're kidding!" She crosses the room in a dozen long, energetic strides to look more closely at the large, gilt-framed canvas.

"I'm not." He would like to stand next to her but he doesn't want to make her feel like he is following her every move.

"And why exactly do you have her squirreled away in your bedroom, where no one can see it?"

"It has always been here. I never thought to move it."

Electra looks around the room at the dark decor, and a light dawns. "You didn't decorate this room to your tastes?"

"Heavens, no. I don't believe anything has been changed in this room—except the linen, of course—in the last hundred years or so—not since that painting was hung."

The rest of the house has prepared her for this magnificent setting but she has felt shy of looking too closely at his room. However, if it doesn't reflect his tastes, if it is preserved as a museum like the rest of the house, her reservations disappear. Standing in front of the Sargent, she remarks, "It is curious this painting was hung in the bedroom in the first place. Sargent was famous in his own day."

"I know." He can't resist. He comes to stand beside her. He can feel the electricity from the sleeve of her dress against the sleeve of his shirt. "But the story goes that my great-great-great grandfather threw a fit of jealousy when he saw the portrait. He couldn't have it destroyed, that would have offended both his wife and Sargent, but he cloistered it in his bedroom as too intimate to be viewed by visitors to the house."

"It looks fairly decorous to me," she says.

Julian leans toward her and whispers, "Look more closely."

"Is her dress cut too low? Is that the problem? It's too revealing?"

"No, women of her day allowed a fair amount of cleavage in the evening. But look more closely." He takes her arm and moves her closer to the portrait. "See?"

Electra shakes her head. She can't see anything inappropriate in the portrait.

"An erect nipple," he whispers in her ear.

"No! That's a pleat in her dress, the top of a dart."

"That's exactly what Great-Juliet is reported to have said, but her husband couldn't be convinced. He said it would be hung in his bedroom or not at all."

"This was their bedroom then?" She looks around with ever increasing wonder, as the preserved becomes personal. She takes in the details of the frescoed ceiling, the intricate cast iron lamp hanging down from the center of the tall ceiling, the splendid, luxurious drapes tied back from the windows.

"It was his bedroom, yes, and after that, his son's bedroom when he married, and my father's bedroom when his parents died, and now mine. But come with me." He leads her to the western alcove of the large room, and turns a key in a door. "This was where Great-Juliet slept—and all the Berryrose wives after her, including Mother." He pulls back the heavy drapery, reaches his hand in to flick a switch, and then lets her pass.

Electra feels she has entered into a twilight zone between reality and a flight of imagination. The furnishings have been draped with dust cloths; but that only makes the frilly, diaphanous decor seem occupied by ghosts. She believes she can smell generations of French perfume lingering in the air. She moves back toward the door, not wanting to linger in what feels like a time warp, in case she gets caught and can't pass freely back into her own life.

"I know a lot of couples sleep in separate rooms," she says, when they have returned to Julian's room, and have closed the door to the past. She reclaims her seat by the open window, and pulls aside the fluttering, gauzy fabric, preferring the unfiltered sunlight rather than the softer, veiled view. "But it seems to be missing the point of marriage, don't you agree?"

"I do," Julian says, coming to sit beside her on the divan. His cat has entered the room in their absence, has jumped up onto the foot of his bed. He hopes Electra won't notice him. Some people are intolerant of animals in the bedroom. "But times were different. Marriage was more about combined estates and lineage than intimacy."

"My *Nonna*—my Italian Grandmother—told me a few years ago that her husband had never seen her without clothes, that even their most intimate moments were veiled in low lights and lingerie."

"I doubt Father ever saw Mother without high heels," Julian laughs, but it is the sound of perplexity rather than humor. He watches his cat stand up to stretch, then jump down from the bed and walk toward them boldly. "You can't share the same bedroom and always maintain that decorous pose."

"What a tiring job it would be to wear a mask in your own house, in front of your own husband." Electra reaches down and offers her hand to be appraised by the cat. He rubs his face against her fingers, and then jumps onto the sofa between them. Her hand meets Julian's as they both reach to stroke the cat, and she has to contradict the urge to pull away. "Isn't marriage about intimacy," she says, "about revealing yourself; making yourself vulnerable, trusting that the person you married won't betray the confidence?"

"You make it sound so easy—" He watches as his cat positions himself onto Electra's lap, surprised that his finicky pet would choose to befriend an unknown. "And so tempting." He watches to see if she minds the cat's familiarity, and is relieved when she doesn't try to dislodge him, but starts to caress his fur. "But is marriage ever the way you describe it?"

"I think it must be." She pauses, her hand poised over the cat's back. "Otherwise, what's the point?"

"Well, children, of course. The family lineage to carry on."

"Yes, of course. We might risk extinction if everyone waited for the right person to come along." She shakes her head, as if dislodging an unwelcome thought, and focuses again on the furnishings in the room. "So you haven't changed a thing?"

"I don't really feel it is mine to change." He shrugs, running a hand along the gilt-carved sofa on which they sit. "In a sense, I'm just the custodian in a long line of tradition." He appraises the ornate canopy bed, as if seeing it for the first time, through her eyes, and is filled with what can only be called fondness for its delicate drapings. "Until I was born, when my mother had complications that required she deliver me in hospital, all my forefathers were born in these rooms, either in this bed or the one in the adjoining room. Does that seem so strange?"

"Not entirely, no. My father was born in the same bed that his father was born in. Before that, his grandfather was born in the same house where his ancestors had lived for four hundred years."

"You do understand, then."

"My father would agree with you entirely."

"I am maintaining this house for my sons and their sons."

"That's what my father says, too, although he has only daughters. On the other hand, my mother would say that each generation has the right, the responsibility, to add their personal imprint, to leave a trace, so that future generations can see the stratum of civilization. The earliest Christian churches were built on Greek temples, whose proportions and dignity weren't razed but were allowed to evolve into a new holiness."

Julian brightens. "I *have* changed the bedside lamps."

"You have good taste," she says, a laugh colliding with a yawn.

"The original lamps were impossible to read by," he says, "not enough light," and then, as if afraid the additional light isn't enough, adds, "I also had the kitchen remodeled when Father died. Come, I'll show it to you, if you'd like."

"And then let's walk until it's time to leave for the airport. Otherwise I may have to curl up on your bed with the cat to sleep."

CHAPTER
FOURTEEN

Christine is feeling restless. For a third of her life she has worked at an accelerated pace, close enough to the center of fiery issues that her senses have burned with purpose. Yesterday, as she repeated *Round and Round the Garden* for the thirtieth time, drawing a circle on Anna's little palm, then Elle's, she felt an Arctic wave of resentment descending from the cold north, colliding with warm, maternal currents, creating an emotional whirlwind that surprised and disturbed her. Thomas is at work, surrounded by intellectual dialogue, and she is at home, supervising Lego construction, pregnant again. She misses their old life, when she and Thomas resolved real issues together.

These days, she can't resolve anything. Her sister has called again, asking when she will come up to Sweden. Christine can't travel now, and even if she could, Sweden wouldn't be the destination of her choice. As she watches the Italian news, she translates into English, into Swedish, French, German, an exercise to keep herself from going stale, like stationary bicycle riding to keep a runner's muscles fit. The other day she couldn't remember a word and panicked. She needs to get back to work or she will lose all the ability she has worked so hard to acquire. She pulls out her dictionaries but is interrupted by Anna who can't find a shoe. The search for the lost word is replaced by the search for the lost shoe. In the afternoon, when she has a minute to resume the search, she can't remember the word she was looking for.

Last week Christine set up an interview in town. She risked her life in traffic to arrive at her appointment on time, only to be kept waiting for almost half an hour for a meeting that lasted less than ten minutes, with a man who couldn't be bothered to look her in the eye once he saw she was pregnant. He mispronounced her name, even though Christine isn't far from the Italian *Cristina*. She could have just as easily left her résumé with the receptionist. He half rose from his chair as she stood to leave, his handshake as disinterested as the bored expression on his perpetually tanned face. At the door, when she turned to say a final goodbye, he didn't bother to look up. He was on the phone, enthusiastically making plans for dinner at a new *enoteca* in town.

Anna picks up her mother's reluctant hand from where it rests on her slightly distended stomach, and tries to initiate the finger rotating against her palm. Christine yields, even though she wishes they would choose another book, something a little more advanced, more suitable to their age. She forces herself to reintroduce enthusiasm into the tired game. She loves her children and can't imagine her life without them, but what she can imagine is a little intellectual activity more challenging than the repetition of a five line nursery rhyme and the mechanics of OshKosh buckles.

"Allegra?" Christine steps into the next room. "Would you be free to babysit Friday night?"

"*Perché no?*" She barely looks up from folding the children's clothes, but her surprise lifts her voice a couple of notes. They never go out in the evening.

"We won't be late." Christine takes the folded outfits and stacks them neatly in the drawer. The clothing no longer seems impossibly miniature to her, as it once did. She examines the overalls Elle wore yesterday, impressed that the grass stains have washed out of the knees. The girls are growing so fast they outgrow their clothes before they can stain them. She wonders if the child growing in her womb will emerge to wear these clothes.

"Be as late as you want," Allegra says, reaching down to tickle Elle, to distract her before she unfolds the stack of towels Allegra has just folded. Elle climbs into the plastic laundry basket, and Allegra pushes it along the floor while manufacturing engine revving noises.

Allegra's boyfriend, Giorgio, is a sous chef at the St. Regis Hotel, and is rarely home before midnight. Christine knows that Allegra is saving the money she earns babysitting so they can eventually open a little restaurant together. Allegra also loves to cook, and when the twins are sleeping, she is happy to give Rosa a hand in the kitchen. Several times, Christine has found Allegra engrossed in Rosa's collection of hand-scratched recipes, transcribing ingredients into a notebook in her neat, steady hand.

On Friday night, Christine kisses her daughters and leaves the twins with Allegra an hour before Thomas is due home from work. She immerses herself in a hot bath scented with exotic, Mideastern oils.

Christine is still master of the quick change act. In the old days, she and Thomas could pack their suitcases and be at the airport in the time it takes her now to give the twins their evening bath. These days, she moves from one mundane task to another, in constant fast forward movement, like those cartoon characters that run in place. She does a lot but does any of it add up? By the time she emerges from her bath, as she wraps a large soft towel around her body, she feels both relaxed and energized. She is looking forward to her evening with Thomas, as much as if she were a young girl anticipating a first date. She changes her dress twice before deciding upon a dark blue knit, with gold buttons on the left shoulder. Her tummy shows more than she likes—she looks fat rather than pregnant—but even that bulge is agreeable tonight. She takes time with her hair, puts on her favorite jewelry, even applies a little more makeup than she usually wears.

Thomas is surprised to find Christine dressed to go out. He has arrived home late and tired. He has been looking forward to a quiet evening at home. "Sorry," he says, "I forgot." He looks at her to see if there is any chance of changing their plans, then jumps up with borrowed energy to keep his wife's look of expectancy from fading. "Do I have time for a quick shower?"

"Our reservation is for eight."

"Right then." He pauses to kiss her lips, to lay a hand on her slightly bloated tummy. "I'll be ready in five."

His hair is still damp as they drive east to Maiano, to the tiny trattoria where Thomas brought Christine the first week they moved to Florence, almost two and a half years ago. They haven't been back since, and Thomas can feel his exhaustion as he parks the Saab at the side of the restaurant, wishing they could have stayed home for a quiet evening.

"Thomas, look!" Christine says in a whisper, her soft voice exuberant. "No, don't turn off your lights. Look there!"

It takes Thomas a minute to locate the object of his wife's excitement. Perched on a telephone line, directly in front of their car, is a baby owl, its talons tightly gripping the wire while the rest of its dignified little body sways in time to the wind.

"Isn't it amazing?" Christine says, her voice filled with wonder. Her hand has found its way into his. "It looks just like Elle's stuffed owl."

"It does," Thomas whispers, even though the windows of their car are closed, and the white, fluffy owl can't hear them. He watches the perfectly formed little barn owl, an exact replica of his daughter's favorite stuffed animal—even the size and the wise, knowing expression are the same! He has often held Elle's toy owl and has pretended to make it screech, which makes it that much easier to imagine the suppleness of this owlet's plumage, as if he had held the real bird and not the toy in his hands. Breathlessly, he watches it sway dramatically on the high wire, a bright-eyed, tightrope walker giving its debut performance in the spotlight of his car's unblinking headlights. "I wonder if I can take its photo without frightening it?" he asks. Furtively, he pulls out his phone from his pocket, flicks on the camera option, and raises it to his eye in time to witness the owl's abrupt departure.

"We might as well go home now," Christine says, wrapping her shawl around her shoulders as she opens the car door.

"Why?" Thomas, who would have been happy to go home a few minutes ago, is now disappointed at the thought of concluding the evening before it has begun.

"It's not going to get any better than this," she says softly, in the same reverent tone she has used to appraise the bird. "This is undoubtedly the best course of our meal, the *tiramisù* of the evening."

"I'd be willing to try for additional good fortune."

"And I'd be willing to prove you right."

As they walk through the arbor into the old, dark-walled restaurant, they see the city of Florence in the distance, nestled like jewels in a crown valley. They are at the same altitude, more or less, as they are from their house in San Domenico, but the view here is off-centered. They are viewing the city from the east rather than the northeast, and even though the buildings they see are the same—the Duomo, the Campanile, Palazzo Vecchio, Santa Croce—the altered perspective makes them seem new, almost like Christine and Thomas are visiting the celebrated city for the first time.

"So tell me, how is work?" Christine says, after they have ordered their meal. The waiter has poured a dark ruby red *Pinot Nero* into Thomas's glass. Christine has been drinking water instead of wine since she became pregnant but the color is so tempting she takes a sip from her husband's glass.

"Frustrating," Thomas says, passing her the basket of warm *schiacciata*. "I am teaching others how to address the world's problems instead of doing it myself."

"That is what teaching is, I believe." She breaks a tiny piece of the flat, salty bread, and puts it into her mouth, wiping the traces of olive oil from her hands onto her napkin. "Isn't there stimulating conversation with the students?"

He considers. "Some." He dips his bread in oil, and leans forward to put it into his mouth.

"The other professors?"

"There are some good minds. I would do better to focus on them. But there is a lot of posturing, too." He shakes his head and his hair falls onto his forehead. "Prima donnas who wear their tenure like Oxford Dons in scarlet and navy robes." His voice grows excited. "They sit in their offices, compose their scholarly papers—which are as far removed from the real problems as Tibet is from China. They have an undisguised contempt for teaching, as if it were beneath them. On the whole they avoid contact with students, as if they were contagious."

"You make it sound terrible."

"Shoot me if I ever become like them."

She raises her hand, the forefinger pointed toward him, and cocks her trigger thumb.

He feigns being hit, a bad John Wayne imitation, which catches them in laughter as the waiter sets between them an enormous platter of Tuscan smoked meats, pâté, olives and crostini. "Today has been particularly frustrating," Thomas says, spearing an olive. "I attended a seminar this afternoon—eight professors, two students." He twists his wedding ring nervously. "The students were so intimidated, they barely asked a question, let alone voiced an opinion. The professors were even worse. There was this one guy who could have been straight out of central casting—tweed, elbow patches, the pipe, and his attitude was even more predictable. Extremely boring."

"You should have spent the day playing *Round and Round the Garden* with Anna and Elle."

Their eyes meet, and they laugh.

"Remember when we had real things to complain about?"

"I do. I don't mean to sound ungrateful but the truth is—" Thomas takes a sip of his wine "—I miss my old work." He sets down his glass, twirls the liquid in its large bowl. "And I miss working with you."

"I can say the same." She lifts her hand, which has been resting on her stomach, as if an answer could appear from her palm. "But what can we do?"

"Do you mind terribly being at home with the girls?"

"No, not at all." Her fingernail finds its way into her mouth but she catches herself before she can chew on it. "But I would enjoy it more if I had, say, three or four hours a day of intellectual stimulation. Even a few days a week, time to miss our daughters, to look forward to seeing them again, rather than sneaking off for fifteen minutes to read and feeling guilty about it."

"This pregnancy is badly timed."

"This pregnancy is what it is." She still doesn't know if she should be happy about it or not. She is taking it one day at a time, trying not to let either fear or hope get the best of her. "I always wanted to have lots of kids, but having two proves more demanding than I could have imagined."

"Your pregnancies are a lot more difficult than we thought, too." He doesn't want to introduce doubt into their new arena of hope, but he knows how trying her miscarriages have been. He has reached across the table, has taken her hands in his.

"If I am honest," she says, "I have to say I miss the intellectual stimulation of work." He nods in agreement. "Tommy, I miss working with you."

"Come join me, then, even if it is just a few hours a day."

"Really?"

"Really."

"I could walk over after Allegra puts the girls down for their morning nap."

"I could come back home with you for lunch." They are smiling, plotting an adventure. "You can remind me of the good things that are happening each day at the Institute, and I can—"

"—distract me from my rosary of *Round and Round the Garden*."

"It's not a long term solution," Thomas says, moving his silverware to make room for a platter of steaming *tagliatelle* and *ragù*.

Christine adjusts her silverware, as well, and inhales the familiar fragrance of *ribollita*. The vegetable soup thickened with day-old bread is so dense it can be eaten with a fork. It's a winter dish and this will be the last time she has it until next year. The waiter pauses to dribble olive oil over the soup, a delicate design of pungent green, but when he offers to grind fresh pepper over her bowl, Christine raises her hand to stop him.

"We don't need a long-term solution, darling," she says. "I have no doubt that things will right themselves in the future. We just need to find a way to maneuver ourselves through these next few years."

"Will you be all right adding another baby to the confusion of the household?"

"I think I will be OK with whatever happens. If I move forward with this pregnancy, I will—" She looks at him across the table, so eager for her happiness.

He waits for her to continue but her silence is long, even for her. He completes her thought. "And if we don't, we have a rich, enviable life as it is."

She nods her agreement to his wise, knowing words. Once again she is grateful that he has shed light on her fledgling thoughts, has spoken the unarticulated words she hasn't known how to voice.

CHAPTER
FIFTEEN

They are sure they will miss the marriage ceremony. The kids haven't awakened from their nap, and Christine is reluctant to wake them, knowing they will be cranky through the evening if their nap is interrupted. At the last minute, Allegra shoos Christine out of the house. She will bring the twins down to the church on the bus or across the Arno Valley on the tram, when they are up, fed and dressed.

Christine, Thomas and Julian park their car just in time to see Elizabeth arrive at the church in an open, horse-drawn carriage. Her father, tall and dignified in tails, escorts Elizabeth into the church. As they are too late to be seated, they watch the wedding ceremony from behind: the lovely, nubile backs of the bridesmaids as they traipse one after another down the long central aisle of the church. They watch Electra, tall and tanned after her sojourn in Argentina, solemn and pensive on the occasion of her sister's marriage. They watch as Elizabeth pauses at the entrance of the church, as Elizabeth's mother arranges the veil and the long train so that it won't catch on its passage to the altar. As she kisses her daughter, and then kisses her husband, Christine feels a lump growing in her throat. She closes her eyes and feels her mother's hands, as if adjusting *her* veil, kissing *her* cheek, sending Christine on her way down the aisle. She feels tears brim and blinks them away before they can ruin her makeup. She focuses on the back of Elizabeth's mother as she is escorted down the aisle by the groom's brother to her place in the first row.

Elizabeth is splendor incarnate in her cream-colored gown, but what strikes Christine about the bride is an absence of extraneous movement. Elizabeth has stood perfectly still while her mother has fussed over her, while her father speaks. She nods agreement in a single gesture, almost as if she is conserving her energy for a long and significant journey. Christine would have been chewing her nails, twisting her engagement ring, fidgeting with her bouquet, but Elizabeth is as motionless as a work of art sculpted to preserve this moment in perpetuity. When the organ music changes from Beethoven's *Fur Elise* to Handel's *Largo*, Elizabeth glides forward, her hand resting lightly on her father's pinstriped arm. Christine waits for the father to deliver the bride to her future husband but that doesn't happen straight away. He stands between them, like a host at a party, presenting two people to their fates. An usher whispers in Christine's ear, "I'll take you to your seats now."

The ceremony is traditional high church and brief. The service is delivered in English, despite the majority of Italian guests, except for the reading, Corinthians 13, which is spoken in Italian. Christine has no difficulty translating the Italian into English, and is as moved as if Paul had composed his words for her personally.

> *Though I speak with the tongues of men and of angels, and have not charity, I am become as sounding brass, or a tinkling cymbal.*
>
> *And though I have the gift of prophecy, and understand all mysteries, and all knowledge; and though I have all faith, so that I could remove mountains, and have not charity, I am nothing.*
>
> *And though I bestow all my goods to feed the poor, and though I give my body to be burned, and have not charity, it profiteth me nothing . . .*

Christine is pleased that they have used the King James version instead of a translation which substitutes the word *love* for *charity*. It is a natural option, especially at a wedding, but for her, who spends her days in active contemplation of charity, the choice is ideal. A world without charity is impossible to imagine and yet—it exists all around her.

When I was a child, I spake as a child, I understood as a child, I thought as a child: but when I became a man, I put away childish things.

For now we see through a glass, darkly; but then face to face: now I know in part; but then shall I know even as also I am known.

And now abideth faith, hope, charity, these three; but the greatest of these is charity.

There is no communion, Christine notes, and even more surprising, no photographer to distract. The church is full; even the side pews are all occupied, but the wedding vows have not been absorbed by the crowd. They resonate throughout the large church as if carried by heavenly acoustics or reproduced by an echo, as if gaining volume from their own conviction. Seated toward the rear, Christine can hear their vows as clearly, as distinctly, as if she were standing in their place at the front of the church.

Thomas squeezes her hand. He, too, is moved by the vows, as if remembering their own exchange. He leans over and kisses her softly as the bride and groom exchange rings. Christine can see that Julian is also moved. For Elizabeth and Stephen, who have been already married in the eyes of the State, today's service is merely a formality, but the joy that radiates from them as they walk down the aisle, toward the bright spring light that awaits them outside the church, tells Christine that there is nothing rote about this ceremony. Today they have raised their voices in front of God, family and friends. Today begins their life as husband and wife. *Grattis på din bröllopsdag,* she thinks to herself.

Allegra is in the front garden of the church with Elle and Anna when the wedding party exits, and Christine is alarmed to find them sitting one in front of the other on the horse reined to the waiting carriage. She walks to them, as quickly as she can in heels on gravel, to remove them from the horse before they can draw attention from the bride and groom.

A woman stops her with a touch to her sleeve. "They aren't bothering anyone," she says. "On the contrary, they will make nice photos for the wedding album. Are these Elizabeth's twins—Elle and Annie?"

"They are."

"Which makes you Christine." The two women join hands. "I am Elizabeth's mother."

"Kate Griffitts."

The older woman shows her surprise. "I am."

"I am a huge fan of your work. My mother had all your Diva books."

"I am not sure even I have them all, they've been out of print for years."

"Elizabeth is absolutely lovely. Congratulations. You must be so proud."

"We love Stephen. We couldn't have hoped for a better partner for Elizabeth."

"Mother!" Electra calls from across the courtyard, gestures back toward the church. "Photographs!"

"Sorry. On duty." She raises her eyebrows and smiles. "I will look forward to seeing you up at the house."

Buses have been chartered to transport the guests up to the villa for the evening's party but Thomas figures he'll fit his family and Julian into the Saab, as he doesn't know how long the twins will be able to behave. He unlashes the car seats and stores them in the boot and Christine and Allegra seatbelt the twins onto their laps. Julian sits up front beside Thomas, GPS navigator in hand.

"Thanks for keeping the children during the wedding," Christine says to Allegra "Did you see anything of the service?"

"Yes, it was lovely," Allegra says. "Almost like a dream."

"Lovely Pippa," Julian sighs.

"Careful, Jules," Christine says from the backseat. She is trying to keep her dress from getting wrinkled but it's a losing battle. "One day you will slip and call her Pippa to her face, and then you will be sorry. Best to keep your confidences to yourself."

I wonder if I can ask for her first dance, Julian thinks, and then turns to look back over his shoulder at Christine. She is smiling. She knows what he is thinking, even if he stays silent. "I remember this car having more pickup," he tries to change the subject. "Is it getting old?" he laughs.

"This Saab is twenty-four years old," Thomas says proudly, admiring the still modern interior, the plush black leather seats that heat up on cold mornings. "She's slower because I had her switched to methane. €50 to fill the tank instead of €110."

"Isn't there a danger of not finding fuel?"

"Not in Tuscany. Methane is everywhere."

T hey are among the first to arrive at Villa L'Antica. A field kitty-corner to the front gate has been mowed and a parking attendant waves them in. Thomas stops. "We might need a quick getaway. Any place we can park so we won't be blocked?"

The dark-skinned man stares at him incomprehensibly. Christine opens her window: *"Cerco un posto facile per uscire."*

The man smiles and directs them to a spot close to the exit.

"Do we need their stroller?" Thomas asks, as they leave the car.

"I'll come back for it later, if we do," Allegra says, hoisting their bag onto her shoulder. "Let's let them run for awhile."

The villa stands tall and stately inside an ancient fortress wall which is surrounded by far-reaching groves of olive trees. Torches have been positioned along the parapet and have already been lit in anticipation of dusk. Spotlights illuminate the upper limbs of an ancient cedar of Lebanon and the other secular trees in the garden. In the inner courtyard, a string quartet plays Handel's *Water Music*. Christine looks to Thomas, to see if he's noticed it, too, but he and Julian are deep in conversation. Usually, at a large gathering, Thomas knows everyone, is surrounded by colleagues with whom he discusses the issues at hand, but tonight he doesn't know anyone beyond the principal players. It occurs to her, with a twinge of sadness, that her husband, underneath all his political savvy, his charismatic façade, suffers from shyness. His professional commitment pushes him past a natural reserve, but tonight, deprived of his purpose, he doesn't know how to start a conversation with strangers. She is glad Julian is here to keep him company. After all these years, she finally understands the base of their friendship.

She would like to move closer to the musicians, in particular to hear the cello's contribution to this watery music, but she doesn't want to leave the view, not yet, not with the light shifting dramatically, turning the far hills violet where the sun still shines. Here, on the south side of the valley, opposite from where they live, the sunset occurs behind westerly hills. All along the Arno Valley, the sun reflects its last rays, charging the pale blue sky with streaks of orange and pink. Across the valley, up in the hills of Fiesole and San Domenico, and Monte Morello, the façades of the Renaissance villas glow warmly with reflected light. The lighting is so different on this side of the valley it is like witnessing another city altogether.

"I wonder if we can see our house from here?" Thomas says to Julian, but Julian's attention is trained on the front gate, awaiting the wedding party that has been detained at the church for photographs.

Drinks are being offered in the inner courtyard where the musicians are performing. Hors d'oeuvres are being served from large banquet tables stationed throughout the garden. Waiters circulate with heavy silver trays balanced on upturned palms. The two hundred guests who filled the church to overflowing sparsely populate the garden. That will change later as the evening chills and people move inside the more confined space of the villa, and again later, after dinner, when the inner courtyard will be transformed into a dance floor. But for the moment, because of the size of the garden, there is no crowd; no one nearby to mind the children's antics. There are other children in the garden playing a game of badminton with a babysitter: the serious little Italian boy who carried the rings down the aisle, the six-year-old flower girls, one Asian, the other Eastern European, probably Russian, who tossed rose petals on the aisle runner. Three older Austrian boys have found a soccer ball and are kicking it between themselves in a distant corner. Elle sees an orange cat and runs after it. Christine warns Allegra, "Keep them out of the Italian garden, if you can." The temptation of a cat and the low hedged maze may be more than her daughters can resist.

The stringed instruments stop abruptly and are replaced by a trumpet's herald, which is answered in kind by a pheasant's honk rising from the fields below the house. Christine laughs at the call and response, and then turns serious as the wedding party arrives.

Elizabeth and Stephen sweep through the garden as victoriously as if they had just set the sun themselves, followed by Elizabeth's and Stephen's families, bridesmaids and ushers. Their progress across the garden is slowed as they stop to speak with every guest they encounter. Christine touches the arm of a waiter on his way to serve them. "Make sure you have a glass of juice for the bride."

"I've got it," he says. "Thanks."

Elizabeth chooses a glass of Champagne rather than juice with which to toast her husband, her family and her guests. Her father thanks everyone for joining them on this joyful day, and welcomes them all into their home. He raises his glass to his daughter and her husband, and then clinks it against his wife's glass: the clink of Baccarat crystal resonates clearly across the garden like an orchestra's cymbals. He touches his glass to his mother's, a tiny, well-appointed woman in her nineties, and then before drinking, raises it high to include the entire assemblage. There will be other toasts this evening but this first one has served to release a tension, to let the wedding party relax and enjoy themselves and their guests, as if this were an end-of-summer party instead of a wedding, a beginning.

Christine doesn't mind standing alone. She assumes her habitual wallflower pose, content to watch the dynamics around her. She studies the happy couple and smiles. Every time Stephen takes an hors d'oeuvre from the tray and puts it into his mouth, someone new approaches him with a greeting or a question. Elizabeth knows better than to try to eat. Christine hopes she has had something to eat before her father picked her up from the St. Regis hotel to escort her to the church. Right now, she is clearly too excited to eat. She has taken the long veil she wore in church and has slung it low over her arms, like a shawl. Her hair is still up, held in place with miniature silk flowers and crystal beads, but tendrils have been unclipped to curl down around her long, regal neck.

Christine turns to Julian, who has come to stand at her side, and starts to comment on the beautiful bride, but Julian is looking elsewhere, farther back into the wedding party, fixed on the tallest of the bridesmaids. "Someone has certainly caught your attention."

"I know. I hope I won't embarrass myself, but I can't stop looking at her."

"You know how to disguise your emotions, Julian. You are English, for Heaven's sake."

"It doesn't help seeing her like this, at a wedding, surrounded by happily-ever-afters. I feel like proposing."

"Let's keep it our secret," Christine says. "You remember what happened the last time you acted in haste."

Julian nods, although he knows his feelings for Electra aren't anything like his feelings for his first wife. In its best moments, his failed marriage had never felt pure, had always felt forced. It had been born from need, a sense of ought. "Right then. I won't ask for her first dance."

"I'll dance with you, Julian, and if your toes aren't ruined, then you can ask Electra to dance."

Elizabeth's mother, Kate Griffitts, comes to sit beside Christine. "Your children are asleep upstairs."

"Oh, thank you for checking."

"Your babysitter is playing cards with our babysitter and the other children. I don't think any of them speak the same language, but they seem to be getting along well enough."

"Thank you. You have saved me a trip upstairs."

"You aren't a dancer?"

"Actually, I love to dance. But I am pregnant and that seems to have offset the little coordination I once had."

"You are barely showing."

"Just enough to feel fat."

"I remember that stage." Kate smiles. "I was quite self-conscious."

Christine doesn't say anything. She has never progressed beyond the self-conscious stage to where she was obviously pregnant instead of in need of an exercise class. She wonders if this pregnancy will be different. Some days she is sure she will deliver this child, as if it depends on will alone. Other days, she is sure she will miscarry, like all the other times. Her optimism-pessimism are two faces of the same coin: she can't sit on the toilet without checking for blood, but every morning she wakes up to find she is still pregnant, she is convinced she will carry this child to term.

She doesn't need to share this seesaw ride with Elizabeth's mother, especially on the day of her firstborn's marriage.

"They are nice looking together," Kate offers, and when Christine looks up, about to agree that the bride and groom are indeed lovely, she finds the comment has been directed toward Julian and Electra who are dancing together, slightly removed from the central crush of the dance floor. It is a slow song, a sentimental journey into the early forays of the 20th century.

"Oh, Julian. He's a dear."

"You know him well?"

"He's my husband's closest friend. Our summer cottage in England is situated on his property. Your daughter is in good hands."

"England." Suddenly Kate understands Electra's promise at the church to visit her sister often; regularly. "It is a moment like this that makes me wish I hadn't stopped photographing people."

"Elizabeth said you had moved into nature. Why did you shift?"

"A hundred reasons, a million years ago." Christine's silence lets her continue, unhurried. "I stopped seeing closeness in people. It all seemed artificial. Even that most intimate relationship, mothers and daughters, felt forced. More about matching hair ribbons and lopsided Tiffany hearts dangling from invulnerable necks."

"I remember the photograph you took of Princess Diana with William and Harry. It was perfect in every sense."

"It was my last official photograph of mothers and their children. The occasion, as I remember it, was fraught with tension." She reads the questions Christine is too discreet to ask. "Diana was lovely and her children adored her, but she was a bit like a lion defending her cubs against the palace hyenas, all those interfering sycophants who had their own ideas of how she should pose with her children. I remember thinking, how can she stand it? Years later, when *my* mother-in-law tried to interfere with some little thing I did, like feeding the children before the eight o'clock dinner hour or questioning the way I had dressed them, I remembered what Princess Diana had to put up with—"

"You met the Queen?"

"I met the Queen once, yes, but not on that occasion. I won't pretend I had privy to Diana's relationship with her mother-in-law. But the people who surrounded Diana, and interfered with her motherly instincts, they gave me a good point of reference for my own little problems. Later, when I had children, it didn't stop me from minding my mother-in-law's interferences, but it kept them in a healthy perspective."

"There is always an interesting story behind a work of art."

"To be honest, I am just pleased when the work of art, as you call it, is successful."

"So why did you stop?"

"Photographing the future Queen, with her young Princes, that's about as close to the top as one could hope to rise, no? It should have been the ultimate artistic experience, but it left me feeling empty, depleted, as if they were hoping I could give them something to make their fairy tale real. You say the photograph is perfect, but I left Sandringham feeling a failure, for not being able to provide the fable they were hoping for."

A handsome, middle-aged couple pauses to congratulate Kate. Christine watches their exchange, wondering at the ease by which Kate moves between an intimate disclosure to the polite and impersonal. It is a skill she wishes she could learn.

"It wasn't just that," Kate continues, as if they had never been interrupted. "My dissatisfaction had been building for some time, but Sandringham was the straw that broke the camel's back. The more my editor glorified in the slick image, the more my agent found me other *important* assignments, the more I was moved toward the messy, which you find everywhere in nature but almost nowhere with humans."

"You obviously haven't photographed children like mine."

"Actually, I have. I snuck a shot of them sleeping upstairs, all intertwined, like they were still sharing the same womb."

"You're kidding."

"I'm not."

"Could you show me the photograph?" She wants to ask more. She wants to ask if Kate could photograph her as their mother. She doesn't dare to ask, this woman has just explained why she has detoured from a successful professional career, but Christine believes a photograph could help, as if providing the missing link of those absent nine months. It could help to see herself in print with her daughters, as if they had been born from her body.

"Eventually," Kate says, fiddling with the string of pearls around her neck. "I don't shoot with a digital camera, I only use film." She twists the pearls nervously. "As soon as the confusion from the wedding settles, I will develop the negatives I took tonight. If they are any good, I will be happy to give one to you."

"How can they be anything but perfect? You are the celebrated Kate Griffitts."

Kate laughs. "You would be surprised how many failures I have hidden in my negatives file. But somehow I have a good feeling about your darling twins. Let me call you when Lizzy and Stephen have left."

"Where are they going for their honeymoon?"

"They aren't taking a honeymoon now. Lizzy has to be back in surgery on Thursday. Stephen just started in a new department, and can't take off time now."

"Not even a few days?"

"A few days, yes," she nods. "Tomorrow they fly to Sicily for three days. We stocked their little house full of food and sunscreen."

"I am sure they will better appreciate a few days of quiet after all these festivities, more than an adventurous honeymoon."

"Yes." Kate remembers how tired she had been on her own honeymoon, how much better it would have been if she and Niccolò had gone somewhere to be quiet together instead of moving from city to city. "They mustn't be tired when they return to work, and they can look forward to a belated honeymoon, perhaps during their Christmas holidays. They have been talking about a trip to the Galapagos."

The music has changed but the genre is the same: another sentimental slow song. Christine says, "You may have another wedding to plan."

"Willingly." Kate gazes fondly at her younger daughter dancing closely with Christine's neighbor. "But I won't call the caterer yet. Electra is very difficult to please."

"That's as it should be, especially when one is choosing a mate."

"Last year she invited a nice young man to our home, someone we thought she was interested in. Sweet, cute, they looked nice together, but he neglected to stand up, to greet me when I walked into the room, and I could see by the expression on Electra's face that she had crossed him off her list."

"She's not entirely wrong."

"These days no one stands up when a woman enters the room."

"Perhaps, but if it's important to her, she is right to respect it. You wouldn't want her staying with someone who embarrassed her sensibilities. It's the small details that reveal compatibility."

At the center of the dance floor, Christine observes the groom dancing with his bride's grandmother. The struggle is evident, if one watches closely, as if the grand dame isn't content to let him lead but wants to steer him to her music.

"Electra is that way with everything," Kate continues. "Try taking her shopping for shoes! She will visit every shop in Florence and still won't have found what she's looking for."

"I'm a bit the same way," Christine admits, looking down at her feet, "which is why my shoes are never quite in style." She studies Elizabeth dancing with her father. They are almost standing still in the middle of the dance floor, talking more than dancing. He may have given her away this afternoon, but his love for her hasn't diminished. It shines as brightly at a distance as it did when they arrived at the church.

"I shouldn't complain. I was thirty-one when I met Niccolò. I was so picky I probably would have never married if fate hadn't placed him right in my path for me to trip over."

"That is my story, too," Christine says, redirecting her attention to Electra and Julian. "They do look nice together."

"I wonder what they are talking about," Kate says.

Before she has time to speculate, Thomas approaches. "May I dance with the mother of the bride?" he asks, resting his hands on his wife's shoulders.

"If you don't mind leaving your lovely wife alone."

"I can probably convince her to save a dance for me. Darling?"

"I am happy to sit here. I will enjoy watching the two of you dance."

A moment alone allows Christine to give her undivided attention to her surroundings. There is a medieval sense to the garden, lit as it is in torchlight. The only electricity outdoors is aimed into the upper boughs of the ancient trees; indoors, the light from the chandeliers is diffused, like moonlight behind a cloud. The softer light transforms the wedding guests, and their formal attire transports them into a previous epoch. Only the very short dresses of the younger guests belie the illusion of the bygone era.

The villa has undoubtedly hosted innumerable parties throughout its centuries. The tower rising up out of the center and the fortress wall that surrounds it are probably 15th century. The shape of the house itself, and the stonework around the windows is most likely 17th century. The façade could use a coat of paint, Christine notices, but then so does their house on the other side of the valley. These old houses need more attention than twins, and considerably more money.

Christine tries not to think how many villages could be fed with the money spent on tonight's party. She has to be careful not to let her dedication to charity ruin a lovely celebration. The truth is, even in countries where poverty is the main course at the banquet table, people all over the world spend too much money on weddings.

Almost as quickly as Thomas escorts Kate to the dance floor, Christine is joined by Electra and Julian.

"Not dancing?"

"Not at the moment."

"I was hoping we would find you free." Electra sits beside Christine on the wrought iron bench, her hands cupped together, as if containing a good luck charm she wants to protect. Julian pulls forward a chair to face them. They are flushed with excitement.

"You two look like you are plotting a coup."

"We are. And we want your help."

"What country are we going to overturn?"

"All of them, one by one, by rescuing their children."

"I've convinced Electra to come work with me," Julian says proudly.

"I've agreed to give it a try," she qualifies, opening her hands to liberate the secret, as if releasing a ladybug. "I've never done anything like this, and I don't know if it is my cup of tea."

Julian is touched by her English turn of phrase. "She is going to coordinate the conferences we host at The Surdans. We've already talked about the first one."

Electra nods excitedly. "I would suggest we start small, to identify the glitches before we fill the house with people."

"How small is small?" Christine asks. Their enthusiasm is contagious; she can feel it infecting her.

"Fourteen people. Fifteen, counting Thomas. Sixteen if you will agree to participate."

"You want translators, then?"

"Not for the first meeting. It would be easier to start with participants who all speak English. But we thought you should be there, as much for the ideas you can contribute as for your common sense."

"It would be hard to manage with the children."

"Bring them with you—and your babysitter. This should be an extension of our lives, not an excursion away from it. We're talking about children, aren't we? It wouldn't be a bad idea to have a couple of healthy prototypes running through the fields."

"Do you know that I am pregnant?"

"I didn't." She looks for evidence but doesn't find it. "But that doesn't change the fact that if I am going to succeed organizing this first meeting in a very short period of time, I am going to need your help, both here and in England."

"You are going to need to be in England a fair amount of the time," Julian says to Electra, his face turning red as a beet.

"Don't worry, Jules; I don't intend to leave you stranded." If Electra has noticed the blush, she has chosen to ignore it. "I will be there as much as I'm needed. But much of the work can be done online, and Christine lives just across the valley from me. She knows better than anyone the level of quality you are seeking from these meetings. I would think Christine is the key to the success of these meetings."

"Thomas is the expert, I'm just—"

"We will consult Thomas every step of the way, but I've seen you, Christine, sitting back, watching, making note of everything that passes in front of you."

Julian nods his agreement, the heightened color in his face and neck beginning to fade. "Eventually, when we move into larger numbers, when we start to invite non-English speaking participants, you can coordinate the translators."

"Something I know nothing about," Electra says. "But at the beginning, we will keep things simple."

"And you are prepared to finance this meeting, Julian?"

"He won't have to," Electra saves him the question. "Lizzy and Stephen have requested that donations be made to their favorite charity in lieu of wedding gifts. The box at the entry is full of envelopes. I can surely convince them that we should be their favorite charity."

"There's no need for that," Julian says. "I agreed to finance this conference, and I am a man of my word."

"And I have a few ideas to fund subsequent conferences."

"Yes, excellent ideas," Julian adds.

"You two sound as if you have been conferring for months."

"Two dances," Electra says.

"And she hasn't stepped on my toes once." He smiles at his joke. "Tell Christine your scheduling plan."

"Meetings will start early in the morning over breakfast. There will be time for a stroll through the gardens before lunch. Discussions will continue over lunch, to be followed by a rest period. In the afternoon, outdoor exercise, an excursion—"

"—to High Beach, for example," Julian adds. "Or Waltham Forest."

"Talk before dinner. At dinner. After dinner, but early to bed. Once the ideas have been proposed, they need to be considered, not rehashed endlessly over drinks in a smoke-filled room."

"It sounds refreshingly healthy."

"The next morning, meetings will start early in the morning over breakfast, etc. What doesn't work with this strategy, we can adjust in time for the next conference. We thought to schedule one every other month. What do you think? Do you think it can work?"

"*Let me not to the marriage of true minds admit impediments.* Let's find Thomas. He will be thrilled."

"Yes, find Thomas," Electra says. "It looks like Elizabeth and Stephen are ready to cut the cake."

CHAPTER
SIXTEEN

"This is the second sunrise I've spent with Electra, and I haven't kissed her yet."

"Coffee or tea?" Christine puts toast and marmalade on the table. She and Thomas drove home just after midnight with the girls and Allegra, but Julian stayed for the sunrise breakfast. He doesn't look worse for his lack of sleep. On the contrary, Christine thinks he's never looked better. And taller.

"Better make it coffee."

"What time is your flight?"

"I thought to postpone it until tomorrow, if you and Thomas can put up with me another night."

"We would be delighted." Thomas will be happy to have more time with his friend and Christine will be happy to see her husband with his closest friend. She only wishes Anne were in better form. She, too, should be enjoying Julian's presence.

"I would like to see Electra again," Julian says. "She is free today after she drives her sister and brother-in-law to the airport at noon."

"You don't think she will want to nap after lunch?"

"Undoubtedly, but she's agreed to have dinner with me tonight." Color rises from his neck to his face, as if he's confessed a secret. "I want to clarify as much of the plans for the first conference before I leave tomorrow," he adds, hoping to dilute his embarrassment.

"You are here for lunch, then?"

"Yes, if you'll have me."

"I will tell Rosa. I am sure it will be fine."

At noon, Thomas and Christine bring Julian into the sitting room to join Anne for a drink before lunch. Anne is pleased to see Julian, but when Rosa gathers her sewing to leave, Anne becomes agitated. "Stay where you are," she commands.

"But Signora, you have company now, and I—"

"Stay!"

Rosa hovers. She has spent a lifetime following commands. She is used to doing what she has been told, but usually the rules she is asked to follow don't breach her sense of propriety. She knows she mustn't stay but she doesn't dare disobey a command.

Thomas steps in. "Mother, Rosa has things to do."

"I said she is to stay." Anne is embarrassed but that doesn't diminish her insistence.

"But lunch?"

"Someone else can cook."

"Let Rosa go, Mother. Otherwise, we won't eat. Do you want Julian to go hungry?"

Reluctantly, Anne lets Rosa go, possibly because Julian's presence has embarrassed her into good behavior. Nonetheless, she frets in Rosa's absence. She twists the rings on her gnarled fingers. She moves her watch up and down her too thin wrist. She listens to Thomas's recounting of the wedding, nodding at the appropriate times, but it is clear she isn't listening. She perks up a little at news of Julian's plans for conferences, and recounts in detail a meeting at The Surdans shortly after her marriage to Ian.

Thomas notices that when his mother is dwelling in the past, she doesn't seem old. Her memory is flawless. In the present, he hardly recognizes the person who has taken her place. He wonders how much she is aware of her decline. How can he ask? The question itself is offensive.

After lunch, while Christine, Julian and Anne are in the sitting room with the children, Rosa stops Thomas in the hallway to confide.

"I can't leave her side anymore without a litany. If I so much as leave to go to the bathroom, she starts: 'You don't care if I fall, you don't care if I'm alone, you don't care—'"

"I am sorry, Rosa. Christine and I will try to spend more time with her ourselves. It can't be agreeable for you—"

"It isn't really the abuse that worries me, although of course it isn't pleasant, but how am I expected to cook? I can prepare my sauces in the morning, before I bring her tea, but if I leave her an hour before lunch, she frets. She gets angry with me. It isn't in my nature to go against her orders, but when her orders are unreasonable, as you saw before lunch," Rosa throws up her hands, as if presenting her case to heaven. "When she gets like that, I don't know what I am supposed to do."

"We will find a solution, Rosa, even if we have to hire another cook."

Rosa looks alarmed. "Another cook in my kitchen? Wouldn't it make more sense to find her another companion?"

"I don't know if she'll accept anyone else, Rosa. The important thing is to keep Mother from upsetting herself."

Julian is nervous about calling Electra. He shouldn't be. She made it clear this morning that she would look forward to hearing from him today, but he keeps finding excuses to postpone the call. First, he's afraid he'll call too early, to wake her after the big celebration of last night. Then he's afraid he will interrupt her lunch. After lunch he's afraid he'll interrupt a nap or a family conversation. What if his call is answered by a housekeeper who speaks Italian only? Truth is, he's just afraid.

He's afraid she will discover the truth of his intentions, understand that he wants to meet with her to discuss more than the conferences at The Surdans. He feels himself a fraud, and he is sure that a smart girl like Electra will see through him straight away, will find him as transparent as glass.

After lunch, Thomas hands him his phone and insists he dial. "Now or never, Jules. If you don't call at two o'clock, you can't call again until five. Do you want her to think you've forgotten your promise for dinner? She'll make other plans, and you will have changed your flight for nothing."

Julian picks up the phone but hesitates.

"Call her. She won't bite."

Electra answers on the second ring.

"Is this a bad time to call? Are you still at lunch?"

"Not at all. I just got back from driving Lizzy and Stephen to the airport."

"Right." He has forgotten. If he had remembered, he would have had another reason not to call. "Have you eaten?"

"We had a late breakfast—a late second breakfast, that is," she says, her voice bright with laughter. "I was getting ready to go riding. It's such a beautiful afternoon."

"Riding?"

"There is a stable a stone's throw from my house. There is a great trek up into the hills. You don't ride, do you?"

"I do. I do," he says, unable to hide his enthusiasm. "But I'm afraid I don't have my riding gear here."

"I can find you gear, if you like. What size boot do you wear?"

Julian is very excited. He had dreaded the quiet across the table, the inquisitive eyes; the need to fill the silence with words, but riding will give them something to do. "What time shall I be there?"

"As soon as you can. The earlier we start, the longer we can ride. The horses need to be back before dark."

"I'll leave now. I'll be there in the time it takes to cross the valley."

Electra in jodhpurs and boots is a different version from the Electra as bridesmaid, Julian thinks, or Electra travelling through London, for that matter. There is a well-established stain on the inside of one knee, but otherwise she cuts a clean, no-nonsense figure. Her glorious hair is tied back in a high ponytail, and still it falls halfway to her waist.

She doesn't leave him much time to study her. "Would you like to change here or at the stables?"

"Either way."

"Change in my room, then." She hands him the sports bag with the riding gear. "Ignore the state of the house— everyone is relaxing after the wedding—"

"Understandably," he says, but he doesn't find evidence of the disorder she mentions, except for a collection of dog toys under the dining room table. "It was a marvelous party. I would like to thank your parents again."

"They are ferrying friends to the airport, saying goodbye to the out-of-town guests." She shows him into her room. "They may be here when we return. I'll wait for you downstairs."

He doesn't want to take long but he stalls a moment to study her room. It is brightly lit, with large southeasterly windows. There is a ladder in the corner of the room, which leads to a loft, which holds her bed, he assumes, since the room he is changing in is set up as a sitting room. On one wall there is an enlarged photograph of the child Electra running through a field of wildflowers with her sister, and beside it a more serious photograph of her sister giving her a hand up into a tree. There are photographs everywhere of Electra and her sister, and although it isn't a medium he understands well, he has to admit that the quality is professional. Exceptional. If he were slightly farther away, he would swear they were oil paintings. He folds his clothes neatly and sets them at the end of the sofa, then wonders if he should put them into the sports bag so Electra isn't obliged to invite him up to change after riding. He doesn't understand why he is so uncertain with her, but he is.

"Ready?" she asks, "for the ride of your life?"

"I am."

"Would you rather walk to the stables or drive?"

"As you prefer."

"Let's drive then. Afterwards, I am always glad I brought the car."

"I saw you had a lot of photographs of you and your sister in your room. Is it hard to have her gone?"

"Not anymore, no, but at the start it was really hard." She throws their gear into the trunk of the car. "We were very close and then she was gone, off to university. The next minute, she had a boyfriend." She seats herself behind the wheel and turns on the ignition. "Even though I liked Stephen, it was hard at the beginning to share Lizzy with him."

"How long have they known each other?"

"Seven years. They have been living together for six of those years, but they decided to wait to marry until they were both practicing doctors. They had seen friends' relationships suffer the transition from medical school to hospital practice, but Stephen and Elizabeth are stronger than ever."

"They are a lovely couple."

"Yes. They are lucky to have found each other."

Electra parks her little FIAT at the edge of the stables. She introduces Julian to Roberta, the owner, who queries him about his riding experience. Electra translates. Julian tells them that he has been riding all his life, that he owns horses; at present he has two, a Pinto Dutch Warmblood and a four-year-old black Quarter Horse. From the look in her eyes, he can see that Electra is pleasantly surprised, but she doesn't say anything, and when Roberta asks him to ride twice around the corral, he is afraid he will somehow disappoint Electra, not live up to her expectations. He is excessively relieved when the trainer gives them the OK to begin their walk. Often Roberta accompanies Electra when she rides into the hills, but today she stays behind to give a lesson to another rider in the corral.

"I hope I don't get us lost," Electra says, as they disappear into the woods.

"I have a GPS on my phone."

"Good. Set this as the starting point, just in case."

Julian had hoped they would be able to talk as they ride, but the path is narrow and his horse is happiest when it is following Electra's mare. A tailgater, literally, if this leisurely stroll can be interpreted as moving out the gate.

How different it is to ride in Tuscany as opposed to riding in Essex. Here, the hills slope gently but insistently up into a thick forest, the leaves overhead are bright green with spring's first full flush. Nature is so abundant, the fecundity is almost embarrassing. He hates to admit it but his beloved Epping Forest pales by comparison to these seductive Tuscan hills. He feels a traitor, and has to remind himself that not every forest provides a view of London in the distance, giving nature such an alternative backdrop. He thinks he has reinvested soundly in his national pride when their horses round a bend and the city of Florence presents itself below in the valley, bisected as it is by a late afternoon iridescence on the Arno River. As they ride to the top of the hill, Florence shrinks to the size of a cameo, its precise, now miniature lines seemingly etched in shell.

There are times when they are isolated from everything except themselves, their horses, and the trees. Because of the limitation of the narrow path they are following, they walk or trot their horses. They duck their heads to avoid low-hanging branches, and eventually cross over an old wooden footbridge to emerge into an open pasture, as green and familiar as any English pastoral painting. An early Turner, Julian thinks, before the painter's colors turned dark and menacing, or perhaps more like an early da Vinci, he considers, allowing his eye to follow the perfect, classical lines of uninhibited nature as light marries shadow in a perfect union. Julian hurries his horse forward, he wants to share his thoughts with Electra, but before he can reach her, Electra nudges the flank of her mare with the heel of her boot, coaxes it into a canter, and all comparisons, all thought of talk, shared or singular, give way to the simple physical thrill of an unrestrained gallop.

Just past a tabernacle that pays homage to St. Zanobi, Electra swings her leg over her horse and jumps down, as energetically as if she has been resting all afternoon rather than riding. Tethering her horse and Julian's securely to a branch, she scrambles up a rocky pathway, ducking low to avoid the overhanging growth. When Julian finally catches up with her, she is standing at the edge of a small lake. It isn't as significant a body of water as is his lake; nonetheless, it has its appeal. A raft of Mallards disappears into the tall reeds crowding the edge of the pond, leaving a faint ripple in the otherwise still water. Although he can't see any wildlife, the air is animated with raucous mating calls.

Julian lowers himself onto the bank beside Electra, stretching his legs out beside hers, the toes of their boots pointing up at the soft blue sky. Clouds float overhead but don't pause long enough to block the sun. The day is warm. If he were another kind of person, he would take off his shirt and let the sun warm his pale skin.

"I have a confession to make," Julian says, shifting on the stony shore to find a comfortable position. He tosses a pebble into the lake and watches it ripple.

"Should I be afraid?"

"I hope not." He tosses another rock and watches the new ripples intersect with the old. "I am a bit of a dilettante."

"How do you mean?" Electra skims a stone across the surface of the lake. Together, in silence, they count how many times it bounces.

"I just mean, I am not like Thomas." He tosses another stone, and listens to its deprecating *kerplunk*.

"I hadn't assumed you were like Thomas. Not that I know either of you well enough to judge." She skims another rock and smiles when it bounces one more time than last. "But why is being different from Thomas a problem? Is there a competition between the two of you?"

"No, not at all. I just mean to say that I don't have his convictions." He tries to skim a stone but it sinks after the first bounce. "I am willing to host conferences at The Surdans, I am happy to do my part, but I want it to be a part of my life, not the whole of it, the way it is with Thomas."

"I see." She collects a handful of smooth, flat stones from the ground, polishes each one between her thumb and forefinger, as if a slight layer of dust might inhibit the next successful skim.

"I just didn't want you to get all excited about this project I've proposed and then find I'm a fraud."

"A fraud?" She looks up from the stones in her hand, looks him directly in the eye.

"Not devoted, like Thomas."

Electra turns her attention to a distant point across the lake to where she wants her next stone to land. With a subtle flick of the wrist, she skims each of the stones in her hand, one after another, hardly pausing between each stone. When she has finished, she dusts her hands together lightly and turns back to Julian.

"I am glad you told me," she says. "It makes things easier for me." She picks up another stone, polishes it quickly and skims it across the lake. He waits for her to speak and when she doesn't, he worries that he has spoiled everything. If only he had stayed silent. If only he had kept his own counsel. When would he learn that people—especially women—don't like to hear the truth.

"Electra?"

She skims another stone. When she finally decides to speak, she doesn't look at him but stares at the distant spot where her last stone has sunk. "When I was a child, my mother brought me to this lake. We usually spent our summers in California with my American Grandmother, but for some reason we had to stay in Italy that year. I don't remember why. As a solution to the heat, my parents brought us up to this lake quite often. By then both Lizzy and I knew how to swim pretty well. We had taken lessons for years at the pool near Grandmother Claire's house, in Rustic Canyon, so my mother felt confident she could swim across the lake with both of us at the same time. So we started off and everything was fine, but about halfway across, Lizzy started to lose her water sandal, so she stopped to try to fit it back on her foot. I was oblivious to what was happening and continued swimming. My mother didn't know if she should wait for Lizzy or swim ahead with me."

"Every parent's dilemma. What did she do?"

"She swam after me. She figured I was the younger child, I was less experienced. I was more in need of her help than my sister was."

"Good thinking."

"Yes. Of course. But it left me with a permanent fear of too much responsibility. I mean, if something had happened to Lizzy, it would have been my fault."

"Or your mother's, who made an informed but difficult choice."

"Yes, but you see, her decision to swim ahead was because she considered me less capable than my sister."

"Or perhaps younger? Less experienced, as you said. How old were you?"

"Six or seven?"

"Your sister was eight or nine? Wouldn't you do the same thing?" he asks. "I believe I would choose to stay with the seven-year-old, trust that the nine-year-old would be all right."

"I would, too. I am not saying my mother made a mistake. The reason I am telling you this little tale is that it left me with a fear of assuming full responsibility, an uncertainty that I can't seem to rid myself of, no matter how many times I cross a lake."

"Is it that important what your mother thinks of you? You are a grown woman, obviously talented."

"The problem isn't my mother. She is quite vocal in her praise and trust in me. It's that I worry that I might not be up to the task if I am given too much responsibility. If this project were the be-all and end-all to your life, it would make it much harder for me to work with you. But if you will be satisfied to make a small contribution through the efforts we exert, rather than trying to resolve the world's hunger issues, then I am your girl."

"You are my girl," he says, and hopes she wouldn't notice the deep blush. "So you are not disillusioned that I am a dilettante?"

"Honestly, I am enormously relieved. I am not focused on one thing as my sister Lizzy is, or your Thomas. But that doesn't mean I can't accomplish something significant, in my own small way. I can think of a dozen ways in which we can help Thomas without giving up the essence of our own lives. For example, the products you grow on your farm—"

"Don't ask me to become a merchant. There are certain responsibilities, limitations, that go with my title."

"Yes, *Precious*, I know."

He thinks she is being coy, but then he remembers Denise's drunken remark about his title and his facetious response.

"Is there anything stopping you from establishing a nonprofit organization, directing the proceeds towards Thomas's projects?"

"Nothing that occurs to me at the moment."

"Good." She stands up and dusts the back of her jodhpurs. "Shall we continue our ride? Or is there something else you want to tell me?"

Julian looks out at the lake. It has become familiar in the short time they have been here together, and he is tempted to curtail their ride to stay here longer. There are many things he could tell her. "How can you tear yourself away from this spot?"

"Pretty, isn't it?" She bends down to skim a last stone. "But wait until you see what's around the corner. Prepare yourself for an eye feast."

CHAPTER SEVENTEEN

Electra has an idea, but before she calls Julian or Christine to discuss it, she wants to present it to her sister.

"Don't tell me you are still sleeping. Come on, it's one o'clock."

"Only noon here, but I'm glad you called. I really don't want to sleep through my one day off. I'm getting up. Talk me awake."

"I have had an idea," Electra says. "And I want your input." She can hear the closet door opening, a rattle of hangers, something being pulled over her sister's head. She can see her, as clearly as if they were still living in rooms across a common corridor, as if the cross-current of air flowing from the open windows in Elizabeth's old room into Electra's room was the same current of air that carried their conversation.

"Do you mind if I eat breakfast while you tell me?"

"Go ahead," Electra says, hoisting a small suitcase onto the sofa and unzipping it to pack. "I am used to your crunching dry cereal like a hamster. The only difference is that now you are a married hamster."

"Tell me your idea." A refrigerator door opens and closes. There is the sound of juice being poured—and spilt. "Oh, shoot."

"You know I am helping to organize this conference with Julian," Electra begins.

"Yes. How is it going?"

"Good," she says too quickly, and then qualifies. "Well, it is more complex than I thought. I hadn't counted on having to pick up people from the airport, coordinating schedules. I kind of assumed adults could transport themselves across London but no—"

"The more important the people, the more service they expect. Is it getting the best of you?"

"No." She opens the top drawer of her dresser and selects undergarments for three days, then thinks better and adds another two pairs of everything, in case Julian wants her to stay longer. "Things are going pretty well. There will be some unanticipated last minute details, but Julian is hiring extra staff, at least for the first conference, so we can quickly set right any oversights."

"Sounds good." Lizzy is more awake. She brings her bowl of cereal into the living room and makes herself comfortable on the sofa.

"You want to hear something totally bizarre?" She doesn't wait for an answer. "Remember Denise? That girl Julian—"

"How could I ever forget Denise?"

"She called him the other day, wanting to know why he hasn't called her. Apparently it isn't the first time, either."

"Poor Julian."

"Yes, poor Julian." She folds two pairs of trousers and two skirts into the bottom of the suitcase, and then adds her jodhpurs. The last time she was in England she had to borrow a pair from Julian. They weren't a bad fit but not exactly flattering. Maybe she will leave a pair there. Julian's horses are dying for exercise, the property is extraordinarily beautiful, and a long ride is the perfect way for them to conclude a hectic day of organizing. She wonders if she should bring along her second riding cap to leave as well, but decides against it. She doesn't want to make it seem like she's moving in. "The woman is positively Kafkaesque. Denise—or, *The Menace*, as Julian calls her, doesn't realize how strange her behavior is."

"Or perhaps she is trying to convince Julian that his response to her is wrong," Elizabeth says, "by acting like everything is normal."

"Hadn't thought of that," Electra says, tucking her hairbrush into a side pocket.

"What *is* his response?"

"Why, he wants nothing to do with her. He refers to her as 'the drunken bore'. Or 'boar', I'm not sure which. I'll have to ask him to spell it next time her name comes up."

"Scary woman."

"Yes. But Julian thinks it is funny. He's not pulled in. He plays befuddled but he's not. He's surprisingly clever."

"The powers of manipulation are only as great as our desire to be manipulated."

"Are you cracking open fortune cookies for breakfast?"

"I am!" She crunches loudly in her sister's ear. "So what was your question?"

"Do you think it would be a good idea, since we are talking about children's rights, to include you and Stephen in the conference?" Electra adds three carefully folded silk blouses and two cotton tops to the suitcase. A jumper, in case they walk in the evening. She can wear her blazer on the plane, which will save space, even though it's really too hot for a jacket in Italy. What else will she need?

"You flatter me, Electra, and I would jump at the chance to attend your conference, but I think we'd be out of our league. Hold on, I'm being paged." She is back in a minute. "From what I can gather, Thomas has Very Important People on his list."

"I was thinking the conference would be more interesting, and ultimately more beneficial, if it were interdisciplinary. You know, throw in a doctor—"

"Like throwing a Christian into the lion's den?"

"You and Stephen spend your days, *every* day, helping people, and *you* specialize in children. You could offer a practical approach to the discussion instead of more theory."

She starts pacing as she talks, the length between her room and Elizabeth's, which is kept ready for visits or guests. "For example, you know all about the programs that send doctors into underprivileged countries. You know what works. You know what goes wrong."

"Much of what I know is theory, too. I mean, I know some of the doctors who have participated in these programs. I have spoken with colleagues about their time on the Mercy Ships and a couple who have been a part of *Médecins Sans Frontières*—but I haven't gone myself yet. Nor has Stephen."

"Do you think it's a bad idea?" In the bathroom Electra finds a cosmetic bag in the top drawer—it is Elizabeth's but she won't mind if she uses it—and fills it with a few necessary items. The last time she was in England, Julian suggested she leave her liquids, so she wouldn't have to worry about transporting them on the plane. It felt peculiar stowing her things under the sink in the bathroom she uses, almost as intimate as if she were lining things up beside his in the medicine cabinet; but he had been right, it is easier to travel without worrying about 100 ml. containers in sealable transparent bags. Perhaps there will be room after all in her suitcase for her riding cap? She takes Elizabeth's Japanese silk robe from the back of her bedroom door. She has privacy at The Surdans. Julian has given her a suite of rooms at the opposite end of his house, but better to bring a robe, just in case. "So what do you think?"

"I don't know. It could be interesting."

"I just thought it would be useful to have a pediatrician on board. You know more about children than anyone invited to the conference. I thought you could give these big brains a little practical advice."

"I might feel more comfortable if you invited me as a point of reference, someone who could answer their questions, rather than a participant. Otherwise, I would surely be out of my league."

"And Stephen?"

"He's not even a pediatrician."

"But he's a doctor. And the smartest person I know."

"Perhaps you should ask Thomas. He knows us both well enough to decide if we'd be able to contribute or distract from the tenor of his meeting. We will come if we can be of use—if we can get time off from work—but we don't want to crash a party just because my baby sister is drafting the invitation list."

"I am meeting with Christine this morning, but I wanted to ask you first. No point in asking if you aren't willing to come."

"Are you kidding? We'll be there in an instant if we're welcome. Thanks."

"Thank you." Electra will feel more secure about everything if her sister is present.

"How is everything else? Mama says you are spending more time in England than you are at home."

"Mama exaggerates, you know." She waits for her sister to contradict her but the only sound on the other end of the line is a muffled munching. "But yes, I have been in England quite a bit. I'm on my way up again this afternoon."

"You could call, you know," Lizzy admonishes.

"If you were ever home," Electra counter-scolds.

"Are you borrowing my clothes?"

"I am." One of the skirts and two of the blouses are Elizabeth's. "How did you know?

"I've installed a micro-chip in your suitcase." They laugh. "You have more clothes than I do, why do you borrow mine?"

"I don't know. I just feel prettier wearing your clothes."

"You are pretty no matter what you wear. Wait, I'm being paged again. Don't they know this is my day off?" She is back in a minute, without having lost her train of thought. "So you like working with Julian?"

"Yes, he's great, but—"

"But—?"

"Lizzy, I think he likes me."

"Of course he likes you. How could he not?"

"But I mean *like*, as in interested in me, you know, as a girlfriend or something."

"Is that a problem?"

"It could be."

"Do you like him?"

"I do. Very much."

"Has he kissed you?"

"No—" She isn't sure how much she wants to confide. Elizabeth tells everything to Stephen and she might mention something to Christine, who could mention it to Thomas. A game of telephone is all she needs right now. Besides, what is there to tell? That he leaned forward at the end of a lovely evening and might have leaned closer if she hadn't pulled back. That she is to blame, that she kisses him on both cheeks whenever he picks her up at the airport, that his kisses goodbye, while always chaste, are increasingly familiar; that he lingers a moment longer than the usual double-cheeked peck. And so what if he were to kiss her, what is the big deal? She isn't sure she doesn't want him to.

"Would you rather he was not serious? A player? Trifling with your heart?"

"No."

"Then what is the problem?"

"It's nothing to do with him, really, but with everything that surrounds him. His house is the size of Buckingham Palace."

"I know. I've seen it. It's not a problem unless he expects you to clean it."

"People bow to him, for Christ's sake."

"Listen, sissy. It's not as if you are marrying into the Royal family."

"Don't cross your bridges before I can burn them. No one has said *anything* about marriage."

"I can think of worse places to live. Instead, you are being offered Buckingham Palace without the immobile guards," she is gaining momentum, "without the noisy London traffic, without gossiping employees."

"The Surdans is as quiet as Villa L'Antica, and Gregory is a sweetheart. So is Marion," she adds, "as long as I don't dull his kitchen knives."

"And Julian?"

"He's a sweetheart, too." She can't tell her sister, she can't tell anyone just yet, not even Julian, especially not Julian, but she fears she is falling for him. It frightens her terribly, as if the fall were physical, a free fall leap of faith from the tallest mountain, arms spread, falling into the unknown. "I'm just not sure I am up to the task."

"He wouldn't be offering if he thought you weren't his equal."

"You think?" She closes the top to her suitcase and zips it shut. "What should I do?"

"Practice your curtsy. You used to be really good at it."

She'll need more than a curtsey, Electra thinks. She'll need to trust the thermals to carry her to safety, as if she had wings to soar and the strength to keep herself alight. She better bring her riding cap, after all. She's going to need all the protection she can get.

CHAPTER EIGHTEEN

Christine is helping the girls finish dressing for their trip into Florence when she has the idea to invite Anne to join them. She leaves them each with a hairbrush and a headband and makes her way through the house into Anne's quarters.

When was the last time Anne went into the city? When was the last time she has left the house? Christine is shocked that she can't recall even one trip away from the property in the two-and-a-half years she's lived here, and as she searches her memory, she can't recall a single time Anne has stepped out of the house, into the garden, in the last year. She rarely comes downstairs anymore, except for meals, and when she does, she's likely to closet herself into the library. An open window seems to be as much of an excursion outdoors as she's willing to take.

She knocks on her mother-in-law's door and hears the invitation to enter: *"Avanti!"*

Christine peers in and blinks into the shadows. Anne is still in bed, propped up against a mountain of pillows, holding a ridiculously large cup of tea.

"Can you even lift that cup to drink?" Christine asks.

"Just barely. It was Thomas's idea. He has insisted that I drink three cups a day, and he thinks I won't notice that the proportions have doubled."

"Would you like me to open the curtains?" Christine moves toward the windows. "It is a gorgeous day today."

"Yes, thank you. Just a little." She squints at the brightness. "Perhaps a little less."

There is a bird in the cypress tree outside her window, whose mating call is shrill like a whistle, even through the closed window. He's been calling since dawn, and he is beginning to drive Anne crazy. She doesn't know what she will do if he finds a responding mate.

Christine sits beside Anne's bed in the mostly darkened room. "I am taking the girls into town today. I thought you might like to join us."

"Oh, no," Anne says, automatically, without considering the invitation. The bird calls again: *chiri chiri chiri chiri*. With the window open, it sounds like he's inside her head. "It will be much too warm in town."

Christine folds her hands on her lap, gathers her determination around her like a shawl against the cold. All winter Anne has been complaining about the humidity. In the spring she complained about the cold and the rain. She has used the inclement weather as an excuse for declining every invitation to leave the house. But today there is nothing to fear: the sun is warm but not yet hot, there is a slight breeze but no wind. The sky is cloudless; there is no chance of rain. Christine is determined to transport her mother-in-law into the glory of this perfect day.

"Come with us, Anne. It will do you good to spend the morning in Florence. I am taking the girls to the Palazzo Pitti to see the jewelry in the *Galleria degli Argenti*. I have promised them an ice cream afterwards and a walk through Boboli Gardens."

"The Pitti has too many stairs, and I could just as easily walk in my own garden; it is better kept than Boboli." The bird calls again, shrill like a referee's whistle.

"Yes, of course," Christine says. "It's just an excuse to visit the city. We can change our plans. What would you rather do?"

The light from the windows hurts Anne's eyes. She would like to discard this cumbersome ceramic cup and drink her tea from something that doesn't strain her wrist to lift. She would like to close her eyes and be done with all these aches and pains. She can't see Christine's face clearly enough to read her expression, but she imagines that these are not the answers she is waiting for. The insistent bird calls again: *chiri chiri chiri chiri.* Its repetition is wearing her down.

"How soon were you planning to leave?" Anne asks, setting the half-empty cup on the bedside table. Anything is better than listening to that relentless bird. "How long do you plan to stay?"

"We will leave when you are ready," Christine says, trying to keep the surprise out of her voice, "and we will be home in time for lunch. Shall I call Rosa to help you dress?"

"No, thank you." She folds back the covers and moves her legs over the edge of the bed. Her feet don't quite touch the ground: she has to let go, let herself slide, trust she won't fall the last several inches to the floor.

Christine is astonished by how fragile her mother-in-law has become, a wisp of down escaped from its goose feather duvet. She averts her eyes from the insubstantial form in its gossamer nightgown but can't avoid the sense of embarrassment at being witness to her mother-in-law's decline. Anne gropes her way into her dressing gown and gathers the belt to tie it firmly around her waist. She turns her back on her daughter-in-law, as if dismissing any need for compassion or pity. "If you can be patient while I dress, I will take the girls to *Piazza della Signoria.* I have been craving the chocolates at Rivoire."

The twins have been well behaved behind their too tall parfait glasses, and the few drops of ice cream that have splattered onto their dresses have been removed easily enough with *acqua gassata* and a little rubbing. When their spoons scrape against the bottom and come up empty, they ask if they may leave the table. Christine sees that the sugar from the ice cream is making it impossible for them to sit still, and as Christine is in no hurry to bring Anne back into her reclusion, she lets them run in the piazza. She takes a package of crackers from her purse, and gives it to Anna and Elle to feed the pigeons. She also checks to make sure she has hand gel in her purse. She adjusts her chair so she is beside Anne, looking out on the piazza to keep an eye on her daughters.

Anne has selected an assortment of chocolates. She deliberated over each filling—*crema di nocciola, pasta di mandorle, ciliege,* and *rhum,* as if savoring each filling as she pronounced its name to the waiter. However, the ordering seems to have fulfilled her appetite, and after eating one, she has ignored the rest. They are beginning to melt; are losing their form. Christine moves the plate out of the sun as she listens to her mother-in-law reminisce.

"Ian and I used to come here regularly—almost every evening in the season—for an *aperitivo.* It was only a ten-minute walk from the Consulate, very pretty along the Arno at the end of the day. Florence wasn't crowded like it is now when Ian was stationed here. There were fewer people, fewer tourists. Certainly fewer tourists wearing *shorts*," she says, investing considerable disdain in a single syllable. She adjusts her large sunglasses so they sit higher on her nose. "Especially in the evenings, people would stop here to meet before going to their parties, their dinner engagements. It was like a club. All the waiters knew us: they knew how Ian would want his gin and tonic. They knew without asking that I would want Champagne, well chilled. Even then," she gestures to a nearby table, "there was a group of very old ladies, as vain as peacocks, I remember. Expatriates, many of them, but so provincial they might as well have stayed at home with their Brahmin husbands. Boring, every one of them."

"It must have been hard for you to find peers," Christine says, noting that the *old* women at the neighboring table are at least twenty years younger than her mother-in-law. "I imagine it was hard to find people who had travelled as much as you had, people who—"

"I wasn't the snob, darling. I have always been happy to converse with anyone who has something of interest to say. But I have never been tolerant of people who recount what they have had for lunch, as if it could possibly be of interest, nor have I been impressed by the name-dropping of fancy hotels, which seemed to be the only subjects of conversation those women knew." She loosens the silk scarf at the neck of her blouse. She is wearing a favorite Roberta di Camerino suit, but the light wool is too hot for July. "No. Forgive me," she says, "I have forgotten another area of expertise: how shrewd they were in slandering their dearest friends— behind their backs, of course." She shakes her head, and then pushes her glasses back against her glistening nose.

"Fortunately, I found companionship in Florence, a few individuals with really formidable minds and an elevated hand of Bridge." She lifts her *Martini Bianco* and sips carefully. "Which is why I suggested we move here after Ian retired. Ian loved his game of Bridge and was willing to indulge me, as long as he could have his *piéd a terre* in Knightsbridge. Nothing more than a studio, really, but how he loved that London apartment, so high up it felt like a tree house perched in the arms of the great oak trees in Ennismore Gardens." She frowns, then reaches into her purse, pulls out a case and mirror and applies a coat of lipstick. "But we didn't live there long enough to see the leaves change color, and after, well, I was relieved to return to Florence, to leave that noisy city, to enjoy a few solid friendships. I have been happy here." She frowns.

Christine wishes she could do something about the smear of lipstick on Anne's front teeth, but there isn't anything she can say that wouldn't be offensive. She turns away and focuses on her children, two brightly colored, low-flying kites bounding across the piazza, as happy chasing pigeons as if they might catch one.

A group of older tourists, undoubtedly Swedes from their height and their sunburnt skin, follow the clipped-heeled pace of their guide across the square. Christine feels an inexplicable urge to join them, if just for a moment, to hear her language up close. She restrains her odd impulse, moves her gaze away from the group, back to her children. She sees Elle followed by Anna approaching a dapper horse reined to its carriage. He suffers the crowd and the noise, his head deep in a bucket of feed, not unlike the elegantly dressed man at the table next to them who is burrowing deeply into a triple scoop of ice cream.

"Do you believe in Hell, Christine?"

The question catches Christine off guard, and she wonders if she has heard the question incorrectly. She sets down her glass of lemon tea and looks to her mother-in-law, trying to fathom from where this question has come. "How do you mean?"

"Eternal damnation. If a person has lived a lie, for example. Do you believe it exists?"

"This is a hard question." She looks at her mother-in-law, who is clearly waiting for an answer. "I believe we are held accountable for what we do with our lives. If we have done wrong, I believe we must pay for those wrong-doings. If we have tried to do good, even if we haven't succeeded completely, I believe we are rewarded. How the bill is tallied up I can't begin to guess, although I don't believe there is a physical place, with fire and brimstone, where people are poked by the prongs of a devil's pitchfork."

"And how important an offense would you gauge a lie to be?" Anne asks.

Christine doesn't like being asked to judge. "A lie depends on its content and its context. If I tell you I like your dress when I don't, well, that can be forgiven as a social nicety, but if I cheat on my husband and lie, well, that would be more difficult to support in the final accounting."

"But if cheating on Thomas, for example, brought him great happiness—"

"I don't see how it could."

"For example, if you slept with another man so you could give him a child."

"But Thomas wasn't the problem; it was I who couldn't carry a child to term," she says, placing a hand on her stomach.

"But hypothetically—"

Christine doesn't know where this conversation is going but it makes her uncomfortable. "Hypothetically, I suppose, if the end justified the means, a lie could be forgiven. But Thomas—for example—would have difficulty accepting a child born from an infidelity."

"What if he never knew about the infidelity?" Anne asks.

"If the lie were never acknowledged," Christine says, watching Anna and Elle twirling themselves in the center of the piazza, pinwheels of dazzling primary colors. "As in, if he didn't know, it couldn't hurt him?"

Anne nods. "If he never knew."

"I am not Saint Peter," Christine says, "I do not hold the keys to Paradise, but as long as the intention is in earnest, and no one is hurt by the betrayal, as long as the liar is convinced of the altruism of his or her act and never feels the need to confess the lie, well, perhaps even a significant lie like adultery could be forgiven. Hypothetically."

"Hypothetically." Anne repeats, sipping her Martini. "Did you ever hear the story of how I met Ian?"

"Yes," Christine says, smiling, happy to move onto an easier, happier subject. "Thomas told me you were both waiting for blind dates and you mistook each other for the person you were supposed to meet. It is a marvelous story."

"Yes." She pauses for a moment, as if wondering how much she should tell. "At the entrance to the park in Boston, I saw the man I was supposed to meet. I recognized the rolled umbrella, the drooping moustache my classmate had described. However, at the other entrance to the park, I saw another man who was clearly waiting for someone he didn't know—another arranged date. In a split second, I made the decision that changed my life: I walked purposely past the droopy moustache, toward Ian, held out my hand and said, 'Here I am! I hope I haven't kept you waiting.' He accepted my hand and replied, 'Not at all,' the glint in his eye betraying that I was prettier than he had been led to believe his date would be. 'Shall we walk?' I suggested, taking his arm, as if I were entitled, leading him out of the park, out of eligibility. As we left the park, I glanced back to see another young woman approaching Mr. Droopy Moustache. I hoped with all my heart that they would have a lovely evening together."

Christine has set down her glass on the table too abruptly. It makes a hard clink, glass meeting glass, but nothing breaks. "So you knew?"

"I did. It wasn't the right thing to do. I knew that even then, but I thought, why waste an evening with someone who doesn't interest me, why take that first step toward disappointment when I knew at a glance that Ian would be fun, at the very least. And I was right. We were the right match."

"But Thomas told me the mix-up hadn't been discovered until you and Ian were halfway through the meal."

"I was careful to steer the conversation in the direction I wanted it to go. It's an old trick: get a man talking about himself and pay attention. Women have forgotten how to listen, how to ask a leading question."

"What did Ian say when you confessed?"

"What on earth makes you think I ever burdened him with a confession? I saw the girl he was supposed to meet. He would have been bored to tears. I saved us both a fruitless evening." She nods with conviction. "I made him happy."

Christine looks out across the piazza, to the Loggia dei Lanzi populated with carved Renaissance marble, and acknowledges how hard it is to distinguish between myth and historical fact, regardless how beautiful it is. A lie is like the smear of lipstick on her mother-in-law's teeth: it doesn't bother her because she doesn't acknowledge its existence. Only Christine knows, and she isn't going to tell.

She looks at her children, and is reassured by the simplicity of their mundane pleasures: happy for something to chase, happy to be chased, in equal turns.

"Are you happy here?" Anne asks, unexpectedly. "In Florence?"

"Yes," Christine answers, simply and honestly, as surprised by this new question as the last, although relieved that it is easier to answer. She lifts her eyes to appraise the magnificent *Palazzo della Signoria* itself, its stately tower straining her neck muscles as she follows its line high against a bright Tuscan sky. She looks around the piazza for the group of Swedes but they have moved on.

How different Italy is from Sweden, she thinks, where the old structures are too often knocked down in favor of what is new and modern; where no matter how much construction there is, it is nature that dominates; where one cannot help but see the forest for the trees.

Christine has been lying to herself, avoiding a truth. She watches her daughters running toward her and sees that Elle is carrying a stunned pigeon in her hands. She sets her napkin on the table, pushes back her chair and stands. She needs to go home. It is time to lay her ghosts to rest. "I am happy here," she says, and realizes it is true. "And I will be even happier when I return from Sweden."

CHAPTER NINETEEN

"Mother?" Thomas finds her in the library, surrounded by open books, as if in the middle of a research, as if she could see what was written on the pages. "I was thinking to invite a few people to dinner on Saturday night, if you don't have any objections."

"I don't know, Bunny. I am not in the mood for company." She closes one book, then another. "Having you and Christine at the table is about as much confusion as I can deal with right now."

"We wouldn't be dancing on the tabletop, Mother. We wouldn't be hanging from the Murano."

"I didn't think you would." She smiles, despite the dull ache in her forehead, and closes the last of the books on the desk. She can't complain of a headache, it isn't that intense, just a dull ache from morning to night. To be honest, it leaves her exhausted. "What would be the purpose of your dinner?"

"Partly social, partly work. We are organizing a conference at Julian's estate in October. We have concocted a short list of participants but we need to halve it again. It would be an occasion to throw out ideas."

"Who were you thinking to invite to the dinner?" Maybe she could take another aspirin? They don't do much but perhaps she can expect a little relief.

"Julian and his collaborator, Electra Aragona. Her sister, Elizabeth—you met her and her husband last winter—"

"Yes, the doctors."

"Exactly. I thought to invite their parents, as well. You may have heard of their mother, Kate Griffitts?"

"The photographer?"

Thomas nods but she can't see him. "They invited us to Elizabeth's wedding. Christine thought it would be nice to invite them back." He takes a chair beside his mother. He wonders what she has been doing in here. "I thought to invite Martin Gould from the Institute, and Simon Cathaway—they are in the law department with me, and are both seriously committed to Children's Rights."

"You should probably include their wives, if you want to keep it a social event rather than a conference."

"Good idea." He stacks the clutter of papers on the desk. He doesn't know what they are, but regardless of what they are, they needn't be in disorder. "It's the end of term; it would be nice to say goodbye before everyone leaves on summer holiday."

"You might want to hire a caterer. It may be too much for Rosa alone." She collects the papers and tucks them into a folder, then slides them all into the center drawer of her desk. Yes, she will take another aspirin before lunch.

"I can call Ciabatti, good idea. Do you think Rosa could serve?"

"You are up to twelve. Tell Ciabatti to bring another server. If you decide to serve fish, you can use the Limoges."

"Are you certain, Mother?" She has always been a little possessive about her belongings, but about these dishes she has been particularly ungenerous. She hasn't brought them out for family use since Father died. Even when his father was alive, the Limoges was reserved for extraordinary occasions.

"You will join us for dinner, Mother?"

"Thirteen at the table, I don't think so." She pushes her chair back from the desk and swivels it so she is facing the sun. It strikes her as ironic that her favorite room in the house has become the library, since she can no longer read a word that is printed in the books lining the walls. But the chairs are comfortable, the scent of the leather bindings is a familiar reminder of the stories within, and the light in the room is soft on her eyes, less harsh than from the other rooms in the house. It was Ian's favorite room, and if she stretches her imagination, she can still see him seated in the big arm chair by the window. "Besides, I would embarrass you at the table, Thomas. I can hardly see to find the food on my plate." She shudders at the image of spilt food down the front of her dress, unable to see to correct the situation. "I will join you afterwards, if it isn't too late, for a cognac."

He sits in the chair opposite his mother. He can't argue with her. She puts up a good front but if one is paying attention, it is clear she can't see. At lunch he noticed that she filled the sugar spoon to sweeten her coffee but half fell into the saucer instead of her demitasse. He didn't say anything, he didn't need to. She knows how sweet her coffee is supposed to be and frowned at the taste. She also couldn't find her blood pressure pill, and had to grope for it on the tablecloth. "It should be an interesting group," he says, not wishing to dwell on unhappy thoughts. "Electra has proposed we invite Elizabeth and Stephen to the conference, to give a practical edge to the talks, to keep the discussions from getting bogged down in theory."

"I think she has a good idea, but perhaps you could carry it a step further." She rises from her chair, steadies herself, and as securely as if she could see, moves deliberately to the shelves behind the desk. "When I was young, poets and philosophers and even painters were invited into society— and not only to liven it up. Think back: almost all the Romantic poets were deeply committed to politics." She reaches up onto the shelf and retrieves a book, places it on the desk so Thomas can see it. "Many of them were invited to The Surdans when Julian's ancestors were in power." She places a second book beside the first, *Poetical Essay on the*

Existing State of Things, as if she could read the title. "Shelley was probably the most politic of all the Romantics. He considered poets to be the unacknowledged legislators of the world."

"But weren't his efforts without result?" Thomas challenges. He picks up the volume, flips through it, as if looking for a large red mark evidencing failure. "I seem to remember he was called the *Ineffectual Angel*?" Thomas moves to the shelves behind the desk, tidying the books as he reads the names. The Romantics have been pulled out and not replaced properly, unruly company in death as they were in life. "And wasn't Byron of little consequence, as well, even though he was a Lord and spoke up in the House? Come to think of it, Blake and Coleridge were also politically engaged but without consequences."

"You are right, up to a point, Thomas." She stops his hand from tidying the books. "Perhaps they didn't change laws but surely they influenced their friends, the politicians."

"Wordsworth," Thomas says, his hand caressing the spine of a collection of poems. "He was a political activist when he was young." His hand lingers on *Prelude*. "He wrote 'it was a blessing to be alive in those days' but he ended up betraying his juvenile ideal for a regular paycheck as a postal worker."

"The way you present it, one might conclude that the Romantic effort to influence politics has been one of their many failures." She brings out a copy of *Walden Pond* and places it on the desk. "But Thoreau's civil disobedience and Gandhi's passive resistance were inspired by Shelley." She taps a finger against the spine of *Masks of Anarchy*. "Which was the first modern argument for nonviolent resistance." She moves away from the bookshelves, seats herself in the chair by the window where she can feel the sun on her face. "It's absurd to say the poets haven't influenced the course of history. Only the illiterate politicians are immune to their influence."

Thomas nods his assent but his mother isn't waiting for his approval. He doesn't really believe the point he is presenting, but it will help him clarify the slant to the conference if he plays devil's advocate to his mother's

250

romantic idealism. And it is great to see her engaged in intellectual conversation again. Maybe her new medicines are beginning to work.

He misses Christine. He wishes he could have gone with her. He has always wanted to explore Sweden, to get to know her country, her people, beyond the immediate family and hometown, but she was determined to go alone. *Another time*, is what she told him. So he is home without her, in charge of his mother and the twins.

What a job it is having full responsibility for the twins! He has been an active parent since he and Christine brought their daughters home from the hospital. He has helped to feed them and change them, has held them when they were afraid or angry or in need of comfort. He has encouraged their first words as well to help them understand when it is best not to speak. But his parenting has always been joined with Christine's and alone he finds himself treading water in a very large lake, his life raft nowhere in sight.

He isn't alone, not in any real sense. Allegra takes care of the girls when he is at work, and gives him a half hour's reprieve at the end of the day to change out of his role of professor, into *Daddy!* Rosa brings him an *aperitivo* and a bowl full of toasted almonds as his daughters are ushered into the living room. They climb onto his lap as he listens to their excited recounting of their day, press against him as if close physical contact is an essential part in the sharing of their news. As he appraises Anna's careful drawings, admires the precision with which she has cut out and pasted her designs into a book, she touches his arm, strokes the side of his face, as if repaying him for his words of encouragement. He finds words of praise for Elle's drawings, too, an elaborate, abstract interlocking of bold black lines, and she smiles at him as if indulging his need to reassure her, then scrambles off the sofa to collect a ball she has stashed behind an armchair. From the comfort of the sofa, Elle tosses the soft foam ball into a wastebasket across the room, scoring ten hoops out of ten while Anna has difficulty gripping the ball with two hands. Elle is carefree and oblivious; Anna is serious and a bit too careful where she sets

251

her feet. He marvels yet again that they could have come from the same womb.

It's always the same, night after night. Anna loses interest in the ball and patiently constructs a tower of blocks, which Elle knocks down after the last cube is in place, a game they repeat as long as Anna is willing to rebuild. They climb over him as if he were a jungle gym, and when he is tired and they begin to fuss, he reads to them to quiet their attention before dinner. They each choose a book, always the same books, *Are You My Mother?* whose title disconcerts him, and *Make Way for Ducklings*, which he bought for Christine at the start of her first pregnancy. They pretend to read with him, reciting the words they have long since committed to memory. He chooses a poem, something easy, something catchy, like Kipling's *If*, that they can play with over dinner. In Christine's absence, his mother has permitted their presence at table. The alternative would be that someone would have to dine alone.

It isn't that he is alone with the twins that much, it is more the idea of carrying the full responsibility for their well-being. If he were another kind of parent, he could sit them in front of the television instead of taking them out after dinner to chase the fireflies, or let them eat Nutella for breakfast instead of cooking them oatmeal. If he were another kind of parent, he could give in to a tantrum instead of working through it, but if his job is to educate them into thoughtful, conscientious adults, and if he takes his job seriously, well, that's a big responsibility to deal with alone. He will be relieved when Christine returns home at the weekend.

Thomas's father didn't play with him as he plays with his daughters. His childhood memories don't include a suit and watch-chained father down on his knees, fitting together Lego pieces. The minutes they spent together in one day would probably not have resulted in an hour, but when Thomas did speak to his father, his father listened, as if he had all the time in the world to dedicate to his son. His father made him feel valued—and therefore valuable—and in Thomas's own small way, as he plays with his daughters each evening, he is paying homage to his father. He is passing along that gift, as if his daughters hadn't been denied the pleasure of knowing their grandfather.

His mother continues her train of thought, recaptures his attention. "I remember dinner parties where the politicians were at odds with the painters and the poets, where the philosophers were threatening to overtake the government from the Prime Minister if he didn't do something—how did they say it—*imaginative*! How often the Romantics were quoted—and still are."

"You are referring to the famous salons of the 1840's?"

"I'm talking about London in the fifties, New York in the 60's, The Hague in the 70's. People didn't always agree but discussion is different from disagreement. Ideas thrown up into the air filter down to become part of the ruling process. Politicians work for power and short-term interests, poets struggle for eternity. Mix your academics and historians with poets and painters," she says. "Like gin and tonic, the effect is invigorating." She smiles at a long ago memory that has eclipsed her headache. "Fill the house with poets and artists, Bunny! Take back the practice of Open House from the real estate agents. You will be pleasantly surprised by the ideas that surface."

"Surely then there would be dancing on the table, swinging from the chandeliers."

"Light reflects differently from broken glass, darling. Just watch! You'll see things you had never imagined seeing."

"You've always been imaginative."

"Better too much imagination than too little."

CHAPTER TWENTY

She can't look at the lake. She can't stop looking at the lake. She sits on the porch at her parents' house and wonders why she is here, why she felt the sudden, adamant urge to return to her childhood home.

In the sixteen years since her parents have been gone, her sister's family has transformed the house. Even if much of the furniture is the same, even if some of it is still positioned where their parents had arranged things, everything has been transformed by family clutter so that the austere feeling of her parents' home has been totally eclipsed. Even the insistent ticking of her father's formidable clocks seem subdued in comparison to her sister's large and noisy family.

Christine's sister, Janelle, fluctuates between being a very relaxed, indulgent parent and a malevolent tyrant. She doesn't nag her kids to pick up the clothes they leave scattered around the house, as their mother did, nor does she feel inclined to pick things up and put them into their proper place, as Christine tends to do. Instead, she lets the mess accumulate until she can't walk through a room without tripping on a skate or a basketball jersey, then unleashes a tirade that brings everyone running—even her husband, who is just as unconcerned and responsible for the mess as the kids are—a cyclone of activity and apologies that clears the room of its mess as effectively as Hurricane Bob. For several days the surfaces can be seen again, the upright piano is recognizable as having a keyboard and a bench, the floor is clear and relatively safe, if one doesn't trip over the gym bags in the entry hall (which Janelle doesn't count as mess); if one can avoid the loose floorboard or the curled carpet corner. One must tread carefully these days, Christine thinks, in her parents' once immaculate home.

Meals are loud and boisterous but mostly congenial. Christine tries to establish some kind of relationship with each of her sister's six kids but she has trouble distinguishing Jarrett, the tall blonde nineteen-year-old from Jakob, the tall blonde eighteen-year-old. Jarod, sullen at sixteen, doesn't engage in conversation with adults. Joelle, the twelve-year-old, competes with the three- and six-year-olds, Jaycee and Jenna, for time on her parents' laps, but cries when her brothers call her a baby. The table is crowded and noisy but no one is listening to each other. Janelle prepares quantities of food and sits down: that's the end of her responsibility. Her husband, Jamie, praises the food his wife has prepared, and that seems to be the extent of his responsibility. The kids bring home their friends, which makes it more difficult for Christine to keep her nephews and nieces straight. No one asks her why she has come for a visit. No one asks her anything, except to pass the *räkor* and *raggmunk*. Seated at the head of the table, feeling unprepared to fill her mother's place, Christine herself isn't sure why she has come to Sweden, and it is hard to make sense of her impulsiveness amid the confusion and noise of her sister's home.

The food is familiar, haphazard versions of their mother's favorite dishes. Christine can taste an inkling of what motivated her return as she bites into the fried potato cakes, the flavor of lingonberries filling her mouth like an awakening memory. When she steps outside, settles herself into her mother's old rattan chair on the wide, graceful, wraparound porch, she is given another memory, the smell of just mown fields: seasoned hay mingling with fresh pollens.

And just beyond the mown grass lies the lake, if she dares to look, calm and inviting, seductive on the surface, but dark and menacing beneath, a current so strong it doesn't help to struggle. She can't look at the lake. She can't stop looking at it.

"What are you doing out here all alone?" her sister asks. "Don't you want dessert? I've made Mama's *Kladdkaka*."

"In a little while, perhaps."

"In a little while there won't be any left." She laughs. "Not with that brood." Janelle pulls a rocker closer to her sister's chair. Its arm is loose but she bangs it back into place, then settles so close that the arms of the chairs are practically touching. "Jamie is taking the kids out onto the lake. There will be fireworks on the pier. Why don't you come, too?"

Christine shudders. "Won't it be dark soon?"

"You forget. It won't be dark until dawn."

"Aren't those storm clouds?"

Janelle appraises the sky. "I doubt it." She leans back, lifts her heavy legs onto the edge of the porch railing. "I'll stay here with you. It will be nice to have a little quiet."

"I am fine alone. Don't feel obliged to stay."

"Are you kidding? My baby sister comes up for the first time in years. You think I want to miss a minute of your visit?" She scoots her chair closer, and when she rocks, the arm brushes Christine's chair and makes a grating sound. "I've set aside some things for you. I'll bring them out as soon as the Js leave."

Kids pour out of the house—ten of them, Christine counts. They all raise a hand to wave as they race across the lawn, down to the edge of the lake where the boat is docked. Only the baby, Jaycee, comes to kiss her mother goodbye. She reminds Christine of Anna and Elle, and is unnerved that there is only one of her. Momentarily, she is sorry she didn't bring the twins. They should know their cousins, but as soon as she imagines them into this chaotic setting, she is relieved they are not here: not out on the lake at night.

She wonders now how her mother kept her and her sister safe, kept them from the dangers of the lake. In some of her earliest memories Christine plays outdoors, alone or with her sister. She can practically hear her mother in the kitchen. How could she have been sure her young children weren't toddling toward the edge of the lake, to drown before she noticed they were missing? And then she remembers: her mother and father had constructed a long stretch of free-standing fence. They created a large enclosed area in which Christine and Janelle were free to play. When they wanted to leave their play area, they were taught to ask: Mother, may I? Christine recalls that her father responded to the question as readily as their mother. It was a game but it kept them safe; and probably kept their parents from worry.

Christine is wondering how all her nephews and nieces will fit into the boat when their father, Jamie, propels a second skiff out of the boathouse and aligns it beside the first. Kids clamor in, the older boys and their friends in one boat, the younger kids with their father. Joelle argues with her brothers but they won't let her in their boat; she must ride with the little kids. Gear is thrown into the hull. Christine can hear the counterpoint of their voices as the two boats distance themselves from the shore, and then it is quiet again, quiet enough to hear the lake lapping at the shore, the call of a Siberian Jay in the soft night sky.

Her sister is right, she has forgotten the night sky that never darkens but remains twilight well past midnight. In July, the days are already beginning to shorten. The sun will set tonight around ten-thirty, whereas she remembers, as a child, as a teen, being out on the lake, like Janelle's kids tonight, to watch the setting of the midnight sun. She finds it disconcerting, in a way, to be sitting in daylight after dinner, as if the *Glögg* Janelle is pouring is an *aperitivo* instead of a digestive. There are no stars visible. Yes, she has forgotten the excursions out onto the lake after dinner, the camaraderie of friends and family, the noise. What she lets herself remember is like an old silent film: the scene plays a little too fast, but the dialogue is missing; the sentiment is overacted, melodramatic. She has let the sad ending dominate the entire story.

"What do you have to show me?" she asks, curious what her sister can reveal of their lives together.

"Where do you want to start?"

Her sister leads her back into the house. She is a little unstable, Christine notices. She poured her first *Glögg* as she was preparing dinner, and has consumed enough to drown a sailor. Christine isn't drinking—her pregnancy is too precarious as it is without sabotaging it with *Glögg*. But she and Jenna, the three-year-old, are the only ones abstaining tonight. Another thing Christine had forgotten.

Janelle brings her into what used to be her father's study. It, too, has been kept the same but is transformed by a new generation of clutter. A computer sits incongruously on top of her father's old, solid desk, surrounded by a modem, a printer and a scanner, connected to their respective tangle of cords. An ironing board and a stack of wrinkled clothes crowd a corner of the room beside a large, cumbersome television. A sewing machine is covered in plastic, under the window where her father used to sit in the early evenings of her childhood. Christine hears before she sees that her father's favorite clock is silent. From the thick layer of dust that has accumulated at the base of its glass, it would seem that it hasn't been wound in ages. The pendulum hangs askew, has stopped in mid-beat, as if waiting for permission to *tock*. It is painful for Christine to be in this room. She doesn't know if the clutter helps or makes it worse.

Janelle sits behind her father's desk, and Christine is struck by the injustice of it all, as if a cuckoo has claimed the nest in its rightful owner's absence. Christine knows she is being absurd. Their father is gone. It is right that Janelle uses the house for her family. But the absurdity returns: it is not Janelle who is to blame, but her father. He abandoned them long before he should have given up the right to his desk. How old would he be now? Something keeps her from doing the simple math. Whatever his age, he should be here, helping with his grandchildren, keeping his elder daughter from drinking too much.

"You look like you've seen a ghost, Christy. Are you sure you don't want something to drink?"

She shakes her head. "Doesn't it bother you to sit at *Far's* desk?"

Janelle stops sorting through a box on her lap. "I guess it did, at the start. I kept this room empty—kind of like a memorial to *Far*—but when Jaycee was born, we needed the room upstairs, so I moved my *office*, if you can call it that—" gesturing toward the sewing machine, the ironing board "—in here. I've gotten used to it." She brings out a smaller box and starts to unwrap it. "I can see it bothers you."

"Yes. I wish it didn't," she says, stopping herself from biting a fingernail by picking up a photo from Janelle's desk. "Isn't it odd how much Jenna looks like Elle? Or is this Jaycee?" She reaches into her purse for a photo of Elle and Anna to show the resemblance.

"That's not Jenna, Christy, that's you, when you were almost four. With *Far.*"

"That's impossible." She holds the photos side by side. "I was never this pretty."

"You were. You are." Janelle takes the photo and studies the picture of Elle and Anna. "And your children look exactly like you did at their age." Janelle hands Christine another frame. "Here is a photo of *Mor* and *Far*, if you want to take it home with you."

Reluctantly, Christine accepts the photograph and glances at it quickly, then looks again more closely. She recalls this photo. It sat on the piano in the living room. She never noticed her resemblance to her mother. It is disconcerting, she thinks, biting her nail before she can stop herself. Like looking in the mirror. She looks at her sister but the resemblance isn't there. Janelle hands Christine another photo. It is of her parents at Christine's graduation from *Ecole de traduction et d'interprétation*. She calculates quickly, a year before their deaths. She forces herself to look into the faces of her parents, and is astounded by how young they are. Her mother? It is like looking into a mirror of the future, to see what Christine will look like in ten years. She studies her father's face. Thomas is nearly as old as the man in the photograph. How healthy they look! She turns the photograph over and lays it on her father's desk. Such a lie!

"Why does it upset you to look at them?" Janelle asks.

"I feel betrayed, I guess. Not by her—she couldn't help that she became ill. But Far—I still don't understand how he could have—" she forces herself to say it, "ended his life. Didn't he know how much we would need him?"

"He saw what *Mor* went through—"

"We all saw it—it was horrible."

"He said he couldn't stand for us to go through it again."

"He said—what?"

"He was ill, Christy."

"What do you mean, *ill*?" she says, throwing as much contempt into the word as she can muster. "Wouldn't I have known if he had been *ill*?"

"Not if he tried to keep it from us, from you."

"Unwell like *Mor*?"

Her sister nods, once. "He had leukemia, too, but refused chemo."

"Why didn't I see it?"

"He did everything he could to hide it."

After a long pause, Christine makes herself ask. "How did you know?"

"I was cleaning out *Mor's* medicines, and found the same prescriptions on his side of the medicine cabinet. It was just a matter of time."

"And you never thought to tell me?"

"He made me promise."

"When does the patent on a promise run out?"

"Today, I guess."

"And not before? Jan, sixteen years have passed."

"Be fair, Christy. You didn't want to know. Any time I started to speak of *Mor* and *Far*, you changed the subject."

"It was painful. First we lost *Mor,* and then *Far*, he—well, it felt like he robbed me of my right to mourn *Mor*. I had to divide my sorrow between them both, but I was so angry at *Far*. How could he have left us, when we needed him?"

"You know how he was." She looks down, loath to be the keeper of her father's shame. "He needed to be strong, invincible. He wouldn't have permitted himself to waste away like *Mor* did."

"How much of this is speculation on your part?"

"I spoke to him the day he died. It was our usual conversation, about the weather, about the kids, but I thought it was peculiar that he told me to take good care of you, to take care of myself." She is trying not to cry but the tears have a will of their own. "We talked about the storm coming up. He said it was a good storm, the right end to a difficult summer. How could I have known what he was talking about?"

"But leukemia? Both of them? Doesn't that strike you as a little far-fetched?

"Do you remember the project *Far* worked on in the plant up north?"

"Vaguely."

"Do you remember that *Mor* stayed with him for six weeks?"

"No." She thinks back. "I was away at university." How could she have been so self-absorbed?

"It wouldn't have made any difference if you had known. I knew, but I didn't think anything about it. I was absorbed in my life. Jarrett and Jakob were babies, I was pregnant with Jarod—" Her thought trails off. "Besides, what could we have done? Nobody understood the danger until it was too late."

"All this time I assumed—"

"Does knowing make things easier?"

"I don't know. Maybe not." She lifts the photo and looks at her parents, studies their expressions, as if for a clue. "I don't understand any of it. I watch Thomas's mother, at the end of her life. She can't see anymore, she's got terrible arthritis. She can't remember things. Her parts are rusting, like an old automobile, but she will rattle on until she runs out of gas or gets a flat. I suffer the humiliation of her demise." She looks at the photograph in her hands. "I wonder which is worse, losing a parent early, as we did, all at once, or undergoing the slow, disrespectful process of old age?"

Janelle shudders. "What a terrible choice." She refills her glass with *Glögg*. "I want to die in my sleep on my hundredth birthday."

"With all your teeth! Who wouldn't?" Christine pours herself a drop of Glögg. She takes a sip, and then sets the glass down on the edge of her father's desk. "But perhaps we are mixing apples with oranges."

"How do you mean?"

"For an old person, it is of course better not to suffer the final humiliations. It would be better to be spared those final horrors. Death is easier to accept, perhaps, because the child sees the parent relieved of suffering, is willing to let them move on. But when a parent dies young, like ours did, they are robbed of a full life and we are left with years of regret."

"And then there is *Far's* decision—" Janelle says.

"*Fader's unilateral* decision threw a monkey wrench into the works. The worst of it all—" she is presented with several alternatives but goes toward the one that has bothered her most, "—is that it confused our mourning."

"I know," Janelle says. "I didn't know what to feel, grief or anger—"

"Or a sense of betrayal?"

"I know. What can I say?"

"Is there anything to say?"

"Quite a lot, really. Now that you are finally here."

"Like what?"

"Like half this house is yours? Half the furnishings. Half of everything."

Christine laughs, an incongruous note that reverberates like a slap in the face of her sister's seriousness. There is something humorously absurd in the concept of half of everything. How would they divide the stately grandfather clock, down the center or top and bottom? Surely the top half would be more valuable, with all its intricate inner workings. Father's collection of Goebel figurines, which he bought for their mother but kept on his shelves: they would shatter before they would let themselves be shared. Christine knows she is being ridiculous but she can't stop herself from laughing as she imagines dividing and thus destroying every possession in her parents' house. She looks out the window, hoping the night's infinity will restore her reason, will reinstate her seriousness, but how can she make sense of anything when it is so light so late? And where, for God's sake, are the stars?

"Christine, you're crying."

Suddenly, she is impatient to return home. She envisions her daughters asleep, and Thomas, undoubtedly outdoors, watching the stars, waiting for one to drop through the sky. She looks back at her sister, who is watching her with a concerned expression clouding her pale, moon-shaped face. "I would like to have *Mor's* books, if you don't mind," Christine says, wiping tears from her eyes. "And two pieces of *Mor's* jewelry, to pass on to Elle and Anna."

"I'll show you what there is," Janelle rises heavily from her chair, opens an overhead cupboard and brings down a box. "You can take your pick."

Christine opens the box, and is confronted by a faint scent of mint, a reminder of her mother. She looks down at the pieces of jewelry, and selects the strand of black pearls her father had given her mother when Christine was born. In an adjoining compartment, there is the strand of white pearls, a gift to commemorate her sister's birth. "Would you mind if I took these two pieces?"

"Not at all. I doubt my daughters will ever wear pearls."

Christine closes the box, and hands it back to her sister.

"And something of *Far's*?"

Christine stands and stretches. It feels like she has been sitting immobile for years. She looks around her father's study, admires the stately grandfather clock, and remembers how pleased he had been when he found it for sale at a farm auction. It would look nice in the library in Epping Forest but she can't bring herself to transport it out of this room. She looks at the shelf behind his desk, trying to see if there is something to take home, a pleasant memory she can transplant from this house to hers. Her eyes flicker over the framed brass medallions on their beds of dark velvet, to the row of golf trophies in need of polish. She bends down to look at the Goebel figurines until she finds what she is looking for. "I'll take this, if you don't mind."

"That?" Janelle steps back to open the glass. "Of all of *Far's* things, why would you choose a damaged cricket?"

CHAPTER
TWENTY-ONE

August in Epping Forest wins hands down over August in Florence, where the heat of the summer settles in to stay, and even the riotous thunder clouds that threaten the city each afternoon fly high over head, increasing the humidity but never giving relief from the insufferable heat. Epping Forest, instead, has been lovely and fresh all month. At the end of August, the days are noticeably shorter, have reached that equatorial moment in which daylight and darkness share equal status, an equilibrium that won't last long but which is reassuring at the moment. In the evenings now, when they lie out together on the thick picnic blanket to watch the cascade of falling stars, they all wear jackets and huddle close together. The nights are chilly enough to warrant an extra blanket on the bed, but still warm enough to permit an open window. They have been here for three-and-a-half weeks, and will stay another few days, to give Florence a chance to freshen itself, to shower off the heat and humidity, to dress itself again in crisp, fresh air and clear, unveiled skies.

Everyone has claimed a corner of the garden for their own this August. The twins have staked out a grassy patch equal distance between the study Thomas has improvised beneath the elm tree on the far side of the patio and the hammock Christine has hung between the two sturdy poplar trees near the edge of the river. The children's mat is littered with their toys, dolls and stuffed animals, all of which they talk to with equal enthusiasm. They ignore a lack of response or supply it themselves, as they also charitably ignore the anomalous proportions of baby dolls the same measure as stuffed puppies and Bad Wolf hand puppets. When they are tired, they lie down among their toys to nap, and when they awake, they resume their play. They bring their inanimate friends back to life with a gregarious, princely kiss, as if none of the players, principal or secondary, had been interrupted by an interval of sleep.

Thomas has been following their example. He works to prepare his autumn lectures until he is tired, and then switches to writing up the notes for the conference in October, until the lines begin to blur. He naps until he finds himself awake, and reads Auden or Wordsworth until his mind is awake and ready to work. While he is reading, Christine brings out platters of fruits and vegetables, and he nibbles unconsciously until he notices the plate is empty. A pitcher of mint tea is replaced without his noticing, before he can build a thirst, and the pitcher is empty again, without his realizing he has been drinking. It has been a wonderfully relaxing holiday. The rhythm of living without a routine has restored everyone's internal clocks.

Christine moves among the children, the hammock, the house and Thomas. Sometimes he looks up to see that the hammock is weighted down and swaying slightly, with two arms visible above the rim, a book suspended. At other times, Christine curls on her side—he can see her knees forming a bulge on the side of the netted fabric—to sleep, and then the only movement is a gentle rocking from a gust of wind. She, too, has accumulated a pile of books on the table beside her hammock, Proust's *Swan's Way*, which she starts every summer but can never progress beyond the second chapter; an assortment of poetry, Rilke, Millay, Keats and Eliot. She keeps an assortment of notebooks for various projects, a journal, a scrapbook, and more recently, notes for the conference. In their own separate ways, they are preparing for the conference in October. They don't want to lose the last of their holiday to work, but it is best to make notes as they occur rather than finding themselves rushing to clarify concepts at the eleventh hour.

Thomas's mother had been right: the combination of artists, doctors and professors who had enlivened their dinner party in Florence was precisely the kind of conference Thomas hoped to achieve in October at The Surdans. Their little gathering in Florence has given him food for thought all through the month. No one danced on the table, and no glass had been splintered, but ideas had reflected across the Limoges dishes as if a mirror had caught the light and flashed insight from eye to eye. Not everyone had agreed; in fact, there had been a passionate disagreement between Professor Cathaway, a renowned liberal on sabbatical at the European Institute, and Kate Griffitts, who upset everyone's sense of the politically correct by agreeing with Julian when he spoke of his embarrassment, his chagrin, when he encountered gypsies begging on the street in Florence. Everyone listened politely to Cathaway's barrage of platitudes against Julian's social insensitivity, until Kate interrupted to defend him by recounting a personal episode at the train station in Florence.

She had been left waiting for a friend's late train, she said, and as she stood at the steps to the station, her attention had been captivated by a young gypsy with a sleeping infant in her lap, a variation on a mother-and-child theme too familiar for her to ignore. True, many people passed by without acknowledging the girl—which in Kate's opinion was the greatest grievance against humanity, that someone could walk past an open hand and not fill it. But for every ten that passed unseeing, one stopped to drop a coin into the girl's hand. Kate couldn't see the denomination, but if half the charitable people gave the girl a one euro coin and the others gave her only twenty cents, Kate calculated the girl made more than forty euro in the hour Kate waited for her friend's train.

What infuriated Kate, and what elicited an angry huff of disbelief from Cathaway was that late the same evening, when Kate brought her friend back to the train station, she encountered the same gypsy and the same sleeping infant. Kate figured, even if they kept the child awake all night, it couldn't sleep through the roar of a train station ten hours a day without being drugged. She could not give money to anyone who drugged a child to keep it quiet.

No one at the dinner party, including Cathaway, had pretended to have a ready answer to the problem of the gypsies on the streets of Italy, and everyone had agreed, even Cathaway, that if they couldn't address a problem right under their noses, what hope did they have of resolving a more obscure problem in an unfamiliar culture such as Asia or Africa. Martin Gould was visibly discouraged until Kate Griffitts offered a viable suggestion: if someone would organize an auction—Thomas remembered she looked purposefully at her younger daughter, Electra—she would donate an original signed photograph of one of her Divas. An enticing sum could be given to the gypsies who were willing to enroll their children in school, and another sum added if the child maintained regular attendance. Kate's husband, Niccolò, suggested she photograph the gypsies and their wide-eyed, wide-awake babies, to promote the crusade, photographs that could be sold to finance the same project in other Italian cities. At the end of the night, despite a few splinters of disagreement, a viable project had been born that would begin to address a problem that everyone had been complaining about but which no one had begun to resolve.

At the end of the evening, Thomas had credited the success of the evening to his mother, who had reminded him of past traditions. Suggested by Anne and encouraged by the other guests, Thomas and Christine resolved to initiate open house dinner parties every third Thursday of the month when they returned to Florence, hoping to produce a bountiful Thanksgiving harvest of ideas that would help to put an end to the politically incorrect reality of starving children.

As a result of that initial dinner party in Florence, Thomas has come to understand the tone he would like to set for their first conference in England.

The flapping of dry sheets on the clothesline catches Thomas's attention, like enormous flags of surrender. He puts down his notebook and pen and pulls himself out of his ladder-back chair. There isn't much daylight left, he is surprised to note, and he doesn't want the drying process to reverse itself with the onslaught of evening's humidity. He moves across the lawn slowly, reluctant to acknowledge the end of another day.

Thomas unpins one corner of a stiff white sheet and folds it in half so it won't drag along the grass while he unpins the other corner. He wonders if he can convince Kate Griffitts to accompany him and Christine to Ethiopia next year. Those poor kids have been photographed by many of the charity organizations, but not artistically, not by someone of Kate's repute. He glances over the lawn where Anna and Elle have been dressing and undressing their dolls. "Anna?" he asks. "Where is your sister?"

"Dunno." Anna barely looks up from the rubber band she is twisting around her doll's ponytail.

"Christine?" Thomas looks toward the hammock at the edge of the river but it is swaying in the wind, empty. He drops the half-folded sheet into the laundry basket and walks toward the house. "Christine?"

Christine appears at the door to their cottage like the proverbial housewife, wiping her hands on the corner of her apron.

"Is Elle with you?"

"No, she is with you and Anna."

In less than a heartbeat, her relaxed air charges, as decisively as if she's been struck by lightning. "Elle?" she calls, running across the lawn. Instinct takes her toward the river. "Elle? Elle!"

It hasn't rained much this summer and the river is low, but the current is swift, too swift for a child. Thomas orders Anna to return indoors and runs along the bank, upstream, his bare feet cutting open against the stones along the bank. He hears Christine's voice farther down the river, calling. He raises his own voice to call but he can't produce a sound. His throat has contracted with raw emotion, has strangled his attempt to speak. His daughter's name is blocked inside of him and refuses to rise.

Dear Lord, Christine prays, sliding down the sandy ridge to look more closely under the footbridge. *Bring her back to me unharmed.* She trips over a collection of tangled branches and falls up to her knees into the icy water. She flails against the current, admonishing her clumsy, ungainly self until she succeeds in pulling herself out of the water, trying to gain sure footing on the slippery riverbank. Her heart knocks violently against her rib cage, banging to break free of its containment. The water is much too cold for Elle, she thinks, shaking. Elle is always cold, even in summer; is always pushing herself into Christine's arms for warmth; her little feet cold, her hands icy. *Please Lord, give me back my baby,* she prays. "Elle!"

A small voice inside her counsels: G*o back up the river*. But Thomas is upstream, she reasons; surely she should search where he isn't looking. She stumbles downstream, moving as quickly as her graceless body and the shifting sediment will allow her to lift her heavy, clay-laden feet.

Again, she hears the voice inside her: *Go back up river*, but she doesn't pause to listen. She won't give up looking downstream until she has rounded the bend in the river. She has to keep looking, has to keep hoping, has to have faith that she will find her obstinate, headstrong, independent little girl before it is too late. Doggedly, she continues downstream.

A loud voice reverberates inside her head. *Return upstream.* Christine stops herself abruptly, as if pierced through her icy heart with an arrow. She stands still to listen, to gather further instructions, but the only sound now is of water rushing headlong over timeworn stones. Deliberately, she steadies herself against the current, and reverses her direction. With surprising, unprecedented calm, she pulls herself up the steep bank so that she can walk more easily along the riverbank. She studies the steep embankment, looking closely into the tangle of branches at the water's edge. Her eyes survey every possible form, every movement as she passes the miniature sandbars, the halfhearted beaver-attempts to dam. She doesn't understand why she has changed direction, but she continues back toward the house. She stays close to the river but is not slowed by its current, as if she is following in someone else's footsteps along a sturdy, secure path.

A hundred meters from the house, near the veteran beech pollard, where the river drops shortly in its only semblance of a waterfall, she finds Elle lying in the mud.

"Thomas!" she screams. "Thomas!"

She doesn't wait for help. Christine slides down the steep bank, stumbling over an interweaving of sticks and accumulated branches, which interfere with but don't slow her progress. In an instant she has Elle gathered into her arms, is lifting her stunned daughter, scratched and covered in mud but apparently unharmed. Christine staggers back up the bank, will and determination propelling her forward under the heavy, stupefied weight of her child.

"Thomas!" she cries, pressing her daughter against her chest as she runs across the lawn to the house. "I have Elle."

Thomas is beside her by the time she reaches the door, and together they bring Elle indoors. Together they carry her upstairs and undress her as the water runs to fill the bathtub.

Anna stands at the bathroom door. "Didn't we have a bath this morning?"

"Yes, but Elle needs another one now."

"Can I have a bath, too?" Anna asks.

"Perhaps afterwards, darling. Let's clean up Elle first."

"What on earth could she have been thinking," Thomas says to Christine when he returns downstairs. Elle has been washed and rubbed vigorously, and dressed in warm pajamas. Thomas has tucked her into bed and has stayed with her until he is sure she is asleep. He hasn't been able to speak until now. His fear—he has to face what it was—has left him mute. Fortunately, Christine has kept her wits about her. He is surprised by how poorly he has performed in the face of an emergency. He hopes nobody has noticed.

Christine has put on water for tea, and is refilling the wood burning stove with sticks of kindling to start a fire. She wants to make sure the house is warm and dry for Elle. If they are lucky, they will escape this misadventure with only a few bruises, without anything more serious than a running nose.

Anna hangs back at the entrance to the room, her thumb in her mouth, a habit they are trying hard to break.

"Anna. Come sit with me," Thomas says, patting the cushion beside him on the sofa. "Do you know what happened?"

Anna nods.

"Tell Daddy." He moves over to make room. Christine brings the teapot and cups and a plate of Tepparkakar biscuits to the table near the sofa, and sits on the other side of Anna.

"We see this big nest fall from the tree," her arms make a sweeping motion over her head and down to the ground. "Elle want to see if there is baby birds. I told her wait. She don't listen."

"Didn't you think to come find Mommy or Daddy?"

"No," she says, simply. "I fixing Angel's hair." She reaches for a Cardamom biscuit, and then pauses. "Am I a bad girl?"

Thomas wonders where she learns these phrases. They don't sound like anything Christine would say, or Allegra. "You are a good girl, darling. A wonderful girl. But we need to keep an eye on each other. Help each other."

"I sorry." Her hand hovers over the plate of cookies, uncertain if she is allowed one.

"Nothing to be sorry for." Christine hands her a biscuit. "You haven't done anything wrong, and Elle is fine."

"Did she see baby birds?"

"We can ask when she wakes up."

That night, after dinner, after both girls have stayed up later than they should playing interminable hands of *Go Fish*, Christine collapses against Thomas, her resolve depleted. "I wouldn't care ever to repeat a day like today."

"Not in a hundred lifetimes." He wraps his arms around his wife and leans his head against hers. "We are going to have to keep a closer eye on Elle."

"And Anna. Next time she might be the one to wander off."

"We need to teach them to swim."

"Will that be enough, Tommy?" She snuggles closer. "This isn't a lake. The water is swift. The bank is high. I think it's a miracle she's alive."

"Do you think we must fence ourselves in?"

"I am wondering if that will be enough." They sit together with their shared concerns, their arms overlapping like their individual doubts. Christine wants to speak but she can't find words to describe the voice that led her to Elle.

Days pass before Christine is calm enough to recount her strange experience to Thomas, and when she does, her voice is as incredulous as if she needed convincing herself. "It was the strangest thing, Tommy. I can't understand where the voice came from, and the more I tried to ignore it, the louder it became, the more insistent."

"A guardian angel, perhaps?"

"I wouldn't know how to explain it, or what to call it. All I know is that it spoke up when I was in need, and kept insisting until I listened."

"All I can say is that I am glad you heard it. For myself, I was in such a state; I doubt I would have heard Gabriel himself if he had trumpeted in my ear."

Christine feels the change physically before she grasps it mentally. She has been carefully not consulting her calendar these last several days, but her body has been keeping track, like a Swiss guard in Harlequin dress: four months to the day and the watch-clock sentry has deemed it time to throw open the gates. Her uterus contracts sharply as she pulls herself from bed to the bathroom, doubling over beneath cramps like the four monthlies she's missed, concentrated together to intensify the message. She grabs for a towel but it is too late. There is blood everywhere. The doctors say this cramping is the same process as the start of labor. She wouldn't know. Birth is something she has only read about, something she has fallen short of time and time and time again. She is going to have to make sure this never happens again.

The last times she has miscarried, she has rushed to the doctor, but today she piles towels beneath her and climbs back into bed. She knows there is nothing to be done. She would rather suffer this indignity in private than subject herself to the cross-examination of cold-handed, rubber-gloved medical staff. She doesn't even call Thomas. She can hear him downstairs with the children. When she doesn't appear for breakfast, he will come up to find her. Eventually she will have to share the news. In the meantime, she curls up like the fetus she is losing, and tries to quiet her sense of failure.

She listens to the murmurings of the girls with their father. She can tell what they are doing by the sounds through the floorboards, the dragging of a chair to the table, the clinking of an orange juice glass, the sound of a spoon against a cereal bowl. A family in its morning routine. Joe Crowell could be delivering the paper. Howie Newsome could be delivering the milk. She wonders if anyone fully appreciates these ordinary moments. *Maybe the saints and poets do, she thinks, maybe they do some.*

By the time Thomas comes to find her, she has expelled the mass. He sees the bloody towels and understands what has happened. His face reflects the sorrow she felt at the start, before she had come to terms with it. "We aren't meant to have a child of our own," she says, as he sits beside her on the bed.

He nods, rubs his hand over her shoulder, touches her hair. "It seems we are meant to give Elle and Anna our full attention, to help them grow securely, without the distraction of a brother or sister."

"They will have brothers and sisters everywhere we go, in all the children we manage to help."

They are gaining strength from each other, reassurance passing between their clasped hands. But when Christine looks into Thomas's eyes and finds tears, her resolve breaks. "I would have loved to have given you a child that was ours."

"You have. Two. And they want their mother, as soon as you are ready to see them."

"In a minute. In just a minute." She dries her eyes with the back of her hand, and then dries her hand on the sleeve of her nightgown. A trace of mascara smears the arm but it doesn't matter. She will have to throw away this nightgown anyway; she will never succeed in getting rid of the blood. With resolve, she says, "I am going to have my tubes tied, Thomas. I can't go through this again."

"You must never go through this again," he agrees.

"I have up to twenty years ahead of me before I stop ovulating." The thought of another aborted pregnancy fills her eyes again with tears. "Pregnancies are hard on the body."

"And the spirit." He squeezes her hand. She hears him humming, hears the words to this familiar song, even though he hasn't spoken them, even though he isn't aware that he's humming: *my one and only love.* "You don't need to have your tubes tied, Christy. You've had enough trauma already." He makes a cutting motion with his fingers. "I'll have the operation."

"I wouldn't enjoy being married to a eunuch," she says, stopping the tears.

He cringes. "Not the operation I had in mind. A smaller snip should resolve unwanted pregnancies."

"Are you sure? It's so permanent."

"Permanent is our goal, isn't it?"

"But what if something were to happen to me? You are still young, you could remarry."

"Nothing is going to happen to you, and even if it did, I am not going to remarry. We have our children, we have each other. The subject is closed."

She must have dozed. There is a tap at the door, a whisper. "We can come in, Mommy?"

"Of course," Christine tries to sit up, brushes back her hair, dries her eyes. If she keeps the room in half-light, maybe they won't see that her eyes are red.

"We brought you tea," Elle says proudly, holding one end of a precariously balanced tray.

"And toast."

"And marm'lade!"

They stand at the edge of her bed, awaiting the invitation to jump up. Clearly, Thomas has said something to them, just enough to keep at bay their habitual exuberance. They slide the tray onto the edge of the bed, inching it forward, waiting for her to tell them to stop. She can see expectation in their faces, like a poised arrow waiting to be released. However, she doesn't know what question they want to ask, and even if she could discern their question, she isn't strong enough to hold up the target so they can hit it.

"Thank you for this lovely tray. I was just wishing I had some tea and toast."

"Is you sick, Mommy?" Anna asks shyly.

"A little unwell. Nothing serious." She picks up a piece of toast and nibbles a corner, making appreciative, reassuring noises. "But I think I will rest this morning, if that is all right with you."

"We was going riding," Elle reminds her. She is standing at the foot of the bed, half-hidden behind her sister, as if ready to bolt, if there's a need.

The thought of riding is excruciating. She cringes.

Thomas is at the door. She hasn't seen him. She doesn't know if he's been there all along or not. "I just spoke with Julian," he says, stepping into the room. "He and Electra are happy to take Elle and Anna riding this morning. Can you girls ready yourselves?" They nod, in unison. "Quickly?" The breakfast tray teeters dangerously as they scamper from the room.

"We'll give you a quiet morning," he says, adjusting the tray so he can sit beside her on the bed.

"I think that would help." She closes her eyes. She can feel a crust of salt accumulated at the edge of her lower lashes, like a Mediterranean shoreline in August. "I should be better when you all return."

"I am just going to run to the pharmacy." He has called Elizabeth, who has told him what medicine will make Christine more comfortable. "I won't be long." He sees the beginning of a protest forming on her face. "Don't worry, I will let you sleep. I have work to do downstairs in the library."

"You won't mind? It's a beautiful day. You should be outside, with the girls."

"I would rather be inside with my beautiful girl. Try to eat something. I'll collect the tray when the girls are dressed and ready to go. Then you can sleep."

The thought of sleep is overwhelmingly appealing but she makes herself sit up a little more so she can drink her tea. It has been overly sweetened with honey, either the heavy hand of one of her daughters or Thomas's attempt to increase her blood sugar. Scattered over the tray are little hearts raggedly cut out of yellow legal paper, on the backs of which she finds fragments of notes Thomas has scribbled for next semester's lectures. The toast is buried beneath marmalade. She forces herself to take a bite, and is surprised to find she is hungry. By the time Thomas returns to take her tray, she has finished both slices of toast and all the tea.

"Kiss Mommy goodbye," Thomas coaches, ushering the girls into the room.

Christine feels the comfort of their wet lips on her dry skin. She will sleep now, she thinks, and awaken renewed, as if none of this ever happened, as if it were all a bad dream.

When Julian and Electra bring the twins home from riding, they find Christine ensconced in a corner of the sofa, reading.

"We took them out for chicken wings," Julian explains, "and they seem to have gotten a little messy."

Christine is so happy to see them, she feels like crying. She does. Anna runs out of the room before Christine can explain her tears of joy. Elle runs after her.

"Thomas?" She starts to get up.

"Stay where you are. I'll get them tidied up. Jules, there is tea on the table. Electra, would you care to pour?"

Electra brings her tea cup and sits in an overstuffed chair near Christine. "We had a wonderful ride," she says, refilling Christine's cup. "I had Anna ride with me. Jules kept Elle with him."

"Elle kept urging us to go faster," Julian says, bringing his tea to the sofa. "She knows no fear. You may have to lock her up when she reaches adolescence."

"Sorry they got so dirty," Electra says.

"They get dirty—that's part of their nature."

"Sorry about your loss," Electra says. She knows she must say something, but she feels awkward.

"Yes, terribly sorry, love," Julian adds.

"It wasn't unexpected," Christine says.

"That can't make it any easier," Electra answers.

"Actually, it has. I have had time to come to terms with it—"

"But still—" Julian turns an empty palm upward.

"Yes, well—I will be all right. I—"

They hear noise on the stairs, little feet followed by bigger, heavier steps.

Anna rounds the corner in a rush and Elle follows. They have had their clothes changed, their hands and faces washed. Anna runs to Christine but slows as she nears. Clearly, she's been cautioned about her mother's delicate condition. She thrusts out her hands, and gives Christine her doll. "You can have Giovanni. He can be your baby."

"You are my baby," Christine says, and opens her arms to receive a hug. "And you, too, Elle. Come to Mama."

"After—" Elle says, slipping past, disappearing into the pantry.

"What are you looking for, darling?"

"A jar, like Julian."

"Oh!" says Electra. She and Julian exchange conspiratory smiles. "Maybe I should help her?"

"Why would she want a jar?" Christine asks, her question offered to anyone who has an answer.

Julian explains. "Electra had the idea to put a large glass jar in my entry hall, where visitors can toss the coins jingling at the bottom of their pockets, the collected sum going to our anti-hunger crusade."

Electra continues: "The idea is that if everyone has a jar in the entrance to their home, it would be an easy, daily reminder to be charitable—just an emptying of the coins in the bottom of our pockets. The accumulation would be immediately visible, and when the jar is full, the donor would know that a child's future has been improved."

"The trick is going to be to have everyone start a jar, like those yellow ribbons around the old oak trees welcoming back the armed forces."

"It's not a new idea," Thomas says, pouring himself a cup of tea. "UNESCO organized a loose change campaign to save Abu Simbel and other Nubian shrines in 1964. They were surprised by the amount of money that came pouring in from all over the world. One woman even sent her gold wedding band."

"People want to help. No one wants children suffering, but lots of folks mistrust charity organizations."

"Too many of these organizations have the reputation of spending the money on administration, not giving enough of it to the children in need."

"But the glass jar is transparent," Electra says.

"Where would the money go?" Christine asks.

"Elizabeth and Stephen send their money to Medic to Medic," Electra says, "an organization that helps keep hardworking students in medical school."

"Medic to Medic is good," Thomas confirms, "even if the money isn't going directly to hungry kids—"

"Those future doctors were probably hungry kids themselves."

"One good doctor serves hundreds of people in need, and certainly medical care for the poor is as important as food."

Electra says, "I send my money to an organization that teaches Indians how to build irrigation systems so that they won't move from their villages to the already overcrowded slums of Calcutta when the crops fail due to lack of rain."

"Are they successful?"

"Absolutely. In some cases, they have two harvests a year instead of one. That money doesn't go directly to feeding children but it is a better solution in the long run."

"That's vitally important. The last thing we want to do is have a generation of children waiting for pennies to arrive from Britain."

"GranAnne has pennies," Anna says. "Lots and lots." Everyone looks at Anna. The non-sequitur quiets them.

"There are details to work out," Electra says.

"The details *will* be resolved, long before the jars are full."

Elle brings a canning jar into the room. She shakes it but it doesn't sound. Thomas empties the coins from his pockets—two pounds, forty-six pence. Elle rattles the bottle again. "Pretty!" she says, offering the jar to Julian.

"Sorry mate, I've already emptied my pockets in the jar at our house." Electra gets her purse. She too has dropped all her coins into the glass jar in Julian's entry hall. She slips a five pound note into the jar. "Pretty noise?"

"Pretty," Elle nods.

Thomas hums *Pennies from Heaven*.

And Christine smiles, forgetting her loss, forgetting she ever had anything to be unhappy about.

CHAPTER TWENTY-TWO

When they return to Florence at the beginning of September, they find Anne unwell. She doesn't come down for lunch, and when Thomas visits her in her room, the heat is so high he has difficulty breathing. He wants to open a window. It is warm outside, and he thinks the fresh air will do more good than harm. But Anne stops him. "I can't get warm," she says, gripping the neck of her quilted bed jacket. "I'm eternally chilled."

Thomas leans forward and touches his lips to her forehead, as she had done to him throughout his childhood. She doesn't seem to have a fever. He runs a hand over the blankets on her bed. "You shouldn't be in bed, Mother. You should be moving more."

"Why are you always telling me what I *should* do?"

"I'm concerned, Mother." He sits back in his chair, crosses his legs. "It isn't good for a person to stay in bed." He leaves out the significant adjective in his phrase—an *old* person. "Inactivity can cause clots, Mother."

"About suffering, they were never wrong—"

"Who, Mother?" He wonders if she's already seen the doctor. Her already diminutive figure seems terribly small under a mountain of bedcovers, insignificant.

"The Old Masters, how well they understood suffering—"

"Understood what, Mother?" He has to stifle the urge to yell at her, to insist that she make sense. He wants to cry out in frustration—or pull out his hair.

"How it takes place, while someone is eating or opening a window, or just walking along."

"Mother?"

"Leave me now—you have somewhere to get to. Sail on. I would like to rest."

That afternoon, Thomas brings in a masseuse, thinking it might improve his mother's circulation, help her to warm up, but Anne won't let the woman touch her. "The idea of being pummeled right now is the epiphany of torture."

Epitome? Thomas thinks. On another occasion, he would have fun teasing his mother about her malapropisms, but she looks pathetic huddled under her covers like Red Riding Hood's Grandmother awaiting the wolf. He hasn't the heart to tease her. "I will take the massage myself then, as the hour has been paid for."

In the evening, Christine and Thomas come down to dinner to find the table again set for two. Rosa prepares a tray of soup, crackers and weak tea, but when they finish their meal and visit Anne in her room, the food on the tray hasn't been touched. The soup has formed an unappetizing glutinous gel over the top, and the sodden tea bag has made a stain on the napkin that looks like the State of Iran.

"You should eat something, Mother."

"There's that word again, *should*." She coughs, a deep, disturbing rumble, like thunder at the edge of water. "You should stop telling me what to do."

"I don't like the sound of that cough, Mother. I think we should phone the doctor."

"I just need to rest. I am so tired." She coughs again, a raucous rumbling of solid battling against liquid. "Take away the tray," she says breathlessly, forcing an order out despite a shortness of breath. As camouflage to her labored breathing, she busies herself adjusting the covers; but as she turns on her side she coughs again, deeply. "Go. Let me rest now. Please."

"What are we to do?" Christine closes the door quietly behind them.

"I will call the doctor."

"It's Friday night. Will you find him?"

"I have to try."

"You don't think it's just a cough?"

"I don't know. This afternoon she was speaking nonsense. 'The Old Masters, how well they understood suffering—'"

"Darling," Christine says, "That's not nonsense, that's Auden."

The doctor's presence angers Anne but she is too frail to send him out of the room. He checks her blood pressure, which he finds oddly low, despite Anne's complaint of a too rapid heartbeat. He measures her temperature by inserting an aural thermometer into her ear. His bedside audience reads his reaction in the twice repeated movement of his Adam's apple when he looks at the LCD reading. "How are you feeling, Signora?"

"Generally unwell," she states the obvious. "Exactly how much fever do I have?"

"Enough to melt the tarmac," he says. "We are taking you to the hospital."

They take turns visiting Anne in the hospital but it is Rosa she wants to stay with her. Anne whimpers like an abandoned puppy when the nurses insist that Rosa leave at night. Thomas considers speaking with the doctor, asking special permission for Rosa to stay, but Rosa stops him. "It isn't that she appreciates my company, sir. All she does is complain and criticize me, as if I were responsible for her present condition."

"I am sorry, Rosa. I had no idea."

"I try not to take it personally. I know she is annoyed at being unwell, not really at me. It isn't easy being blamed, all the same. If I stay longer in the evening, I won't be of any use the next day." She twists her gnarled hands. "Besides, who will cook for you and *la Signora* Christine?"

Thomas is ready to pronounce Allegra's name or Christine's, but he understands before he speaks that having someone take over Rosa's kitchen duties will only augment her conflict. Allegra has been happy to help out in the kitchen, but she has confided to Thomas that Rosa has criticized her for putting things away in the wrong place. Thomas understands that there is a cat fight in the making, if he isn't careful.

"I will sit with Mother this afternoon," he says. "You go home to prepare dinner. Give Christine something tempting to bring Mother to eat tonight. Something she can't say no to."

Rosa licks her lips and rubs her hands. She is already concocting what she can bake that Anne can't refuse. "After I cook dinner, I can feed the children, if Allegra wants to prepare her lovely brioche for *la Signora* Anne's breakfast tomorrow."

Thomas smiles. If only the rest of the world's problems could be so easily resolved.

Anne's problems, too, seem easily enough resolved. "In this day and age, pneumonia isn't the life threatening illness it once was, as long as it is treated in time," the doctor pontificates. "You were smart to call me when you did. Our Anne here would have been seriously ill if she had waited another day."

Anne tolerates the doctors and nurses and their invasive treatments because she has no other choice, but she doesn't like them any more than she likes strangers addressing her by her first name. She resents them looking into her handkerchiefs and praising her mucus when it turns from a brackish green to yellow, as if she's been awarded a blue ribbon for phlegm in a Gargoyle's State Fair. Rosa is increasingly annoying and insists she put on the oxygen mask so that she can recover and return home. The antibiotics make her sick to her stomach, but at least the sweating and shivering have passed. On the whole, she is bored and wants to go home. People keep moving her glasses and the television remote control, and how is she expected to drink if she can't find her water glass and straw?

Thomas finds her without her oxygen every time he enters her hospital room. "Mother, don't you want to get better so you can come home?"

"Not particularly."

"Not particularly what?" His concern is compromised by annoyance. "Not come home or not get better?"

"Your choice. Two sides of the same coin, really."

"Mother, please." He looks for an empty surface on which to place the containers of food Rosa has prepared. "Try to make sense."

"Try to hear the sense of what I am saying. I didn't want to come to hospital in the first place."

"Didn't you hear the doctor?" He opens a dish of Rosa's ravioli with wild boar sauce, hoping the fragrance will stimulate his mother's appetite, and positions it on the tray in front of her. He refills her glass with fresh water, and turns the straw in her direction. "You might have died if we hadn't brought you in."

She ignores the food as if it weren't there. "If it isn't this time, it will be next. The most I can hope for is a short reprieve, not restored health."

Thomas sits down reluctantly. He leans his arms on the side of her bed, leans forward and takes her hand. "Eventually we will all die," he says, as patiently as he can. "But we try to postpone that inevitability for as long as possible."

"The inevitability has overstayed its advantage."

"Pneumonia needn't be fatal, Mother." He stands up abruptly, angry. "You heard the doctor."

"I'm tired, Bunny." She pushes the tray away, as if bothered by the odor. "I want to stop."

"What about your grandchildren?" He paces the room, twists the pole that flicks up the blinds, sees his mother wince, and readjusts it so the light isn't in her eyes. "Don't you want to see them grow?"

"I can't see them at all, Thomas. I can't see anything anymore."

"You can still let them know you love them. You can still receive their love."

"I have loved too many children in my life." She closes her eyes and settles back against the mound of pillows. *"I have not turned away leisurely from the disaster."*

"Auden again?"

She nods. *"But I heard the splash, the forsaken cry. I saw something amazing, a boy falling out of the sky."*

"While everyone else had somewhere to get to," Thomas adds, *"and sailed calmly on."*

"I remember how those children looked at me, as if I were their sun. Every movement I made I saw reflected on their faces."

"It's unrealistic to expect—"

"I see how you look at me, Thomas. I may not remember what day it is, but I will never forget how you used to look at me."

"And how was that?" he asks wearily.

"With admiration. With love."

"The way a child looks at his parents." He can't argue with her point. It is empowering to be revered, even by a child—especially by a child. "The way Elle and Anna look at me—at you."

"Not even the twins look at me that way." Her eyes are dry, her tone is descriptive and without self-pity. "I stopped seeing admiration in your eyes—"

"Mother—"

"—long before I lost my sight." She fumbles for her handkerchief, feels the cough before it surfaces. It racks her

286

body, as if something deep inside was seeking release. "I am not blaming you, Bunny," she continues, when she can speak again. "The woman you loved and respected has gone. This tired old husk is just waiting for a strong wind to blow it away." She looks at an unseen object in the distance. "I am relieved Ian never saw me like this. Decrepit." She shivers, repulsion rippling through her body. She composes herself, and then adds, "I am equally relieved I never had to see him old and incapacitated. What a gift it is to cherish his memory intact."

"I am sorry, Mother." Resignedly, Thomas sits down beside her bed. She takes his hand, as if she were offering comfort instead of receiving it. "You are right—at least about all those children. They really did love you."

"I've done something important with my life. How can I have regrets that it is over? I have loved—and have been loved."

"I know."

"And more than by any of them, by you."

"Without a doubt," he says, smiling. "Your constant playmate."

"We did have fun, didn't we?"

"We had a blast."

"It isn't fun anymore, Bunny. I am reverently, passionately waiting for the miraculous next birth. I'm ready to stop this life."

"I'll miss you. Doesn't that count for anything?"

"There always must be children who did not specially want it to happen."

"Mother, you must stop quoting Auden."

She folds her hands obediently on her lap. "I knew him, you know. I tried to convince him to adopt a child."

"You're kidding."

"I am. But I might have. That was the kind of person I was. Admit it, Bunny. The Mother you loved has been gone for years."

CHAPTER
TWENTY-THREE

Christine is trying to keep the children quiet so that Anne can rest. Until Anne returned from the hospital, Christine always assumed that her mother-in-law couldn't hear the children in their playroom. However, if Christine can hear Anne's racking cough, she must assume that Anne can hear them playing. Laughter to a person who is unwell can't be amusing. Christine has closed all the doors and is trying to teach the twins the art of mime.

She has found two large, brightly colored scarves as her prop, and they have been letting her wrap the scarves around them in various styles for the last half-hour. Elle walks toward the full-length mirror at the far end of the room with a scarf trailing behind her like a Zorro cape. She pivots and does a series of funny little bows, then returns to Christine, who has just finished tying Anna's scarf in the same fashion and has sent her swaggering toward the mirror. Next, Christine ties the scarf over Elle's head like an old Befana witch, positions her fingers into claws and sends her toward the mirror, as Anna returns for the same transformation. Christine is beginning to run out of ideas but the girls keep coming, so she invents as she goes, twisting the scarf to make bunny ears, twirling it around their waists like swarthy pirates carrying imaginary swords. She paints their lips with bright red lipstick and puts the shawls low on their shoulders like Spanish dancers. Elle stops when she arrives at the mirror, distracted to see herself in lipstick. She throws off her scarf and presses her lips against the glass, leaving a row of diminishing red imprints. Anna picks up her sister's discarded scarf and brings it back to Christine.

"Do you want to keep playing?" Christine whispers.

"Yes," Anna says, handing her both scarves.

It is easier to be creative with two scarves and Christine fashions a long skirt and cloak for Anna, who marches proudly toward her sister, who watches her pass with an expression of admiration.

Anna passes again, and Christine reassembles the two scarves so that they are a poncho and loose fitting trousers, tucked up into her belt. Anna parades proudly to the mirror, twirls in front of Elle, and returns to Christine.

Christine throws the scarf over Anna's head so that it covers her forehead and ears, a colorful nun, with the other scarf clashing brightly into a Sister's robe. Christine puts her hands together in prayer, and Anna walks solemnly to the mirror, pirouettes in front of Elle, who grabs the scarf from her sister's head, pulling her hair, causing her to scream.

"No, Elle!" Christine hurries to separate her daughters, but they are hitting each other, already crying. "No hitting, Elle. Anna, stop."

"Mine," Elle says, pulling the scarf from her sister. She says something else that Christine can't understand.

"Behave, Elle."

Elle fusses and continues to pull on the scarf. Anna is fussing now, too. They are both making enough noise to wake their Grandmother.

"Would you both like to be sent to your room?" Neither of the girls is listening to her. "Mommy is one minute from losing her temper!"

Anna unwraps the scarf, throws it down. "Smelly Elle!"

Elle wraps the scarf around her and cries, runs to the other end of the room and smears the lipstick kisses with her scarf. "Smelly you!" she screams, as she leaves the room.

Anna cries and climbs into her mother's arms. Christine holds her until they are both calm. "What happened, Anna? You were playing so nicely. What went wrong?"

"Elle want her scarf."

"Why didn't she just say so?"

"She did."

"Why did you call her smelly?"

Anna repeats the phrase, obviously delighting in the rhyming words. "Smelly Elle!"

"That isn't kind, and you must never say it again."

Suddenly, Anna doesn't want to be held anymore. She wants to play. "Can you tie up my scarf again, Mommy?"

The repetition is going to kill her, Christine thinks. She struggles to imagine how this damned scarf can be tied in yet another way but can't for the life of her. "Why don't *you* tie it up, Anna? How would you like to wear it?"

Anna wraps it around her shoulders and gropes her way toward the mirror. When she returns, Christine asks, "What is your costume, darling?"

"I was Grandmother Anne," she closes her eyes, pretends to be blind, her hand extended, groping. "Where I put my glasses?" she says, in a frighteningly accurate imitation of her Grandmother.

"You must never do that in front of your Grandmother," she reprimands.

"OK," she says, twisting her scarf in another design. "But she can't see me."

Christine is beside herself when Thomas returns home. She tries to mask her desperation but she isn't successful. She explains the problem with Elle and the scarves, and then reports Anna's cruel imitation of her Grandmother.

Thomas doesn't think either is a big deal. He is tired, too, has had a long, frustrating day at the Institute, a long week made longer by his mother's poor health. He has been looking forward to coming home, but he hasn't expected to be showered with problems. "Anna couldn't be cruel if she wanted to be. She just hasn't learned the art of deception, yet. But don't worry, she will."

291

"But what about Elle? I almost spanked her, I was so annoyed. And Anna said that she had tried to explain but I hadn't heard her."

"Mother's illness is upsetting us all," Thomas says, pouring them both a glass of wine, their Friday night ritual. "More than we realize."

"I can't understand half of what Elle says," Christine admits. "She makes lots of noise but doesn't say much."

"She doesn't speak clearly." Thomas removes a book and a blanket from the sofa and seats himself at one end. He pats the cushion beside him and Christine comes to sit with him.

"I haven't wanted to admit it," Christine says, sipping her wine.

"We haven't needed to." Thomas picks up the books at his feet. He marks them with a bookmark and sets them neatly on the end table. "As long as Anna is around, Elle always has someone to interpret for her."

"Thank God for Anna." Christine takes the blanket and folds it in thirds, and then places it over the back of the sofa. "She is quick to translate for her sister when we don't understand she needs it."

"I think that's our mistake," Thomas says. He leans back, and finds a doll's arm. "Have you been looking for this?" He tosses the loose appendage across the room, and claps when it lands in the toy box, like a basketball through a hoop. "We need to ask Elle to express herself more clearly, instead of expecting Anna to interpret."

"Do you think she should be tested?" Christine tosses a badminton birdie but it falls short of the toy box. Peeved, she gets up to retrieve it. "To see if it is a problem?"

"No, she's not even three. Mother said I didn't speak clearly until I was five. Some people say I still don't speak comprehensively." He laughs. "Don't worry. Nothing serious has happened."

Christine takes a sip of her wine. "Something odd happened today with your mother."

"What?" Thomas stretches out on the sofa, lays his legs over Christine's lap. It will keep her from getting up and he likes the feel of her hands on his legs. They will have to get up soon and send Allegra home, but the evening will be easier, and more enjoyable, if they have a few minutes alone together first.

"I found her flipping through old appointment books, as if she were looking for something important, but when she heard me, she became embarrassed—"

"Mother and you both know she can't see."

"Well, yes, even if she's never admitted it to me."

"She's been a bit more candid with me."

"Anyway, she gave me this year's book, the big leather one the bank sent her, and asked me to see if she had any appointments."

"Odd. She would be the one to know. She's the only one who writes in that book."

"But there was nothing written in the book, Tommy, nothing at all. I flipped back through it twice, thinking I might have missed something. I told her, 'Anne, there's nothing here.' She said, 'I remember when I had to write my appointments in the tiniest hand, otherwise there were too many things to fit onto one page.' She showed me an older book and every page was full of her scribbles. Then she said, 'I don't know which is worse, the days so full they all run together—no time to reflect between events and appointments—or all these empty pages, with nothing planned, too much time to reflect.' I started to say something to reassure her but she wasn't listening. She said, 'Both ways, the time is lost, just holes in the calendar.' I had to leave. She made me so sad."

"I wonder if she was quoting again."

"I don't know. Perhaps."

"Poor Mother. You know, she had quite the reputation for cleverness."

"I can imagine," Christine says, then thinks of the sad old woman upstairs. "Or not. I never really knew her as you describe her. She has seemed tired for all the years I've known her."

"She changed when Father died. As if her flame had shown brightly in order to light his presence. But when I was young, she was the one who people came to see. She was the dynamic force behind the man in office. Father was honored, no doubt about it, but I wonder now, would he have been so revered if he had married another woman."

"If he had met the woman he was supposed to have met in the park with the Boston ducks."

"If she had met the man she was supposed to meet."

"I think she did. I think he did."

"We should—" she starts to move his legs off her lap.

He jumps up with renewed energy. "Let's bring the children into the dining room with us tonight."

He catches her by surprise. This is the first time he has suggested it. "Do you think they are ready?"

"Probably not, but we can have Rosa wash the tablecloth if they soil it. Come on, it will be fun. No point in living in this big old house if we don't use it."

"I'll get their booster seats so they can see over the edge of the table."

"I'll pay Allegra. Is she coming in tomorrow?"

"No, she has the weekend free."

"Good. It will be nice to be just the four of us."

After dinner, while Rosa repairs the damage to the dining room, and Christine pays a quick visit to Anne, Thomas brings the girls into the sitting room, and puts music to play on his mother's stereo.

When Christine joins them later, she finds that Thomas has taught them one of his favorite songs.

Thomas interrupts his song to explain. "I have been repeating the lyrics until both Anna and Elle know them by heart." He sings:

> *Ev'rybody loves Saturday night.*
> *Ev'rybody loves Saturday night.*
> *Ev'rybody, ev'rybody, ev'rybody, ev'rybody,*
> *Ev'rybody loves Saturday night*

Christine can hear the underlying lesson. Thomas is working on Elle's pronunciation.

Ev'rybody loves Saturday night

"What is that word, darling? *Night*—it finishes with a *t*, like thumb starts with a *t*."

"Thumbelina!" Anna says.

Thomas hugs Anna and wiggles his fingers. "What is this one called, Elle?"

"Thumb."

"And this?" he taps his chest.

"Heart."

"And what am I wearing?"

"A tee-shirt!"

"That's a girl. Now sing it for me?"

Anna wants to sing too, but she hasn't inherited her father's ability to carry a tune. She marches through the lyrics like a woodcutter chopping a tree, hitting each note at exactly the same spot. However, her enunciation is perfect, and her memory for the words is infallible. Elle's tone isn't pitch perfect either but she corrects her mistakes and gets back on key quickly. They know what she is saying because they know the simple words themselves, but Christine wonders if someone unrelated would be able to understand. Just for fun Christine sings the same line in Swedish:

Alla älskar lördag kväll

and she is stunned when Elle repeats it back verbatim. Astonished, Christine repeats the line, which Elle sings back perfectly. Her pronunciation isn't greatly improved in Swedish but it is unquestionably better than her English. More to the point, Elle's intonation is perfect.

"Try another language," Thomas says softly, bringing Anna onto his lap. "Try Italian."

Christine sings the first line *Tutti amano sabato sera* and Elle repeats. Christine repeats the line again and Elle sings it more clearly. By the fourth and final line, Elle is enunciating the words perfectly.

"Try German."

Christine starts to sing, *Eider man hat dem Samstag abend,* then stops herself. "Do we really want her singing in German?"

"Right, then. Try French."

Christine sings the first line, *Tout le monde aime Samedi soir* and Elle is singing along before she can start the second line.

"If I didn't know better, I'd say the DNA was surfacing. In what other languages do you know this song?"

"Well, Nigerian...."

"Nigerian?" Thomas looks at her incredulously. "Why on God's Earth?"

"It's a Nigerian Folk Song," she says simply, then sings.

Bobo waro fero Satodeh,
Bobo waro fero satodeh,
Bobowaro, bobowaro, bobowaro, bobowaro,
Bobowaro fero Satodeh

and Elle mimics the sounds with astonishing precision.

"Something's happening," Christine says to Thomas. She kisses Elle on the top of her head, and then repeats the gesture with Anna as they move off the couch. In a family of twins, there can never be just one kiss, one compliment, one endearment. "If nothing else," she continues, watching her daughters as they search through the toy chest for something of interest, "I now understand that Elle has a gift and not an impediment."

"She will still need to be able to speak clearly in English. People are going to want to understand her."

"Of course. But think how much easier it will be for us to help hone her gift rather than correct a handicap." She unfastens her hairclip and exchanges it for Anna's headband, so that Elle and Anna aren't wearing their hair in the same fashion. "I have also just understood that Anna and Elle will move along diverse tracks."

CHAPTER TWENTY-FOUR

It rained last night, and the last traces of summer have been washed away. Christine looks out over the Arno Valley and sees clouds rising from the basin floor, water evaporating, a reverse cloud process. She wonders if the warm weather will return, or if this is the first of the cold that will accompany them through the winter. Last night she put extra covers on all their beds but still found the girls in bed with them this morning. She was grateful for the extra body heat. How those little bodies radiate!

She contemplates putting away their light summer clothes and bringing out their sweaters and jackets, but every year she has changed their wardrobes at the first weather change, the weather has laughed at her and has reverted immediately. Perhaps it would be worth the effort to have a few more weeks of sun? She pulls down a sweater for herself and Thomas, the white Irish fishing sweater she loves, and searches for a couple of sweaters for the girls, too. Maybe she can find room in their dressers for clothes for both seasons. The walk she had planned for the morning will have to be postponed until the ground dries. If they have to stay indoors today, Christine figures, she might as well try to organize their clothes.

She pulls down a big box of old clothes that Anne gave her last spring for dress up, and rummages through it, enjoying the feel of crushed velvet and taffeta in her hands. It will be a perfect distraction for the girls while she packs and unpacks clothes. She puts on a large, floppy hat and calls to her daughters. "Who wants to dress up?"

Allegra has the morning off as she worked late last night. Thomas and Christine were at a dinner that Electra had arranged with a group of expats living in Florence, local people interested in children's rights. Most of the evening had been a pleasant waste of time, but toward the end of the evening, she had spoken to a couple who were not only serious about their wish to help, they had ideas and funding to back it. Christine has agreed to meet them for drinks this evening with Electra. She hopes Thomas will be able to join them.

Anna and Elle are wholly absorbed with the costumes in the box, and Christine has time to work. She removes the lightweight summer outfits and puts them into a big box, leaving out the little tee-shirts and cotton trousers that can be used mid-season, if it warms up at all. From time to time, the twins arrive in a new costume, wanting her approval. She puts on the airs of an important fashion consultant and praises their choices as if they were auditioning for Valentino's replacement.

Christine doesn't even bother to check if anything can be worn again. They are growing so fast, nothing she puts away now will fit them next spring. She boxes everything up to give to her favorite charity—a local group of women who collect Italian summer clothes to bring to Kanpur in India each year. The winter clothes she packs neatly into a separate box which she has decided she will keep for Elizabeth's first child. She fondles a favorite little dress that Rosa made in two different colors, blue with white smocking and white with blue smocking, and knows that she will keep a few things, just as her mother did, to remind the twins when they are older just how small they once were.

Christine has found herself thinking about her mother in the past several weeks. Odd bits of memory pop up like arbitrary, unannounced visits: the time her mother prompted her for a third grade spelling test or bought her a new herbal shampoo she had been wanting. Christine hasn't tried to make sense of the memories, has just been grateful for their appearance, but today, as one memory after another floods her mind, she wonders why the reminiscence after a long, empty interlude.

It could be anything. It might be her hormones bouncing back to earth or Anne's pneumonia stirring up memories of her mother's illness, although the dissimilarities are greater than the similarities. As cruel as it is to think, Anne is an old woman at the end of her life, and pneumonia is a tired body's response to its declining ability to function. Christine's mother was in the prime of her life, struck down by an aberrant illness that had nothing to do with the natural process. What do these two endings have in common?

Christine doesn't know which is worse, the long, drawn-out ending that makes one look forward to the release by death, or the abrupt loss that keeps all its suffering for after the person has gone. Ideally, if one could plan the perfect ending, it would be to live one's life to its fullest, then lie down to rest and not awaken. But even as she drafts this scenario, she knows it isn't ideal, not for those who are left behind. It seems the suffering is a necessary part in order to let go of loved ones. Would she want to keep Thomas with her longer, if she knew he was suffering? A little longer, yes. Time to say goodbye. Time for one last embrace. Time to erase any last regrets.

But how long is a little longer? A day? A week? A month? A year? She knows she would want to keep him with her for as long as she could. An impossible balance between love and loss. Is there ever the right time to say goodbye? If she were ill, she would want her ending to be swift. But how fast? A day? A week? A month? A year? The faster she disappeared from Thomas, the longer he would have to mourn alone. Despite the impossibility of concluding this bizarre discourse, she understands that both parties are destined to suffer, unless they are indifferent. Loving someone is being willing to let them go, not postponing the inevitable. Or not?

Elle runs to her in an oversized hat that Anne must have worn to someone's wedding a half-century before, holding up a photo for her scrutiny. "Mommy, I finded a picture of us in your tummy."

Christine understands that this is the moment she has been waiting for, the first question. She is surprised it has happened this young, but since Thomas told them she had a baby in her tummy—and then had to explain the reversal of that story—their interest in babies in tummies has come up in doll play and bedtime stories. She reminds herself to answer their specific questions, nothing more, nothing less. She wishes she could involve Thomas in the conversation. He would know what to say. But he is spending the day with his mother and mustn't be disturbed.

Christine studies the photo. It takes her a moment to remember which pregnancy this was. From the look on her face, which is filled with uncompromised happiness, she assumes it is her first pregnancy. The tall mountains in the background make her think the photo must have been taken in Nepal. She frowns at the memory. They had taken a large gourd and had tucked it under her sweater, to make her look more pregnant than she was. She had never shown like that in reality.

How she had blamed herself for not staying home, had insisted she was invincible, could travel with Thomas to the far corners of the earth without compromising her health. How sure she had been that some foreign bug had caused her first miscarriage. She carried that guilt with her well into the second pregnancy, staying at home, a little compulsively it might be said in retrospect, staying out of cinemas where she might contract an illness, walking instead of riding a crowded bus, washing her hands obsessively. All for nothing, it turned out: her body betraying her again, rejecting the foreign body inside her at precisely four months. She had lost her baby again, and had lost months of travelling and working with Thomas, all for nothing.

Anna is tottering toward them in too-large, too-high-heeled shoes. "Mommy, we is in your tummy, look!"

"You ladies look like you are dressed for a tea party. Come, we'll have cookies and tea and I will tell you about that photograph."

They had been hungrier for biscuits than details. Once they knew that it wasn't them in her tummy, they had lost interest. They didn't ask who had been in their mother's tummy nor why he or she wasn't here to play with them; nor did they ask to see photos of themselves in her tummy. The only question they asked was how many of Rosa's *biscotti di Prato* they could each have.

T he day Boots had her kittens, Anna wanted to know how babies were born. This time Thomas is with Christine, and with a quick glance over their heads he mouths *be specific*. In terms they can understand, Christine explains that a mother and a father come together to create a little seed, that grows into a baby inside the mother's tummy.

"In your case," Thomas explains, "the mother and father nurtured two seeds, and you grew side by side in your mother's tummy."

Christine continues. "When you were fully grown, and tired of being crowed into one small place, you pushed your way out of your mother's tummy."

"You licked us clean, like Boots?" Anna wants to know.

"No, with human babies the hospital nurses do the washing up, and then they give the clean babies to the mother to hold."

"Were we tiny like the kittens?"

"A wee bit bigger," Christine answers.

"Were our eyes squeezed shut?"

"They were. But you opened your eyes more quickly than kittens do."

"Can we keep the kittens?"

"Can we?"

Thomas and Christine smile conspiratorially. They know Rosa will feed the cats, regardless of what they say. "The cats can live in the garden."

301

"But if it rains?" Elle wants to know.

"We will keep a window open in the cantina. They can come and go as they like. Would you like to see the kittens again? Will you promise not to frighten the mother?"

CHAPTER
TWENTY-FIVE

Anne sits by the window in her bedroom. She can't see the view, can't see her reflection in the glass, but the sun feels good on her face. It's an autumn sun, she can tell from the angle it slants through the glass at midday, and it doesn't burn her eyes the way it did in summer. She coughs. She doesn't need her sight to know the color is bad, but despite it all, she is feeling better today than she did yesterday.

She presses the intercom button that summons Rosa, and asks her to invite Christine and the children to her room. She hasn't wanted visitors, but if she doesn't invite them in now, when she has a bit of energy, there may not be another occasion.

"Grandmother!" The girls chorus, twins in all things.

"How are you feeling, Anne?" Christine ushers the girls in, but lingers at the door. The girls have been playing dress-up again, and Christine has let them stay in their costumes, hoping to elicit a smile from her mother-in-law.

"Better, thank you. Come in."

"Make a wish!" Anna says, handing her Grandmother a perfect halo of white dandelion seeds, which Anne crushes as she grasps to understand what it is.

"You could blow me away with one wish," Anne says. Before anyone is tempted to correct her, she continues, "I would like to play a game with the girls."

"Dress up?" Elle asks. She puts her hand on her waist and juts out her hip, mimics a model's pose for her grandmother, but the gesture goes unnoticed.

Anne pats the cushion beside her on the window seat, and the girls clamor to sit beside her. "We are going to play jewelry shop," she says. "Christine, please hand me the beauty case beside the bed."

Christine knows this beauty case: it contains all of Anne's jewelry. She brings it to her mother-in-law and sets it carefully on the table next to where she sits.

"Do you girls know how to take turns?"

"I do!"

"Me, too!"

"Then we will begin shopping right now." She reaches into her pocket for a handful of pennies, and separates them from the collection of pills she's stopped taking. She hands a pile of pennies to both of her granddaughters. "Who would like to go first?"

"Me!" Two hands shoot up in the air. "Me!"

"Christine, you are going to have to help me, dear."

"Since you have given them coins, let's flip a penny." Christine borrows a coin from Anna. "Heads or tails?" Thomas has taught them this ritual, which resolves all sorts of questions from first baths to bedtime stories.

"Elle has won and gets first choice." Anne opens the lid to the beauty case and instructs her granddaughter to choose her favorite piece. Elle picks up an enormous gold bracelet with emerald and diamond accents. Anne fingers the piece and reminisces, "Ian bought me this the year we were at The Hague. I had admired it in a shop window on our walk home from some function, and he must have gone back the next morning to buy it for me. It was on my plate at lunchtime. That's how it was. He might forget my birthday or an anniversary, but if I saw something I liked, it was mine. I learned to be careful about admiring things out loud."

"My turn?" Anna says, worried.

"Not so fast," Anne admonishes. "Elle hasn't paid me yet."

Elle gives her grandmother a penny, and reconsiders, adds a kiss, as she has been taught to do when receiving a gift.

"Now it is your turn, Anna."

Anna takes longer to decide and selects another bracelet, as substantial as her sister's but entirely diamonds. Christine swallows hard, as she listens to her mother-in-law's recollection of the provenance of this piece. She hopes she will be able to explain to the girls that these are not playthings, not to be confused with the costume jewelry they are used to mauling: the brightly colored pop beads; the long strands of fake pearls. Decades will pass before they will be old enough to wear these important pieces. She is not even sure she herself could pull it off.

"My turn?" Elle asks, holding up another penny.

"Let's give your mother a turn first."

"Me?" Christine answers, incredulous.

"She don't have pennies," Elle says.

"She'll be in my debt then," Anne says.

"I am deeply indebted, and always will be."

"Then choose," Anne says, already beginning to tire. She isn't sure how long she will be able to play this game with her granddaughters. She lifts the top drawer of the box to reveal a second layer, like chocolates. "Anything your heart desires."

Christine thinks, *I would like you to get well again, really well, to be the woman you used to be, before you got tired and old. I would like you to see again, to see how beautiful your granddaughters are, how adorable they are dressed up in your old finery. I would desire you to be the mother Thomas remembers and loves.* Her eyes cloud, her sight blurs, her prayer recedes. She reaches into the box and selects an Art Deco baguette-cut brooch she has always admired, more extraordinary for the craftsmanship than the value of the carats. It isn't the most important piece of jewelry in the case, or the most valuable, but if she's to accept a gift from her mother-in-law, it should be one she has always enjoyed seeing her wear. She also wants something she will be able to wear without feeling self-conscious.

"Ian inherited this pin from his mother," Anne says, when Christine hands her the brooch. "I've always loved this piece."

She doesn't let go, and Christine begins to wonder if she's changed her mind about giving it away, the way she is holding it, weighing it, running her fingers over the rectangle-shaped diamonds and sapphire inserts. Abruptly, she thrusts out her hand, bumping against Christine. "It's yours now," she says resignedly. "Wear it in good health."

"I will think of you every time I wear it."

"I hope you will wear it every day."

Elle holds up a penny. "Now me?" she asks.

"Yes, darling. Now you."

Christine finds two shoe box tops and lines them with cotton batting from Anne's bedside table, so the pieces her daughters are acquiring won't bump against each other and scratch. She sets a little table beside Anna, whose shoe box lid keeps falling off her lap, and helps Elle organize her growing collection so that there is space for the various pieces. Elle's pieces are multi-colored. She hasn't restricted herself to a single gem. She has chosen jewelry that houses gold and diamonds, diamonds and sapphires, emeralds and pearls. Anna, on the other hand, has selected no gold, no emeralds, sapphires, rubies or amethyst. Her shoe box lid holds only diamonds. They refract light from the window and bluster blindingly. Christine can imagine their luminescence against a simple, black velvet evening dress.

"If you are getting tired, Anne?"

"I believe I am." She closes her eyes and asks, "How many pennies do you girls have left?"

"One," Elle says.

"Two," says Anna.

"You can each choose another piece and then we'll close shop." Anne rests her head against the wall while her granddaughters make their final choices. She doesn't bother fingering what they have chosen, and she is too tired to recount another story. She has enjoyed this game but she is looking forward to getting back in bed. "Now you, Christine."

Christine comes forward to select a second piece, but Anne closes the box. She holds it on her lap, her hands grasping the handle, and then with a strength she didn't know she still possessed, she hands the box to her daughter-in-law. "Here. The rest is for you."

Christine receives the beauty case as if she's been given a treasure chest. It weighs in her hands as much for the significance of the gesture as for the weight of the jewels. As she staggers under the weight of the gift, she notices that her mother-in-law looks lighter. "I don't know what to say," Christine starts.

"You are a good wife to my son, an excellent mother to my granddaughters. You are the most precious jewel of all."

Christine wishes she could leave the room and quickly, to maintain her dignity and not dissolve into tears in front of everyone. "Thank you, Anne." It isn't enough to match the magnitude of the occasion but nothing she can say will be enough. She repeats the inadequate phrase. "Thank you."

"You will help the girls take care of their jewelry?" Anne moves back toward her bed, fumbles with the covers.

Christine steps forward to assist. "I will." She folds back the covers so that Anne can enter more easily, then pulls them up; adjusts the pillows behind her back, somehow keeping back the tears. "We will put things away securely for the next couple of years, won't we girls? We will wear Grandmother's jewelry when we are all grown up."

"I will sleep with that charming image," Anne says, resting her arms on top of the covers.

"Come on, Elle. Anna? Let's let your Grandmother rest now."

"Thank you, Grandmother Anne," Elle says, leaning up to kiss her grandmother's papery cheek.

"Thank you Grandmother," Anna repeats, adding her kiss. She takes the last penny out of her pocket and slips it into her Grandmother's hand. "If you wants to buy things back."

She could have slept all afternoon if Thomas hadn't awakened her to make her get out of bed to sit. The lunch that Rosa has brought sits untouched on its tray. She has no appetite for anything but sleep and doesn't understand why they keep waking her to give her food she doesn't want. She would like to go back to bed but Thomas insists she sit up, even though she has had her heparin shot against clotting. She is tired and is considering disobeying orders to sit in the chair when she hears Thomas's footfall in the hallway. She fumbles for the oxygen hose to fit into her nose but the door to her room opens before she can accomplish her deception.

"Would you like help with that, Mother?"

Thomas tries to keep the annoyance out of his voice, but they both know what he is thinking. He had inserted the oxygen tube against her will an hour ago, but she removed it as soon as he left. They both know she will do the same again, yet he can't leave her alone.

She recalls the half-dead plant Thomas kept on his window sill one long ago winter, a January poinsettia that had lost all its leaves, which she had placed by the trash in the alley. He had watered and nurtured that dying plant throughout the long winter, and in spring, when it showed its first green, he made her admit she was wrong. She had agreed with him, and had marveled at its rich foliage, but a part of her continued to believe the plant would have been better off left to die. In nature, a dormant period is to be expected, but she would hate to be kept alive after she had lost her foliage. She must be firm with Thomas or he will insist on keeping her alive beyond her season. "Let's not insist with the oxygen, Bunny," she says gently.

Thomas sits down beside her at the window. He remembers the various windowseats around the world where they passed their hours together, like *miradores*, safe indoors, watching the world perform its wonders just beyond the looking glass. She had read to him, had kept him company, in every country they had visited. She had taken his small hand as they ventured out into the folly, had tried to help him interpret the marvels they encountered. He realized later that she had shielded his eyes from the things he was too young to see, but later, when he was old enough, those things became part of her narrative, as well. He had never felt afraid in her company. He had found the world an exciting place, its arms wide open and welcoming if he ventured forward, unafraid to look.

He looks at his mother beside him on the window seat. A ray of sunlight breaking through a rainy day has mercilessly highlighted the web of wrinkles on her face. Where has the dynamo gone? When did she leave? Why didn't he notice?

Change: by the time we notice it, how long has it been present? When does love atrophy with the weight of obligation? When does it become a burden, a test of tolerance? Who has replaced his mother with this old, white-masked geisha sitting so still beside him, as if afraid to move? Who has forgotten to redden her lips with color?

He looks out the window at Florence in the distance, at the Brunelleschi dome rising magnificently above the red tile roofs of this beautiful town. In a large city, like London, he thinks, where the buildings are tall and the view eclipsed, it is easier to get turned around, to lose one's way. It is comforting to have the Cathedral in view from wherever one looks: a focal point by which one can find one's way through the narrow, pedestrian streets.

A large red umbrella and a pair of matching boots emerge from the loggia. From the way it moves across the garden, Thomas gathers it is Anna. An instant later, another oversized red umbrella and boots stumble to catch up. It is a comic sight: two umbrellas and four boots traversing the garden. He would like to share it with his mother, to make her laugh, but she can't smile at what she can't see.

He hums to himself, and then can't stop himself from singing:

If you want the things you love you must have showers
So when you hear thunder don't run under a tree
There'll be pennies from heaven for you and for me

He sees her frown and stops singing. "Would you like me to read to you, Mother?" Their roles have reversed but their lives are the same. It is the change that they hold onto that has become habit, their routine. "Is there something you would like to hear?"

"Would you bring me—" she pauses to let pass a fit of coughing "—my children?"

"Elle and Anna? They are in the garden. I'll—"

She stops him from rising by laying her hand on his arm. "No, *my* orphans." She coughs again deeply, a noisy release of air that quakes her entire body, like it has hit a minefield. "Bring me the albums."

Thomas carries a heavy stack of photo albums into his mother's room. He hasn't brought them all, she won't be able to see them anyway, but if she insists, he can return to the library for the rest. The futility of the errand weighs on him as much as the books in his arms, but there is so little he can do for her, it might as well be this as something else.

"Where shall I set them, Mother?" Every surface of her room is covered: bottles of medicine, ointments, measuring spoons; a box of syringes and a roll of cotton; disinfectant; bottles of water, which she isn't drinking, Thomas notices. He wonders how she has been taking her medicine. He pushes the blood pressure apparatus to one side, next to the spare oxygen tank, and deposits the albums on her dresser top. "Which one do you want?"

"The first one," she coughs, "the one that starts with Rikki."

Thomas swallows. This is going to be more painful than he had thought. He looks out the window at the wind in the trees. Just the other day it was summer. Overnight it has turned cold and rainy. He wonders if he can postpone this unpleasant journey into the past by claiming work responsibilities. He looks back at his mother, sees her face lifted, turned slightly toward him, waiting, and he knows he can't disappoint her. He opens the first album to the first page, and there is his nemesis, looking him straight in the eyes and smiling. Thomas studies the boy who has haunted him all these years, but can't find anything that speaks of the lies or the desire to play with fire. He sees only the falsely bright smile, the attempt at bravado, nothing that he hasn't seen a hundred times in the villages he has visited.

He flips a page and recognizes a street boy from Naples wearing that same disguise of streetwise overconfidence. Thomas remembers the family his mother found to adopt him. There is a letter stuck into corner angles with a later photo of the same boy, holding a *laurea in giurisprudenza*. Thomas wonders if he ever became a judge. He should look him up. He flips the page and recognizes another child, then another. He has never looked at his mother's photographs, not even when she laid them all out for him to see, page after miraculous page in these albums. He carries it to her, opens the book so that its pages are turned to face her, but she waves it away.

"Read me the names of my children," she says, leaning her head back against the wainscoting and closing her eyes. "Slowly," she cautions, resting her hand on his. "I want to see each of them clearly, one last time."

CHAPTER TWENTY-SIX

"I have developed the photograph of your daughters, and would like to bring it to you today," Kate says to Christine, "if you aren't busy."

"I am alone with the children this morning." She doesn't explain that her babysitter's schedule has become erratic since Allegra and her fiancé have started catering parties. She is expecting Allegra to tell her that she will quit soon to work full time with Giorgio, once he quits his day job at the St. Regis. In the meantime Christine is happy for whatever hours Allegra can give them. It is easier now that the children are older. Christine isn't overwhelmed by them, as she was when they were newborns. She thrills in their company. In January, when they turn three, they will start nursery school, and she will have time to pursue her work again. She already knows she will miss them. "It will be impossible to have an uninterrupted conversation, but I would love to see you, if you don't mind the disruption."

"I remember interrupted conversations."

They laugh, a splash of Champagne in two slender flutes. "Do you remember when they stop?"

"Do they stop?" They share another drop of laughter, the foam overflowing. "What time should I come?"

313

"Whenever you like. The girls and I have been making biscuits. The last two trays are in the oven now."

"I am making cookies to bring to you!"

Christine has time to tidy up the kitchen in the three-quarters of an hour it takes Kate to drive across the Arno Valley, and to change the girls out of their flour-dusted and butter-sticky clothes into clean outfits. She dusts herself free of flour as the doorbell rings, and hurries down the stairs to find that Elle and Anna have already opened the gate.

"I would like to offer my condolences," Kate says, after she has greeted the children and has watched them run into the garden in pursuit of a very fat, slow-moving cat. She follows Christine into the loggia where the lemon trees line the back wall, where they will receive sun all winter but not frost. Christine has moved a small round table so that it sits in a rectangle of sun. "I only met your mother-in-law that one time we were here for dinner," Kate continues, "but it was easy to appreciate the woman she had been."

"She was a grand person," Christine says, sitting next to Kate so she can look out onto the garden, to keep an eye on the children. "Would you like to know what her last words were to me? *'Anticipate each goodbye, as if it were already behind you like a winter that's passed.'* Rilke."

"A remarkable woman."

"Yes. A bright light burned out." Christine needs to replace the end image of a tired old woman who died in her sleep, with the vital woman she had been for the majority of her life.

"How are you managing?" Kate doesn't want to dwell on unhappy subjects, but neither can she ignore what needs to be said. "I heard you lost your baby."

"Yes, well—" Christine sits up straighter, tucks her legs beneath her chair. "It wasn't unexpected."

"Does that make it easier or harder to bear?"

"I can't say really. I've never not miscarried." She attempts a little laugh, but it doesn't illicit a smile from her guest. "We are, how can I say—adjusting. You know how the Rilke poem continues? *...underneath these winters is such an*

314

interminable winter, that only by hibernating can your heart survive. I think that describes our state. We are hibernating, until we can make sense of our loss. Losses."

"Understandably."

"The girls can't quite grasp the concept of death—which is just as well. They keep asking when their grandmother will return. It is all quite disconcerting, especially for Thomas." She had overheard him that morning in his study, reciting Rilke's sonnet to Orpheus:

> *climb ... the way a singer climbs,*
> *in a voice rich with loss and celebration of that*
> *pure connection.*
> *And here, below ... in the empire of bitter endings,*
> *be the clinking glass that, even as it shatters, rings.*
> *Be ... just this once, be all you were meant to*
> *become*

"I can imagine how hard it is for all of you. It couldn't have helped to have had the conference so close after the funeral."

"We were tempted to cancel the conference, to postpone it, but Thomas decided to go ahead with it." Christine waves her hand over a plate of cookies to vanquish a dragonfly, and then stops herself. "Electra and Julian had worked so hard, all the participants had their flights booked, had programmed their time to attend the conference. Perhaps if it had been the fourth or fifth conference we could have postponed it, but Thomas feared we wouldn't be taken seriously if we cancelled the first one." The dragonfly settles on the edge of the table, a delicate damsel dressed in iridescent blues and greens. Sapphires and emeralds, Christine thinks. "In the end, it was Thomas's decision, and he chose to honor his mother's memory by moving forward with the charity work she had instilled in him, rather than staying home and indulging his sorrow in private."

"Your husband is an extraordinary man."

"Yes, he is." Loss, they both agreed, is a private ordeal, not an excuse to postpone their commitments. "Still, there were moments." Christine moves the tea and biscuits she has prepared from the trolley to the table. "Thank goodness Electra was there, making sure everything ran according to plan." In spite of herself, the image of Electra sending everyone off on bicycles makes her smile.

Kate brings a round tin out of her bag and sets it on the table. "My contribution. What we Americans do best: Chocolate Chip Cookies."

"Lovely." Christine lifts the pot of tea. "Lemon or milk?"

"Lemon, please." Kate selects a *Pepparkarkor* biscuit from the pretty blue and white plate. "It was kind of you to invite Elizabeth to the conference."

"Elizabeth and Stephen were helpful, too. They were only there for one night—they couldn't ask for days off—but they fielded important questions that would have otherwise fallen onto Thomas's already burdened shoulders."

Elle runs from the garden, her movements awkward and slowed by the cat in her arms. "Mommy, can we have a biscuit?"

"Are you asking for you and Anna or for you and the cat?"

"Me and Anna."

"Would you like to picnic under the arbor?" Christine wraps two cookies into a napkin and hands them to her daughter. Kate wraps chocolate chip cookies into another napkin and hands them to Elle. "Can you manage all that?"

Elle brightens, hoists the cat higher in her arms, and tucks the napkin-filled cookies into the front of her bib overalls. The two women watch as Elle runs back across the garden.

"So, all things considered, you would say the conference was a success?"

"Yes, although it is hard to determine success in a field as vast as children's rights. There is so much work to do, even a big step forward measures painfully small in light of what needs to be done."

"How true."

"We invited participants from many fields, which made for lively debates. One man in particular, Ole Sorensen, is a real Renaissance man: a poet, musician, writer—of journalism, theatre, children's literature, art and architectural criticism—"

"My goodness!"

"Yes, a powerful intellectual. He became the unofficial leader of the group."

"You never know what will happen when you put people together."

"True. The dynamics of a conference shift according to who is present, especially in a small conference like this one. Sorensen raised some interesting observations although I doubt if they will lead to anything practical. He ran off on a tangent about the presence of *evil* in the world. It is an intriguing concept, and although I disagreed with him at the start, I ended up seeing his point."

"Which is?"

"That evil can and does exist in its own right."

"Just as a person can be born good, he can also be born evil?"

"Precisely. It doesn't all depend on social malfunctions, as I had assumed. Anyway, none of us got to bed early that night. We stayed at the dinner table long after the candles had burnt out." She remembers the circles under Thomas's eyes, was surprised that he hadn't curtailed the discussion, had just let it run out of steam of its own accord. "But Electra had us up on time the next morning, with lots of hot coffee and fresh croissants, and the staff were as cheerful as if they had been given a day off instead of working overtime."

"Electra told me she was helping you plan another meeting."

"Yes, for the week after Christmas. We are working on the academic calendar, since many of the participants are professors. I need to call Electra. Is she in Florence?"

"No. She's stayed on in England. She called yesterday to say that she and Julian would be coming down next week." Kate sets down her tea and frowns.

"You don't look thrilled."

"It's an awfully busy time of year for us, that's all. We try not to have guests at the end of October, when we are preparing for the harvest."

"Grapes or olives or both?"

"Fortunately, only olives, but it's still a tremendous undertaking for us." She helps herself to another cookie. "To be honest, I was counting on Electra's help to organize the workers, but I won't feel free to ask her to help if she has company."

"I imagine Julian would love to help harvest olives."

"You're joking?" Kate looks into Christine's face for an expression of irony. "I would never think to ask."

"You'd be surprised. I often find Julian wearing a bee's bonnet, cleaning the hives himself, or wiping down his horse after he rides. He's a bit of a Renaissance man himself."

"I would have assumed he was squeamish about getting his hands dirty."

"That is what he would like us to believe. He has a title, a reputation he feels obliged to maintain, but Julian isn't lazy—and I suspect he'd do anything Electra asked of him."

"They do seem to have grown rather close."

There is a question in her statement that Christine doesn't know how to address. At the conference, despite the professional facade, Christine had seen hints of intimacy, a shared smile, a private joke, a lingering gaze when they assumed no one was watching. Christine might not have noticed it herself if Electra hadn't brought her into her confidence. The day before the conference started Electra realized that they had prepared one room too few to host their guests, and rather than send the staff into a tizzy of last minute cleaning, rather than asking to use the spare room in Thomas's cottage, she changed the sheets on the bed in her room and moved in with Julian. It was only for one night, to accommodate her sister and brother-in-law, but after they left, when Christine passed Electra's room, she saw it wasn't in use.

How much of this information can she share with Electra's mother? Kate seems open-minded but it isn't Christine's place to share Electra's personal details. Tactfully, Christine changes the subject. "How good of you to stop by for a visit. You must be terribly busy."

"No, not at all. Now that the wedding has passed, until we begin the harvest, the only thing that dictates my schedule is the light."

"How delightful." Christine tries to imagine a day dictated by light. "My day is ruled by the routine—or lack of routine—of two small children." She gestures out into the garden where Anna and Elle are dressing the cat in their doll's outfit.

"I remember those days, the need for a schedule—and an alarm clock."

"The dreaded alarm clock."

"Until the girls were grown, we were up every day of the week at six-thirty—even Sundays, as our dog couldn't grasp the concept of a day off—to have breakfast together before we drove them to school. The best thing about having grown daughters is that the alarm clock is never set. We wake when we want to. We've even trained Clover to sleep later in the mornings." She sets down her tea cup and reaches into her large purse. Carefully, she brings out a manila envelope, and lays it on the table, where Christine can reach it.

"I can't wait." Christine knows what is in the envelope. She has been looking forward to seeing the photograph of her children, as if she will be seeing them for the first time. Her expectations are unreasonably high, she knows, and she prepares herself for disappointment.

"You have barely started." Kate takes another biscuit. She loves the fusion of ginger and cinnamon. She watches Christine's excited reluctance as she carefully opens the flap to the envelope. Kate feels the same way when she develops her prints, that moment of excited tension before the photograph presents itself from the tray of chemicals. Sometimes the photograph is as she has imagined it to be, but just as often she has captured something she hasn't known she was seeking. She wonders if Christine's eye is keen enough to catch it.

"Oh my goodness," Christine says, when she finally has found the courage to slide the photograph out of its envelope. "How did you capture this?"

"To be honest, I didn't notice until I developed the print. I saw their arms crossed one over the other, which made a lovely symmetry, but I hadn't realized what they were doing when I took the photo."

"I have watched my babies sleep a thousand times, and I have never seen them sucking each other's thumbs."

"You know the expression, *as close as twins*—" She doesn't finish her sentence. "So what story shall we put behind your photo?"

"What do you mean?"

"The light is perfect, as soft and as fresh as on Raffaello's Madonna. I thought I could photograph you with your daughters, if you don't have anything better to do."

CHAPTER TWENTY-SEVEN

"You're kidding?" Thomas is unloading a demijohn of newly pressed olive oil that Julian has driven across town from Electra's farm. "What convinced you? What decided for you that Electra's the one? Other than her golden hair?"

Julian slams down the boot of the car with more force than necessary. He isn't entirely familiar with Electra's car yet. He dusts his hands on the front of his trousers. "It was the way she poured tea."

"Tea? You're kidding."

Julian holds open the front gate, and then shuts it after Thomas has passed through. "You know the service I have? Greatest-grandmother's arm-breaking silver? I can barely lift it, and when I do, the tea always spills down the nozzle when I pour. At least as much goes out of the cup as in."

"Yes, I seem to remember." Thomas has rested the demijohn on the table. Later, after he has filled the container in the kitchen, he will store the rest in the cantina. "But what does Electra have to do with the price of tea in China?"

"She saw I was having trouble pouring the tea, and without a blush, she wiped up the spilt tea with her napkin, took the pot from me and finished pouring our tea herself. She said, 'My mother has a tea pot that does the same thing.

The trick is not to hurry, to pour slowly, to not let it get ahead of itself. After all,' she said tenably, after she finished filling both cups without spilling a drop, 'we are drinking tea, which is meant to be relaxing. We're not racing toward a finish line.'"

"And that's what decided it for you?"

"It is," Julian answered. "And you know another thing? Electra's grandmother has taken a fancy to me. She's a funny old bird, quite a lot like my grandmother, actually."

"I remember her from Elizabeth and Stephen's wedding."

"I have invited her up to The Surdans. Electra warned me she doesn't travel anymore, but you know what? She's accepted the invitation. She has asked Electra to accompany her."

"What will you do with her? From all I've heard, she won't be an easy guest."

"Oh, sugar! I'll treat her like the Queen. *'Have you come far?'* Maybe I'll even introduce her to the Queen. Whatever it takes to win Electra's affection."

"I think the Queen will have little to do with you winning Electra's affections."

"I think you are right. This girl and I are going to make it to the finish line together at a very comfortable pace."

"Have you told her how serious you are?"

"Not yet. But I hope to next weekend, if the occasion arises. You'll be my best man?"

"Always have been, always will be." He smiles at his friend, pleased as peaches at his overdue good fortune. "You may have Electra's entire family present at The Surdans."

"How's that?"

"Electra and I have convinced Kate to photograph the hungry mothers and children of the world."

"Unbelievable!"

"I told her that the book sales alone will feed a small village. She has agreed to start with the children in Naples, with the gypsy mothers on the streets. If it works out as we hope it will, she and her husband will accompany Christine and me to East Africa in the spring."

"Absolutely brilliant. Good that you and Christine will travel again. What will you do with the twins?"

"Didn't Electra tell you? Elle and Anna will be staying with you two."

"Goodness! Where?"

"Here. Electra thought it would be easier on the twins to not move them. Besides, she wants to get the feel of Mother's house, if we are going to reinstate the Open House."

"How's that?"

"Monthly gatherings that can build support for our causes. Electra has agreed to help organize it."

"Won't it be a lot of work?"

"Is it a lot of work for you at The Surdans?"

"It is, and I have the staff. You can't expect Rosa to feed everyone, can you?"

"Rosa has suggested we hire Allegra's fiancé to handle the dinner parties. He's used to cooking for crowds, and he has started a small catering business of his own. Allegra can help, too."

"Anne would be pleased to think of her house full of intelligent, motivated people working to resolve this long-overdue problem."

"Our Fathers would be pleased."

"Who art in Heaven. I can almost see them smiling down on us."

"Elle? Anna? Your mommy and I would like to talk with you."

Anna scrambles down from the window seat where she has been reading to her stuffed owl, James. Elle drops a handful of glass marbles into her pockets, dusts her hands on the front of her tee-shirt, and walks to join them. "Are we naughty?" she asks.

Thomas wonders again where they learn these phrases. "Of course not. Mommy and I just want to talk with you."

Thomas boosts Anna up onto the sofa next to Elle, and sits beside her. Christine has brought a pitcher of milk and cheese toast to the table, trying to downplay the importance of their reunion. She seats herself beside Anna, then reconsiders and lifts her daughter onto her lap. She has thought long and hard about how she would like to start this conversation, and even though she has worried that it might link an unpleasant occasion with an important event they will face together, she has decided to proceed with her example. It gives her a solid point of departure.

"Do you remember when you went too close to the river, Elle, and fell and scratched your arms and legs?"

Elle nods once, keeps her chin lowered. "Baby birds."

"That's right. Do you remember what Mommy and Daddy did after that to help keep you and Anna safe?"

"Mother may I?"

"That's right. We put up that long fence around the edge of the lawn, and if you wanted to leave the enclosed area, what did you have to do?"

"We ask: 'Mother May I?'"

"That's right," Thomas proceeds. They had created a large enclosed space that wouldn't feel like a playpen but which would give the girls clear boundary lines. "Did you like the game?"

"Yes!" they chorused.

"Did it keep you safe?" he asked.

"Yes!"

"Your Mommy and I want to build another Mother May I fence, one you can't see but which you can always count on to keep you safe. Do you want to play?"

"Yes!"

"OK. Here are the rules. Whenever you find you have a question—"

"A question about anything—" Christine leans forward to add.

"All you have to do is ask, and we will be here as quickly as we can with an answer for you. Does that sound like a fun game?"

"Yes!"

"OK. Let's start our game. Do you remember when Boots had her kittens?" Thomas begins.

"They was tiny!" Anna says, reaching for a piece of toast.

"Tiny!" Elle cups her hands together, measuring their remembered size.

"And do you recall when you asked if you had been little like that?" Thomas continues, his words offered slowly and evenly spaced, as if wanting to allow time between the words to digest what he's saying. "You asked if your eyes were squeezed shut, like the newborn kittens."

Anna nods, scraping the melted cheese from the toast with her bottom teeth. Christine reaches over to stop her, but Thomas intercepts her hand.

"And do you remember when we explained how the kittens were born? How they came out of their mommy's tummy?"

Anna and Elle nod, their attention divided between their father's words and their afternoon snack. Christine wonders if they are listening, if they are following Thomas's train of thought.

"Do you remember when Boots disappeared," Thomas continues, slowly, patiently, "and Rosa found another mommy cat to adopt the kittens, to feed them?"

"But-tons!" Elle pronounces clearly, the hint of a pause between the two Ts.

"We had lots of kittens!" Anna recalls excitedly.

"Six kittens," Elle remembers.

"And do you remember how much Buttons loved Boots' kittens, how she loved them like they were her own?"

"They drinked her milk," Anna recalls.

"They did," Christine confirms, confident that this discussion is proceeding well. "And they loved her as much as she loved them, even though they weren't born from her tummy, even though they were adopted?"

"Where'd Boots go?" Anna wonders.

"We can't be sure, honey," Thomas takes over. "She might have wandered off, smelling some delicious cat food, and couldn't find her way back home. We don't know exactly. But whatever her reasons, it wasn't because she didn't love her kittens. Wherever she is, I am sure she is happy that her babies have been adopted into a loving, happy home."

"You two darling girls are a little like Boots' kittens," Christine says, suddenly in a hurry to deliver her carefully prepared speech. "You were born from another mommy's tummy, but she had to go away, so Daddy and I asked if we could be your parents."

"Did you give us milk?"

"We did!"

"Did you lick us clean?"

"Not exactly. The nurses in the hospital made sure you were all clean before they wrapped you in pretty pink blankets so we could hold you. You were both so tiny," she duplicates the hand cupping gesture Elle has used. "We could practically hold you in the palms of our hands."

"We's adopted," Elle says.

Christine and Thomas look at each other, surprised and impressed that Elle has made the link. "Why yes, you are. Do you know about adoption?"

Elle nods. "Rosa say to Alle's boyfriend we's adopted, like Thumbelina."

"But we's bigger than Thumbelina!" Anna insists indignantly, wiggling her thumbs.

"I don't want to be little like Thumbelina," Elle says, frowning, "always and always."

"You mustn't worry," Thomas says. "You will both grow to be much bigger than Thumbelina. You already have. You'll be more like Mommy and Daddy."

"You are only like Thumbelina because she wasn't born from her mommy's tummy." Christine caresses her daughters' arms, trying to convey the depth of her love with a physical gesture. "Do you know how much your daddy and I love you? Do you know how happy you have made us, coming to be our daughters?"

The girls nod.

"Can I have more cheese toast?" Elle asks.

"You may." Christine passes the plate, and Elle takes another triangle. "Do you have any questions?"

Elle shakes her head, concentrates on the toast.

Anna purses her lips together to make a tiny O, and then says, "Mother May I?"

326

"You may."

"Was Boots our mother?"

"No. Boots is the kittens' mother." Christine understands that this conversation is the first of many. The girls are too young to understand, really. They have grasped more than she and Thomas had anticipated. They have begun an ongoing discussion that will develop and diverge as the girls grow older to understand the more complex concepts of adoption. The questions will continue for as long as they are a family, will alter as the girls come to terms with the nature of their situation. Christine and Thomas will tell them everything they want to know. The only fact they have decided to conceal is that they were found in a trash bin. No good can come from divulging that bit of history. But the rest of the story they will happily share. Today they are just initiating the conversation. Christine continues, as simply as she can explain. "Your mother is a woman, like me."

"Beautiful, like a fairy princess?"

"She must have been very beautiful if she looks like you and Elle."

Elle wiggles out of her parent's embrace, jumps down from the sofa and runs out of the room.

"Where she go to?" Anna asks.

"Elle? I don't know. Thomas, can you go after her?"

"She'll come back." He turns his attention to his other daughter. "Anna, did you want to know where Elle went or your birth mother?" Thomas tries to clarify.

"My bird mother."

"We don't know," Thomas confesses. "But one thing I know for sure is that she would have stayed with you if she could have. I am also sure she went away for her own grown up reasons, not because she didn't want to be with you."

Christine continues quickly, before the lump in her throat makes it impossible to speak. "We are very, very happy that she gave both of you to us, so we could be a family together. I hope you are happy to be our daughters."

Anna nods, and then asks, "Can I have milk?"

"Like Boots? No, I am afraid not, darling," Thomas replies, discouraged by the repetition, afraid that Anna is too young to understand such a complex issue as adoption.

"No, in a glass, like Mommy."

"Of course you may." He reaches for the pitcher. "You may have anything you want, like your Mommy."

Elle runs into the room, waving *Are You My Mother*?

Thomas is perplexed. "Do you want us to read to you now, Elle?"

"No, *I* read." She turns to the last pages of her favorite book. "*You* is my mother," she points to Christine, and then to Thomas. "And *you* is my mother, too." She reaches her hand toward the last triangle of toast on the plate. "Mother, may I?"

"You may."

CHAPTER TWENTY-EIGHT

"**D**o you remember how hot it was the last time we were here?" Thomas asks, getting into bed.

"How could I forget?" Christine pulls the mosquito netting around them, double-checks that all the openings around their bed are closed. She clips it closed with the clothespins she's brought with her, a trick Thomas taught her the first time they travelled together to Africa. Instead of the usual gifts of ballpoint pens and bars of chocolate, Christine has brought the women of the village packs of sturdy wooden clothes pegs, remarkable for their simple diversity. At home Christine uses the pins in a variety of ways: from securing closed a half-full bag of flour or cereal to marking their water glasses with initialed pins so they each won't dirty more than one cup a day.

"It's odd," Thomas remarks, lifting his pillow to make sure there isn't a mosquito or scorpion stowed away, waiting an opportune occasion to sample his blood. "It's the same time of year as when we were here last—what was it, six years ago?"

"I can't recall. Everything before the twins has become a blur. Let's call it b.c., before children, and start counting anew from when they were born."

He ruffles her hair in a way she doesn't like, especially when it is hot, and the wisps will stick out until tomorrow when she can find the comb in her suitcase. "It's still terribly hot, but it's much greener than last time, too." She adjusts her pillow behind her head and lies down beside Thomas. "It's almost like the passing of the old chief ended a drought here, like he was hoarding the little rain there was all for himself."

"With the old chief, anything was possible."

She switches off her little flashlight to conserve the batteries, and speaks into the abrupt darkness. "You like the new chief, then?"

"I rather do, as much as I was prepared to not like him." Thomas finds her hand in the dark.

"He has agreed to work with us, then?"

"He has. He will allow four women from the village to attend the nursing school at Unity University. In addition, he will allow us to sponsor two men to study medicine at Addis Ababa University and six men to enter the Integrated Water Resources Development program in the engineering department."

"All related to him, I am sure." She wishes there were a breeze; the air inside the mosquito netting is as still, as thick, as a swamp. For a moment, she transports herself to Sweden to let a cool, fresh breeze from the lake caress her skin. As long as she is indulging in imaginary travel, she pauses in Epping Forest and finds the cold air filled with a fine, penetrating rain. She allows herself to stop briefly in Florence for a peek at her daughters, and finds them getting into bed, waiting for Julian or Electra to read them one last story. Mentally, she kisses them good night, sends them bouquets of sweet, peaceful dreams, and reminds them they will return home shortly.

"Undoubtedly related," Thomas says. "And certainly all brothers to the women he has selected." He starts to scratch a bite but stops himself; wills himself to ignore the itch. "But it doesn't matter. As long as he lets them study, doesn't take the money we provide for their schooling for his own private use." He brightens up as he remembers another successful

330

negotiation. "He has agreed to let the village school teacher instruct the girls as well as the boys. Even if they don't learn more than the repetition of old tales and scripture, at least it will elevate their status from mere chattel."

"You think you can trust him?"

"We don't have any other choice in a situation like this but to trust. I have stipulated that the students he has chosen must send us monthly progress reports. I believe everyone understands that continued funds depend on serious, consistent studies. If we can qualify two of the four women, and four of the eight men, this village can take a significant step forward in resolving its health problems, and will bring us a step closer to feeding the children."

"The new chief didn't offer to sell you any children this time?"

"No. And did you see how he insisted he pose with all his children, including his daughters, before he allowed Kate to photograph his wife and youngest child?"

"Kate is going to have an impressive new book, if the photographs develop as I suspect they will."

"Quite different from Divas and Daughters," Thomas says.

"Yes, Chiefs and Future Chieftains. She doesn't seem to mind getting her hands dirty, does she? And her husband spent half the night chatting with the chief's mother, even though neither understood the other's language. Perhaps he has figured out a new source of power in this village!"

"Kate is going to be a major player in our campaign against poverty," Thomas says. "It's amazing, really, how much an individual can do."

Christine nods, a gesture lost in the dark. "Did you see the girl and the baby that Kate photographed right before dinner? The baby couldn't have been more than a couple of days old."

"Yes." Thomas shifts onto his side so that he is facing his wife. He can still see her, even though the room is very dark. "And the mother couldn't have been older than fourteen."

"But the Chief let her be photographed. I saw him nod at her when Kate had finished the shoot. His father never would have acknowledged a woman in public."

331

"Yes. I am much more optimistic about this village than the last time we were here," Thomas says, stifling a yawn. "I even saw a flowering plant at the doorstep to one of their huts."

"I am more optimistic, too," Christine says, catching the yawn as if it were contagious. "I was so at odds the last time we were here." A wave of weariness washes over her, and she knows she will sleep, despite the heat, despite the persistent buzz of mosquitoes on the other side of the net. "Now I can't think of anything that's missing from my life."

"You aren't too homesick for Anna and Elle?"

"I miss them terribly," she admits, envisioning them in their beds, also giving in to sleep. "I can't wait to tell them everything I've seen this week, to hear what they have done in our absence; what special sights they've seen with Julian and Electra. And one day, soon, I hope we can bring them with us. We must make sure they see how these people live, Tommy, so they won't be tempted to take their good fortune for granted."

Epilogue

*H*er hair has grown long again but not enough for braids. These days she tucks it behind her ears, or if she's at work, she ties it back with a rubber band. When she's serving lunch to the people on her ward, she has to wear a net. It makes her feel odd to walk around with a shower cap over her hair but those are the rules, so who's she to make waves. Braids would be an easy answer but she's got out of the habit of braids when her hair was short. They were part of being young, she thinks, then laughs. Tomorrow is her seventeenth birthday. She feels older than most of the patients lying in hospital, but not quite as old as she felt when she was young.

At the end of her shift, she locks up her work clothes in her locker and changes into her regular clothes real fast so she can get to school on time. She hurries into her jeans. Her days are ruled by the clock. She gets docked if she's late to work; she gets marked if she's late to school. She pulls her sweater over her head, tugs it down, and stuffs her notebook into her backpack.

She likes her afternoon class. The teacher is young and pretty and she makes Jo feel less like a loser. She smiles at Jo when she comes into the classroom, like she's done good just showing up on time. Jo will get her diploma at the end of this year if she doesn't mess up. Her teacher said she was smart enough to continue with school, university even. Now there's *an idea! But Jo already has plans. She wants to become a nurse someday, but before that, she's aiming to be a nurse's aide. The work's the same as what she's doing now but the pay is double. She likes bringing food to the new mothers. She doesn't even mind the cleaning up part, although she's always squeamish if there's blood.*

She's figured out a lot since she's come to work with these women having babies. Not all of them are happy to be mothers, and some of them give their babies away, like she did. But some of them can't wait to hold their babies, even though Jo can see it hurts to shift around in bed, to make room for their babies. Jo doesn't want a baby, not yet. She has plans. She's OK living with her sister for the present, especially now that Jackie's bloke has stopped coming 'round to bother her. She wants an apartment of her own, with a nice sofa that isn't stained, and a pretty kitchen table with flowers in a pot that isn't cracked. But first, she has to finish school.

She passes the nursery and studies the tiny forms in their beds. Twins was borned last night, and she lingers a minute to admire their double image. Twins was what she had, she now knows, and that ugly thing wasn't a deformed baby like she had thought but after-birth. For the ten millionth time, she wonders how her babies are. She doesn't know where they are, and Jackie isn't telling. She doesn't even know if they was boys or girls.

She dreams of them sometimes, as if she could actually see them, two girls, with blond hair like hers, and finds them happy and carefree in a family that can feed and love them. They would be three by now. As she leaves the hospital, she gathers the coins from the bottom of her purse and tosses them into the big glass jar at the entrance. Impressive how many more coins it has each day, she thinks, pulling up the hood of her parka against the January wind and snow, like a bright and shining future for her elsewhere babies.

Lynn Rodolico divides her time between Tuscany and Sicily. She is married and has two grown daughters.

For questions and comments,
visit Lynn Rodolico
@
www.lynnrodolico.com